After Anatevka

MITCHELL G. BARD

Prologue

After a while, carrying one's possessions, no matter how meager, can feel like the weight of the world. I hope you won't mind if I sit and rest a bit. It will give my family a chance to catch up.

And why, you may ask, am I here instead of back there with my wife and children? Well, to tell you the truth, I had to get away from them for a few minutes.

I know it's a terrible thing to say, but we've been walking for days and even the most patient of sages, Hillel himself, would be ready to jump off a bridge after hours of listening to my children whine and my wife kvetch.

The kids are tired and hungry, so who can blame them. My wife, my darling Golde, on the other hand, has no excuse. She is the Lord's answer to prayers I have never uttered.

The burden of responsibility for them is weighing me down more than this old rickety cart and knapsack. The family I can't put down, the rest I can, so, with your permission, I think I'll lean the wagon against this rock. I have to balance it so these old wooden wheels are not under too much strain. If the cart gives way or the sides burst, we will be left with only what we could carry.

Don't think that I'm complaining, because I'm not. When the authorities came with their little piece of paper telling us we had to leave Anatevka, the place we called our home all our lives, we had to sell whatever we could and take only what we needed on our journey to the promised land they call America.

Instead of reclining in my rocking chair and reading to the children, poor old Tevye is slumping on this tree stump talking to himself about his misery.

It's not as though I'm suffering alone. You can hear the muttering and sobbing down the road as our little band of refugees sloshes through the mud toward an uncertain future.

Look what has become of my family. Their clothes are already tattered and their faces sooty from the dust kicked up during the days of walking. My Golde has the strength of an ox, not to mention the disposition, but she will not protest in front of the children. That bag she's shifting from one shoulder to the other holds all our remaining clothes. Her voice carries over the racket of our little multitude and pierces the air like a shrill bird.

"Come along children," she screeches. "We've got to catch up to your father to make sure he doesn't make off with all my pots and pans."

When I think about Golde and her pots and pans rattling on the old stove I can almost taste her cabbage borscht. The memory just makes me hungry, and the pots and pans don't satisfy me. What they do is weigh down the cart.

I'm so exhausted I'd fall off this stump if I closed my eyes for a second. We can't afford to rest, though, with the sky darkening. About the only thing that would make matters worse would be for it to rain before we find shelter. Should I bother the Almighty with a request as trivial as keeping my family dry? No, there are more serious questions to ask.

"Dear Lord, was everything else in the world going so smoothly that You decided it was time to play some mischief on your old friend Tevye? Don't get me wrong, it's not that I don't like attracting Your attention; it's just that it might be more fun to play with someone else for a change. Why not pick on poor Rothschild? He wouldn't mind an edict from the authorities to leave his home, he has enough houses. He could just move from one chateau to another. Rothschild probably wouldn't even have to pack his bags, someone would pack them for him, or he could use the clothes he leaves at the other houses."

"But who am I to question Your infinite wisdom? When You told our father Abraham, 'Get thee out of this country,' he left his home. So now You think I'm Abraham. I'm flattered, believe me, but it wouldn't have been too upsetting if You thought less of me and let my family stay in Anatevka."

"You are the Master of the Universe. I don't even have a home to master. The mayor, the cousin of mules, Ivan Poperilo, is now living in my house."

"All right, I know it's a tradition for Jews to wander. It's been passed from generation to generation, from father to son, or, in my case, daughters. Without tradition, life is as shaky as – ah; this is one custom I think I could do without. I know, I know. I should put my faith in You and trust that all is for the best. But how can it be for the best that poor old Tevye should have to take his wife and children and all he can carry and move from his home?"

Do you think God is listening to me? As if He has nothing more important to do than listen to my problems. God probably was watching and laughing when I sold my poor horse. After serving me so well for so long, Subotin treated it as though he was being asked to pay for the plague.

"Do you call that a horse?" Subotin said, looking at it from all directions as if he expected to find an extra leg or a tree growing out of its backside.

"What do you think it is? A clock?" I asked.

"Tevye, if it's a clock, its time has run out."

"My friend has more years left than you do."

"Well, I don't know how much time I have, but if this pitiful beast you call a horse was any older we'd sell it to the French as a relic left behind by Napoleon."

After insulting my horse, he offered me such a pittance I was tempted to make it a gift. But I was too weak. I took the money. Now the coins jangling in my pocket remind me of the life I am leaving behind.

Why shouldn't God laugh at Tevye? He moans like an old woman. But do you think it was easy to sell a lifetime's worth of possessions? Every dish, every stick of furniture was more than mere clay or wood. They were memories. Cups that my daughters first drank from, pots that Golde brought from her parents' home when we were married, pillows that were sewn by my mother. My rocking chair, the one I sat in to comfort the children.

Ah, my children. God has truly blessed me. They are more valuable than all the world's jewels. Millionaires can keep their diamonds, so long as I have my gems, my daughters.

"Tevye, what are you doing?" Golde shouted.

"What do you think I'm doing, visiting the Tsar?"

"You should wait for us!"

Is it any wonder God made Adam before Eve? If he hadn't, Eve would have told God how to make man.

Never mind, I was saying that I remember when we first got the rocking chair. It was after Tzeitl, my first, was born. She hardly cried at all. She was strong from birth, as tough as any diamond. No wonder she defied our tradition and chose the penniless tailor Motel Kamzoil as her husband. The match I arranged with the butcher Lazer-Wolf would have assured her food on the table, but I can't say I blame her for not wanting to marry a man as old as her papa. I wish Tzeitl and Motel were here, sharing this delightful walk through the countryside of our fatherland. But we could not afford to take them with us, so they have taken a different path and headed for Warsaw.

Motel took his new sewing machine and says he will work hard, but soon they will have another mouth to feed. My Tzeitl doesn't grumble. She says she's the happiest woman in the world. Someday they will earn enough money, she tells me, to join us. God willing, it will happen before the *mashiach* arrives.

My second daughter, Hodel, is my ruby. I can hardly speak of her. Like all my daughters, she's a beauty, like Queen Esther. Now she could cry. She started to speak her mind from the moment she arrived in the world and never stopped. And smart. Instead of playing with the pots and pans in the kitchens, she was always looking through my books. She was the only girl in the village who could read and write both Russian and Yiddish. If she were not a woman, she might have become the greatest scholar in Anatevka.

Hodel was smitten by the revolutionary I brought into the house to teach the younger children. We called him Feferel, peppercorn, because he looked like one, short, dark and homely. He was full of confidence, with a quick, sharp tongue. His real name was Pertschik, the son of a cigarette maker. He wanted to change the world. Unfortunately, the authorities like things the way they are and arrested him. Now Pertschik is in prison in Siberia and Hodel waits for him. She washes clothes to earn a few kopeks and goes to the prison every day to see if they will let her speak to him. In her letters, she writes about how Pertschik will change Russia when he is released. Such a girl. I can still see her face the day we parted at the train station. The strain showed in her tearful eyes, the tautness of her cheeks, her knitted brow. She didn't want to leave us, but she knew her place was with her husband. I pray that was not the last time I will see her.

We had another child, with eyes the color of emeralds. She was so sickly as a baby; we had to stay up all night with her and feared she would not survive infancy. Even now, the terrible memory comes back of her and the gentile peasant Fyedka Galagan begging me to listen to them. I cannot say anymore, or even speak her name, because she is dead to us now.

God has decreed that my family should serve him from different places, but I still have three pearls: Schprintze, Beilke and Teibel. By the time little Teibel was born, the old rocking chair was full of nicks and cracks and one leg was so worn down it wobbled back and forth. As long as we are all together with my beloved Golde, we will be all right. As the Good Book says, "Better is a dinner of herbs where love is, than a fatted ox and hatred with it."

So, now, just because I express a little optimism, a new curse is brought upon me. Up ahead, three men are coming this way and they are not coming to wish me a good journey.

"Dear Lord, is this Your answer to my prayers, to send thieves to rob me of my last possessions? No, no, You would never do that to Your old friend Tevye, would You?"

Of course God would not do such a thing. But why would a trio of *schlimazels* be walking in this direction? They certainly don't look like Jews with their clean-shaven faces and uncovered heads. They're dressed even worse than the rest of us, like real peasants. Maybe they were told about the houses abandoned by the Jews of Anatevka.

I can see them more clearly now. One looks a little like Motel, reed thin, hair tousled under a blue worker's cap and thick spectacles pushed up a huge, crooked nose that resembles a goose's beak. The second is short, maybe as tall as my shoulders, but stockier than me, with a barrel chest and powerful looking arms, like a blacksmith's. He has the kind of round face that looks like it is accustomed to storing food. Their expressions are as different as their physiques. The muscular one has a blank expression and the other a huge grin.

The third one is different. He could be my age. Not much hair visible under his cap, bushy black eyebrows and a jutting chin that reminds me of Hodel in one of her defiant moods. If he's a Russian, he's been away for some time because his complexion is too dark even for someone from the spas at this time of year. He's also much taller than the other two, and dressed more neatly, in clean khaki trousers and a blue shirt buttoned to the top. One sleeve dangles beside him. God would have to really be in a mischievous mood to send a one-armed bandit after me.

So they're probably not thieves. Even from a distance, though, I can see a crazy look in their eyes, the one Pertschik got when he started ranting about changing the world.

I think I've rested long enough. It's time to reunite with my beautiful wife and children.

"Stop! Please stop! Don't run away. We mean you no harm," one of the men shouted from behind me.

I've learned that whenever someone tells me they mean me no harm, I should run in the other direction, so I started pushing the cart as quickly as the wobbly wheels would allow.

An instant later, the three men appeared in front of my cart. I tried to go around them, but each time I turned, they moved to block my path.

"*Shalom aleichem.* I am Moshe and this is Simcha," the muscular youth said, gesturing to the thin boy.

"Moshe and Simcha are Hebrew, not Russian names."

"You are correct, Reb?"

"Tevye."

"You are correct, Reb Tevye. We have changed our names."

"Why?"

"Didn't Jacob change his name to Israel?"

"Forgive me, but you do not look like the righteous father of our people."

"How do you know? When did you see him last?" Moshe replied.

"Is that why you've come, to mock me?"

"No, no. Pardon my friend," said Simcha putting himself between me and Moshe. "He has a quick tongue, sometimes a little too quick."

I didn't like his gap-toothed smile. He looked too happy for someone walking along a road in the middle of nowhere.

"We didn't change our names for any divine reason," Simcha continued.

"Is this your way of rebelling against your parents?"

"No, Tevye. And I believe our parents, of blessed memory, would approve."

"I don't understand."

"We are like you, my friend," Simcha said. "We have been driven from our homes. Our parents were killed in a pogrom."

"You grow up, go to school, and work in one place all your life and then, suddenly, it's all gone," interrupted Moshe. "The authorities tell you to pack your bags and go. Go where?"

"Exactly. I lived in Anatevka all my life. My father lived there, and my father's father, and his father, and. . . ." I could hear my voice begin to crack. My new companions looked at me sympathetically. I cleared my throat.

"I raised a family and had a business. It wasn't much, but it gave me time to read the Holy Book. Now, if I were a rich man. . . .Oh what's the use of thinking about it? Now I have nothing but the clothes on my back and what I could fit in this wagon, which I hope you have not come to take."

"Take?" Simcha looked genuinely confused. "Oh, you thought we were coming to rob you."

"Even if we were bandits, you know what Reb Tevye?" Moshe said with a little too much familiarity. "We still couldn't take your most precious possession."

Now it was my turn to be puzzled.

"He's talking about your family," Simcha said.

"I'm afraid I don't even have all of that. My oldest daughter Tzeitl went with her husband to Poland and —"

I stopped myself in mid-thought. Why am I telling strangers my business?

They must have sensed my discomfort because they didn't ask me to finish the story. The one who called himself Simcha instead asked, "Where do you plan to go?"

"America. I have family in New York and I can get another horse and maybe deliver milk again."

"America is not the place for you," said Moshe.

"Who are you to tell me where I should go? Just because you took his name doesn't make you Moses. Don't you know how to show respect? America is the land of opportunity."

"Tevye, it is all talk. America is where all unhappy souls go," Simcha replied shaking his head. "It's a paradise of fools."

"And Russia is a hell of wise men," Moshe chimed in.

"In America," Simcha continued, "you will be a Jew in a Christian land, a minority, just like in Russia."

"But there is no Tsar, no pogroms. My brother-in-law says he prays in a big, beautiful synagogue and studies with the learned men every day. He lives in a nice house and is surrounded by Jewish neighbors."

Simcha was still smiling, but shook his head again. "That may be true now Tevye, but for how long? You used to be able to pray and study among your friends in Anatevka too. Now look what has happened. Tevye, you know how Jews have been treated in Christian lands in the past; why should America be any different?"

"It's diff —"

"It's not different Tevye. In America you will be a Jew in a Christian society," Moshe repeated.

I began to feel even more despondent. The kernel of optimism that the dream of America represented was fading. Their words made me feel as though the weight of the cart was on my back.

"Where else can I go?"

"You can come with us to your motherland, to Palestine," Moshe answered, waving his arms as though he had the highest bid at an auction.

"Palestine?"

Simcha now became animated as well. "Yes Tevye, Palestine. Palestine is our real home. We can go back and rebuild the Temple and the Kingdom of David. As the Bible says. . . ."

"I know what the Bible says. As the Lord said to Abram: 'Leave your own country, your kinsmen, and your father's house and go to a country that I will show you. . . .'"

"'I will make you into a great nation," Simcha added, "I will bless you and make your name so great that it will be used in blessings."

"For someone who dresses strangely, you know the Bible."

Moshe grabbed my arm. "Tevye, God has taken us from our homes so that we may go to the land of our forefathers. There we can work to build a state of our own, a Jewish nation where all of the people will speak Hebrew. We have taken the first step, a small one, by changing our names. I have chosen Moshe, after our leader Moses, for I plan to lead our people in the fight for freedom. We will not be slaves in our homeland. We will be the masters."

Moshe suddenly released my arm. Just as he did, a group of soldiers on horseback came racing past. I bowed and doffed my cap. My show of respect was rewarded by a splattering of mud from the horses' hooves. As I brushed myself off, I could see the others had been quick enough to get out of the way.

"And while my friend here mobilizes our people to fight," the tall one said, the grin still firmly in place as though nothing had happened, "I will be content to work the land and build the country from the ground up. That is why I chose the name Simcha, because this labor of love will make me happy. I was trained in Minsk at one of Jonathan's centers and now I am ready to enter the Promised Land. Come with us Tevye."

"Jonathan? Who's Jonathan?"

"I am Jonathan," the one-armed man answered. "I have set up training centers around Russia to prepare people to work on collective farms to build our state."

"So Jonathan, you too have a tongue. And what will I do in Palestine? I will be like the original Moses, a stranger in a strange land."

"What will you do?" Jonathan shouted as though he were talking to a multitude. "You will live! And you will not be a stranger because you will be with your people in your homeland."

"You don't need to yell," I whispered, holding my throbbing head and looking back at Golde. She had a hand to her ear and was craning her neck, obviously straining to hear the conversation.

"I will live, you say. Living is good. But how will I feed my family?"

"Ah, that's the best part," Jonathan answered. "If you come with us to the kibbutz, all your needs will be satisfied. You don't need any money. In return for your labor, you will receive food, clothing and shelter. Your children will receive an education and, best of all, you will receive all these benefits while helping us to build our homeland."

"Such a deal. I receive everything I want just for working."

"No Tevye," Jonathan continued, still speaking loud enough to be heard in Moscow. "You receive everything you *need*. Unlike this country, where they quote Marx, on the kibbutz we live out his maxim, 'from each according to his abilities, to each according to his needs.'"

"I know about my needs, I'm not so sure about my abilities."

"Don't worry," said Moshe, "everyone has a function on the kibbutz and the *chaverim* will help you as you help them."

"The *chaverim*? It sounds like some kind of skin disease."

"No, a *chevra* is a community characterized by love. In Hebrew the people who live together are called *chaverim*."

"Love, eh? It's spread all the way to Palestine?"

"The work I do on the kibbutz," said Jonathan, "is a labor of love."

"And what about time for study? I work so I may have time to go to the synagogue and pray."

"I must tell you honestly, Tevye, we are not bound by rituals," Jonathan said without a trace of regret.

"You have dispensed with our traditions?"

"Not dispensed, revised for a new time, our time, a time to rebuild the Jewish nation."

"You're heretics," I said and tried to push my cart away from them.

Jonathan held up his hand. "Wait. Please. Do you know what the Hebrew word *avodah* means?"

"Yiddish I know."

"*Avodah* means labor *and* worship. We practice what my friend A.D. Gordon calls *dat ha-avodah*, the religion of labor. We honor the Almighty by our work. We will sow the seeds a handful at a time until we conquer the land of Israel."

"Jonathan, you sound like my son-in-law who used to tell me it was the rich who were impoverished and those who toiled with their hands who stood first."

"Your son-in-law is a wise man. He too should join us in Palestine. Is he with the family?"

"No, he's been rewarded for his work by standing first in a Siberian jail."

"I am sorry. But Palestine is not Russia, Tevye. We will control our own fate in our homeland."

This Jonathan has an answer, a loud one, for everything. "I don't wish to be impolite, but what is it that you do?"

"You insult our friend," Moshe said. "He is a hero and a *vattik*, a founder of the kibbutz."

"It's all right Moshe. It's a fair question. I suppose you're referring to this." Jonathan used his good arm to hold up the empty sleeve. "I lost it in the war with Japan. It wasn't so heroic, believe me. But you ask the wrong question. The question is not what I do, but what Palestine requires. I will do whatever the nation demands. Is a hammer needed? I will be that hammer. If a well must be dug? I will dig it. Do we require policemen to protect the nation? I will put on a uniform. I am ready to do anything and everything!"

"That is quite a speech, but our faith requires deeds, not words."

"It's not just talk," Moshe said indignantly, and stood in front of me poking me in the chest with his finger.

"Jonathan has established training centers in Minsk and Simferopol. People like us, who have graduated from his schools, are going to Palestine and making the desert bloom."

"That is a miracle I would like to see."

"Come with us and you *will* see it," Simcha said with so much enthusiasm I thought he might burst if I agreed.

"I must admit I've been drawn toward the Holy Land for a long time. I would love to pray at the Western Wall, visit the Tombs of the Patriarchs and stand beside Mother Rachel's grave. I have dreamed of following the footsteps of Moses up Mt. Sinai and gazing upon the River Jordan."

"Those dreams can become a reality. Palestine is a small country, a fraction of the Russian empire," Simcha burbled. "From here, God has to strain to hear your prayers. From Palestine, you can whisper in his ear."

I stood dumbly, scratching my beard and considering what these men were saying. On the one hand, I thought, I can go to live in America and probably make a good living. On the other hand, they are right. I will be a Jew in a Christian land. Who knows what the future may bring. On the other hand, Palestine is such a barren, desolate land. There is nothing there but sand and camels, and if there are camels, there must be. . . . And Arabs. We will still be a minority, even in our homeland. On the other hand, how can I pass up the opportunity to live in the land promised to Abraham, Isaac and Jacob? Not even Moses was permitted this blessing. As the psalm says, "If I forget thee, O Jerusalem, let my right leg go weak in the knee."

I looked into their expectant faces and finally shouted, "I will go with you!"

"Wonderful," Moshe said.

"We will return to the land of milk and honey and be free of the Tsar," added Simcha.

Putting his arm around me, Jonathan squeezed my shoulder and said, "We will work and we will build a Jewish state, just as Herzl foretold."

"May God be with us," I said. "Now all I have to do is tell Golde."

I

Surprised to find me back in a barn?

It's as Marx decreed, "From each according to his ability," so where else would Tevye the dairyman be?

Even without the socialist idol, how long do you think I could stand to be away from a cow's teats, enjoying the sound of fresh milk squirting into a bucket? But this is not *any* cow in *any* barn; it's nothing like the one I had in Russia. This is a Palestinian cow in a barn built by Jews on a kibbutz in the Promised Land.

I shouldn't tell you, but the cows actually came from the Arabs. At first no one could figure out the secret to milking them. They would lie down or kick over the pail. Finally, we learned to milk them at night.

All right, so it isn't a Jewish cow. Soon, we will have those also.

Arab cows are not the only difference between Palestine and Russia. Everything is distinctive here. The sky is bluer. The sun shines brighter during the day. At night, the stars twinkle over head like a sea of Sabbath candles. The air smells sweeter. Even the dung is fragrant.

My mother told me different is not necessarily better. She was right.

The Lord said we would inherit a land of milk and honey; what He forgot to mention were the bee stings that would come with it. Speaking of stings, the swamps here have mosquitos the size of dogs — and they carry malaria. So far, thank God, I have not caught the illness. Others have not been so lucky, so, unfortunately, one of the first things built here was a cemetery.

Is it any wonder that so few people have come here, despite the lure of living in the Holy Land? Most of the country does not look special, unless you're impressed by desolate, sandy deserts, and craggy, rock-strewn hills. It is even difficult to find water. We dug a well, but it's infested with frogs. Sound nice?

I can see why this land was promised to the Jewish people — no one else would want it.

But do you think I'm complaining? Not Tevye. How can I be unhappy in the land of my forefathers, of Jewish kings, prophets and sages? It's just that I was expecting something a little more like the Garden of Eden, especially after listening to the stories of my new friends Moshe and Simcha. The entire journey on the fourth-class train to Odessa, and then, for nearly two weeks, while I was hanging my head over the side of the ship crossing the Black Sea, they spoke of a land where bright flowers bloom, fruits and vegetables spring from the earth like weeds and the women are so beautiful Solomon could not choose between them.

Only Jonathan, who actually had lived in Palestine, tempered their enthusiasm by explaining that Palestine was a garden of dust that would only flourish after years of hard labor, but my friends would not be denied their fantasy. They were not even discouraged when we saw our homeland for the first time. The long sandy beach of the coastline looked like nothing more than the edge of a desert. As we got closer, we could see a cluster of mud and sandstone houses perched precariously on rocky cliffs.

When the ship anchored, Arabs in long white robes came out to greet us in little rowboats that looked so shaky everyone was afraid to get in them. Finally, when Jonathan got in the first boat, others followed. We rowed ashore through sharp, protruding rocks to the port of Jaffa.

The minute my feet touched the holy soil of Palestine, I kissed the ground and said a prayer of thanks, "Blessed art Thou, Lord our God, King of the universe, who has granted us life and sustenance and permitted us to reach this time."

I could hear other people singing songs of praise, the way Miriam did when she crossed the Red Sea.

As we walked onto the dock, schlepping what was left of our belongings, a crowd approached.

"Look," Simcha said, "hundreds of people have come to welcome us."

It wasn't until later that Jonathan admitted that the multitude had come to take the next ship out. This paradise we were entering was so popular people were lining up to leave.

I have to admit Jaffa was not my idea of the gateway to Eden. Jonathan led us through a filthy bazaar, where we were accosted by dark-skinned Arab shopkeepers hawking fruit, clothes, pots and trinkets. It smelled worse than my old barn. Beggars covered with sores sat on steps, weakly holding out withered hands. Sadder still, were the emaciated children wandering the streets, dressed in rags and covered with flies.

You might be wondering how my Golde reacted. Well, when I first told her that we were going to Palestine, she fell on her knees, clasped her hands and thanked God for giving her the opportunity to see the Holy Land. Then she asked what we would do when we got there. I told her what Jonathan had said, "we will live!"

"I'm living now," she said. "How will we eat?"

I explained about the kibbutz and Marx and she started carrying on like a chicken chased by a butcher. I told her the pioneers were mostly men, so Palestine was full of single *chalutzim* looking for wives. "And not only that," I reminded her, "Ephraim the Matchmaker said he was also going to Palestine."

Knowing she would find a familiar face, one devoted to bringing happiness to her children, satisfied her until we got on the boat, then she started again with the questions. If I had not been so sick, I might have jumped overboard.

So, what do you think were Golde's first words after setting foot in our homeland, where not even Moses was permitted to walk?

"Well Tevye," she said, "you wanted to come to Palestine. Here we are. Now we can go back."

And if you think she was excited when we arrived, you should have heard her after we reached the kibbutz. She acted as though I had taken her to another planet.

"There's nothing here, just sand and wind and rocks," she whined. "Where will we sleep? In those tents? I could light the Sabbath candles, puff out the match and blow the whole thing down. For this we left Russia?"

"This isn't the kibbutz," I reassured her. "It's just a camp outside the kibbutz. Wait, you'll see there are houses and trees and gardens and orchards."

"Not yet," Jonathan interrupted, still shouting even though we were right beside him. "This *is* the kibbutz. But all that you have dreamed about will be a reality after we build it."

I thought maybe Jonathan had lost more than his arm in the war. He was delusional.

"God promised us a land of our own, he didn't say anything about houses being here waiting for us," Jonathan said.

"But what about the land of milk and honey?"

Jonathan laughed. "Golde, we have cows and bees. They will do their part if we do ours."

And so we did.

It was not easy, and it seems like more than a lifetime has passed, but today, as you can see, we have a barn with cows that provide us milk. Someone else is collecting the honey from our bee hive. Many of the *chaverim* still live in tents, but we now have houses also, nothing fancy like the dachas in Yehupetz, but they are comfortable. They're also a lot sturdier than the clay huts we first bought from the Arabs to replace some of the tents. One day I was getting dressed and a strong wind blew my house away. I stood half-naked in the cold while the rest of the kibbutz stood by laughing hysterically.

Now Golde and I qualify as *vattikim*, founders of the kibbutz, so we were among the first allowed to move into the new wood cabins. This is real luxury! We have one big room with an iron bed covered by a seaweed mattress along one wall. Our closet consists of eight nails in the same wall. The kibbutz just started a carpentry shop, so, eventually, we will have some real furniture. For the time being, we use *pachim* for everything. We get these five gallon tin cans from the British. You can cover them with a blanket and use them for chairs and tables or cut them open and use them for garbage cans or flower pots.

Slowly, we are transforming our surroundings as well. The toughest task has been to drain the swamps and to try to rid ourselves of the mosquitoes, gnats and sand flies. So far, we've drained some of the area, but the mosquitoes still outnumber us. When the watchmen go out at night, they have to wear long pants and shirts, hats, veils and gloves to protect them from the swarms. The only other defense is to smear Vaseline everywhere so the pests will stick to the skin and, even then, we usually can't escape from being bitten. You can always tell who was on guard duty by the people scratching themselves at dinner the following day. We initially put the cows nearest the swamps; it's not that we want the poor animals to be sick, but we thought the mosquitoes would kill them first and spare us.

We planted trees between the rocks and now there is the beginning of a forest. Our orchards are yielding oranges, grapefruits, apples and olives. And flowers are everywhere you look on the kibbutz. Red and pink cyclamen, wild poppies, cornflowers, yellow jonquils, freesias, crimson dahlias. Everyone has their own garden. Of course, my Golde's is the most beautiful.

And what has become of Golde and the children? Well, Golde was also given an assignment according to her ability, in the kitchen. Most of the women in the kibbutz protest against cooking and cleaning. They want to be equals with the men, paving roads, planting forests, harvesting crops, guarding the kibbutz. Can you imagine such a thing?

Men and women are equal, but they have different roles. God granted women the power of reproduction and the patience and strength to raise children.

Try explaining that to the younger women. They squawk if they're given "women's work," but Golde is quite happy in the kitchen.

As for my daughters, they're blooming like the flowers we've planted in the desert. After Simcha and Moshe *hocked me a chinek,* Golde and I agreed to give them Hebrew names.

Schprintze we renamed Shoshana, because she is as beautiful as a rose. Her hair is reddish brown like her grandmother's. Her eyes are the color of chocolate, but always look moist, as though she is on the verge of crying. She smiles often, but it is a tight-lipped, nervous grin. Shoshana was always a more sensitive child than the rest. Even the mildest teasing from her sisters would cause her to collapse in tears. That is why we were all surprised by how she seemed to mature after we arrived on the kibbutz. Shoshana joined the other young women who refused their initial assignments and set out to prove she can work harder than any man. She is the first person to reach the orchards in the morning, sometimes as early as three, and the last to return in the afternoon.

Teibel, the next oldest, is an angel. We named her Devorah after the prophetess and judge in the Bible who inspired the Israelites to defeat the Canaanites. She inherited her father's good looks, long dark black hair, bright green eyes and a wide mouth with thick lips. When she smiles, you can see all her teeth and those around her can't help but return the smile. Fortunately, she did not inherit her father's appetite, so she has remained thin, but sturdy, like a eucalyptus tree. Devorah may be the strongest of us all. Shortly after we arrived, she became deathly ill with malaria, but God watched over her and she recovered. She is also sensitive, but not in the same way as Shoshana. Devorah's tenderness comes out in the way she treats God's creatures, from the most irritating insect to the most revered person. Now she works in the infirmary helping Dr. Susser heal anyone, or anything, which is sick.

My baby, Beilke, we call Sarah after the mother of our people. The Bible says Sarah died when she was "one hundred and twenty and seven years." The rabbis teach us that her age was written in this way because when she died Sarah had the maturity and wisdom of a person who had lived one-hundred years, the freshness and beauty of a woman at twenty and the innocence and sweetness of a child at seven. Our Sarah is wise beyond her years, beautiful and innocent. Her hair is lighter than Devorah's and curlier. She also has green eyes that sparkle like a drop of water in sunlight. Sarah is quieter and more thoughtful than her sisters. She is still too young to work all day. Most of the time she is in school with all the other children.

Why, you might ask, didn't Golde and I change our names? I've been a Tevye so long I would feel as if I wasn't the same person anymore if I had a different name. As for Golde, it's tough enough remembering the kids' Hebrew names; I didn't want to start over with a new wife also.

Finding Hebrew names for the children was easy; all we had to do was consult the Bible. Learning to speak the language was more difficult, but we had no choice. The minute Jonathan stepped foot back in Palestine, he refused to speak in any other language. At first, no one could understand him. Soon all the business of the kibbutz was conducted in Hebrew. It was a struggle, but now our whole family is fluent enough to get by.

Golde's biggest concern is that our daughters will not find husbands since Ephraim the Matchmaker decided to live in Tiberias instead of the kibbutz. I'm not worried. Tevye's daughters are known for their beauty and they will be found.

Not having a matchmaker isn't the only thing that's different about life here. The children, for example, do not live with us. They live in a special children's house. The kibbutz philosophy is that children belong to the whole community and not the parents alone. Still, we get to see them during the afternoon after work, and again in the evening. At night, the dormitory is locked and mosquito netting is put over the children's beds.

The separation from our daughters was the toughest thing for Golde to accept. We don't even share meals. All the children eat together while the rest of the *chaverim* eat in a big dining hall. Golde and a few other women cook for everyone. That she likes, but food is so scarce the meals she makes are hardly worth looking forward to: chickpea mush, cereal, herring and her famous cabbage borscht. We rarely eat meat and, when we do, it's usually canned beef bought from the British. A *chaver* only eats chicken if he is ill or the chicken is sick.

In the best of circumstances, leftovers show up in different forms in all future meals until they are gone. The meals are worse when our crops do well. We had a surplus of carrots once and our resourceful cooks used them for carrot salad, boiled carrots, carrot soup, carrot jelly, stewed carrots and candied carrots. My skin was turning orange from all the carrots I was eating.

To be fair, meals are much better than they were at the beginning. At first everything was cooked in a pot over a fire fueled by dried thistles and cow-dung. Smoke used to get in everyone's eyes and I don't even want to tell you what the smell was like. The only water came from a distant well infested by frogs.

In Anatevka we had a tradition for everything, what to wear, when to eat. Here on the kibbutz, we have a committee for everything: a planning committee, an education committee, a cultural committee, a welfare committee, a security committee, a work assignment committee, a nominating committee, a smokers committee, even a landscape committee. And we even have a tradition about committees.

You think I'm kidding? Let me tell you what happened when I received my first honor to serve on a committee.

As Jonathan warned before we left Russia, the kibbutz is not very committed to our religious traditions. Still, I was determined to maintain my own level of observance and to persuade the rest to fulfill as many of God's six-hundred and thirteen commandments as possible.

Since the *chaverim* recognized me as a learned man, Menachem, the chairman, invited me to be a member of the education committee. Of course, I said, I would be honored.

"What's the matter with you?" Menachem replied angrily.

"What do you mean, what's the matter with me? You asked me to be on the committee and I would like to be on the committee."

"But you're not supposed to say that you want to be on it."

"Then why did you ask me?" I said feeling thoroughly confused.

"Obviously, because we believe you have the ability to contribute," Menachem said.

"So why shouldn't I accept?" I shouted, thinking he was trying to make a fool of me.

"You don't understand. Here, no one is considered more important than anyone else. No one aspires for prestige."

"So I should not feel honored that you asked."

"That's right."

"Maybe I should feel insulted."

"Not exactly. But when you are asked to join a committee, you should say, 'I don't want to.'"

"But what if I do want to be on the committee?"

"Then you say, 'I don't want it.'"

"And that means that I really do want to be on the committee?"

"Correct."

I was beginning to understand why Menachem was chairman of the education committee.

"So," I said to him, "what do I say if I really don't want to join the committee."

"No one on the kibbutz turns down the opportunity to serve the community; it would mean placing one's own desires above the needs of the whole."

It all became perfectly clear. And that is how I ended up on the education committee.

What do I do with this great privilege? Mostly go to meetings. The *chaverim* love meetings. We talk about what subjects should be taught in school, how they should be taught and who should teach them. We discuss programs for the adults, study sessions on Hebrew poetry in the Spanish era, Zionist philosophy in the nineteenth century, Hegel's interpretation of Marxism and, at my insistence, Talmud. We talk and talk and talk.

The biggest fight we've had came after my daughter Sarah told me about her lesson from Exodus. When explaining the passage where God first speaks to Moses, the teacher informed the class that "God" was a theoretical notion.

God theoretical? If Jews do not believe in God, what makes them Jews?

Well, I had quite a row with the Marxists on the committee before we agreed that the Bible would be taught without any commentary regarding the existence of God.

Can you imagine?

My rebbe would be horrified, but Pertschik would be proud. He always said the poor man is more important than the rich, and that the worker is most important of all. He should only know how important I've become.

If my committee doesn't have a meeting, our evenings are usually quiet. We play cards or chess, read, write letters. Every Saturday night, after the Sabbath, we have a town meeting. It's held in the dining room, which is made of tin salvaged from abandoned British army installations. It leaks, so when it rains, our discussions are often interrupted by people running with pots to catch the torrent before it floods the room. When it's dry and hot, we spend our time swatting the swarms of flies.

In Anatevka, the papa made decisions for the family. Here, everyone gets to have their say and then the whole kibbutz votes. Whatever the majority decides, the rest of the *chaverim* must accept. And we must decide very important issues, such as whether men and women must share showers, why the taste of soap remains in the dishes after they are washed, the construction of a bench for older people to sit on and the amount of time each of us will be allowed to stay in the bathroom.

You probably think I made up that last item, but it was on the agenda. Since so many of us share living space, the lavatory is one of the few places to find privacy. Sometimes you have to stand outside waiting, for hours it seems, for the person inside to come out.

In case you're wondering, the debate on this subject went on for hours. Some of the women argued they needed more time than men. The men insisted that they be given equal time. We had votes on five minutes, six minutes, seven, it was ridiculous. Finally, a majority agreed to limit visits to the bathroom to nine minutes. The best part is that the assignment committee now has to find someone to keep track of how long people stay in the water closets. You can bet there'll be a fight for that job.

Adapting to the kibbutz philosophy has been particularly hard on Golde. She can't get used to the idea that what's yours is mine and what's mine is yours. All her life, she made clothes for her family, but here that is the job of the people assigned to work as tailors and seamstresses. The women are given one good dress every two years and a plain dress every other year. I am privileged to receive three pairs of Sabbath pants and four shirts. But you don't get to keep the same clothes. When you pick up fresh clothes from the laundry, you are given whatever is on the top of the pile. Sometimes I send a shirt and pants that fit perfectly to the laundry and get back those belonging to a *chaver* six inches shorter, so the pant legs reach just below my knees and my arms barely fit through the shirt sleeves. On other occasions, of course, the sizes are too big.

This brings me to the subject of some of the characters on our kibbutz. In Anatevka we had our share, Ephraim the matchmaker, Lazer-Wolf the butcher, Menachem-Mendel the entrepreneur, and, of course, our beloved rabbi. Here, we must have the Noah's Ark of the human race and, if you want to know the truth, there are a few people I wouldn't have let on the boat.

Take Yitzhak, the *chaver* from Warsaw. He refuses to wear shoes because he says our feet should get used to the soil of our homeland.

Enoch the Bee Keeper scares everyone to death. He'll rub his face with wildflower petals and let thousands of bees land on his eyes, nose, and face. He even lets them crawl in his mouth. I shudder just thinking about it.

We're scared in a different way by Oren the Inventor. He's always trying to build new contraptions to pick crops faster or dig deeper ditches. The *chaverim* run when they see him coming because his inventions usually make more work for them. I wasn't smart enough to bolt when he brought his milking machine to save me from this chore. He said the nozzle attaches to the cow's teats and sucks the milk out into a pail. All I would have to do, he told me, was collect the milk from the pails. Oren turned it on and held up the nozzle to show me how strong it could pull. The crazy thing began to suck up everything in its path: hay, rope, the fringes of my *tzitzit*, my hat.

When Oren finally tried to attach the machine to the cow, it kicked him in the head and knocked him silly. He's persistent, so I'm sure he'll be back to try again. Hopefully, when I'm on kitchen duty.

Then we have Eitan and Uzi, the resident ideologists. They have a quote from Marx for everything. As for the Bible, they don't know borscht. "Religion is the opium of the people," they repeat at every opportunity, parroting their hero. To them, socialism is the highest form of human achievement.

Simcha is a pioneer. He volunteers for everything. When we need a road, he joined the construction crew. When we started replacing tents with houses, he became a carpenter. Whatever the kibbutz needs, he wants to help, just like his mentor Jonathan.

Jonathan is revered as a *vattik*, a founder, but he works as hard as anyone, alternating between the fields and the chicken coops.

My other friend, Moshe, is referred to as "The Militant," because he is always warning of a coming confrontation with the Arabs. He went off for military training and now is responsible for kibbutz security. He's organized watchmen and, if Jonathan allowed it, would run the kibbutz like an army unit.

We call Gideon "Mr. Big" because he always wants to do everything in a grand way. The economic committee was discussing the purchase of ten sheep. Gideon jumped up and said, "Let's buy one hundred, and goats too."

On the kibbutz, we usually have shortages of just about everything — except mosquitoes. So we are forced to ration food, water, you name it. Whatever is being rationed, Laban the Miser hoards. If we're only allowed three bars of soap a month, he'll save twelve.

Then there's Shmuel the Bell Ringer. Now how we came to have a bell ringer is a story.

When we first came to the kibbutz, no one wanted to use a bell. Eitan and Uzi said it was wrong, that bells were for factories not a *kvutza*. They argued it was too impersonal. So, when it was time to eat, the cook would come out to the courtyard and scream "meal time" until her voice gave out.

That was not so bad. The real problem came when we were sleeping. Whoever was assigned the night watch would walk into our tent and yell, "Wake up! Wake up!" If you didn't respond immediately, he'd come over to your bed and start shaking you until you got up and dressed.

The lack of privacy finally upset enough *chaverim* that a vote was taken and the decision made to use the bell. The next problem was to assign this thankless job to someone. Fortunately, Jonathan knew the perfect candidate.

Shmuel is still a young man, in his twenties, but when he was in Russia, during the revolution, an explosion destroyed most of his hearing. It also blew off one of his arms. Jonathan was naturally drawn to Shmuel and brought him to the kibbutz. Since one is missing a right arm and the other a left, they sometimes put on skits for the *chaverim* where they put a sheet over themselves and attach a pumpkin to a broomstick for a head and pretend to be one man.

Their performances can be hilarious, but Shmuel's bell ringing is no joke. Never have you seen a person who takes more pride in pulling a string back and forth. Maybe too much pride. It seems like he's clanging at all hours of the day and night. But it is not random noise. No, you have to memorize a whole code because different sounds have distinct meanings. For example, three long rings means it's time to milk the cows, five long rings are a call for a meeting, two sharp rings followed by a pause and two more sharp rings indicate it's time to eat and a rapid, constant ring is the alarm. Then there are the times Shmuel decides to try to play music with the bell and you're not sure what is going on. First, you start to run to the dining room, then to the barn, then to the fields and you end up going in circles until you realize it's just another of Shmuel's compositions.

We haven't come up with names for everyone, but it's not for lack of trying. Hyman, for example, is like the sun; he thinks everything revolves around him. Whatever happens on the kibbutz, Hyman will tell you how it affects his life. One of the animals is sick, Hyman will have extra work. The cucumbers are ripe; he'll be forced to pick them out of his salad. A hole in the fence has been found, he won't be able to sleep worrying about intruders.

And, of course, we have certain types of people you can find anywhere, Faiga the Gossip, Natan the Nudnik, Timur the Know-it-All.

Since we arrived, the kibbutz has been a veritable sea of tranquility, except when it comes to the issue of jobs for the women. As I mentioned before, the women here don't want to be confined to cooking and cleaning. No one except my Golde wants to work in the kitchen. Actually, that's not quite true. One crazy woman came here from America and volunteered for cooking duty. Her name is Bernice. She and Golde look a little bit alike, but Bernice is *meshugana*. She is always trying to change things in the kitchen.

First, she started to feed everyone oatmeal for breakfast. She said it was "nutritious," but we just thought it was baby food. Then Bernice decided the enamel coffee mugs we drank out of were too chipped and dirty, so she bought glasses. They were certainly nicer to drink from; unfortunately, within a couple of weeks most were broken and the *chaverim* were forced to drink in shifts from the handful that was left.

Come to think of it, Bernice is the least strange of the women in the kitchen. Another woman, Maya, tried to change the routine of washing the dining room floor. Since it was built, it had always been scrubbed the same way, from the east wall to the west. Maya decided to start from the west wall. The other women were so upset, they left in protest.

And then there's the famous Chana Leibowitz. One Sabbath she decided to make a rice kugel for dinner. When people ate it, they thought it tasted better than usual and wanted to know what ingredients she used. Chana told them it was a secret recipe she had just discovered. Actually, she couldn't figure out why it tasted the way it did so she checked the rice sack and found out it wasn't rice.

Guess what was in the sack? It was birdseed. Can you imagine? Suddenly, all the *chaverim* ran for the door and started spitting kugel out on the ground. It was quite a scene.

With all the *meshugas*, being here in Palestine is a dream come true. To the west is Jerusalem, the holiest place in the world. Someday, hopefully soon, I will go to pray at the Western Wall, and visit Rachel's tomb. The Patriarchs are buried just a few kilometers from here and Mt. Sinai is in the desert to the south.

God has decreed that my family should serve him from different places, and so I must do what he has meant for me to do here.

"What is that?" you ask.

It's a good question.

I think that my role may be to keep our traditions alive here on the kibbutz. As I told you, the *chaverim* believe that work is a religion. They don't cover their heads or wear prayer shawls. Most refuse to pray or study the Scriptures. Golde and I do our small part to try to bring a little *yiddishkite* to the community. For example, on the Sabbath eve, Golde makes sure white tablecloths are set out for dinner with wildflowers neatly arranged on each table. I always wear my finest white shirt and after our meal say the *Birkat HaMazon*, the blessing after the meals. Then I sing Hasidic songs I learned in Russia. At first, people looked at me like I had come from Mars. But, soon, a few *chaverim* started to join in. Before long, the whole kibbutz — except Eitan and Uzi — was singing along with me, turning the evening into an especially joyous time.

Maybe the most frustrating thing is that I can't get the *chaverim* to stop working on the Sabbath. They have a million excuses: if we don't work, the crops will be ruined by the sun, wind, rain. We don't have enough workers. The milk will sour, the fodder will rot. They exhaust me with their arguments. But I will not give up, not on this tradition. Observing the Sabbath and keeping it holy is one of God's most sacred commandments, it is one of the Jewish people's greatest contributions to civilization.

You hear that? It's Shmuel's latest composition. I think he calls it "Ode to Lunch." I have to go in now.

Ay!

One thing is the same here as in Russia. If you don't watch where you're going, you still step in the same piles.

2

Living in Palestine, it's easy to wonder just what it was that God promised to the Jewish people. I told you we decided to keep the cows between the swamps and the rest of us so the mosquitoes would get them first. Well, it worked. The cows caught the plague and the herd was wiped out.

It's not the end of the world. We'll just be drinking a lot of goat's milk for a while.

Simcha volunteered to go to Holland to try to buy some new cows. In the meantime, the work committee has decided Tevye should help pick apples.

On a beautiful day like this, it's a good job. I get to work in fresh air for a change, and the breeze is strong enough to prevent the sun from baking me. Beautiful yellow butterflies are flitting about and a flock of starlings just flew overhead. The best part, though, is that I get to be with my beautiful daughter, Shoshana, who usually works here in the orchard.

Actually, it's a little embarrassing. I fumble around in the leaves and strain to pick the fruit while she just hauls the apples down by the handful. If all, no, make that any, of Oren's inventions worked as well as Shoshana, the kibbutz would be the most productive in Israel.

She takes her work very seriously, so I don't get to talk to her much. Besides, Shoshana is preoccupied with someone else.

"You know you don't have to prove anything to anyone," Chaim said from the base of the ladder as Shoshana gave him a fistful of apples.

"What do you mean?" She didn't look down as she worked. Grabbing two and three apples between her fingers, Shoshana could strip a tree in minutes.

"You know exactly what I mean," Chaim said.

I didn't like the way he was staring at the muscular, slightly scarred leg in front of his face.

"What are you doing up there Tevye, taking a nap?"

Oh, did I forget to mention that I have the privilege of being paired with Timur the Know-it-All?

"Why don't you come up here and I'll wait for you to bring the fruit down?" I shouted.

"Tevye, You know I'm afraid of heights."

"Yea, yea. Afraid of work is more like it," I mumbled.

"What's that Tevye?"

"There's nothing like working in the outdoors, Timur."

"You're right, except for the heat and the bugs."

I let a bunch of apples drop and that sent Timur scurrying and gave me a chance to return my attention to Shoshana's conversation.

"You don't think I need to work hard because I'm a woman, right?" Shoshana said before tossing a rotten apple at Chaim's head.

He ducked just in time.

"No, I don't think you have to work harder than the men to prove you can do the same job."

"I'm not —"

"Come on, Shoshana. If someone else is out here at four, you get up at three-thirty. If they come at three-thirty, you're up at three. When it's time to quit, you insist on working ten more minutes."

"I like what I do."

"That's great. It really is. But the whole point of the kibbutz is that we share responsibility, and no one — male or female — has more than anyone else."

"Don't lecture me on kibbutz philosophy. We both know the difference between rhetoric and reality."

"All right, all right," Chaim interrupted. I should know better than to argue with you. Ever since you came from Russia and were put in my class, I've had a tough time getting a word in edgewise."

Shoshana climbed down the ladder a few steps so she was face to face with Chaim. "You manage very nicely, Chaim Danziger. The only way the teachers could get you to shut up was to throw things at you."

"You've changed a lot since our first days in the high school together, Shoshana."

"How so?"

"When you first arrived in Palestine, your skin was yellow like Jerusalem stone. You were so thin I tried to give you my ration of meat and vegetables because I was afraid you might be blown away by the Galilean winds. The holy land has done wonders for you."

"Chaim, is this your idea of charming me?"

I watched the children and wondered if Chaim saw my daughter the way I do; if he thought of fireworks when he looked in her eyes. He was certainly right about the way the new environment invigorated Shoshana. Within months, her skin was tanned by the sun, she gained weight and developed into a mature woman. Once Shoshana began working, she grew strong and her muscles taut.

I didn't like the crooked smile on Chaim's face when he looked at her. I noticed Shoshana moved up a step so he couldn't look down her blouse.

"You know all about me and my family," she said, quickly grabbing all the apples at the center of the tree, "but you've never talked about yours. So many people here have been tragically separated from their families, like me from my sisters, I've always been afraid to ask you."

"So what has given you the courage to ask now?"

"Maybe it's the way you've been looking at me lately."

"What do you mean?"

"You look like you'd eat me if our rations ran out."

Chaim laughed to conceal his embarrassment. "I think I'd do it long before I starved."

"If you could."

"Yeah," he mumbled.

"What's that?"

"Quiet, your father's pretending not to listen from behind that tree."

"I know. If I try to tell him to mind his own business, he'll suddenly quote socialist philosophy to me about how everyone's business belongs to the kibbutz."

"And probably back it up with a quote from the Bible."

Shoshana laughed. It hadn't taken long for everyone to get to know her father.

I could barely hear what they were saying. Timur was telling me all about the different varieties of apples, why some were green and others were red, why green ones might be either sweet or sour. Timur was a font of mostly useless information.

"What do you want to know?" Chaim asked.

"Well, how about if we start with the basics," Shoshana said. "Where does your family live?"

"They're in Tel Aviv."

"Brothers or sisters?"

"Nope."

"Why did you leave?"

"You're a very nosy girl."

"I got that from my mother. Besides, this isn't a place that encourages privacy. If you'd rather not talk about it."

"It's okay. I'm just a little sensitive about family matters. It's not that easy to leave your family."

"I can't imagine leaving mine. It's hard enough being separated from my sisters."

"Well, I never imagined leaving home until I began to read the writings of our greatest thinkers."

"You mean Rashi and Maimonides and scholars like them?"

"No, not those medievalists," said Chaim, making me grimace. "I'm talking about people who understand the problems of today, humanists who understand the value of work. Men like Syrkin, Borochov, and Gordon."

"Until I came here, I'd never heard of them."

"Of course not, Shoshana. You were still reading texts written hundreds or even thousands of years ago. They tell you how to be Jewish in alien lands but they don't tell you how to be Jewish in your own land."

I don't like this boy. What does she see in him? He's got Pertschik's arrogance, but not his intelligence. He's shorter than Shoshana, even when she's not on a ladder. His ears stick out over the sides of his cap like a donkey, and he could probably balance the ladder on the end of his nose.

"You're napping again Tevye."

"Who could sleep with you down their reciting the history of apples? Fear or no fear, Timur, you're going up the next tree."

"I don't think you'd want the consequences on your conscience Tevye."

If Simcha doesn't get back here soon with the new stock, we may have to bury more than dead cows. And I thought Natan was a *nudnik*.

"So, now I have read what your great thinkers have written," I heard Shoshana say. "I don't recall any of your great writers teaching that you have to leave your family to be Jewish in your own land."

"No, but they do teach that what is important is labor. It is labor that binds a people to its land and to its national culture, which in turn grows out of the people's soil and the people's labor."

Shoshana climbed down the ladder and she and Chaim moved it to the next tree.

"As you said before, Chaim, I'm a believer in working hard. Don't your parents believe in work?"

"Oh, my father works, but only for profit. He cares nothing for the value of labor or the land. My father is a greedy capitalist who runs a factory and exploits his workers. The workers don't earn the value of what they produce. But that's not even the most important thing. He could be a greedy capitalist in America, he should not be here. He doesn't understand the spiritual ties we as Jews have to the land — this land. He's only concerned with making money."

"As a girl from a poor family, let me tell you that it's no sin to be rich. I could suffer with the burden of a few extra piasters in my pocket."

It was nice to hear my daughter had inherited something from her father.

"You see, you haven't gotten over the idea that money is necessary for happiness," Chaim said.

"I know that it's much easier to be unhappy without money than with money. At least rich people can afford to complain."

"Shoshana, haven't you learned anything here on the kibbutz? All of your needs are met. You don't have to exploit anyone else's labor. All you have to do is work and you receive food, clothing and shelter. What more do you need to be happy?"

"Better food, nicer clothes and a house of my own."

"It's that desire to have more than your neighbor that leads to inequality, injustice and war. When we eliminate classes, we will have a just society. Here, in our homeland, we have an opportunity to achieve justice and equality for all."

"And what about the Arabs?"

I couldn't wait to hear Mr. Marxstein's answer to that one.

"Why should they be treated differently? We can all live together peacefully."

"Do you think they feel that way, Chaim?"

"We have to show them we mean no harm."

"Time to move Tevye," Timur shouted.

"Fine. But you're going up on the ladder this time," I said climbing down. "And don't start kvetching about your fear of heights. You can start with the lower branches and I'll take the higher ones."

"But —"

"Forget it, Timur. Help me move this."

Timur and I moved the ladder to the next tree. I was mainly interested in staying close enough to Shoshana to hear what she and Chaim were saying.

"Tevye."

"Up!"

Timur gingerly stepped on the bottom rung of the ladder as if it were covered with jagged glass. He went just high enough to reach the lowest apples.

"What does your father think about you being here?" Shoshana asked Chaim.

"He's furious. He thinks I'm wasting time. He wants to groom me to inherit his business. Why would I want to push paper and meet with bankers? I don't think my father has ever touched his fingers to the soil. He couldn't tell you the color or texture of the ground he walks on each day. Servants do even the most menial tasks for him. I'm not sure if even dresses himself anymore."

"You sound bitter, Chaim."

"I'm angry that he's not doing his share to build our nation."

"Don't you think every Jew has a role to play? For some it may be to farm the land, for others to build roads, for some to negotiate with the British and for a few to create industries?"

"He hires the Arabs to do his work, Shoshana. We can't rely on others to build our homeland, especially the Arabs."

"What happened to everyone being equal?"

"That's the point. Where is the equity in hiring Arabs to do our dirty work for us? As Jonathan says, we must be willing to do whatever is required to build our state."

"Perhaps you're right."

"Of course I'm right."

"Now you sound like my father, Chaim." I saw her look in my direction. "Doesn't he, Papa?"

I tried to hide behind the tree trunk.

"Tevye, what are you doing?" Timur shouted as apples began to fall to the ground where I had been standing.

"Didn't you say something about the worker deserving the fruits of his own labor?" Shoshana asked Chaim.

"I didn't use those words, but that's the idea."

"Good, I think I'll collect my payment." Shoshana picked two apples. She tossed one to Chaim and sat on the top of the ladder and began eating. "As the proverb says 'the worker's hunger works for him; for the mouth urges him on.'"

"So Shoshana Zalman, now we learn the truth. It's really your belly that motivates you!"

"Very funny."

"You know, you're beginning to sound like your father."

"What do you mean?"

"You're quoting from the Bible all the time."

"No I'm not."

"Yes you are."

"Really?"

"Yes."

"Learning Torah is the most important thing to him. I think he's disappointed I've never been as good a student as my sisters."

"Then I'd hate to be stuck in the orchard with them."

Shoshana laughed.

"You'd better not let anyone see you slacking off like this. They might think women need extra breaks."

"You," Shoshana said and threw the core at him.

It hit him in the chest and he pretended to be hurt, reeling backward as though he'd been shot. They were both laughing when I heard a cracking sound. One leg of the ladder splintered. Shoshana fell backward. She ended up in Chaim's arms.

"Nice catch," she said breathlessly.

"You know we never let the ripest fruit hit the ground. I'm just glad you ate a light breakfast."

"I'm glad you were here."

She kissed him.

He pulled away.

"What's wrong?"

"You know public displays of affection are inappropriate, Shoshana."

"It's a good thing we're not in public." She kissed him again harder.

"Hmm," I cleared my throat as loudly as I could. Obviously, fruit was not the only thing growing in the orchard. It took all my willpower not to run over and separate the children.

The reminder I was nearby was enough to send Chaim scurrying back to the toolshed for another ladder.

"Oh Papa," Shoshana said with a stern look on her face. "It was just a harmless kiss."

"That's what I thought before Tzeitl was born."

"You shouldn't be spying on me."

"Spying? Who's spying?"

"You were," Timur said.

"Who asked you? Take a break while I talk to my daughter."

"All right. It gives me a chance to get down from this ladder before I get sick."

"Timur. . .Ah, never mind. Listen Shoshana," I said, taking her by the arm and walking away from the tree where Timur was now sitting. "The committee assigned me to this job. It's not my fault the cattle died and I was taken from my beloved barn."

"Yes, I know how you miss talking to the animals and having the chance to be alone with God."

"Shush! You know better than to take the Lord's name in vain."

"I —"

"Shoshana."

"All right, Papa."

"Must you wear such short shorts and such a flimsy shirt? You are tempting that boy."

"I hope so."

"Are you mocking me, Shoshana?"

"Oh, come on Papa. I thought we were long past this argument. That business about modest dress was nonsense even before we came to work in the broiling sun. I'm certainly not going to wrap myself up to conceal my charms just because of some old tradition from the freezing *shtetl*."

"Some old tradition! Some old tradition!" I felt the blood rushing to my face.

"Papa, the boys looked at the girls even then. Long sleeves and skirts didn't stop them."

"But it didn't encourage them the way you girls do now, running around half naked."

"Please! Why are you starting with me? You know this is the way everyone dresses here and that I'm not about to change now. What's really bothering you? Is it Chaim?"

"No. Chaim's no worse than the rest of the socialists here."

"That's a fine thing to say, Papa. Whatever happened to *lashon harah*?"

"Who's gossiping? It's the truth."

"All right. What is it, really?"

"It's just that you're getting older. That's all. With your sisters gone, you're the oldest, but I still think of you as a little girl. Seeing you with Chaim the Socialist just reminds me how much I miss Tzeitl and Hodel and . . . and that you've grown up. You'll see when you have children of your own how quickly the time flies."

"We can't stay children all our lives, Papa."

"I know. But I wish you could."

3

It's like the good old days in Russia. Just me and my feeble horse and dilapidated cart delivering a load of bread and milk. The *chaverim* have been making bets on whether the rickety wagon will collapse before the old mare dies. I think the odds are about even.

You're right; the days in Russia weren't so good. Could you imagine me wearing shorts in front of all the rich people in their dachas in Yehupetz? Or even to the poor people in Boiberik? My knees are not much to look at, I admit, but Shoshana finally convinced me it's too warm to spend all day in long pants and boots.

In Russia the seasons were cold and wet, cold and muddy, and freezing and snowy. Here it's beautiful most of the time. True, the summer is so hot you can see waves of heat rising from the ground. All right, we also have our share of mud when it rains in the winter, and these iron wheels sink, so that I have gotten stuck more than once, but the weather is still paradise compared to Anatevka.

Whatever the conditions, I enjoy the peace and tranquility of being alone in the country. Thankfully, Simcha brought back some cows from Holland to replenish our herd and I was able to get out of the orchard and away from Timur. I do miss being with Shoshana, but she and Chaim started to work farther away from me so I couldn't eavesdrop on them. Anyone with two eyes in their head can see where their relationship is headed, but I don't want to think about it now. What good would it do? On the kibbutz, I have even less control over my daughters than I did in Russia.

That's just one of the things I haven't grown used to yet. Another is our choice of clothes. I was never very concerned about my appearance. As I've gotten older, I worry more about my *dis*appearance.

Still, I like to choose what it is I will look terrible in. Here, a committee even tells you what you can wear. I was forced to wear these shorts. All right, they didn't hold me down and tie them around my waist. But it took some getting used to. The *chaverim* made fun of me wearing my prayer shawl and keeping my head covered. They say those traditions are antiquated, from another time and place where Jews had to distinguish themselves from the *goyim*. No, I said, showing respect for God does not get old or become obsolete. The closer we are to him, the more reverent we should be.

These socialists, with their visions of a world where everyone is equal, want to do away with everything that has kept us a strong people for generations.

"We will start our own traditions," they tell me.

I admit I don't know how all our traditions got started, but even a simple man who does not have the vision of our Jonathan, can see that you don't just throw away something that has worked for centuries. Who is man to make all the rules? I have seen what the edicts of men can do and I prefer to place my trust in the Lord.

It's funny. I used to dream of being the most learned man in my village, a person everyone would come to for advice and now I am that person. I admit I've changed. It was necessary to be part of the community. But, you know, I've changed them a little bit too. Now the kibbutz celebrates most of the holidays; before, the only festivals were ones associated with harvests. At first, I studied alone, but today I lead discussions once a week on the *parsha*. It's not much, but it's a start.

Still, I miss our old rabbi. It's been many years since I last saw him and yet I can see his face clearly. His long grey beard and stern expression betrayed by eyes that sparkled with excitement at even the simplest question. I remember how he used to bang his fist on the lectern to make a point, and how he would shout: "Tevye, Hillel was able to explain the entire Torah on one foot. You are always trying to do the same; the trouble is your other foot is always in your mouth."

Ah, our rabbi. Such a learned and righteous man. And now I am playing the role, but lack the knowledge and the spirit. I pray for God to give me the wisdom to answer the questions my friends ask. I always have a response, but I don't think it's the same one the rabbi would give. Watch, here comes Natan the Nudnik. He always asks questions the Almighty Himself would not want to answer.

"What are you doing out here on the road, Natan?"

"I came to find you."

"Natan, I'll be back at the kibbutz soon."

"It couldn't wait."

"All right, Natan," I said climbing down from the cart and taking out a canteen. "Water?"

"No, thank you," he said, dismounting his horse.

"*Nu?*"

"Tevye, I am deeply troubled."

"What's wrong?"

"Tevye, I'm deeply troubled."

"What is the trouble?"

"Tevye, I'm deeply —"

"What is it already?" I shouted inches from Natan's face. Then, more calmly, I repeated, "What is it that is troubling you?"

"Tevye, do you know if birdseed is kosher?"

"What?"

"Is birdseed kosher? We all ate the kugel Chana made and now a few of us have begun to wonder if we have committed a sin."

"Still this nonsense with the birdseed?" I took a last drink, closed the canteen and started to get back into the wagon.

"Please Reb Tevye. I'm deeply —"

"Troubled. Yes, I've figured that out Natan." I turned back toward him, scratched my beard and tried to look thoughtful.

"This is a very difficult question you pose, Natan. I wish we had a rabbi here to answer."

"But Tevye, you are our rebbe. Who else would possibly know?"

"You have a point. So I will give you an answer. The Good Book says that we shall not eat birds of prey — or birds that treat their food as do birds of prey."

I could see Natan was confused. That was progress, so I spoke more quickly. "Since birds of prey do not eat birdseed, it must be kosher."

"That makes no sense. Birds of prey don't eat pigs either, but that doesn't make pork kosher."

"You miss the point, Natan. It is not what the non-kosher birds eat that matters, it is what the kosher birds eat. Chickens are kosher. Chickens don't eat pigs, but they do eat birdseed. Excuse me now, I have to get home."

I jumped up onto the wagon.

"Wait, Tevye."

"*Shalom*, Natan. We'll talk again later," I said and whipped my horse. The cart started to pull away.

"Tevye!"

I waved over my shoulder.

Natan threw up his arms.

See what I mean? After spending time with Natan I'm reminded that humans have been talking like asses for thousands of years, but not one ass has ever spoken like a human.

It's not easy being the man who people come to with their questions. How can I complain? Now I have the time that I always wanted to study and pray. So we don't have a synagogue. When I face Jerusalem, I know it is just beyond these hills. Could I really be closer to God in a building?

And for every Natan, there's a child who truly seeks the way of the Lord. If I were not here, who could they go to for guidance? Jonathan, our leader, only talks about planting, growing, building. He says his soul is nurtured by the soil and his labor.

Jonathan may not be a scholar, but he is a good man. He envisions a Jewish state with hundreds of thousands, maybe millions of people. His dream is nicer than most of mine, I have to admit. But take a look around. What is here? Who is here? It's like Anatevka. We have our own little circle, but the Arabs outnumber us almost ten to one. So far they haven't bothered us and we haven't bothered them, but how long will that last?

We've made progress draining the swamps near the kibbutz and planting our orchards. But, for now, it's little more than a tiny oasis. Bernice, the American, told me a famous American writer named Mark Twain visited Palestine and wrote about never seeing a soul, and the land being so desolate he couldn't imagine life. It's a desert. Dirt, rocks, sand, swamps. Jonathan doesn't have to worry about us running out of things to do to make this the paradise he envisions.

Still, I wouldn't trade this wilderness for any city. What, with all their cars, brick houses and trash? Your ears are bombarded by noise and your nose by the foulest smells.

Here, all you can see for miles is dirt, hills, grass and trees. Open space. The only sounds are the buzzing of bees and flies, the chirping of birds and the croaking of frogs. The smells are the fragrances of wildflowers. I look up and instead of seeing chimneys belching smoke, a gorgeous blue blanket covers me with God's rays.

Before I realized what was happening, I found myself in a different kind of blanket, surrounded by Arabs on horseback. They had crept up on me so stealthily I didn't hear them coming. Now they forced me to stop my wagon.

I had seen Arabs many times while making deliveries in the village, but I had never spoken to one. These Arabs were clad in robes with kaffiyehs partially covering their dark faces and daggers visible in their belts. They looked at me as if I were a stray animal that had wandered from the herd.

"Good day to you," I said pleasantly.

"You will come with us," the one I took to be the leader said menacingly.

Before I could respond, the Arabs began riding north, away from the kibbutz and the village, pulling my horse and wagon with them.

"If you don't mind, I think I'll ride with you," I said.

We rode in a direction I had never been, with no sign of humans. I could see what the American Twain had meant. It was the kind of desolate landscape I imagined surrounded Hodel in Siberia. Instead of snow, however, this expanse was covered with dust, rocks and weeds and I felt as though I might melt rather than freeze.

In the distance, I could see a long tent with goats and sheep grazing nearby. A herd of camels was tied to a post. As we got closer, I saw a group of children running around chasing a chicken. Four women were standing around a pot that reminded me of our old dunghill fires.

I suppose if these men wanted to hurt me, they would have done it already; still, I can feel my knees shaking like a humming-bird's wings.

When we reached the tent, the Arab who had spoken earlier, gestured for me to enter. I climbed down from the wagon and gave a little bow to each of the men on horseback before walking into the tent. It was not an elaborate structure, just canvas held up by poles buried in the ground. An old man in a white aba and red checkered kaffiyeh was seated on the carpeted floor beside a hookah. He had a weather-beaten look, darker than most Arabs I've seen, with a deeply lined face. A young man, perhaps Devorah's age, sat beside him. His skin was just as dark, but his face was smooth, with a neat black moustache covering his upper lip. While the old man sat looking relaxed, the younger one was coiled like a cobra poised to strike.

"*Salaam aleikum,*" the younger Arab said. "Welcome to the tent of Sheikh Jabber. I am his son, Ali. My father does not speak Hebrew so I will speak for him."

"*Shalom aleichem.* I am Tevye, from Kibbutz —"

"I know where you're from."

"You do?"

"Of course."

"May I ask how?"

"We have watched you come and go making your deliveries."

"Oh."

"Would you like some tea?"

"Yes, thank you."

Ali clapped his hands and a young girl covered from head to toe in a black robe appeared and placed a round brass tray in front of me with a small cup and kettle in the center.

I could barely see her eyes, but saw them stare at me for just an instant before she backed away.

"Thank you," I said, watching her leave the tent and join the other women beside the cauldron on the fire.

"*Shokran*," Ali said to me.

"What's that?"

"It means 'thank you' in Arabic. If you are going to live among us, you should learn our language."

"Is that why you know Hebrew?"

"Yes. My father sent me to a school to study. He foresaw the coming of many Jews and thought it would be useful for me to know how to talk with them."

"Your father is as wise as he is generous."

Ali did not translate my compliment and the sheikh showed no sign of comprehending.

"What are you doing here?" Ali asked.

"What do you mean, what am I doing here?" I repeated.

"Did you not understand my question?"

"I understood. I thought you knew that your friends brought me."

"No, you do not understand. I mean what are you doing on my land?"

"Your land? I was on the road to the kibbutz. We purchased this land."

"Fool! All of the land belongs to the Arabs of Palestine."

"Is that why you steal from the kibbutzim?"

"Steal!" Ali shouted and leaped toward me, pulling a dagger from his robe. "How dare you say such a thing in my house?"

The sudden outburst surprised and frightened me, but I couldn't do anything but recoil. I was completely at his mercy.

I could see Ali's eyes burning with hatred and began to recite the *Sh'ma Yisrael*, hoping God would let me finish this last prayer before I died at the hands of this crazy man.

Then Sheikh Jabber barked some command in Arabic. Ali hovered over me until his father spoke again. He then slowly returned to his seat, never turning his back to me or letting the scowl fall from his face.

"With respect," I said nervously, "the land where my kibbutz was built was purchased from an Arab who lives in Beirut. I thought he sold most of the land in this area."

"The land of our fathers cannot be bought or sold. You are invaders who are trying to steal our land!"

I didn't want to argue with a man in his own house, especially when that man has a big knife. Ali's demeanor was such a contrast to his father's. While Ali seemed prepared to slit my throat on the spot, Sheikh Jabber just sat motionless with a placid expression. Even when he yelled at Ali, he did it with the kind of authoritative tone an officer might use to give a soldier an order, rather than an angry one. I sensed he did not like his son losing control in front of a stranger.

"Ali, this is the land of my grandparents' grandparents. It is the land promised by God to the Jewish people."

"Our family has lived here for generations. I have never met a Jew."

"And I have never met an Arab."

"There isn't room for both of us."

"Why? I may be a little *zaftik*, but I don't take up too much space. Look around you, we are hardly sardines in a can here."

"I don't know what this means, sardines in cans," Ali replied. "I do know that more of you arrive each day and take more of our land. If you are not stopped, you will steal it all and we will lose our homes."

"But we have no wish to take your homes. We want only to live peacefully in our homeland."

"Our homeland," Ali snarled.

I was searching the sheikh's face for a hint of disagreement. I was hoping that Ali was expressing his own opinion rather than conveying a message from his father. Sheikh Jabber just put the hookah in his mouth and stared at me blankly.

"Would it be so terrible to live together?" I asked. The Prophet Isaiah said the lamb would one day lie down with the wolf. Why can't this be that day?"

"That is fine, so long as you understand that I am the wolf."

"I am happy to share the land with you."

"You still don't grasp what I'm telling you. I *will not* share my land."

"So you didn't invite me here for tea because you wanted us to become friends."

"We Arabs are a hospitable people, Tevye, but you should not confuse this hospitality with weakness. We will drive you from our home. If not today then tomorrow. If not tomorrow, the day after. It took two centuries for us to expel the Crusaders, but they are gone. You too will be forced to leave."

"Ali, you should not be mistaken about our resolve. This land, and no other, was promised to the Jewish people by God Almighty. I have been thrown out of my home once. I will not be made to leave my home again. This time, if necessary, I will fight."

"Then you must prepare for war, because we will not let you stay. My father brought you here to warn you that we will not allow our homes and our land to be stolen. Leave now, before it is too late."

"My people have wandered for two-thousand years, Ali. Those days are over. We are here to stay."

"Then," Ali said, "we will see what the true will of God is."

4

⚜

The Bedouins are a strange people. After threatening me and my people, Sheikh Jabber served the most sumptuous meal of lamb, rice and pita. I was reluctant to eat the lamb, but after Ali's earlier flash of anger, I wasn't about to risk insulting him by not eating. I pretended to enjoy it. Actually, I didn't have to act. I hope God will understand why I violated his commandment to eat only kosher food.

We did not talk while we ate. The sheikh stared at me silently, eating slowly with three fingers. Ali wolfed down his food as if the quicker we were done, the sooner he would be rid of me. At one point the sheikh spoke to his son. If it was meant for me, Ali did not pass on the message.

After this awkward feast, Ali surprised me by announcing that his father wanted to strike a bargain with me. I couldn't imagine what kind of deal he would want, other than to agree to lead my people into the Mediterranean. Then again, it was hard to tell how much of what Ali had said before was his opinion and how much was really his father's.

I was happy to accept his proposal. Ali said his father agreed not to steal — his word was "bother" — from the kibbutz if I would periodically come to report on the attitudes of the Jews toward the Arabs. Ali added he would also be willing to share information about the Arabs.

Apparently, I was the first Jew Sheikh Jabber had ever met, and he considered me a bit of a curiosity, like an animal in a zoo. He wanted to study Tevye and learn more about the Jewish people. I think he also hoped to use me as a kind of spy to keep abreast of the plans for our state. Since I'm not privy to any of the *yishuv's* secrets, I was sure that nothing I could tell him would hurt our cause. At the same time, I did hope to learn more from Sheikh Jabber about Arab intentions, so perhaps I would be forewarned before any violence. Of course, I'm smart enough to know he doesn't plan on giving away any secrets either.

The whole experience was quite nerve-racking. Ali's mood shifts from fury to cordiality kept me off balance. Until the end, I was never quite sure why I had been brought to the Sheikh's tent, or if I would be allowed to leave.

When I rode back through the gate to the safety of the kibbutz, I was still trembling. As I thought more about what Ali had said, my anger rose.

"Merciful God, I believed that when You allowed the Tsar to drive me from my home, my fatherland, it was for the best, since You brought me to the Holy Land. But now the Arabs want to expel me from my homeland. Sure, I know, it's nothing new, the Canaanites and the Babylonians and the Assyrians and the Romans all did the same thing. But You did not let Your people remain in dispersion. You have brought us home. Surely, You would not let us be evicted again. Would You?"

"At least You brought me back safely to the kibbutz. I was beginning to think the horse and cart would give out at the same time and everyone would lose their bets."

I pulled the wagon up to the barn and started to release my horse from the harness. "Here boy. You'll feel better after I relieve you of this burden."

Did you know that talking to animals makes them feel more comfortable? And how do I know that, you're wondering, if they can't speak. I know the same way that I am sure God hears me even though He doesn't respond. If the Almighty won't answer, why should it bother me that the horses and cows and chickens refuse to speak?

See, as soon as you relieve the old boy of his burden and give him an apple to nosh, he perks right up. I wish it was as easy to know how to satisfy the Arabs. On one hand, this is the land God promised to Abraham. On the other hand, the Arabs believe they too are descendants of Abraham, through his son Ishmael. Ali is right, his family has lived here many generations while most of the Jews have just arrived. He should not have to give up his land. Then again, no one is asking him to. Why shouldn't we live together in peace, as we do now? I wouldn't object to stopping at his tent to make deliveries. On the other hand, we cannot force him to accept us as neighbors. On the other hand, I'm running out of hands.

"*Shalom* Tevye," Simcha shouted from across the now green lawn that separated the kitchen from the houses when he saw me come out of the barn.

As soon as I was close enough, Simcha grabbed my hand and pumped it like he was trying to get water out of a well. Then he pulled me to him so he could give me a hug. When he released me, he smiled with his typical gap-toothed grin.

"You look troubled. What is it my friend?" Simcha asked.

"I came here to find peace but God has not willed it to be."

"Tevye, what are you talking about? Look around you. Since you and I came here we have built an entire community from dust. Look at the flowers, the buildings the fields, the orchards. This is happening all around the country. It is just as Jonathan promised. We work and we live."

"We have done all that you say. And it is a good life. A very good life. But we did not come to an empty land. Bernice's friend Mark Twain was wrong when he said no people lived here. The Arabs are here. They have been here for a long time, long before you and I arrived. They don't want us here."

"We mean them no harm. We've been living here beside them peacefully and will continue to do so. They are profiting as much as we are from the work we are doing. Look at how we are developing the land. The Arabs will benefit as the standard of living of everyone improves."

"I know that. The Bible says we should cultivate our neighbor like a garden, but you don't understand. They don't want us to help them. They are afraid we want to steal their homes."

"That's nonsense."

The whole ride home from the sheikh's tent I thought about what Ali had said and searched my memory for some Talmudic references to help me understand his position. It occurred to me that maybe the Jewish people were not meant to return at this time, in this way.

"The Good Book also says if you want something, it can lead to coveting it, which leads to stealing it."

"Wait a minute, Tevye. Are you trying to tell me we're violating the tenth commandment because we want to live in Palestine?"

"The Rambam said that even if you exchange what you want for something that is more valuable, once you've bought it from a reluctant seller, you've disobeyed the commandment. And, worse yet, if you take it by force, you also violate the eighth commandment."

"That's absurd. God promised this land to us and we have lived here for centuries. We cannot covet or steal what is rightfully ours."

"It doesn't matter what we say, it matters only what they think."

"And the sheikh accused you of breaking two commandments?"

"Of course not. I'm just trying to make you see the Arabs' point of view, which is that we want land that belongs to them."

"You're giving me a headache. What's gotten into you anyway, Tevye? Since when are you so concerned about the Arabs?"

Simcha was right. I was now twisting the words of our own sages to support Ali's case. This is our homeland, and has been for centuries, even when only a handful of Jews lived here.

"I'm sorry, Simcha. I'm a little confused after visiting the Bedouin sheikh who lives to the north," I said pointing. "Beyond the hills."

"What on earth made you do that? He could have killed you."

"Let's just say I was an invited guest. Besides, why would they kill an old Jew delivering milk and bread?"

"Tevye, do you know what the Bedouins call us? The 'Children of Death,' because they think it's easy to rob and murder Jews."

"Well, today, at least, they did neither."

"So, tell me what was the sheikh like?"

"I don't know."

"What do you mean? You just told me —"

"The sheikh couldn't speak Hebrew. His son Ali spoke for him. He was a very bright young man. I was treated well. A woman, covered by an aba from head to toe, served me sweet tea and then a tremendous meal. I sat on a beautiful rug in their tent. They even fed my horse."

"So why are you so distressed?"

"Because Ali did not hide his feelings. He said I should not confuse hospitality with weakness. The Arabs plan to drive us out by force."

"They can't. We'll fight. Even now Moshe is being secretly trained to be a soldier by men from the old World War I Jewish Brigade. This isn't Russia, Tevye. This is our homeland, the land of our forefathers, the land promised to us by Almighty God. No one will take it from us."

I felt a little silly standing there listening to Simcha use my own words. What were we arguing about?

"I know. I told this to Ali. The Arabs know our numbers are small and they believe they can drive us into the sea.

Simcha put his hand on my shoulder in a fatherly way. Grinning, he said, "Tevye, he's wrong. You of all people, the only one among us who has regular conversations with God, should know He will not allow it to happen to the Chosen People. I never thought I would have to say this to you, but I'm going to now. Have faith."

His words made me feel better. I straightened up and smiled. "Simcha, you're right. God has promised this land to us and He will not let anyone take it away."

I hugged Simcha with the same gusto with which he first embraced me.

"*Shalom* Simcha."

"*Shalom* Tevye."

As Simcha walked away, I noticed the clouds breaking up and the sun peeking through. Simcha's enthusiasm even affects the weather. "You must like him. He's a good man. And he's right. You have brought us home for a reason. And it is not to let any new Amalekites drive us away."

I winked at the parting clouds and walked inside my house.

Golde was sitting hunched over at the table.

"Such a day I've had, Golde. You would not believe where I was. Guess? You can't, so don't even try. I was in the tent of a Bedouin sheikh. I sat and drank tea and . . . . What's the matter, Golde?"

I suddenly realized Golde was crying. A tear-stained paper fell from her hand.

"What is it? News from Tzeitl?"

Golde lifted her head weakly. She looked different. Even though she worked all day in the kitchen, she spent enough time outside over the years for the Mediterranean sun to bake her skin almond brown. Now, she looked pallid. Loose strands of hair hung from her head where they would normally be neatly brushed. And, for the first time, I noticed gray flecks.

"Golde."

"Terrible news."

"What?"

"I can't bare it. To be separated and —"

"Tell me. What's happened?"

"It's a letter from Tzeitl."

"And?"

Golde just sobbed.

"Do I have to drag it from you the way we do questions from Natan?"

"Tzeitl says violence has spread throughout Russia," Golde said in a barely audible whisper. "The Soviets have become more and more anti-Zionist. They've shut down most of Jonathan's centers."

"Is Tzeitl in danger? What is it already?"

"Pertschik is dead."

"What?"

"The authorities decided to do away with all the troublemakers in the prisons so they could not help incite the people in the streets. They hung Pertschik."

I sank into the chair beside her and put my face in my hands. "Poor Pertschik. He was such a good man. He cared nothing for himself. All he wanted was to help the unfortunate and the lowly. And Hodel, my baby, she loved him so. What she must be going through. If only we were there to comfort her."

"Hodel was crushed. She wrote that the authorities were looking for her. Tzeitl doesn't know what's happened to her. What if she's dead, too?"

"Shh. Don't talk like that," I said. "She's fine. Hodel is strong. She survived in Siberia for all these years; she'll be all right."

Turning away so Golde wouldn't hear, I whispered, "Oh God, please let it be so."

Golde began to cry hysterically. I put my arm around her.

Barely able to speak, she said, "There's more."

"More?" I didn't think I could bear to hear it.

Choking back the tears, Golde picked the letter off the floor and handed it to me. I took it and read past the words referring to Pertschik's death. The handwriting was still neat, carefully drawn. Tevye's daughters are all strong. Then I noticed the letters became less precise, as if Tzeitl had fought to keep her hand from shaking.

"Motel has the coughing sickness," I read and dropped my forehead into my palm.

"He's been working too hard," Golde said frantically. "Tzeitl said he works in a basement that is dark and cold. We should have never left them behind. I can't do anything from here."

"What choice did we have, Golde?"

"They're our children and grandchildren."

"I know, but what difference would it have made if we were there? Would you have stopped the Communists from hanging poor Pertschik — *alav ha-shalom*? Would you have prevented Motel from getting sick? Don't talk foolishness, woman. Motel will recover."

I realized I didn't sound very convincing.

"You'll see," I said more gently. "His hard work will pay off and he will bring the family here to join us. And we will see our grandchildren."

"Our grandchildren. We'll never see them. And Hodel." Golde's wailing made me feel helpless.

"Stop it," I said. "They're in God's hands."

"Pertschik —"

"Pertschik has suffered the same fate as some of our greatest sages. Do you know what the Romans did to Rabbi Akiva? They burned him at the stake. It is not for us to question."

"Tevye, I can't stand being separated from my daughters."

"You have three daughters right here to worry about."

"And I can't even see them. They live with the other children. They belong with their parents."

"It's too late to start this argument again. When we were given the chance to join the kibbutz, Jonathan told us the children would have to live apart. They are almost grown up now anyway; besides, we do see them every day. Look, here comes Shoshana now."

Shoshana entered the house and looked surprised to see me embracing her mother. It was probably because we rarely touched each other in front of the children.

"What's wrong, Mama?"

Golde wiped her eyes with her sleeve. "Nothing dear. I think I'm going to go outside and tend to my garden for a while."

"But it's so hot now. Why don't you lie down and rest a bit before dinner."

Golde forced a smile. She was always cheered by the sight of her children.

"It's all right. I'll only stay out a few minutes."

Shoshana and I watched Golde walk out the door. Shoshana had a look of pity on her face, as if she'd just realized her mother was growing old. It's always a painful moment when children see their parents aging. When we're young, we don't think about what our parents will be like when they get older, but, at some point, a child catches a glimpse of their mortality. Then, suddenly, they understand in an emotional, rather than intellectual way, that their parents will die one day.

"Why was Mama so upset, Papa?"

"It's nothing. You know how she gets sometimes. She misses your sisters."

"I miss them too."

"Of course you do. So do I."

Shoshana came over and hugged me. I looked down and saw the same face looking up at me that I remembered from her childhood. A face full of hope and optimism. I wondered if she and the other young people had any idea about the feelings of the Arabs. They all were devoted to the kibbutz and worked like the Israelites in Egypt to build what they expected to be a new Jewish state. Will they be forced to leave their home as I had, or will they fight to keep what they've built? I think I know the answer.

"And what is new with you, Shoshie?"

"You know I hate when you call me that."

"A father can't have his own special name for his daughter?"

"Of course. But I'm a little old for that one, don't you think?"

"No, you'll always be my Shoshie."

"All right, Papa."

"So, how was work?"

"Every day is another step toward our new state. Chaim says the British will get tired of dealing with us and the Arabs and just pick up and leave."

"Perhaps he's heard this from the Almighty."

"He's a dreamer."

"A dreamer? I don't recall the planning committee creating a job for dreamers."

"Oh, stop it, Papa. He works as hard as anyone. He just thinks that by working and becoming one with the land we will rebuild the Jewish spirit and then the state will follow."

"If he becomes one with the land, I know he'll get dirty. I don't know about the rest."

"Very funny. He's more interested in reading the works of socialist philosophers than religious scholars, but I think you'd like him anyway."

I thought about the conversation I overheard in the orchard and the way Chaim looked at my daughter. I don't think I like him at all, but I suspect that won't matter in the end.

"Actually, Papa, Chaim reminds me a little of someone you know very well."

"He doesn't sound familiar."

"He reminds me of Pertschik. Remember how he used to prattle on about the workers uniting and taking over the earth. I'd love to see his face when he heard you were on a labor committee."

I fell back into my chair and put my head in my hands.

"Have I said something wrong? What is it, Papa?"

I couldn't look her in the eyes for fear of breaking down. I will not cry in front of my daughter.

"Pertschik is dead," I whispered.

"Dead?"

Shoshana knelt in front of me and lifted my head. She could see tears forming in the corners of my eyes.

"But how? Why?"

"They hung him. Why? Who can explain the evil impulse? Why was there a Sodom and Gomorrah?"

"And Hodel?"

"She's disappeared."

"Oh Papa."

Shoshana embraced me again and we held each other tight, but I could not stop trembling.

5

Sooner or later, everyone here gets dysentery. Fortunately, my case has come later. My stomach feels like someone is trying to turn it inside out. At least, I'm not running to the outhouse every five minutes. My daughter insisted I come to the infirmary so she could make sure I was getting enough fluids and have the doctor keep his eye on me. The good news is I get to keep mine on her.

"This is going to feel like a bee sting, but it'll only hurt for a moment," Devorah said to the little boy gazing in terror at the needle the doctor was placing in a vial. She stroked his head gently.

"What's your favor subject in school?"

The boy refused to take his eyes off the doctor.

"You must like something. When I was your age, I didn't go to school. Where I come from, girls usually didn't get to study.

"Really?" the boy said. "What did you do? Were you able to play all the time?"

"Not exactly," Devorah laughed. "I spent a lot of time helping my mother."

"Ouch," the boy shrieked, as the doctor stuck him with the needle. A moment later, Dr. Susser withdrew it and placed a bandage over the puncture.

Rubbing his arm, the boy turned to Devorah. "You tricked me."

"See, it didn't really hurt that bad. It's always better to be distracted. I learned that trick from my father." She looked in my direction and winked.

The doctor pulled a lollipop out of the pocket of his white coat and handed it to the boy. "Here, this should help you recover, Yigal. Now lay back down and rest. I want you to get better, so I don't have to put up with your nonsense anymore."

"You're just tired of him beating you in chess."

"That's enough from you, nurse," Dr. Susser said with mock indignation.

Devorah bent over and kissed Yigal on top of his head.

I watched Dr. Susser walk to his desk and sit down. He's one of the tallest men on the kibbutz, but he walks hunched over like a man twenty years older. He told me once it was some sort of disease affecting the curvature of the spine. The fact that he is almost completely bald, with only patches of thin black hair above his ears also adds years to his appearance.

Dr. Susser was rubbing his eyes under his glasses. Everyone liked him. He had the same calm manner that put you at ease regardless of what you were suffering from. He was another of the *vattikim*, the one who helped keep most of the others alive when they came down with malaria and some of the other diseases that claimed the lives of many early pioneers.

"Tea?"

"Yes, please." Devorah said, taking a chair beside Dr. Susser.

"It's about the only good thing I have to say about the British. They know how to make good tea. Now the Turks, they know coffee."

"You were here during the Ottoman Empire?"

"Yes, I'm on the empire tour," Dr. Susser said with the same monotone he used to talk to patients. "So far, I've gotten to see three, the last two without having to move."

"The first was Russia?"

"Yes. Left after Kishinev."

"That was the time of the first pogroms."

"Hardly the first. One thing all the empires seem to have in common is a hatred for the Jews."

"That's for sure," I chimed in from my sick bed.

"That's enough from you, Tevye," Dr. Susser said. He was the only person on the kibbutz everyone called by his last name. I don't even know his first name. "You're here to rest. And that includes your mouth."

"But —"

"You're worse than the children, Papa," Devorah interrupted. "Go to sleep."

I didn't have the strength to argue, so I listened.

"The British are on our side," Devorah said. "Why else would they issue the Balfour Declaration and offer us a homeland?"

"Geopolitics, my dear. They didn't give a fig for us or our homeland. The British needed the Americans to help them in the Great War. They thought doing a favor for the Jews here would cause the Jews in America to encourage their government to fight on their side."

"So, if we can't trust them, how are we going to get a state?"

The naiveté of the young, I thought. They always think their dreams will magically come true.

"The same way we built this kibbutz, inch by inch, brick by brick. You think the British built this infirmary? Devorah, before you came, I worked out of a tent. Sometimes so many *chaverim* had malaria we had to keep two in a bed. We had to beg, bribe and steal medicine from the British."

"I always thought you were more of an optimist."

"Realist," he corrected. "Faith is important, my dear, especially if one is to live in Palestine. When God picked this land to be our home, sometimes I think he decided to find the place farthest from Eden. But when I see the children, I'm filled with joy. They won't have to know what it's like to be surrounded by anti-Semites. They won't have to live in fear of angry mobs. They —"

Two men burst through the doors of the clinic with a third man between them supported only by their shoulders. The injured man's feet dragged along the ground and his head hung limply. I saw that his chest was spattered with blood.

"Put him on the table there!" the doctor said calmly but with authority. "Devorah, get me hot water, bandages and a sterile scalpel."

Devorah stood immobile, staring at the injured man.

"Devorah, quickly!"

Devorah ran to another part of the infirmary. "Wash your hands and put on a mask," Dr. Susser shouted after her while he and the two men ripped open the wounded man's shirt. Devorah came back with what the doctor ordered. Susser quickly scrubbed his hands in a basin and put on gloves.

"Even though he's unconscious, I want to make sure he stays that way during the procedure." Dr. Susser asked Devorah to get a bottle of ether from the medicine cabinet. "Go ahead and give him a handkerchief full."

Devorah did as she was instructed.

"Ok, let's start. Devorah, hand me the scalpel and stand close on the other side and hand me gauze pads. The rest of you stand back."

I could see Devorah staring at the faces of the men who brought in the man on the table.

"Who are you?" I asked.

The shorter of the two men spoke without looking up. His shirt was covered with the blood of his comrade. I moved close so I could see his face. It was bruised and covered with a mixture of grime and black stubble. Curly hair flowed out of the back and sides of his army cap.

"I'm Shimshon and this is Yossi. We are members of the Haganah."

The one he called Yossi was much taller. He wasn't wearing a hat so I could see he had short dark hair with a growing bald spot in the back. His face was equally soiled and, combined with a beard and moustache, made his face look almost completely black.

"What happened?" Dr. Susser asked quietly as he made an incision in the unconscious man's chest.

"A group of Arabs attacked Petah Tikvah last night." Yossi replied. "We didn't get there until after the killing began. Arik was wounded when he jumped in front of a small boy who was about to be shot by an Arab."

Dr. Susser cut open Arik's chest. He spoke calmly while he worked. "Why weren't you able to prevent the attack?"

Yossi made no effort to keep his voice down. "It was the British commander again. He wouldn't allow us to go to the town even after we told him we knew there would be an attack. We begged him to send troops, but he wouldn't. We had no choice but to take the long road around the back of the city. By the time we reached our people, the Arabs were gone."

"Then the British arrived," Shimshon added.

"The British entered as the Arabs were leaving," Yossi continued. "They came in and said they were going to disarm *us*. Someone fired a shot. To be honest, I don't know if it was one of us or them, but soon the police and soldiers opened fire. Arik was hit. Shimshon and I snuck out with him. We traveled all night to get him here."

"Why didn't you take him to a hospital?"

I could tell the one called Yossi didn't like having to explain his actions. Before he could make a nasty retort, Shimshon said, "Because the British would be looking for us there. Anyone suspected of being involved in the fighting will be arrested."

"How many were killed in the village?" asked Dr. Susser.

"I don't know for sure. Some were women and children." Yossi's voice sounded more disgusted than pained.

"And your losses?"

"We all went in different directions when the British arrived." Yossi closed his eyes and rubbed his forehead. "I'd say at least six wounded. Arik was probably the worst."

"I was wrong," Dr. Susser said mournfully to himself as much as Devorah. "Our children aren't safe even here in our homeland."

"But why would the Arabs do such a thing?" Devorah asked as she handed the doctor a gauze pad. "We get along very well with our neighbors."

"Because they hate Jews little girl. Do you know what they would do to you if they could?"

"That's enough Yossi!" Shimshon snapped. "What's your name nurse, Devorah?"

Devorah looked shocked by the rage in the men. It took a moment for her to respond. "Yes, Devorah," she said finally with as much authority as she could muster.

Lying down, I couldn't see what Dr. Susser was doing. I knew he was good at handling the typical kibbutz injury, a broken toe, a sprain, indigestion, but wasn't sure if he knew how to remove bullets. He acted as though it were no different than removing a splinter.

"Devorah, you have to understand something." Shimshon explained. "The Arabs have lived here for generations and during that time only a handful of Jews settled near them. Now, more and more Jews are coming and the Arabs are afraid we're going to steal their country. A lot of them were happy to sell us their land for outrageous prices and move to other Arab countries. The ones left behind are mostly peasants who believe whatever nonsense religious leaders like the Mufti tell them. They've become even more scared since the British said they would help us build a Jewish homeland in Palestine. Never mind the fact that the British haven't been much help."

I felt like I was hearing an echo of my words to Simcha.

"But the Balfour Declaration says the rights of the Arabs will be protected in the Jewish homeland."

"Silly girl," Yossi said. "The British will only protect the rights of the British. They don't care about Arabs or Jews. While Chaim Weizmann and the rest of the Jewish dilettantes drink tea with the Prime Minister at Whitehall, we're going to fight for our lives. The only way we will have a Jewish State is if we drive all the Arabs out of Palestine."

"That's enough Yossi!" Shimshon shouted.

"But it's their land too," Devorah said. "Even if we wanted to get rid of them, how could we? There are so many more of them than us?"

"No one said it would be easy," Yossi continued, ignoring his comrade. "If you want a sheltered life, move to London with Weizmann."

"You don't make it very easy for a person to operate," Dr. Susser said as he held up a tweezer with a bullet. "Your friend was very lucky. It missed his heart and the major arteries and veins. We won't know for sure for a few days, but I think he'll be all right."

"Thank God. And thank you Doctor," Shimshon said as he hugged Yossi.

"He'll need to stay here for awhile to recuperate."

"How long?" Yossi asked.

"Hard to say. Recovery from a traumatic wound like this can be weeks or months. He'd be better off at a hospital.

"I'm afraid he has to stay here," Shimshon said.

"As you wish. But don't expect him back for awhile."

"I'm afraid we don't have the luxury of time, Doctor." Yossi's tone had turned more sarcastic than angry. "The Arabs aren't going to wait for us to grow stronger."

"I understand."

"We'll be on our way now," Shimshon said, pulling Yossi toward the door. "The British confiscated a lot of our weapons and we'll have to procure some more."

"Procure?"

Shimshon and Yossi both looked at Devorah and laughed.

"Steal," said Yossi. "I know. I know. It's a sin. I'll repent on Yom Kippur. If I'm still alive."

The two men started out the door. Yossi turned to the doctor. "Thank you again. And be careful. If the Arabs' continue their pattern, you will be in line for an attack soon."

"God be with you," Dr. Susser said to their backs.

"God be with you," I repeated from my cot.

"They are very brave," Devorah said, seeing the doctor staring at the door. "But the younger one seemed very bitter."

"He is bitter."

"How do you know that?" I asked.

Dr. Susser slowly walked out the door. I could barely hear him say, "Because he's my son."

6

Can you smell the air? It's strange how something you can't see can fill you with such pleasure. It's like getting a massage from the inside. I have the same kind of feeling when I pray. But do you think I can explain that to my socialist friends here?

"The work nourishes my soul," Simcha tells me.

I'm not sure if he really believes it or just repeats Jonathan's every word. It's not that Jonathan isn't a righteous man, he is, but he insists that time for study only takes away from nation-building.

"What will we have built," I ask him, "if we don't know what God expects us to do? And don't tell me, 'live.' We may exist, but we will not be living if we don't seek guidance from our sages. As Rav Kook says, all our most cherished possessions are vessels of the spirit of God."

"You're right, Tevye," Jonathan answers. "A people with a land are no better than a people without a land, if they do not have the spirit of God. To show you I'm not completely ignorant, I can quote authorities too. It was Rav Landau who said, 'Torah cannot be reborn without labor and labor, as a creative and nation-building force, cannot be reborn without Torah.' I can tell our people how to build, and even why they should work, but I can't tell them how they should live. Not even I am that arrogant."

So Jonathan began to spend time during the Sabbath studying with me. And once the others saw that their leader was not afraid to open a holy book, they too joined in our sessions. Even some of the devoted Marxists put down their manifestos long enough to read the weekly *parsha*. Of course, it didn't take long for new rabbis to emerge. Everyone suddenly was the Rambam. Then the arguments grew worse. Some people wanted their own study groups. It was like the old joke about every Jew needing their own synagogue. Jonathan saw the problem growing and called a meeting of the executive committee. They decided to end the study groups to prevent the cohesion of the kibbutz from disintegrating.

Jonathan apologized to me for ending the sessions. He said I should continue to study and to be the rebbe for the kibbutz, but most of the *chaverim* would be better off sticking to socialist polemics. The followers of Hillel and Shammai fought over every interpretation, Jonathan reminded me, but in the end the rabbis had decided to accept the teachings of Hillel. "We have decided to accept your interpretation, Reb Tevye," he said.

Well, I was filled with pride. I remembered what the rabbi had told me back in Anatevka about being like Hillel trying to explain the Torah with one foot in my mouth. If he only knew the respect I had earned. Yes, I know, he would probably spin in his grave.

At least the committee listened to me when I told them we must celebrate Sukkot, since it is a celebration of the harvest. They're still not that enthusiastic about holidays that aren't related to the harvest or the revolution. But I insisted the children learn what it meant for the Israelites to wander forty years in the desert. That's why I'm building this little booth we call a sukkah.

The Lord said, "For in booths did I make the children of Israel dwell when I brought them out of the land of Egypt." And so each year we build our little sukkahs to remember our ancestors' wanderings. Now, with unrest in the villages, it is especially nice to retire to our sukkah of peace.

The Israelites could see the stars through the roofs of their booths, that's why I'm putting these fronds on top instead of something solid. To tell you the truth, this reminds me a little of where we lived when we first arrived in Palestine. The tents and huts often had so many holes we might as well have been in sukkahs.

We have another tradition during Sukkot. You take a palm branch, a myrtle branch and a willow branch and bind them together. We call this is a *lulav*. And this thing that looks like a giant lemon is a citron or *etrog*. We hold them together and recite a prayer, "Blessed art Thou, Lord our God, King of the universe who has sanctified us with His commandments and commanded us concerning the taking of the *lulav*." Then we wave them in each direction, north, south, east and west, up and down. This little ritual shows our belief that God is everywhere.

We eat and sleep in the sukkah. On the seventh day, at least in the synagogue, all the Torah scrolls are taken out of the ark and the congregants march around seven times with the *lulav* and *etrog*. This day even gets its own name, Hoshana Rabba.

On the eighth day we celebrate Shmini Atzeret and say a prayer for rain.

The most joyous day of the year is the following day, Simkhat Torah. This holiday marks the completion of the annual cycle of Torah readings. On this day, all the Torah scrolls are again removed from the ark and congregants march, sing and dance around the sanctuary with them. This is done seven times, called *hakafot*.

This is the time of year I miss our little synagogue in Anatevka the most, but we've developed our own way to celebrate here that will reflect the joy we feel. We're going to have a torchlight procession and lots of singing and dancing, which the *chaverim* don't need any excuse to do, so we'll start a new tradition.

"Excuse me, Tevye. May I speak to you for a moment?"

"Who is this? Ah, Chaim the socialist. Have you come to help me build the sukkah? This is manual labor, just what you believe we all should do. Here, you can hang some fruit inside," I said, and handed Chaim a carrot, apple and pomegranate.

"I will be happy to help you, but I have something important to discuss first."

"So speak. Can't a socialist work and talk at the same time?"

Chaim stood on a chair in the sukkah and attached the fruit to a string and hung it from a slat in the roof.

"Tevye, we have known each other since you came to this kibbutz from Russia. I grew up in the same children's house with your daughter Shoshana and I work in the orchards with her every day. We are almost like family."

"Yes, almost. One of the things I've always liked about the kibbutz is that everyone is *almost* like family, but, fortunately, they are not part of the family. That way the people you love are close to you and the people you don't love aren't too close."

"You make this more difficult."

"You seem to be having a hard enough time," I snickered, watching Chaim try to attach a string to the pomegranate. "Would it be easier to use a cucumber?"

"No, I don't mean the fruit. You make it more difficult to say what I have to say."

"Well, say it already," I told him as I walked outside to the back of the sukkah. "These walls aren't solid, so I can still hear you."

"Tevye, I would like to have your permission to have Shoshana's hand in marriage."

I stared at the outside of the sukkah for a moment, and then raced back inside. "What was that? I couldn't hear you."

Chaim cleared his throat, but his voice still cracked. "I said I would like to have your permission to have Shoshana's hand in marriage."

I picked up the *lulav* and *etrog* again and shook them in all directions. I pretended Chaim wasn't there and looked for help from the Almighty.

"Are You still here? Haven't I had enough troubles from my daughters and their men? First, a nearsighted tailor, then a revolutionary, then a Russian peasant, and now a socialist who rebels against his parents, gives up a fortune and spends all his time picking fruit and filling my daughter's head with crazy ideas. Is this Your way of reminding me of the trials of the children of Israel when they were in the desert?"

"Please, Tevye. I love Shoshana. We've grown up together, worked together and played together."

"Played together?"

"As children."

I stroked my beard and looked at the boy with the hopeful eyes standing in front of me. This is a match? He's not much to look at; he's not even as tall as my daughter. I've heard him talk a lot, more than even Pertschik used to do when he first arrived in Anatevka, but I haven't seen him demonstrate any commitment to Torah, in word or deed. On the other hand, he is sharing in the work of building our homeland. On the other hand, I have always wanted my daughters to have a better life; Chaim will keep my daughter here and her life will be no easier than it has been. Of course, she'll be close by. Here on the kibbutz, the children usually make their own matches, sometimes they don't even get married under a *chuppah*, they just announce they are moving in together. If I say "no," how will I prevent them from doing just that? I saw Shoshana's eyes that day in the orchard, when the ladder broke and she fell into Chaim's arms. If I say "yes," at least we might have a real wedding.

"At least you asked. I suppose that's progress."

"Tevye, you don't have to worry about your daughter here. It's not like in the old country where the husband had to make a good living to feed his family. On the kibbutz, all our needs will be provided for, we don't need a fortune. And don't worry about my father. I've told him and he asked to meet you. In fact, he would like you to go to Tel Aviv tonight to speak with him."

"Well, it's true you've grown up together. Besides, I've learned my lesson with my daughters. I haven't the strength to fight them. If Shoshana would like to be the wife of a fruit-picker, then it must be what the Almighty wants. Who am I to say otherwise? You say your father wants me to come to Tel Aviv tonight? Is there such a rush that I can't wait until after Sukkot?"

"When I told him my intention to be married right after the holidays, he thought it was important to speak with you as soon as possible."

"Aren't you rushing things a bit?"

"Yes, but Shoshana and I thought nothing could be better than to celebrate the most joyous occasion of our lives at the most joyous time of the year."

"For a socialist, your thoughts aren't so bad. I will go and tell Golde that I'm going to Tel Aviv tonight."

"Thank you."

"You're welcome."

Chaim flew away like a bee that had collected its fill of nectar. So much for getting help with the sukkah.

You're welcome. Do you hear me? That's now the extent of my influence over my daughters' lives. Look at him. The son of one of the richest men in Palestine and he's dressed like a peasant who just crossed the desert. What kind of a boy rebels against his parents and runs away from a comfortable home to work in this paradise? Shoshana was right; he is a lot like Pertschik. But will he suffer Pertschik's fate? At least here he's not alone in his views. On the other hand, what will he offer my daughter? Then again, if Chaim can bring her happiness, who am I to stand in the way? I'd just get trampled anyway.

"Dear Lord, I'm grateful for the blessing of daughters, but are sons-in-law really such a blessing?"

7

Finally, in Palestine we will have a real wedding, not like Tzeitl's when Pertschik broke the taboo against dancing with a woman and then our good neighbors crashed and burned the party.

"A pogrom during a wedding. Dear Lord, I still don't understand why You chose that day of all days to make Your people suffer. All right, who am I to gripe after what the Israelites suffered before you allowed them to live here. What's a couple of broken candlesticks at a wedding compared to wandering in the desert for a generation?"

I've been talking to God about that day for a long time. How can such a thing be for the best? Well, now I can see that it was — maybe. If not for the pogrom, we probably would have never come to Palestine.

We never had another chance to have a truly joyous wedding. Hodel and Pertschik were in such a hurry, they had a quick ceremony with the rabbi and a few witnesses. Then a few hours later, I dropped Pertschik off at the train station in Boiberik. It was the last time I saw him. Not long after, I was seeing Hodel off at the same station. If I think about the way she looked when we said goodbye, I might start to cry.

You probably want to hear about the wedding of our other daughter. It was held in a church. I can't speak about it because she is dead, at least to us. I don't even want to think about it, especially now that I'm in our homeland and my Shoshie will be the first of the Zalmans to marry in *Eretz Yisrael.*

You know what else is great about her being wed here? Her children will be *sabras*, that's what we call Jews born here. Jonathan said the term comes from the Hebrew word for a cactus fruit that is hard on the outside and soft on the inside.

This blessing could not come at a better time. Golde has not been well since the news of Pertschik's death. She has been like a flower that wilts petal by petal. I don't know how much longer she can go on. We all try to cheer her up, to remind her of how much she is loved by the children, and by the *chaverim.* For an instant, her face brightens, a moment of sunlight that keeps the petals from falling, but it is only a respite from the darkness that envelops her. I pray that this news will restore her will to live, but I fear it may be too late.

I entered the house and found Golde sitting in the corner staring blankly out the window. The flower box she had so lovingly tended was now empty. She could not muster the energy to care for anything beyond her immediate family.

"Golde, I have something to tell you. You had better sit."

"I am sitting. What's happened?" she said anxiously. "Has there been another pogrom?"

"No, no. The Arabs have been quiet. What I have to tell you is good news, the best."

"Then why do you want me to sit? It's not about the committee, is it? Or your horse?"

"My horse? Why should I have good news about my horse?"

"Because you spend most of your time telling me about that old mare and the news is never good."

"Never mind, it's got nothing to do with my horse."

"So, what is it?"

"I have given Chaim my permission to marry Shoshana."

"What!" She jumped up and threw her hands in the air as if I'd told her the committee prohibited her from making cabbage borscht.

"What's the matter with you? I thought you would be thrilled that your daughter is going to be married. She will be the first of our daughters to be wed in the Holy Land."

"Thrilled? You expect me to be thrilled that you've given your blessing to the marriage of our daughter to a *schlemiel* — again? Can't you ever say no?"

"Enough woman! I'm still the papa. You're the one who is always so worried about our daughters being married. Chaim is a good man. A hard worker. Besides, he comes from a wealthy family. In fact, I'm going to Tel Aviv tonight to meet his father."

"Chaim, from a wealthy family?"

"Yes, of course. Didn't you hear what I just said? I'm going to his father's mansion to discuss the wedding."

"Chaim, from a wealthy family?"

"Wealthy, wealthy, wealthy! Our daughter is going to be a millionairess."

"Why didn't you say so in the first place? My daughter a millionairess. Oh, thank you God! Thank you!"

"I had a feeling you would like Chaim when you got to know him better." I was glad Golde didn't catch me rolling my eyes.

I gave Golde a hug and kissed the top of her head. Then I started to undress so I could change my clothes for the long ride to the city.

"Not so fast," Golde said, following me. "If he's so rich, what's he doing here on the kibbutz? Why does he live like a pauper, like the rest of us?"

"Who else can afford to live like this, if not a rich man? Unlike the rest of us, he doesn't have to worry that a committee will tell him what he can and cannot have."

"I hate to admit it, but you have a point."

"The great sage has granted me the point. Thank you." I bowed then ducked when I saw her swing a pillow at my head.

"Tevye, this time it will be different. Everything will be perfect. When is the wedding?"

"Right after the holidays."

"But there's so little time and so much to do."

I felt relieved to see Golde so excited. As I'd hoped, marrying off another daughter was the best medicine for her. I pray that the feeling lasts.

"So, get to work," I told her.

"And what are you going to do?"

"I must go to Tel Aviv to meet Chaim's father. When I return, we shall toast our daughter's happiness and our good fortune," I said as I changed into my Sabbath pants and shirt.

"Yes, yes. Enough talking. Go already."

She nearly pushed me out the door.

Well, all I can say is, "Thank you Lord for bringing my Golde back to life."

8

What a glorious day! The sun is shining and the wind is just strong enough to blow the white puffs overhead toward the sea, just as the news of Chaim's proposal whisked Golde's troubles away. And my socialist friends don't believe God still makes miracles? I feel as though I could float with those clouds all the way to the home of Chaim's parents.

"I understand you need a ride into Tel Aviv," Moshe said as I stood staring up into the clearing blue sky.

"Is Tevye's life everyone's business?"

Moshe laughed. "By now, I'd think you'd be used to it."

"But how did the news travel so fast?"

"With Faiga spreading gossip, how long do you think it takes?"

"Faiga. I should have known. If she worked as hard at her job as she does snooping around, she'd be the most productive worker on the kibbutz."

"Quit grousing, Tevye. Do you want a ride or not?"

"Yes, I would like a ride. Where's your wagon?"

"Wagon?" He laughed again. "Don't you realize this is the twentieth century? We have cars and trucks now."

"You mean those mechanical moving beasts?"

"It'll take us a fraction of the time to get to Tel Aviv."

I stood staring at the tin can with wheels he wanted me to ride in.

"It's up to you, Tevye. If you'd rather take a horse."

"No, no. Of course, I'll go with you."

"Great. I could use the company."

Moshe walked around the car and climbed behind the wheel. I stood dumbly trying to figure out how to open the door. Moshe must have guessed the problem and reached over and pulled something on the inside of the door and it popped open.

"It's a new and exciting world, Tevye. You might as well start getting used to it." As he spoke, the car started with a shake and a pop.

"I don't mind new or exciting. I'm just not sure a metal coffin is better than a wooden one," I said, gripping the seat with all my strength.

The car began to roll down the road, jumping over bumps and sinking in holes. Moshe waved to the guard as we drove through the kibbutz gate and headed for Tel Aviv.

I sat silently for a long time, holding on for fear of flying through the front window the first time we hit a big bump.

"Tevye, the seat's bolted to the car," Moshe said, breaking the silence. "You don't have to hold it down."

"Yes, but I'm not bolted down."

"Relax already. It's a lot more comfortable than riding a horse or sitting in a wagon. You're a lot safer too."

"I'll pray for a safe journey just the same."

"I'm surprised at you Tevye. I'd think you would see God's hand in progress."

"I'd feel better if God's hands were on the wheel."

Moshe laughed again as he reached into his pocket and pulled out a pack of cigarettes. He held it out to me and I just shook my head. He pulled a cigarette out with his lips and struck a match against the outside of the car with his left hand to light it. I couldn't decide if it was scarier watching him, or staring straight ahead, unaware of whether his hands were on the wheel.

"Try to enjoy the ride, Tevye. Look out the window and see how much has changed since we traveled this route from Jaffa when we first arrived in Palestine."

"It still looks pretty barren."

"Just wait. Soon you'll see how much a handful of Jews has accomplished. If we were going through Haifa, you'd see a soap factory, a flour mill, the salt works. I tell you it's amazing. Even in Tel Aviv the changes will astonish you. Remember the handful of houses and trees we saw beyond the road from Jaffa? There was practically nothing. Now you'll see rows and rows of houses, a brick factory and the new electric power station."

"Electric?"

"We'll have electricity on the kibbutz eventually. You won't believe it. Instead of lamps and candles, we'll have bulbs to light our way. Machines will be powered by electric engines to make our work easier."

"Really? I will see these things in Tel Aviv?"

"Perhaps. It depends on what you're going to be doing."

"You mean Faiga didn't know?"

"She probably did, and maybe she told everyone else on the kibbutz except me."

"I might as well tell you. It's nice to share good news with a friend anyway. I've given Chaim permission to marry Shoshana."

"*Mazel tov!* That's wonderful news," Moshe said reaching over to clap me on the shoulder.

"What are you doing?"

"Congratulating you. What do you think I'm doing?"

"I mean, why are you taking your hand off the wheel. We'll be killed and I'll never see my daughter wed."

"Stop panicking, Tevye. This car practically drives itself," Moshe said and held both hands over his head.

"Moshe!"

The right front tire rolled into a gully bump and it felt like we were going to turn over. Moshe grabbed the steering wheel and righted the car.

"All right. It can't quite drive itself. I'll bet one day cars won't need drivers. We'll just sit back and tell the machine where we want to go and, boom, a few minutes later, we'll be there. Maybe Oren will invent one."

"If Oren has anything to do with it, the boom will be the sound of the car exploding."

Moshe laughed again and then started coughing. So many of the kibbutzniks smoked now I was beginning to think a permanent cloud might hang over our heads.

"You may be a great prophet, Moshe but, for now, I'd settle for a competent driver."

Moshe gripped the wheel tightly and made an exaggerated expression of seriousness. In the meantime, sweat was pouring down my face, but I was too scared to let go of the seat long enough to take out my handkerchief and mop my brow.

"You were saying Chaim and Shoshana are getting married, but you didn't explain why you are going to Tel Aviv."

"Chaim's family lives there. His father wants to meet me. Probably wants to discuss plans for the wedding and the dowry."

"Dowry? You're not going to need to worry about that."

"And why is that?"

"No one gives a dowry on the kibbutz," Moshe said, tossing the remains of his cigarette out the window. "What good would it do? Everything belongs to the *chaverim*."

"No dowry?"

"What would you give her anyway? You don't have any private possessions to speak of. Besides, Chaim would never accept any-thing from you."

"He would insult his father-in-law?"

"Of course not. He's just a good socialist. The whole notion of a wife's family paying him just to marry would be offensive."

"You're right. I can hear the lecture already."

I just shook my head. Another tradition going by the wayside. By the time we build our Jewish state, I wonder if there will still be anything Jewish about us.

"Do you know anything about Chaim's father?"

That was a good question. About the only things I knew about him was what I overheard him tell Shoshana, and Chaim was not too complimentary.

"Only that he is a wealthy owner of a factory of some sort. Chaim wouldn't say much. I suspect their relationship has not been that great since Chaim joined the kibbutz. News of a wedding will patch everything up."

"Uh huh."

"What's that supposed to mean, Moshe?"

"It doesn't mean anything. I'm just agreeing with you."

I let it drop. Moshe was right about the scenery. After driving through miles of wasteland, we had passed through some small villages that had not existed when we first arrived. I could also see the orchards and fields of other kibbutzim, which appeared to be thriving. It was getting hard to see anything out the windshield; so many bugs had committed suicide Moshe was squinting to see between the blotches.

"You never said why you were going to Tel Aviv, Moshe."

"You'll have to forgive me if I don't say too much, Tevye. Much of the work I am doing now is secret."

"Sounds very mysterious."

"Not really. And it's not that I don't trust you, it's just that the people involved have sworn to keep the information to ourselves."

"I understand," I said, putting my finger to my lips.

"What I can tell you is that we are forming a larger organization to provide defense for the *yishuv*. Things have been pretty quiet recently, but we have no illusions about the Arabs' attitude toward us. Sooner or later, we will have to fight. I want to make sure we're ready when that time comes."

"Sheikh Jabber warned me of a coming war."

"The Bedouin?"

"Yes. Actually his son Ali told me the Arabs would never allow the Jews to steal their country. Do you really think it will come to war? Can't we reach a compromise?"

"Tevye, I hope so with all my heart. To be honest, though, I doubt it. Regardless, we must be strong enough to survive, compromise or no."

"And what's in Tel Aviv?"

"Most of the Haganah's operations are being run from Tel Aviv. I have to meet with some of the leaders."

"Someone named Yossi or Shimshon perhaps?"

"How do you know those names?" Moshe snapped.

"Don't worry, I didn't steal any secrets. And I didn't hear them from Faiga. I was in the infirmary with dysentery when two soldiers brought in a third man injured in the fighting when the Arabs attacked Petah Tikvah."

"Oh yes. I remember that skirmish. We arrived too late. Then the British came and we had to scatter to avoid being arrested."

"We?"

"I was there."

"Well, so were the three men who came to the kibbutz. The injured man's name was Arik and the other two were Yossi and Shimshon."

"I know that you're not a military man Tevye, but I hope you will understand when I ask you not to repeat those names. They are now two of our senior officers and the British would like nothing better than to capture them and ship them off to a prison. And Arik is also on London's most wanted list."

"Why? Have they done something wrong?"

"Of course not, Tevye. They're just trying to defend their people. Unfortunately, the British see that as a crime. Anyway, that's why I'm going to Tel Aviv. Please don't mention any of this to anyone while you're there, or even to any of the *chaverim*. *"Biseder?"*

"Biseder."

I think the discussion about the Haganah made Moshe nervous. He withdrew and concentrated on his driving. That was fine with me. It also allowed me to think about my coming meeting. My mind began to conjure up images of being driven to the factory owned by Chaim's father. I would be the foreman in charge of hundreds of workers. Or maybe he would make me the manager of all his businesses and then ask me to become his partner.

Why should I, Tevye, suddenly deserve to have such an honor, to sit with a man of such wealth? I don't need to share his wealth. I only want to live comfortably in my old age, in my own house in a town where I don't have to ask a committee for permission to do anything. And enough money so I could go to a real synagogue and spend my days studying and praying.

Despite the jarring ride, I must have fallen asleep fantasizing about leaving the kibbutz and working with my new son-in-law's father, because the next thing I knew we were riding down a tree-lined street with many other cars around us.

"You had a nice nap," Moshe said when he realized I was awake. He had lit another cigarette and held it outside while his elbow rested on the window.

"I have to admit it's nice having someone chauffeur me."

"Careful, you're very close to kibbutz heresy there."

"Why? You have great aptitude for driving a car. Perhaps that should be your assignment. I have the ability to be a passenger, so I can ride along wherever you go."

"Well, you can't come with me now. Where do you want me to drop you off?"

"Here," I said, handing Moshe a slip of paper. "Chaim gave me directions."

Moshe glanced at the page without taking his hands off the wheel. I was thankful for that.

"I know where this is. It's not far from here."

We drove past rows of yellowish stone houses and then the buildings began to get bigger and grander. A few minutes later, Moshe stopped the car.

"What's wrong?"

"We're here."

"Here where?"

"At the address you gave me. This must be where Chaim's family lives. Not bad. Reminds me of the dachas in the old country."

I couldn't believe it. I knew Chaim's father was rich, but I didn't think he would be this rich. The house was two stories high. From the upper floor, they could surely see the Mediterranean. The front of the house had columns like a palace. A manicured lawn was in front of the door, with flowers like the finest garden on the kibbutz. A shiny new car was in front.

"Do you know how to get home, Tevye?"

"Yes, I'll wait for you here."

"I'm afraid I haven't been assigned the job as your chauffeur yet. Actually, I don't know when I'll be going back. My business here might take a few days. You can take a bus. It will take a few hours longer, but you'll probably feel safer. Good luck!"

"Thank you. And best of luck to you with your meeting."

Moshe waved and the car sputtered away. He left me standing in front of the house staring as if it were the burning bush.

Oy, oy, oy. I slapped my cheek to make sure I was really awake. I always imagined that this is how Rothschild must live.

A circular cobblestone driveway led to the door, which was nearly twice my height. A giant silver mezuzah hung on the door-post. I knocked.

No answer.

I knocked again harder.

Still, no answer.

I hammered on the door with both fists.

The result was the same.

I walked up to a large window and peeked inside. I rubbed the glass with my shirt sleeve and saw a giant dark-skinned man in a uniform with gold buttons on the front brushing clothes. I banged on the window and winked at him, then started to wave my arms and motion for the man to come to the door. The man ignored me at first, then gestured for me to leave. A maid walked into the room and I repeated these gestures. She disappeared from view. A few moments later, I heard the front door open.

"Can I help you?" said the maid.

"Does Reb Danziger live here?"

"Yes."

"Well, could you tell him that Tevye, son of Reb Shneour Zalman, has come from his son Chaim's kibbutz to see him, and that I have been standing here like a beggar because that baboon wouldn't let me in."

The maid slammed the door in my face.

"Thank you," I said to the closed door. Charming girl.

"Dear God, you made many wonderful creatures. Forgive me for saying these two are less wonderful than most."

The door opened again and the uniformed man motioned for me to enter.

"Wait here," said the man who I could now see was an Arab. He disappeared through a wooden door.

As soon as the servant was gone, I began to look around. A huge crystal chandelier hung from the center of the ceiling. The doors of a living room opposite were open so I walked in and felt as though I'd entered a museum. Everywhere I looked the walls and furnishings were covered by silk, velvet, gold and marble. As I moved, I noticed the floor made no sound. I got on my hands and knees and crawled on the carpet. It felt nearly as soft as a sheep's fleece. Oh, how I would have loved to have such a carpet to roll on when the children were young.

On one wood table, I spied a little porcelain figure beside two silver goblets. It was shaped like a woman, and what a shape. She wore no clothes and made no effort to hide her private parts. To have such a vulgar thing displayed in one's house was an abomination.

So this is what the rich people spend their money on, I thought, and turned away. All right, I took one more look first, but just a brief one.

As I walked about the room, I suddenly became aware of a large number of clocks. Grandfather clocks, clocks that looked like little bird houses, wall clocks of all sizes and shapes. Why does a person need so many clocks? To know when the Sabbath begins and ends one has only to watch the sun, the moon and the stars. Is he worried that four or five clocks might all break at once and he won't know the time? Just then, birds popped out of several clocks simultaneously shrieking, "cuckoo, cuckoo."

"I'm not the one who is cuckoo; it's the person who needs so many clocks," I replied.

These clocks were noisy, but some were also beautiful. I walked over to one and stared at the place where the bird had suddenly jumped out. The little house was obviously carved and painted with a loving hand. Each detail was precise. I wish the builders of my house had given as much care as the one who made this wooden bird's home.

I nearly jumped out of my boots when I heard the sudden shrill cry of another cuckoo bird emerging from its hiding place. I'm used to hearing roosters wake me in the morning, but little mechanical birds screaming "cuckoo, cuckoo" all day would drive me crazy.

Before another clock could attack me, I walked into the adjoining room. Now I found myself surrounded by walls covered with mirrors.

"What's this?" I asked the reflections. It was like being in a room full of Tevyes. A Tevye here, a Tevye there. I'd never seen such a thing. I stuck out my tongue and the Tevyes stuck theirs out at me. I winked and they winked back. I hopped on one foot.

"Excuse me, but what are you doing?" a voice called out from somewhere behind me.

I was still holding my right ankle in my hand. Whoever had spoken was not visible in the mirror, so I hopped around and saw a large man in the doorway wearing a gray suit with a gold chain across the front. He had his hands on his hips and a fat cigar between his teeth.

"Oh, I had something stuck in my shoe and I was trying to get it out."

The man began laughing in a high-pitched squeal that reminded me of a donkey in heat. He stopped laughing as suddenly as he began.

"You must be Tevye. I'm Ludwig Danziger. Welcome to my home."

When he drew closer, I could see Danziger was both taller and wider than me. He had only a few strands of black hair on his head, but it looked like he stretched them to cover as much of his baldness as possible. The end of the cigar was nearly in my face. Maybe he uses it to hold up his nose.

I shook Danziger's extended hand. "Thank you for the invitation. You know your large friend is not very friendly."

"Abdullah? Oh, he is paid to protect me. He has to be careful who is allowed to come in. We can't let just anyone in here, can we?"

Danziger laughed again.

"No, certainly not."

"Come, let's go to my office and discuss business. Abdullah, bring us some tea."

Danziger led me to a staircase. Pictures of what I guessed to be family members were along the wall in silver frames. None of them had anyone who resembled Chaim. I stopped to look at a photo of Danziger standing in front of a palace gate. A woman in a long coat with a pearl necklace and a hat with feathers sticking out stood next to him.

"That's my wife," Danziger said when he realized I had stopped. "In front of Buckingham Palace. Magnificent architecture. Changing of the guards is impressive. Have you ever been?"

I shook my head.

"Didn't think so," Danziger said out of the corner of his mouth before turning his back on me and continuing to the top of the stairs.

When we reached the next floor, I followed Danziger into a wood-paneled room with a huge window. As I'd suspected, it provided a breathtaking view of the sparkling sea. On the opposite wall, above a large oak writing desk, was a giant oil painting of Danziger, complete with cigar in hand. In the center of the room a large velvet couch and two matching chairs, separated by a glass table, were placed so anyone sitting in them could see out the window.

"Sit and make yourself comfortable." Danziger gestured toward the couch.

I sat and sank into the cushions. I closed my eyes and thought it wouldn't be difficult to fall asleep.

"You don't have chairs like this on the kibbutz?"

"I didn't know chairs like this existed."

Laughing again, Danziger said, "I guess you wouldn't, would you?" He reached over to the table and picked up a bejeweled box with his initials inlaid. "Would you like a cigar?" he asked, holding it open.

"No, thank you. I don't smoke."

"A man who doesn't smoke cigars? Don't tell me that you socialists believe cigars are a bourgeois conspiracy against the worker."

It was strange to be called a socialist. That was the way I thought of the other *chaverim*. Now I realized anyone outside the kibbutz would see me as one of them.

"I'm not a socialist and, as far as I know, they don't object to cigars. I don't smoke because I can't stand the smell."

"Is that right?"

I could already feel my eyes begin to water from the smoke.

Abdullah entered carrying a tray with a samovar, two cups and a plate of perfectly round brown cookies.

"Milk, lemon or sugar?"

"Lemon please."

Abdullah put a lemon in my tea cup and left the room.

"Do you know why I sent for you?"

I had a cookie in my mouth and spoke as crumbs fell out. "Yes, to discuss the wedding of your son to my daughter Shoshana."

"Yes, the wedding." He took a big puff of the cigar and blew little rings into the air above his head. "You know Tevye. May I call you Tevye, my friend?"

"Why not, it's my name."

"Good. Tevye let me speak honestly with you."

"Please do."

Sitting so close to Danziger, I began to notice his ruddy cheeks were beginning to sag. His neck already looked like a turkey's. His most disconcerting feature was a single thick black eyebrow that stretched across his forehead.

"Tevye, I'm doing quite a lot of business; in fact, my profits will double this year."

"Well, you know what the Good Book says, 'The more business, the more worries.'"

"I'm afraid I don't know what the Good Book says. You see a busy man like me has no time for frivolity."

"Frivolity?"

"The fact of the matter Tevye is that I'm a very important man. I don't say it to brag, but it's a fact. I'm on very good terms with the British High Commissioner and it is very likely that in the near future I will be getting a visit from Lord Rothschild. Do you understand what I'm telling you, Tevye?"

"Yes, you're an important man who is a friend of the High Commissioner and will be visited by Rothschild. What shall we do when Rothschild arrives?"

Danziger laughed heartily. "I like you Tevye. You're a real character."

"Thank you."

He became serious again quickly. "I'm afraid that does not change things. You see Tevye, it just would not do to have my son marry the daughter of a milkman. Not even a milkman with a business of his own, but a socialist milkman on a kibbutz."

My mind was floating, I was enjoying the tea and cookies and the words didn't register. What was he trying to say?

Danziger walked over to the desk and sat under the grinning portrait of himself. He took a key out of his top pocket and unlocked a drawer. "How much will it take to end this nonsense?" he asked as he pulled out a purse and began placing coins and notes on the desk.

"Nonsense?"

"That's right. Surely, you didn't think. . . . Oh, I see. Well, I'm sure we can pay you for your trouble as well."

"Pay me? Pay me! What do you think I am?" I said jumping to my feet, "a mouse and not a man that I should sit and listen to you tell me that my daughter is not good enough for your son."

"I have nothing against your daughter. You just need to remember who you are and who I am."

"May I remind you, Mr. Friend of Rothschild, that your son is also living on the same kibbutz and that he spends his days picking fruit beside my daughter in the orchard?"

"You don't have to remind me. My son is a little crazy, but it's just a phase he's going through. He'll come back to his senses and return to run my business."

"Excuse me, but I think that it is you who are crazy. Your son understands that there is more to life than material riches."

Danziger leaned over his desk and shouted back, "My son has been corrupted by your daughter and her crazy ideas!"

"My daughter's crazy ideas? My daughter is a beautiful, intelligent woman, whose little finger is worth more than all the gold, silver, clocks and mirrors you have. Crazy? You sir are the one who is crazy to think that Rothschild will come to visit you. The *mashiach* will get here first!"

"Listen milkman, I will not be spoken to this way in my house, and there will be no wedding!"

Danziger came back around the desk and stood over me.

"If my daughter wants a wedding, she will have a wedding!"

"Over my dead body!"

"If necessary."

Abdullah rushed in as the volume of the argument increased. When I saw him, I grabbed Danziger's purse off the desk and shoved it into the big Arab's belly. "Here, buy yourself a few new buttons."

9

The meeting with Ludwig Danziger went well, don't you think?

The whole way home from Tel Aviv, I just kept thinking, what am I going to tell Golde? After all these years of worrying about whether any man would be good enough for her daughters, I have to tell her that Shoshana, our jewel, is not acceptable to Mr. Friend of Rothschild.

"You have to remember who you are and who we are."

His words echoed in my ears like a childhood insult that is never forgotten.

How dare Danziger suggest that he, who is ignorant of God's word, is superior to me and my family? Who is he to decide my daughter's fate?

All right, I understand this is a tradition of sorts. People are supposed to marry within their class. But why should my daughter suffer because of my failings? I don't mind that I'm no millionaire, but would it really be so terrible if one of my daughters should be rich? Is it fair to punish Shoshana for my poverty?

I didn't think I'd ever hear myself say it, but I'm happy to be working on the kibbutz and living humbly instead of sitting around in a house full of clocks and mirrors. Who needs servants who behave as though it is they, and not their masters, who are wealthy, and who treat guests like peasants?

Jonathan is right about the power of labor. As the proverb says, "Wealth acquired by vanity shall be diminished; but he who gathers by labor shall increase."

Working outside in the fresh air, with the bees buzzing and birds singing makes my spirit soar. I can see what I have helped to create, the buildings rising on the hillside, the trees growing through the rocks, the flowers blooming in the gardens. This land was not fit for swine when we arrived. But now, throughout Palestine, Jewish life is blossoming. We now have milk and honey as God promised. And if my daughters are destined to spend their days on the kibbutz, they will not suffer. Like the wildflowers, they will thrive.

I've been sitting here worrying about myself and Shoshana, but I haven't thought about Chaim. He thought he would find happiness on the kibbutz, but now his own father wants to deny him the chance. I'm glad I was not so inflexible with Tzeitl and Hodel. What will he do now?

I guess I'll find out soon, because the poor *schlemiel* is standing at the gate. He's probably been waiting all day for me to return to hear that his father had given his blessing for the match. How do I break the news?

"Tevye," Chaim shouted as he ran out to meet the bus.

I waved. "I'm coming, I'm coming."

"Well, what did he say?"

Chaim's eyes were open wide with the hopefulness of a child awaiting a present on Chanukah.

"Your father is a very important man. That is quite a house he has."

"Yes, I know, but what did he say about me and Shoshana?"

"Let's walk. We'll talk on the way."

"He disapproved, didn't he?"

I could hear the bitterness in his voice, but Chaim didn't sound surprised.

"He was not impressed with the family you wanted to join."

"Bourgeois bastard. Of course not. He thinks he's some kind of royalty and his son can only marry a princess. Don't feel bad Tevye. It's not you. My father wouldn't have accepted anyone from the kibbutz. I'm not sure he thinks anyone in Palestine is in his class, or is good enough for his son."

"You shouldn't talk that way. He is still your father and you must respect him. As the Good Book says, "Honor your father and mother . . . so that you may live long, and fare well in the land God is assigning to you."

"Don't you see that I came to the kibbutz to escape from his arrogance and petty prejudices? Well, this is one time he won't have his way."

"Why don't you try talking to him? I have to admit that I was not very enthusiastic about my older daughters' choices of husbands. To tell you the truth, I was also insistent about making the matches for them. But they came to me and explained how they felt. I could see how much Tzeitl loved Motel, and the bond between Hodel and Pertschik. Even though it was an affront to my sense of tradition, I decided their happiness was more important. Maybe you can also convince your father."

"I'm not optimistic. He's not as understanding as you, Tevye. I will try, but if I fail, I plan to marry Shoshana anyway. I've already told her to work with the committee to prepare the wedding."

"You can't go against the wishes of your father. I can't —"

"Tevye, I'm here against his wishes. Everything I've done for most of my life has been contrary to his ambition for me. I will not let him dictate who I may choose for a wife. And, I mean no disrespect, but you cannot decide for me either."

Chaim walked away. After a few steps, he kicked the dirt with all his might, then continued off toward the orchard.

I wanted to speak, but no words would come out. Is this what will become of fathers and sons in Palestine?

I don't like it. I don't like it at all. A boy defying his father. But what can I do? I can't control my daughters, how am I supposed to control someone else's son?

At least I know now, it's not just my family that has problems.

I still have one of my own. A big one. How am I going to explain all this to Golde?

I 0

Talking to Chaim made me even more heartsick. My stomach
began to tighten and my head throbbed. As I was about to go home
to talk to Golde, I heard loud voices coming from the infirmary. I
decided I was feeling too sick — all right too scared and guilty —
to go home. I went inside and found the source of the noise.

"I'll never be the same," Eitan said, as he lifted himself up from
the bed. "I won't be able to eat without examining my food. I'll
probably start pecking at my plate."

"Quit complaining," Uzi shouted from the next bed. "You're
lucky she didn't put nails in the kugel."

"She doesn't have to. The last time she made mandelbread I
broke a tooth."

"Quiet you two. You're disturbing the commander," Devorah
whispered as she moved from bed to bed checking patients. "He's
the only one who's really sick."

"Tevye, what are you doing here?" Eitan blurted.

"Papa, are you all right?" Devorah asked rushing over.

"Yes, I'm fine. My stomach is bothering me. I thought I'd come in and have you take a look."

"This doesn't have anything to do with your trip to Tel Aviv does it?"

"Maybe. I might have eaten something that didn't agree with me while I was there waiting for the bus."

"That's not what I meant."

My daughter inherited Golde's sixth sense about messages hidden behind words.

"Oh, it really hurts. Do you mind if I just lie here awhile," I said doubling over so that my head was nearly level with Uzi's pillow. He winked at me.

"Okay, come on Papa."

Devorah put my arm over her shoulders and helped me to an empty cot. I held my stomach and groaned.

She pushed my abdomen with her fingers. "Does this hurt?"

"Ah!"

"This?"

"Oh! Yes."

Devorah took a thermometer out of her pocket and shook it.

"Is that necessary?" I asked.

"Maybe you have an infection. I want to check to see if you have a fever."

I started to speak, but she shoved the thermometer in my mouth.

"Dr. Susser's sleeping. Do you want me to call him?"

I shook my head and said out of the side of my mouth, "No, don't bother him. I think I just need to lie down for a while."

"Are you sure?"

I nodded.

She checked her watch and after a few moments, she pulled out the thermometer and held it up to the light.

"Ninety-nine point one. That's just above normal. Why don't you just rest? If you're not feeling better in a couple of hours, I'll wake the doctor."

"Thank you sweetheart. I think I'll be okay after a nap."

Devorah bent down and kissed me.

"You're lucky you didn't eat dinner here tonight, Tevye," Eitan shouted. "You'd have food poisoning for sure."

Devorah put her hands on her hips and gave him a dirty look. "*Sheket*, I said."

Eitan started to speak and I saw Devorah lift her eyebrows. It made me feel good to see how calm and self-assured she had become. She supervised the infirmary the way her mother ran our house in Anatevka.

I knew that Devorah was highly regarded by the *chaverim* for her skills as a nurse and, more important, for her bedside manner. Uzi and Eitan were not the only members who were difficult patients. It was a gift to know how to use the right combination of sympathy and firmness.

Devorah walked over to Arik's cot and sat on the edge. I strained to hear what she was saying.

"They make a lot of noise over nothing."

She smiled and began to change the bandage on his chest. "The funny thing is that most of the kibbutz thought it was the best meal Chana ever made."

"What did she make?"

"Oh, she made kugel again and they think it was made with birdseed."

"Did you say birdseed?"

"Yes. A few years ago, someone accidentally put a bag of birdseed in the kitchen along with the bags of rice. Chana wasn't paying attention to what she was doing — she's more than a little absent-minded — and put birdseed into her kugel instead of rice. When she tasted it at dinner, she realized something was wrong and checked the ingredients she had used. Chana was horrified when she looked at the bag where she thought she was getting the rice, but everybody thought it was delicious. The other cooks came up to her after dinner and asked what her secret was, but she wouldn't tell, at least not at first. The secret was too much for her and she finally confided in someone. I don't know who it was, but soon Faiga, our resident gossip, made sure what she had done became common knowledge."

"So, did she keep using birdseed in her recipe?"

"Well, like everything here, it became an issue for the whole kibbutz. The executive committee called a meeting and everyone got to have their say about the kugel recipe. Even though most people admitted they liked it, they were afraid the birdseed might make the children sick. If you can believe it, a vote was taken and Chana was instructed not to put any more seeds in her kugel."

"I'm glad to hear you have such important matters to discuss here on the kibbutz."

Listening to Devorah retell the story reminded me of how ridiculous socialist life could be sometimes. And the *chaverim* laugh at me when I want them to study the passages in the Torah about things *they* find obscure, like the discussion of the Red Heifer in the Book of Numbers.

"That's nothing." Devorah continued. "You should hear some of the stuff that comes up at our meetings, the condition of the outhouses, the distribution of soap, the type of music that is acceptable."

"You vote on what music to listen to?"

"We vote on everything. Besides being hypochondriacs, Eitan and Uzi are the kibbutz ideologists. They're constantly trying to tell us which composers represent the highest form of music."

"And?"

"And what?"

"Which composers have received their *hechsher*?"

"Beethoven!" Uzi shouted from across the room.

"Chopin," Eitan added.

"Brahms," said Uzi.

"All right, that's enough. The Major gets the idea. What are you doing eavesdropping on our conversation anyway? If you don't be quiet and go to sleep, I'm going to throw you out of here."

I started to chuckle.

"Papa, are you okay?"

"Yes, I just felt a cramp in my stomach," I said, adding a groan for affect.

"Well, you go to sleep too."

"So what are, what were their names again?"

"Eitan and Uzi."

"Yes, what are Eitan and Uzi doing here?"

"People still suspect that Chana purposely puts birdseed in her rice kugel. Those two come in here every time she makes it and complain their stomachs hurt. They scratch the ground with their feet like chickens and cluck instead of cough. Actually, they're very entertaining. I don't usually get much to laugh about here."

"To tell you the truth," Arik said, "I think a birdseed kugel would taste pretty good after some of the things I've had to eat since the operation."

"Really? There's still some left. I could get you a piece."

"No, no," Arik said, holding up his arms with mock horror. "That won't be necessary. I don't think I feel quite up to a big meal like that just yet."

"Of course, I'm sorry," Devorah said looking away and feeling embarrassed. She continued to change the bandage without looking at Arik's face

Arik groaned as she wrapped the clean bandage over the wound.

"Am I hurting you?"

"No. It's just a little sore. You have a very delicate touch. It's nice." Devorah flushed.

"I don't think I'd enjoy one of the women who worked in the fields changing my dressings."

"Why? What's wrong with those women?" she snapped. "My older sister works in the orchard."

"There's nothing wrong with them, nothing wrong at all," Arik said quickly. "They're making a great contribution to the kibbutz and to building the state. I just meant their hands are rough and calloused from the type of work they do. A nurse should have softer hands."

I watched the soldier take Devorah's hand and stroke it.

"And it's not just the texture, it's your manner. I've watched the way you tend to the other patients, especially the children. You are so gentle, yet confident, that everyone believes you can heal them."

She pulled her hand away shyly. "You're starting to make me out to be some kind of angel of mercy. It's sweet, but a little trite.

I'm just helping Dr. Susser. He's the one with the golden hands blessed by God."

"Dr. Susser is a good man. I'm sure he is very skilled. So far, I seem to be getting better and liquid doesn't spray out of the punctures in my chest when I drink, so he must have done something right."

Devorah chuckled. She probably had the same image as I did of water leaking out of holes in Arik's chest like a fountain.

"You have a nice laugh and a kind smile. What I was talking about was not so much healing the body as the spirit. That's your contribution."

"Enough already. You're starting to sound like my father telling one of his *bubbameisers.*"

"What did you say?" I said.

"Nothing Papa. Go to sleep."

This time Arik laughed, then coughed. "Oh, that hurts. Do me a favor. Save the jokes until I'm better."

Devorah had a pained look on her face.

"It's okay," Arik said. "If I laugh too hard I might split my stitches. Say, what does your father do here?"

"He usually works in the barn with the cows and horses. He delivers milk and bread to the nearby villages and kibbutzim. The same thing he did back home."

"Where was home?"

"Anatevka. It's a small village in Russia. We were expelled. All the Jews were forced to leave."

"I know about the pogroms and evictions. Most of the Russian Jews moved to the Pale, didn't they?"

"Yes, I think so."

"So why did you come to Palestine?"

"My father met some men on the road. We were planning to go to live with an uncle in America. The men said we should go to Palestine and help build a Jewish state. My father had always dreamed of coming here and he decided it was the right time. So here we are."

"Just like that?"

"Just like that."

I forget sometimes my daughter was a little girl when we left Anatevka. She remembers life being simpler than it was. I had thought about living in Palestine for many years, so Moshe, Simcha and Jonathan didn't just convince me to change directions on the spot. I was about to point this out when Arik asked another question that I wanted to hear Devorah answer.

"Are you sorry you came?"

"No, of course not," Devorah said. "Russia was horrible. We were surrounded by people who despised us because we were Jews. Besides, the weather was awful, we froze half the year."

"Well, the weather here's better, but that's about it. We're still despised."

"Yes, but one day we will have our own state and it won't matter what others think."

Arik snickered. "If it is God's will, and we fight well, we may have a state. But it will be a very small island surrounded by an ocean of hatred. We will always have to worry about what our neighbors think."

"Aren't you scared to fight? There are so many more Arabs, and your friend said the British help them."

"My friend?"

"Yes, one of the men who brought you here."

"Oh, you mean Yossi. He's a bit of a hothead, but he's a good fighter. He's also right. The British have no intention of carrying through with the Balfour Declaration. What's in it for them? Their main interest is in securing this region within their sphere of interest."

"I don't understand."

"Devorah, the British want to expand their empire. They want access to any resources that might be found underneath the sand and to maintain control over land and sea routes to Africa and Asia. If they deliver on their promise to the handful of Jews in Palestine, they'll anger millions of Arabs throughout the Near East. They can't afford to do that."

"So what's going to happen?"

My daughter is still so innocent. I never told her about my visit with Sheikh Jabber. Maybe it is time I explained that life here will not necessarily be safer than in Russia.

"I'm a soldier, not a prophet Devorah. My guess is the British will try to have it both ways. String the Jews along with promises of independence and do the same for the Arabs. Our leaders will go along, but the Arabs will revolt. They see us as interlopers, foreigners stealing their land. After all, this is their country. They have lived here for hundreds of years, so it's only natural that they would see us as invaders. Why should they share *their* land with us?"

My ears perked up hearing Arik's analysis. It was clear that he understood better than most how the Arabs felt. Maybe he had also met with Sheikh Jabber.

"The British might restrict Jewish immigration in the hope that this will pacify the Arabs," Arik continued. "It won't. The Arabs will never be happy as long as Jews are in Palestine."

"But why can't we live together? The Arabs in the villages around the kibbutz have caused us no trouble; we've been friends for years. I take care of some of their children when they're sick. Even the Bedouins have left us alone, even though I know they've raided other kibbutzim."

I involuntarily coughed.

"Papa, stop eavesdropping."

"What? What did you say? I couldn't hear you."

"Go to sleep!"

"It's okay. I'm not giving away any secrets. The truth is most Arabs are content. In fact, many are moving to the cities with the largest Jewish populations because they've heard the living conditions are better than in their villages. The average Arab wants the same thing as the rest of us, a job, a home, food for their family, peace of mind. Their leaders feel threatened by any improvement in the life of the *fellaheen*. They see their dominance over the peasants being eroded and are determined to maintain their control."

"Can't we convince those average Arabs that we mean them no harm?"

"I'm afraid not. They are easily manipulated, especially by religious leaders like the Mufti. Neither the bourgeois Christian Arabs nor the Muslims will ever accept us and, unfortunately, they can stir the masses against the *yishuv*."

"But it's our land too."

"They can't accept that and won't."

Devorah's face dropped. "So you will fight the Arabs so we can control Palestine."

"I hope not. None of us want that. Right now we're just trying to protect ourselves."

It was easy to see why Devorah was so good with patients. She is gentle, but also willing to listen to everyone. No, more than that, she's genuinely interested in what people have to say. When you are with her, she looks you straight in the eye and acts as though you are the only person in the world that matters at that moment. The ability to make a person feel important is a gift as precious as Dr. Susser's medical skills.

"What can you do?" Devorah asked.

"It is extremely dangerous to talk about."

I saw Devorah lean closer to Arik's face. I strained to hear.

"What are you up to Arik? Tell me."

Arik looked around the room. Eitan and Uzi had finally stopped arguing about the kugel and appeared to be asleep. I closed my eyes and pretended to snore.

"All right, I'll tell you, but you must not repeat this to anyone."

"I promise," she said with what I thought was a giddy voice.

"We're building a secret army. Some of the men fought in the war with the British, in the Jewish legion. Those veterans are training the younger people like me, Yossi and Shimshon. We're also collecting weapons."

"But what will happen if you're caught?" Devorah blushed as she realized she was giving away her feelings.

"It doesn't matter, others will take my place. If we are to survive, we must fight for our lives and our homeland. After what you went through in Russia, you understand what it means for Jews to be persecuted. What would your family have done if they had not been allowed to come to Palestine? This is our home. It is the only place we can ever hope to be safe."

"But look at you. How can you say we are safe here when the Arabs will not accept us?"

"When we have a state, and an army, they will have no choice, and then we will gather all the Jews together here. We won't have peace because the Arabs became Zionists; we'll have it because they fear our strength."

"It sounds a little silly to talk about Jewish power when there are so few of us."

"You're right. But our day will come. Have faith."

"You sound like quite a dreamer."

"I am. But this is the Promised Land and God will see that it comes to pass."

"And religious too. Tell me, are there any women helping in your work?"

"Yes, there are. Here in Palestine, women have an equal role in building our state. Not just on the kibbutz. We can always use more help. But it's very dangerous. If the British catch you, they can send you to prison, sometimes as far away as Africa. It's better for a girl like you to stay with your family and help the doctor here in the infirmary."

"Don't patronize me, Arik."

"I'm sorry, that's not how I meant it. What I was trying to say is —"

"Be a good little girl and stay with your mommy and daddy."

"Would you let me finish, please?"

Devorah was pouting the way she did when she didn't get her way as a child.

"All I meant was that you are playing a very valuable role as a nurse right here."

"But your work is so much more exciting."

Arik laughed softly and nodded toward his bandages. "I could do with a little less excitement. But I'm not sure I could do without you."

I saw Devorah blush.

"When I woke up after the doctor removed the bullet, the first thing I saw was your face, and I felt your hand wiping my forehead with a cold towel. At that moment you were the most important person in the world to me."

This time Devorah took Arik's hand. "Will you go back?"

"Yes, I must."

Arik struggled for words.

"Building a homeland and protecting Jews are causes that are worth dying for. You, Devorah, are someone worth living for. I have never had that before."

A tear rolled down Devorah's cheek.

"What's wrong? Did I say something I shouldn't have?"

Brushing away the tear, Devorah said, "No, it's just that someone once said the same thing to my older sister. He was very much like you, an idealist, a fighter."

"Was? Is he dead?"

"Yes, he was hung in a Siberian prison after the revolution."

Arik smiled and reached up to gently brush her cheek with the back of his hand. "Don't worry, I'm not going to die."

Devorah brought his hand to her lips and kissed it. "You better not."

My head was halfway off the cot as I struggled to hear her last words. Then I fell out of bed and hit the floor with a thud.

"Papa!"

I I

After I fell out of the infirmary bed, Devorah kicked me out. She knew I was faking and said the cots had to be reserved for people who were really sick. I tried to point out Eitan and Uzi were no sicker than I, but she wouldn't listen. I think she was more upset that I was listening to her conversation.

Hearing Arik talk about the future of Palestine did nothing to lift my spirits, but at least his thoughts diverted me from thinking about Shoshana and Chaim. I would have liked to put off confronting Golde forever, but I figured it was better to get it over with quickly.

I didn't have to wait long.

"Where have you been? I thought you'd be back a long time ago," Golde said the instant I walked in the door.

"I wasn't feeling well, so I stopped in to see Devorah."

"You were stalling."

"Stalling?" I said pointing to my chest as if this were the silliest idea I'd ever heard.

"Tell me what happened in Tel Aviv," she said, pulling a chair up and sitting in front of me.

"Nothing happened," I said walking around her. "I went, we talked, I left, and here I am."

She flipped the chair around and yelled at my back. "Tevye, what did you talk about?"

"I'm tired now, woman. My stomach hurts. Leave me alone."

"Tevye!" she shouted even though she had leaped out of the chair and was right behind me.

I ignored her and started to change into my night clothes. Golde was hovering over me.

"Do you have to stand on top of me? Go lay down. We'll talk in the morning," I said getting into bed and pulling the cover over my head.

It was a relief when Golde's breath was no longer making the hair on my neck stand up. But she walked around to my side and yanked the covers off. She stood with her arms folded tapping her foot. I was kidding myself if I thought I could go to sleep.

"Well, it was hard to understand him with the cigar in his mouth," I said sitting up, "but I do recall hearing him say he is a friend of the High Commissioner and that he expects a visit from Rothschild any time."

"The High Commissioner and Rothschild," Golde said clasping her hands together and looking heavenward. "As the Bible says, 'The poor is hated even by his neighbor, but the rich has many friends.'"

"Ah, such a blessing You have bestowed on my Shoshana, to be the bride of a boy from such a wealthy family."

"A blessing," I mumbled.

"What?"

"Yes, our house has been blessed."

"Speaking of houses, what was their house like?"

"It was very big. And it had clocks all over the walls and the tables and the floors."   .

"Clocks?"

"Yes, clocks. Clocks everywhere. I think they had a different one for every hour of the day."

"That's the way rich people live Tevye. They don't like to use anything too much. They wear different clothes every day, they eat on different plates, they even take baths every day."

"Well, I'll tell you two things that never change, Danziger's cigar and his laugh."

"Who cares about that? Tell me about his wife. Did she have a lot of jewels and beautiful clothes?"

"Don't be foolish woman. Even in wealthy families, it is still the papa who makes all the arrangements. I didn't even meet his wife."

It suddenly occurred to me that it was a bit odd that I didn't even see the woman. But I wasn't about to say anything to Golde.

"Go to sleep and stop your nonsense, Golde. We have a big day coming up."

I slid back under the covers with my back to her.

"All right," she said. "Good night."

"Good night."

Suddenly, she leaned over my shoulder. "Did you see any *pictures* of his wife wearing jewels?"

"Golde." I was about to shout at her when I remembered the picture in the stairwell. "Actually, I did. She was standing in front of Buckingham Palace in London. She was just coming back from having tea with the queen and was wearing a string of pearls, a fur coat and a hat with a peacock on top."

"A peacock!"

Golde sounded as though I'd seen her part the Red Sea. At least the image silenced her. That barely lasted an instant.

"Was the peacock alive?"

"No! Good night," I said and pulled the blanket over my head.

"Good night."

The last thing I remember hearing was her muttering, "praise God, a rich husband."

Since I didn't really sleep in the infirmary, I felt waves of exhaustion from the long trip overtake me. As my eyes closed, I saw shadows. The blurry images slowly became clearer.

It is Tzeitl and Motel standing under a *chuppah*. A rabbi is mouthing the words of the wedding ceremony. I can't hear, but his lips stop moving. Motel breaks a wine glass with his foot and now I can hear people shouting "*mazel tov*." The room is suddenly filled with people dancing. Motel and Tzeitl are both being carried in chairs. I can see Golde's face in rapture.

Suddenly, a group of Russian soldiers burst in and start to destroy the wedding gifts, tearing pillows and throwing down candlesticks. Mixed among the Russians are some Arabs who begin to set fire to the room.

"No! No!" I screamed, shooting up in bed. "Not again! Not this time! Not in Palestine! No!"

Golde grabbed my quaking shoulders. "Tevye. Tevye. Wake up. Wake up."

"What, what? What is it?"

"You were having another one of your dreams."

"A dream?"

"Yes, a dream. Would you like me to tell you what it meant?"

"No, No. I'm afraid I don't remember it."

"But you must remember. You were screaming and —"

"I don't remember. I'm sorry. Go back to sleep."

I lay back down. Golde curled up against me. I stared at the ceiling, knowing the dream was a nightmare that could come true.

I 2

Well, in the days leading up to the wedding, I didn't have any more nightmares, but Golde would not leave me alone. With all the arrangements for the ceremony, she still found time to nag me to tell her my dream so she could interpret it for me. When I told you about the characters on the kibbutz, I should have also mentioned Golde the Soothsayer. What made her think she could explain dreams? God only knows.

The meaning of my dream was obvious enough; it didn't require any great wisdom to uncover. She was nervous enough without having to think about some potential disaster occurring in the middle of the wedding. I suspected it was already on her mind anyway. The experience during Tzeitl's wedding was not easy to forget.

I had to tell her something, though, to keep her from driving me crazy. Finally, I said, "Golde, I want to tell you a story about a man who interpreted dreams."

This got her attention immediately.

"A woman once came to Rabbi Eliezer and asked him to interpret her dreams. She told him that she had dreamed the ceiling of her house had collapsed on her. Rabbi Eliezer said, 'This means you will have a baby soon. The cracking ceiling is your womb. The ceiling falling on you symbolizes the pain of giving birth.' His words came true. She had a baby."

"That's a wonderful story, Tevye. Now tell me your dream."

"I'm not finished. The same woman came back to Rabbi Eliezer to have him interpret another dream, but she couldn't find him. She looked all over, but, finally, his students told her he was out of town."

"She was disappointed, but the students said that they could interpret the dream for her. The woman said she had again dreamed of the ceiling falling in on her. The students told her this meant her husband would die and her life would fall into ruin. She was overwrought and went home sobbing."

Golde was listening as though I was revealing a prophecy from the Almighty.

"The poor woman cried and cried for days and no one could make her stop," I continued. "Her husband was so upset about her; he had a stroke and died."

"When Rabbi Eliezer returned from his trip, he heard what had happened. He rushed over to the woman's house. She told him her story. He then asked his students to repeat what they had said to her. Hearing their answer, he was furious with them."

"Why?" Golde interrupted. "They were just doing what they had learned."

"No, Golde they were not. Rabbi Eliezer told them, 'You killed her husband. As sure as if you had done it with your own hands, you have killed the man and ruined her life! You fools! Don't you know that a dream will usually come out the way it is interpreted?'"

That made her think for a moment. Finally, she said, "So, I'll be careful when I tell you the meaning of your dream."

"Don't you understand, Golde? If I had a nightmare and you said it meant something evil would happen, it would. Would you want that on your conscience?"

"But it could be something good, something happy?"

"Do you really want to take that chance?"

Well, Golde was just superstitious enough to be afraid of what she might do, so that was the last I heard on the subject of my dream. Of course, there was no shortage of other subjects on which she could badger me.

As I put on my Sabbath clothes to prepare for the ceremony, I realized that Shoshana is my fourth eldest daughter, but the first who will have a real wedding. Children grow up so fast. Only two more to find husbands for. Then again, why should I worry? So far, I haven't had to do any work. They've all found their own mates.

I have to admit that when she was born, Schprintze was not the most beautiful child. She was also terribly fragile; it seemed that throughout her childhood she was injuring herself. Tripping over tree roots, banging into doors, slipping in the mud. Maybe that is why she has always been so sensitive. If a bird broke its wing, she would bring it home and nurse it back to health. If any of the other animals were sick, she would tend them day and night. By the time we came to Palestine, she had matured and acquired the beauty that Tevye's daughters are known for. The name Shoshana immediately came to both Golde and me when we decided to give the children Hebrew names. And now my beautiful, delicate rose has blossomed into a woman. And since Chaim asked her to marry him, she finally smiles easily. Instead of walking, she's been floating through the kibbutz as though she were in a dream. God willing, she will have an easier time getting married in Palestine with our kibbutz family than her mother and sisters had in Russia.

I'm still not comfortable with the marriage going forward without the blessing of Chaim's father. Hopefully, Chaim will persuade him to accept the reality of love the way my daughters convinced me. Shoshana is optimistic, but in the state she is in right now, she can't imagine that marriage could be anything short of heavenly bliss. I hate to think how disappointed she'll be the first time Chaim fails to notice she has combed her hair differently or uses the wrong tone of voice.

After my little visit to the infirmary, I wouldn't be surprised if we had to plan another wedding soon. I can see that look — the one my daughters all seem to get when they fall in love — in the eyes of Devorah standing next to her patient. I don't know much about this Arik. He sounds a lot like Pertschik, but is obviously more of a fighter and less of a talker.

Why is it everyone here seems to remind me of Pertschik?

Poor Pertschik. If only he could have lived to join us here. He would have found peace. Hopefully, he has it where he is now, with God.

After I got dressed, I walked into the courtyard. Shmuel was ringing the bell. It was a new composition that reminded me a little of the church carillon in Anatevka calling the Christians to prayer.

Golde was oblivious to the sound. She was standing in the middle of the courtyard, pointing this way and that, shouting orders about where flowers should be placed and who should stand where. My little Saraleh was trying to stay out of the way. She looked beautiful in a long, flowing blue skirt and ruffled white shirt. She'd put a flower wreath in her hair. I wish Tzeitl and Hodel could also be here to share their sister's *simcha*. I even miss Motel.

"Dear Lord, will we ever be together as a family again?"

"And who are you talking to now?" Golde said. "On such a happy day, you're bothering the Almighty with your *meshugas*."

"How many such occasions have I had to talk with Him?"

"Do you think God has nothing better to do than listen to you? *I* don't even like to listen to you. The Creator of the Universe must have second thoughts every time He hears from you."

"And since when did you become an expert?" I asked.

"Do you think this blessing was your doing? God, may His name be blessed forever and ever, has heard my prayers and answered them."

"As much as you talk, no one could avoid hearing you."

"Such a man."

Golde turned away from me and spied Devorah and Arik.

"And what is going on over there?"

"What, you mean Devorah? She seems to have performed her own miracle."

"I'm very happy Arik recovered from his wounds, but what do we know about him? What kind of family does he have? Does he make a living being a soldier?"

"Even today you can't enjoy yourself. Interrogate Arik tomorrow. Today, be content with one blessing."

"Maybe I'll just go over and make conversation," Golde said as she walked across the lawn toward Devorah and Arik.

Make conversation. For that she doesn't need anyone.

"*Mazel tov*, Tevye," Simcha said, coming over and slapping me on the back. "The first of your daughters to be married on the kibbutz."

"And her children will be your first grandchildren who are sabras," added Jonathan. "It's a wonderful day. This is our best weapon against the Arabs."

"What do you mean? We can keep up with their birth rate," I said.

"Not with only one wife at a time," laughed Simcha.

"That's not quite what I meant," said Jonathan. "They can't keep out the Jews who are born here."

"True, brother Jonathan. Neither the British nor the Arabs can stop us on our wedding nights. Right Tevye," Simcha said, slapping me again on the back.

"But I'm not sure I can survive all the congratulations," I said, rubbing my sore back. "Speaking of weapons, where's Moshe?"

"I don't know for sure," Simcha said. "Some secret mission. Jonathan, you must know."

"This is not the time, my friends."

Shmuel changed his tune. The bell now was ringing out a fitting song, *Erev Shel Shoshanim.* It begins, "An evening (fragrant) with roses, pray let us go out to the fruit garden, spices and frankincense as a threshold for your feet."

"Ah, here comes Shoshana. She looks radiant," Jonathan said, as he pointed to a horse-drawn cart bringing my daughter into the courtyard.

"Tevye's daughters are known for their beauty."

"And their father for his modesty," Simcha snickered.

It was hard to believe I ever thought this child was homely. Even in the cart, she looked as though she were floating on the wings of angels. The tailor had made a simple white dress that exposed more flesh than Golde liked, but it also highlighted her shapeliness.

Four men held pitchforks supporting a canopy in the middle of the courtyard and all the *chaverim* were in a circle around it. I walked over to the cart when it stopped and looked up at my daughter. Her face glowed through the veil the way the Bible says Moses' face shone after he returned from Mt. Sinai. When my daughters fall in love, they do it with their hearts and minds.

"You look wonderful, Shoshie," I said as I gave her my hand to help her down from the cart. She had a beautiful bouquet of wildflowers in her other hand. "I'm very happy for you." I lifted her veil and kissed her cheek. "You have no idea how much I love you."

She hugged me. "Yes I do. And I love you just as much, Papa."

"My baby," Golde blubbered as she came over to embrace Shoshana and kiss her.

The two of us stood beside our daughter and held her by the elbows. She was so nervous I could feel her shaking. We had to support her to keep her from falling. When we got under the *chuppah* and stood before Jonathan, who officiated at all weddings on the kibbutz, we suddenly realized that someone was missing.

I whispered into Jonathan's ear, "Where's Chaim?"

He looked at me as though I was supposed to know. I looked at Golde and she glared at me. I was afraid that Shoshana would panic, but she seemed unconcerned.

Apparently sensing the tension, Shoshana said, "Chaim told me he might be a little late. He said he was still hoping to persuade his family to attend and he didn't know how long that would take, or if he would have any delays on the road back."

So we stood there. Golde and I stayed beside Shoshana, and we all stared at Jonathan, who tried to keep a calm smile on his face. The sun was slowly setting behind us and the clouds began to turn pink. At first the only sound we heard was the buzzing of the cicadas. As the seconds turned to minutes, the *chaverim* surrounding us gradually began to mumble.

After awhile, I couldn't remain still any longer. I began to shift from leg to leg like I was standing on hot sand. Suddenly, I felt a foot kick me in the behind. I looked over and saw Golde biting her lip. Shoshana looked panicked when people broke into laughter.

Even Jonathan, the most stoic of us all, began having difficulty remaining motionless. The mumbling behind us had increased in volume and people were now speaking in their normal tones of voice.

No one wanted to look at a watch, so we just looked at each other.

Finally, Jonathan said in his usual booming voice, "While we wait, we might as well begin the celebration. Let's have some music," he shouted to the *chaverim* who had brought their instruments.

"Music before the wedding?" Natan shouted.

Golde was horrified.

"It is our duty to make the wedding a joyous occasion. I don't believe there's any prohibition against playing music before the ceremony. Is there, Tevye?"

Jonathan was looking at me knowing the answer he wanted. I looked at Golde and Shoshana. The anxiety on their faces told me that a diversion was preferable to continuing to stand in silence.

"I don't know of any."

"Good," said Jonathan. "Let's begin the celebration. When Chaim arrives, we'll already be in the mood to welcome him."

It only took a couple of minutes for the musicians to get tuned and begin playing. Soon people were dancing the *hora*.

"Why don't you sit and rest a bit?" Jonathan said to us.

"No, I'm fine," Shoshana said, standing in place and continuing to stare at Jonathan.

As long as she remained, he felt obligated to stay at his post. I didn't know what to do either, so Golde and I stood beside our daughter while everyone else danced around the *chuppah*.

"This is the oddest wedding I've ever been to," I heard Arik say to Devorah.

"Something about my family, I think. Nothing ever seems to be traditional."

"You two are next," Sarah said as she approached Devorah and Arik.

"Why don't you find yourself someone so you can be next?" Devorah teased.

"I'm working on it. See that boy over there?"

"Which one? Adam?"

"Yes. He'll be the one. He doesn't know it yet, but he will be my husband."

"He will? Well, go get him." Devorah said.

"I'm going, I'm going. I know when I'm not wanted."

"Your sister is full of spirit and beautiful too." Arik said as Sarah walked away.

"Is that so?"

Devorah put her hands on her hips and had an unmistakable look of jealousy on her face. Arik didn't seem to recognize it.

"You Russian girls don't give us guys much of a chance," he said.

"Why should we?" Devorah said. "If we had to wait for you to come to us, we'd all be spinsters."

"Very funny."

"Come on, slow poke," Devorah said, grabbing Arik's hand and pulling him into the circle of dancers.

She literally was taking matters into our own hands. I suddenly felt a little sorry for Arik. The Haganah didn't train him to deal with women.

Someone then grabbed my hand and pulled me out from under the *chuppah.* As soon as I turned around, I saw it was Simcha.

"It's a celebration. Come and dance."

He didn't give me any choice. Before I knew it, I was in the circle. Kibbutzniks love to dance and I had finally gotten the hang of the hora, two steps clockwise, and one step back. And once I start dancing, I have to admit I lose my head a little. Simcha got me into the center and started doing the kazatske with me.

"Tevye! Tevye!"

My wife's squeal could be heard over the music and laughter. Her voice was like Joshua's shofar; it could make walls crumble.

I broke out of the circle to see what she wanted before everyone lost their hearing.

"What is it, my darling wife?"

"You're getting too old to dance like that. Why don't you sit here with me and watch?"

"Old? Who are you calling old? This is our daughter's wedding and I intend to enjoy it."

"If you want to get any older, you had better stop dancing. Besides, there's no reason to dance since the wedding hasn't happened yet. In case you haven't noticed, the groom is still missing."

"Stop already, you sound like an old hen. You know how unpredictable things are in Palestine. He could have gotten stuck on the road or detained at a road block. Maybe he was slowed by all the money he's bringing from his family."

For a moment Golde was silent. I could see her considering her daughter's newfound wealth. Then she punched me in the arm.

"It's still not right. Dancing is for after the wedding."

"Would you prefer we all stood around staring at each other? Come and join the dancing," I grabbed Golde's hand and pulled her into the circle.

It took a few minutes, but Golde finally began to enjoy herself and was dancing the hora as if she'd lived on the kibbutz all her life. Suddenly the band stopped playing. I had been spinning around in the inner circle of dancers so quickly, I felt lightheaded. Everyone was staring and, for a moment, I thought I was hallucinating, or maybe having another nightmare. Soldiers were all around us.

"I'm sorry to interrupt the festivities," the officer in charge said.

"Your Honor, is Chaim in trouble?" I asked

"Chaim? Who's Chaim?"

"The man who is supposed to be here marrying my daughter."

"I've never heard of any Chaim. We're here for him."

The officer pointed to Arik as a group of British soldiers went to where Arik was standing and roughly grabbed him and brought him to the commander.

"Why?" I asked. "What has he done?"

"This man was seen in Petah Tikvah when the trouble began a few weeks ago."

"That's a lie! He's been here with me the whole time," Devorah shouted.

I gestured for her to be quiet.

"Oh really?" The commander reached inside Arik's jacket and pulled out a pistol. "And does he always carry this to protect you?"

"He has been protecting me," Devorah said, "and he tried to protect the Jews in the village because you wouldn't."

"I'm sorry, young lady, but we have laws about carrying firearms."

"And what about the Arabs?"

"The law applies to them too," the officer answered.

"It's all right, Devorah," Arik said. "They can't keep me away from you for long."

"Forgive me," the officer said with obvious satisfaction, "but we can and will keep you away from here for quite a long time."

"Are you sure there hasn't been a mistake?" I asked.

"There has been no mistake. Go back to your celebration."

The officer nodded and, within seconds, the soldiers were gone, and so was Arik. Devorah ran to the gate of the kibbutz and shouted after him.

"Arik!"

The soldiers threw Arik roughly into the back seat of a car.

"It will be all right," Golde said, putting her arms around her sobbing daughter. "It will be all right. God will see that he is taken care of and that he returns to you."

"Or he will be killed like Pertschik."

"Shah. Don't talk like that," I said as calmly as I could, trying to disguise my own fear. "He will be fine. That Arik is a tough one; he will outlive us all."

"In the meantime there is one less person to do his work," Devorah said wiping her eyes.

"Don't worry, someone else will take his place," Golde said, not understanding what lay behind Devorah's words.

"You're right, Mama. I will take his place."

"What?" Golde said terrified.

"He told me all about his work. It's very important and I want to do my part."

"Are you crazy," I said, feeling more alarmed than even my wife. "You're just a woman. You can't be a soldier."

"Papa, you're so old-fashioned. Women already are in the Haganah. I've made up my mind. I don't know when I will see you again." Devorah hugged and kissed Golde.

"But you can't leave," Golde cried. "We haven't even had the wedding yet."

Devorah turned to Shoshana and hugged her. "I'm sorry Shosh, but I must leave right away, so Arik's friends will know what has happened."

"It's alright, I understand," Shoshana said, trying to suppress tears as she kissed her younger sister's cheek.

Sarah came over and kissed Devorah. "Be careful. You promise?"

"I promise. When I get back I expect you to have Adam begging to marry you."

"I will, you'll see."

Devorah hugged Sarah again.

"Tevye, tell her she can't leave," Golde said.

She was so upset she was shaking. But what could I do?

"I can tell her, but it won't do any good. When your daughters make up their minds to do something, Moses himself could not change their minds with a hundred plagues."

Devorah embraced and kissed me. I felt her warm tears on my cheek.

"You're right, Papa. I have to go now and pack."

I watched my daughter race off to her room. My stomach became knotted; it felt like I'd been hit in the belly with a hammer. It was the same feeling of love and loss I felt the day I took Hodel to the train station so she could go to be with Pertschik in Siberia. I haven't seen Hodel since. Will I ever see Devorah again?

"Life was getting too easy for us, wasn't it, God of Abraham, Isaac, Jacob and Tevye? You had to stir things up. You must know what You're doing, so what can we do but dance."

I looked around and saw everyone staring at me. "Everyone, dance!"

The music began again and the members renewed their dancing. Golde sat on a bench with her head in her hands sobbing. Shoshana stared into space as if she had been awakened from a peaceful slumber and did not know where she was. Her veil was gone and her wedding dress was already soiled. Sarah put her arm around her sister. Shoshana just rested her head on Sarah's shoulder.

Before I could go over to them, I was pulled back into the circle of dancers. I looked toward the kibbutz gate. All I could see was darkness.

I 3

Well Shoshana's "wedding" was a night to remember, or better to forget. I was supposed to give away a daughter as a bride; instead, a different daughter ran away and the bride was left sobbing at the altar.

Would you believe I know a Midrash to explain even this? It's true.

It seems an important man in the town of Kabul invited the great rabbis of his generation to a wedding party for his son. During the meal, the father noticed that the wine bottles on the table were empty. He asked his son, the groom, to go down to the wine cellar and get some new bottles.

The young man went down into the dark cellar and, while gathering up some bottles, did not see that a poisonous snake had slid out from between the wine barrels. The snake bit him and he died instantly.

When the groom did not come back for a long time, his father went down into the wine cellar to find out what had happened. He found his son lying on the floor. The father went upstairs quietly and finished his meal without saying a word to the other guests.

When the meal was over and it was time to say the *Birkat HaMazon,* the Grace After Meals, the father got up and told his guests there would be no more celebration, but that they must join him in saying prayers for mourners, and help him bury the young man.

So, what do we learn from this story?

That no perfect happiness exists in our world. Even times of rejoicing can suddenly turn into tragedy.

This is a lesson Tevye knows only too well. I tried to tell the story to Golde, but she wouldn't listen. I'm very concerned about her. She had finally begun to pull out of her dark mood when the wedding was announced, but now she's falling into an even deeper abyss, muttering all day about her family being scattered, and the shame of a daughter scorned on her wedding day.

Shoshana is even worse. Half way through the morning, when the band finally was worn out and the dancers too weary to continue, the *chaverim* retired, leaving my daughter with words of reassurance about the forces beyond Chaim's control that must have kept him from arriving.

Days passed, then weeks, and still we heard nothing about Chaim. Even Bernice, the American, who has now become very involved in the politics of the *yishuv,* could not find out what happened to him. We all feared the worst, that he had been killed on the road by an Arab band or that he'd been taken away by the British to a prison camp in Africa, as we learned had been poor Arik's fate.

Finally, I decided to go to visit his parents. No one had wanted to go before; since everyone knew they were opposed to the wedding and would likely blame any harm that befell their son on the kibbutz and the woman who lured him from them. But my daughter was withdrawing more each day. We couldn't even get her to eat. From the most energetic *chaver,* the one who felt compelled to outwork the men, Shoshana now had become the feeblest. She had grown and blossomed on the kibbutz, but now she was withering before my eyes. My heart was breaking.

"Why?" I asked God on the way to Tel Aviv. "Why must You make the lives of my daughters so difficult? My life is what it is. I don't complain. I know I have sinned, and the life I'm living on the kibbutz is not exactly the life of Torah, but why should my family suffer? You blessed them with beauty and brains, was that to be in place of happiness? Poor Tzeitl's husband, Motel, is sick. Hodel followed Pertschik to Siberia to see him hung. Another child abandoned our faith. The man Devorah wanted to marry was arrested. And now this heartbreak has befallen Shoshana. What have they done to deserve this? What have I done to merit such punishment for my daughters?"

The whole ride to Tel Aviv I carried on my conversation with God, hoping just this once He would answer, or send a sign to guide me. If I thought the answer would be there, I would climb Mount Sinai. But the only sounds were the murmuring of other people on the bus and the roar of the bus engine.

When I finally reached Danziger's mansion, I knocked on the door. I knocked and I knocked. There was no answer. I went to the window where I had first seen the servant Abdullah, but it was dark inside. I couldn't even see the mirrored walls. It looked like they were covered with sheets. Could it be that Chaim was dead and they were still in mourning?

I went back to the door and banged until my fist began to bleed. Finally, I heard the sound of a latch on the other side being withdrawn. The door slowly opened and Abdullah stood glaring at me as though I were the tax collector. He was dressed in a plain blue aba instead of the gaudy uniform with the buttons. This seemed odd, but I decided not to say anything.

"Do you remember me? I am Tevye, from the kibbutz. I was here several weeks ago."

"Of course I remember you. I'm not stupid. What is it you want?"

"I would like to see Reb Danziger please. Could you tell him I'm here?"

"I'm afraid that isn't possible."

The Arab began to close the door and I threw my shoulder against it. "What do you mean it isn't possible? It's urgent that I speak to him."

"You cannot," Abdullah said and began trying to force the door closed.

I was not going to leave without talking to Danziger and held my ground. "Tell him —"

"He's not here."

The Arab was not going to get rid of me that easily. I continued to push against the door. "What do you mean he's not here?"

"He's left the country."

"That can't be."

"See for yourself," Abdullah said, as he quickly stepped back from the door, causing me to fall forward into the entry hall.

I stood up and dusted myself off. Leaving the haughty Arab behind, I retraced the steps I had taken on my previous visit. In the room where all the clocks had been, the furniture was covered. Some of the clocks were under sheets, and a few spots on the wall where others had hung were now empty. Instead of the chorus of "cuckoos" I had heard the last time, only a few muffled sounds came out from under the shrouds. The room full of mirrors was also veiled.

"Has something happened to Chaim?" I asked breathlessly, running back to Abdullah.

"Not as far as I am aware."

"Well then, why is everything covered up like someone in the family has died?"

"The family has left Palestine for an extended vacation abroad. I was told to watch over the house while they are gone."

"Gone? Gone where?"

"I am not permitted to say."

"What do you mean, not permitted? Where have they gone?"

The Arab just stared down at me.

"All right, can you at least tell me one thing? Where is Chaim?"

"Chaim?"

"Yes Chaim, their son!"

"There's no need to yell, my hearing is quite good."

"Where is Chaim?" I repeated in a whisper.

"He went with them of course."

"He's gone abroad?"

"That's correct."

"As in out of the country?"

Abdullah nodded. He was beginning to look at me as though I'd lost my mind. And he would not have been far wrong.

"And when are they coming back?"

"Mr. Danziger said it would be at least a year. Perhaps longer."

"A year? And what happens when Rothschild comes here to see him?"

"Sir?"

"Never mind."

Abdullah opened the door and stood aside for me.

"One last question and then I'll be on my way. How long ago was this trip abroad planned?"

"Oh, it wasn't really planned, sir. When Chaim returned from the kibbutz to visit, Mr. Danziger flew into a rage. He and his son had quite a row. Finally, he said the whole family was leaving Palestine immediately. They barely made time to pack. Mr. Danziger asked me to ship many of their possessions. I don't think Chaim was very happy about leaving, but he wouldn't disobey his father. Mr. Danziger probably threatened to cut him out of the will."

"So he was more the son of Rothschild than Marx after all. Who can blame him?"

"Sir?"

"Nothing. I'm sorry to have bothered you."

I walked out and looked back at the now deserted house. I just stared at the big door and wondered what I could say to Golde, and to Shoshana. I couldn't tell them that Chaim's father didn't think Shoshana was good enough for his son and had spirited him away to be sure he wouldn't marry the daughter of a dairyman.

The ride home was one of the longest of my life. I was ranting out loud. People on the bus looked at me as if I was a lunatic. I didn't care. I was going to let God know how I felt, as if He didn't know already.

"Being poor is not supposed to be a sin, and yet the sin of my poverty is being visited upon my daughter. It isn't fair. It isn't fair!"

Can you imagine that I am now shouting at God? For even this He must have a reason. Who am I to question? Still. Still.

When I arrived back at the kibbutz, it was already dark. I went to the infirmary. Shoshana had become so weak from refusing to eat; they were trying to feed her intravenously.

I wished that Devorah was still here to look after her sister, but she ran off the night of the wedding and no one has heard from her since. God knows what has become of her. I can't bear to think about it.

Now I could see my Shoshie lying on her side, as thin as the blanket covering her. I walked around to see her gaunt face and could hardly recognize it as belonging to the same person I'd raised.

Her eyes fluttered open as I knelt beside her cot and took her hand.

"He's never coming back, is he Papa?" she whispered weakly.

I stroked her hair, but couldn't answer. I wanted to lie, but I knew she could see the answer in my face.

"I'm sorry, Papa."

"You're sorry? What for, my angel?"

"I've disappointed you and Mama. I was not good enough to marry."

"How could you say such a thing? You are the most beautiful woman on the kibbutz, maybe in all of Israel. Chaim loved you. It was his father who was the problem. And he had nothing against you, how could he? It was me that he couldn't accept."

"I can't stand the pain, Papa. I just can't."

Tevye is not an old woman, but I couldn't bear to see my daughter this way. I pulled her up to me and held her the way I used to when she was a child and hurt her knee after falling down some stairs. But I knew it was not her flesh but her spirit that was injured. And I didn't know how to mend that. I held her until she drifted back to sleep and then gently laid her back on the pillow.

I cried the whole way back to my room. I composed myself before climbing into bed, but then the tears began to flow again. Golde rolled over and put her arm around me.

The following morning Dr. Susser found Shoshana on the floor of the bathroom in a puddle of blood. During the night she had slit her wrists.

I 4

How can I describe my grief? Is there any greater pain than the feeling a parent has after the loss of a child? I cannot sleep. I wander the fields at night alone, looking heavenward but knowing the Almighty Himself could not provide an answer to why this happened that would comfort me.

Shoshie was so full of life, so energetic and happy. How could the vitality be so quickly sapped from her?

I rage at Chaim for being a hypocrite, mouthing Marxist slogans and seducing my daughter, only to cave into the will of his father. A letter finally arrived from Chaim, but I burned it in the fire without opening it.

Listen to me, complaining that a son obeys his papa. So maybe I should direct my anger toward Danziger, whose self-righteousness knew no bounds. But how can I blame him for my daughter's death? He could not know how she would react. If he had given it any thought, would it have affected his decision? Danziger was only following the tradition I myself grew up with in Russia, that children do not decide for themselves who they will marry, and what matches are suitable. The poor daughter of a dairyman would never have been an acceptable mate for the sons of the men in the dachas of Yehupetz.

So who does that leave me to blame? Only Tevye. Why couldn't I have persuaded Danziger that Shoshana was worth a hundred daughters of Rothschild? Why couldn't I comfort my Shoshie, to let her know it would be possible to find love again, to convince her the pain would go away?

Why? Why? Why?

I want to scream to the heavens that an entry in the Book of Life has been mistakenly erased. For what has my Shoshie been sacrificed? What?

Natan the Nudnik, of all people, told me a Midrash that was the closest thing to an explanation I was ever likely to get for this tragedy. He related that on the eighth day of the dedication ceremonies for the Tabernacle, the unbelievable happened. Aaron's two eldest sons, Nadav and Avihu, were suddenly struck by lightning while they were performing the Divine Service. Moses, their uncle, watched in horror as the two young men died instantly. Aaron wept and said, "I and my sons have sinned. This is why God has punished us so severely!"

Moses comforted Aaron, saying, "No, this is not true. The boys died because they were more holy than we are. God used them to sanctify the great Name, because they were among God's most intimate friends. God had already hinted this possibility to me at Mount Sinai. They must have made some slight error in their service, but because God expected them to be perfect and on such a high plane, higher than any of the rest of us, they had to die."

It was some comfort to think of Shoshana as holier than the rest of us, and one of God's most intimate friends. Still, the funeral was unbearable. To see Shoshie in a box. I prayed she would suddenly sit up and tell me everything was all right, that I had just been having another one of my nightmares. But the coffin was as silent as my heart was heavy. I marched behind the casket half hoping the mosquitoes would suck the blood from my body so that

I might join my daughter in the world to come, to ensure she felt no more pain.

The procession of mourners walked silently to the grave site. The only sound was a series of loud, slow clangs on Shmuel's bell.

My feet were so heavy; I might not have been able to move if not for the necessity of holding up poor Golde. When Dr. Susser broke the news to us, she was inconsolable. For the entire *shiva* period she cried. The *chaverim* who shared our grief tried to speak to her, to remind her of the joyous times we spent together, as the Talmud instructs in times of mourning. But she would put her hands over her ears and scream over and over, "No! No! No!"

When it was time for the funeral, she suddenly stopped crying. She leaned against me, but did not react when Jonathan eulogized about Shoshana's contribution to building the kibbutz and to the rebirth of the Jewish commonwealth. Shoshana's actions, he said, were what God meant when he told Isaiah Israel would be a light unto the nations.

"I found a parable that I hope provides some comfort to Tevye and Golde and the rest of us," Jonathan said, his normally booming voice just loud enough for all of us to hear. "A king gave one of his vassals a valuable object to hold for him. Each day this man would lament: 'Woe is me! When will the King come and take back his possession so that I won't be burdened with such a great responsibility?'"

"The same holds true for you, Tevye and Golde. You had a daughter who was beautiful, a hard worker, and an inspiration to all of us. She left the world unstained, pure from sin. Therefore, you must find comfort in the thought that you have returned unsullied the possession entrusted to your care by the King of Kings."

At that point, I could no longer hold back my tears. Simcha came over to support me. It was the first time I could remember seeing him without a smile on his face. I wept like a baby on his shoulder.

When it was my turn to recite the *Kaddish*, I could barely speak the words, "The Lord gave and the Lord has taken away; blessed be the name of the Lord."

The whole time Golde stood stoically. Right up to the point when the coffin was placed in the ground and covered with dirt, she did not shed a single tear. While I sobbed, she watched as each *chaver* took a turn shoveling the earth over the casket. When the last spadeful was thrown over the grave, Golde collapsed in my arms.

Golde has refused to leave her bed since that day. It is said that a merry heart is good medicine, but a broken spirit dries the bones. That is what has happened to Golde. She is beginning to look the way that Shoshana did just before she died. Her little withered body seems to shrink in the bed day by day. I don't know what to do for her. I can't get her to eat. She won't say a word, which I don't have to tell you means she is getting close to death. I was too scared of her reaction to even tell her about the letter that came from Chaim.

Sarah sits by her bedside all day and strokes her hand and cools her forehead with a damp cloth. But not even her daughter's touch can reach the place she has gone. After all that has happened in our lives, we have always had each other, but now, when we need each other most, she is leaving me and I am impotent to help either of us. With our family scattered, and our daughter gone, can I live without my Golde?

No, I cannot. I will not.

"Sarah, would you mind letting me have a few minutes alone with your mother?"

As she walked toward the door, Sarah came over and whispered, "I'm so scared, Papa. All my sisters are gone. I don't want to lose my mother too."

I hugged her and kissed her forehead. I wanted to tell her not to worry, but how could I?

"Go and talk to Bernice. See if she can find out where Devorah is now. Maybe if we can get a message to her, she will come home. That will raise your mother's spirits."

"But —"

"Go Saraleh."

I kissed her again and watched her walk out the door. I've been so consumed with Shoshana's life and death; I hadn't noticed Sarah becoming a woman. Maybe she is the one meant for happiness. I dare not think about it.

When Sarah was gone, I went to the seat she had pulled over to the bed and sat beside my wife. I tried to see what was behind her eyes, but all that was visible was the darkness of a moonless night.

"Golde," I said softly, taking her hand. It felt cold and limp. I held it between mine. "We have had a terrible tragedy. God alone knows why this has happened. But it was His will. We must go on for the sake of our other daughters. Hodel, Devorah and Sarah have no one else to look after them. I know that we have been separated, but I tell you it is not permanent. We will be reunited one day, here in the holy land. I believe it as surely as God gave the Torah to Moses at Sinai."

She gave no sign of hearing me.

"Golde, what will our daughters do without you? What will I do without you? You have been my rock. You will be killing me if you let yourself go."

"I wish words to comfort you would come to my lips, but God has not seen fit to put them in my mouth. I miss Shoshie. I know I will always miss her. But I also know I must go on; I want to go on for the sake of Tzeitl, Hodel, Devorah, Sarah and, yes, Chavaleh."

At the mention of the daughter I disowned, I could see the first glimmer of life in Golde's face.

"Whatever I failed to do for Shoshana, I must make sure I do for them. I am their father and you are their mother. We are all they have. Our time will come soon enough, we mustn't hasten it."

I pulled her hand to my breast and closed my eyes. I spoke as if offering a prayer. "Golde, the Lord said, 'I have put before you this day life and death, blessing and curse. Choose life so that you and your children can live!' Golde, you must choose life! Golde, choose life, please. I need you. We all do."

My head fell on her chest and I began to cry.

A moment later, I felt her tiny, bony hand stroking my hair. I lifted my head and saw a single tear lodged in the corner of Golde's eye. It trickled down her cheek. I brushed it away and lightly kissed her. She began to sob and shake. I put my arms around her and then climbed into the bed and held her. She did not speak, but I felt her arms slowly reach around my back. And then I felt her squeeze me with all the strength she had left.

15

There's a story the rabbi in Anatevka once told me about the great sage, Rabbi Akiva. Once, he went on a long trip. When he reached a village and asked for lodging he was refused. He said, "Whatever God does is for the best."

He spent the night in an open field. He had with him a lamp, a donkey and a rooster. The wind came and blew out his lamp, but he said, "Whatever God does is for the best." Then a lion came and ate the donkey, and a cat killed the rooster. Nevertheless, Rabbi Akiva said, "Whatever the Merciful One does is for the best."

That night, the town was ransacked and the inhabitants were taken away and made slaves. Rabbi Akiva repeated that "whatever God does is for the best."

You might ask, "How could he say such a thing?"

Well, Rabbi Akiva explained, "the light of the lamp, the braying of the donkey and crowing of the rooster might have disclosed my whereabouts to the robbers."

That's a long way of getting around to the news. The Sabbath after I finally broke through Golde's grief, I comforted her as the Bible commands a husband to do. I would like to say that it was my nocturnal charms that helped her come back to life, but it took several more weeks before Golde was ready to work again. Fortunately, her appetite quickly returned. Boy did it return. She began to eat like my horse. Sarah was worried that Golde was having a wild mood swing and was going to stuff herself to death instead of starving. But I could tell she was starting to recover, to the extent anyone can ever really recover from the shock of losing a child. Hopefully, the great sage Ibn Gabirol was right when he said, "Everything that grows begins little and becomes big, except for grief: it starts big and becomes little, until it disappears."

Golde was in the middle of a midday feast of apples, yogurt, cucumbers, bread and jam when Sarah came into the house with a letter. Golde stopped eating and suddenly grew pale. I could tell she was frightened that it would be some new catastrophe that would throw her back into the abyss. She wouldn't even touch the letter.

Sarah started to hand it to me. "No, you read it," I said.

"Okay. It's from Tzeitl," Sarah said softly, sensing our anxiety.

"Please God, bring us good news this once," I prayed quietly.

"Dear Mama and Papa: How is everyone? You can't imagine how much we miss you and long to be in your arms again. The political situation in Russia is growing worse each day. We worry that it will spill over here to Poland. The Jews who thought the worst was over when Lenin died are finding out that Stalin has no greater love for the Jews than either Lenin or the Tsar; he may have less than both."

Sarah looked up at me. I was afraid to hear what might come next, but it was too late to halt the messenger from delivering the message. I smiled and nodded.

"But this is not what I wrote to tell you. You remember that Motel had fallen ill. The hours he works — oh Papa, you should see how hard he works — in the dark, damp basement took a toll and he developed a horrible cough. Thanks be to God, he has recovered. And now I make sure he gets rest and fresh air. The children are growing like weeds. I can hardly believe I'm a mother. It seems like only yesterday I was playing the games that they now play."

I looked over at Golde. Her whole body sagged as if her bones had dissolved. The tension escaped like the air from a balloon. Now a hint of a smile was on her face. It's the happiest she's looked since Shoshana's engagement was announced.

"I can't believe it either. My big sister a mother," Sarah said before continuing to read. "I have wonderful news. Hodel has just arrived!"

"Hodel, ah!" Golde brought her hands to her mouth and shook her head.

"Mama, listen. She is in a surprisingly good mood and has quite a tale to tell. I will let her relate it herself. I can say she looks fantastic and her spirit is unbroken. I can't tell you how wonderful it is to have her here with us."

I could see Sarah fighting back tears. I knew how much she missed her sisters, but she was sensitive enough not to say anything in front of her mother.

"I can't believe it," Sarah said, putting one hand over her mouth, a gesture she got from her mother.

"What?" Golde asked.

"There's more. I am hardly used to having such a string of good news, but, believe it or not, there is something even more exciting for me to share. I am pregnant again! Can you imagine me with three children? I am so happy I feel I could burst."

"Such a miracle," Golde said clasping her hands over her head. "The cycle of life and death within my own family."

It was just as the proverb says, "a bad messenger falls into mischief, but a faithful envoy brings healing." The letter was just the tonic Golde needed. And it didn't hurt me either. Another grandchild. Maybe even a boy, at last, not that there would be anything wrong with yet another girl in the family.

Sarah wiped tears from her eyes and finished the letter. "We are saving our money and one day, sooner than you think, we will join you. But, for now, tell me everything about you and Schprintze, Teibel and little (I bet she's not so little anymore) Beilke — sorry,

I'm still not used to calling them by their Hebrew names. You are in our hearts and prayers. Love, Tzeitl."

Golde took the letter from Sarah and read and reread it over and over. I walked over and kissed the top of Golde's head. She hugged me around the waist and looked up and said, "Oh Tevye, at last some good news. Maybe the Almighty has decided we have suffered enough. This is the beginning of the renewal of our family. I can feel it!"

It was so nice to see Golde smile. She jumped up and flew out the door waving the letter.

"Where are you going?" I shouted after her.

"I've got to tell Chana."

"Who will tell Faiga, who will tell everyone on the kibbutz."

The news, of course, spread quickly. I didn't mind. I've gotten used to everyone knowing my business. The best part is that a single sheet of paper can have such a wonderful influence on a person. Golde put Tzeitl's letter in her pocket and never went anywhere without it. Whenever she thought about Shoshana, or felt down, she would take out the letter and read it over and over.

I was so happy to see Golde getting back to her old self. Tzeitl's letter was like manna from heaven. I pray the good feeling will last.

I 6

"Tevye, hurry up, Shmuel will be ringing the bell soon," Golde shouted from the kitchen.

"I'm hurrying, I'm hurrying."

Now here is one of the true joys of kibbutz life, working with my wife. It's not that I don't like the opportunity to spend more time with Golde, but setting tables, serving meals and washing dishes is not exactly my foremost ability — if you'll excuse me Reb Marx — but we all have to take our turn at what are considered the less desirable tasks.

"Tevye, bring the carts over so we can start loading them."

Another edict from the authority. Talk about turning tradition on its head, the papa taking orders from the mama. It reminds me of the time Moses was asked why he couldn't control his sister. He said, "I can either be the leader of Israel or control Miriam. I can't do both."

"Tevye!"

"I'm coming."

All right, so it's not such a tough job to put some tin boxes on the tables and fill them with forks and spoons and to wheel these little carts around with platters of food, but who needs the complaints. I don't cook the meals, I just serve them, but everybody's got an opinion. The porridge is cold, the eggs are hard, and the tomatoes are soft. The members had food fights like little children until we held a meeting and Jonathan lectured us on the significance of even the most menial jobs, and the importance of treating everyone, especially the kitchen staff, with respect. Well, the scolding stopped the *chaverim* from throwing food, but it didn't stop the grumbling.

Who can blame them? Look at what they're bringing out for lunch: bread with jam, fruit soup and herring. If you think it looks bad, you don't want to know about the smell. Everyone peels the skin off the herring and wipes their hands on their clothes. That fishy smell will be around all day.

The stench of the *chaverim* is hardly the most pressing issue in my life. Actually, I've become a little bit obsessed with the question of justice since Shoshana's death. If I think about Shoshie too much, I might start to cry, and that wouldn't do; my tears might drip onto the food and that would make it even saltier. I'll be fetching drinks throughout the meal.

If only I had more time to study, perhaps I could see things as clearly as Rabbi Akiva. Maybe it is conceited to believe any amount of study would be sufficient to attain even a fraction of his insight. Still, I wish I had Akiva's ability to see that everything God does is truly for the best. How could Shoshana's death really be good? What higher purpose could it serve?

"Tevye, stop dawdling! It's almost time."

If I worked here more often, the committee would probably have to vote on whether to put a window in the kitchen just so Golde could yell at me without opening the door. When she stuck her head out, I could see she was chewing something. Her latest habit is to chew *kamardin* all the time. It's a kind of candy made from boiled apricots. After dwindling away to practically nothing, she's getting a little *zaftik*, but she's happier so I don't say anything.

Don't get me wrong, I like to eat, but instead of filling my belly to avoid thinking about Shoshana, I've tried to nourish my mind, to find explanations for our tragedies in the words of our sages. Many *Midrashim* illustrate that justice is not always obvious, but they usually relate to people getting the rewards they deserve. Take the story about the rabbi who prayed to have the chance to see the prophet Elijah.

His prayer was answered, but when the rabbi asked if he could travel with the prophet, Elijah said, "No, because you will not understand my actions and they will upset you."

The rabbi begged Elijah and swore he would ask no questions if he was allowed to accompany him.

Elijah agreed, but said the first time the rabbi asked a question or expressed astonishment, he would have to leave.

The first place they visited was the home of a poor man whose only possession of value was a cow. The man's wife implored them to come inside to eat and drink and to sleep in their house. After enjoying the couple's hospitality, Elijah got up the next morning and prayed that their cow would die. And it did.

After they left, the rabbi asked, "Why did you kill the cow of this good man?"

"Look, listen and be silent," replied Elijah. "If I answer your questions we must part."

They traveled on and came to a large mansion owned by an arrogant and wealthy man. They were coldly received, given only a glass of water and a piece of bread. They slept in the house and then, the next morning, Elijah saw that a wall of the mansion had collapsed. He restored it.

The rabbi was surprised but held his tongue.

The following evening they entered a town with a large synagogue. They arrived in time for the evening service and were impressed by the velvet cushions and gilded carvings. After the service, the president asked, "Who is willing to take these two poor men to their house?" No one responded, so Elijah and the rabbi slept in the synagogue. In the morning, Elijah shook hands with each member of the synagogue and said, "I hope you may all become presidents."

The next evening they entered another city. The sexton of the synagogue greeted them and notified the congregation of the arrival of two strangers. The best hotel was opened to them and all showed them attention and honor. Before leaving, Elijah said, "May the Lord appoint but one president over you."

Finally, the rabbi couldn't stand it any longer and had to ask Elijah to explain his actions. "Why," he asked, "did you extend good wishes to those who treated us badly but not to those who were generous?"

Elijah explained: "We first entered the house of the poor man who treated us so kindly. Now it had been decreed that on that very day his wife should die. I prayed to the Lord that the cow might die instead. God granted my prayers, and the woman was saved."

"The rich man we visited next," Elijah continued, "treated us coldly, but I rebuilt his wall. If he had rebuilt it himself, he would have discovered a treasure that lies underneath."

"And the members of the synagogue?" the rabbi asked.

"To the members of the synagogue who were not hospitable I said: 'May you all be presidents,' because where many rule there can be no peace. But to the others I said, 'May you have but one president,' because with one leader, no dissension will arise."

"Now, if you see the wicked prospering, be not envious; if you see the righteous in poverty and trouble, be not doubtful of God's justice."

And then Elijah disappeared.

It's a good story, but, ultimately, the good are spared suffering. I ask again, "Dear Lord, how was taking my Shoshie for the best?"

There was a knock at the door.

Perhaps God has sent Elijah to bring me an answer.

The second knock was louder.

Shmuel hadn't rung the bell yet, so the dining room was still locked. We had found long ago that if the door was left open, members would come in at all hours and eat whatever they could find. One night, Bernice prepared a big cake for desert after the Sabbath meal. The next morning she found it half eaten. Afterward, the executive committee voted to keep the doors of the dining room locked until meals were ready to be served.

The knocking continued and grew louder.

Golde finally came out of the kitchen. "What's all the banging? They know they have to wait until we're ready. Go see who it is. Tell them they have to wait."

"Have you suddenly gone lame my wife?"

"Can't you see that I'm working here?"

"And what do you think I'm doing, playing chess?"

"Tevye!"

"All right. All right."

I opened the door and was shocked to see the American. Bernice had moved to Jerusalem a long time ago to be closer to the Jewish Agency and devote full time to the politics of the *yishuv*. I last saw her at Shoshana's funeral. I noticed she had begun to put on a little weight and was starting to look more like a grandmother than Golde.

"Well, are you going to just stand there staring at me?" Bernice bellowed. "A person could age ten years waiting for you to answer. Does it take as long to get invited inside?"

"Come in, Bernice. Come in. I'm just a little surprised to see you. I thought you were in Jerusalem or Tel Aviv with the big shots from the Jewish Agency."

"I was, but you know I can't stay away for long."

At the sound of the American-accented Hebrew, Golde bolted out of the kitchen and came over to embrace Bernice.

"How are you Golde?"

"I'm fine. It's wonderful to see you, Bernice. You look wonderful. Let me make some tea," Golde said, dashing back toward the kitchen.

"That's okay, I can't stay long."

It was too late, Golde was already gone.

"Come," I said, "sit and tell me the news from the big city."

As soon as she sat, Bernice took out a cigarette. It was a habit many of the *chaverim* had acquired. Usually, the smoke made my eyes water.

"So, are we going to have our state?"

"I have no doubt about it, Tevye. But the British won't make it easy. Remember how our good friend Churchill dismembered the Holy Land?"

"I confess, Bernice, I never understood how he could do that to our country."

Bernice smiled wistfully. "He could do it because England was a great power that had just won The Great War. He felt he needed to reward the Arab allies who helped Britain defeat the Turks. So he lopped off four-fifths of Palestine to pay off Abdullah. Poof! All of a sudden, the world has a new nation, Transjordan. By installing handpicked leaders, Churchill hoped to ensure Arab allegiance to the Crown. It won't work, of course, but we have no say in the matter. Our state will be in only a small fraction of our homeland."

Golde came out and put a cup of tea in front of Bernice and sat beside me.

"Why doesn't Churchill say, 'Poof,' and create a Jewish state?" I asked rubbing smoke from my eyes.

She sipped her tea and then gave a little sarcastic laugh. "He needs Arab friends, Tevye. He doesn't give a fig about Jews."

"Didn't the League of Nations give England a mandate for Palestine to fulfill the Balfour Declaration?" Golde asked.

"Of course not! Britain and the other powers control that collection of yentas," Bernice said, waving her hand dismissively. "They just divided the spoils of war. We'll have to fight for everything, hopefully by diplomacy and not force, but the situation here is deteriorating."

"Why? What's happened?" I said before starting to choke.

"You sound like you're going to cough up a lung, Tevye. Have a glass of water," Golde said, pouring me a cup from the pitcher on the table.

Bernice waved the smoke away and finally held her cigarette below the table.

"We've had reports of marauding bands of Arabs coming from the north to steal flocks and set fire to the fields of kibbutzim near the border. Jews in some of the smaller towns have also been attacked. We fear an outbreak of widespread violence soon, so we're going around to all the kibbutzim, warning them to prepare for possible raids. The Haganah is sending people to help train the *chaverim* to use various weapons. This brings me to the real reason I came."

"You mean it wasn't just to bring us such good news?"

"Tevye, you're a good man, but courteous you're not. Actually, I brought a surprise for you. I don't know what's taking so long. Excuse me for a moment."

Bernice got up and walked outside.

Golde and I looked at each other in bewilderment. A few minutes later, Bernice came back.

"You had asked me to do you a favor some time ago, but for reasons that will become clear in a moment, it wasn't possible to deliver. I figured it was better late than never."

Just as Bernice finished speaking, Devorah walked through the door.

Golde and I were so shocked we sat staring with our mouths open. Devorah ran over and embraced us. We had both been too frightened to even talk about her since she'd run off at the aborted wedding.

"Thank you, God. Thank you," Golde muttered through her tears.

I said my own silent prayer of thanks.

"Let me look at you," Golde said backing away from our daughter. "You're so skinny. Aren't you eating? And your beautiful hair, what have you done to it?"

I had been so excited to see her; I hadn't even noticed Devorah's hair was cut as short as a young boy's.

"I've been eating plenty, Mama. Believe me. I just get a lot of exercise. Please sit and I'll tell you everything."

I noticed Bernice give Devorah a look that told her that was not such a good idea.

"Your hair. Oh." Golde put her hand over her mouth and fell back in her chair.

"So, what tales of derring-do have you brought us?" I asked, expecting to hear that she had spent these many months nursing injured soldiers.

"Well, there are some things I mustn't tell. The British have spies everywhere and it would be dangerous for you to know too much."

"Dangerous?"

"She's right, Tevye. I don't even know everything the Haganah does," Bernice said.

"Arik had told me where to contact Yossi and Shimshon, the two boys who had brought him to the infirmary when he was shot. I found them in Tel Aviv and explained what happened. They said the Haganah could use a nurse to discreetly tend to injured soldiers after battles with the Arabs, since they could not take them to hospitals for fear of being arrested by the British. Fortunately, we haven't had many casualties."

"Were you in any riots?" Golde asked. She was holding her hands together in her lap so tightly I could see them turning red.

"No, I stayed at a safe house where they would bring the wounded."

"What's a safe house?" I asked.

"A secret place the British don't know about."

"But what about your hair? Did they make you cut it?" Golde asked again.

"Again with the hair. Let her talk."

"It's okay, Papa. I'll explain. Like I said, until recently it was pretty quiet and they didn't need my nursing skills. But they did need a courier, someone who could take messages to different safe houses, from one unit to another and, occasionally, to smuggle weapons. I don't think it's any great secret that we carried them in our bras and girdles. I'm pretty small, so I never carried much beyond pistols. You wouldn't believe what some of the bigger girls smuggled."

"Devorah," Bernice interrupted.

"Anyway, I only carried weapons at the beginning. Shimshon figured the British were too gentlemanly to search a woman, so he would send me to take guns from place to place. After the Jaffa riots, the police started looking at everyone warily and Shimshon was worried I might be caught. He still needed a courier, so I started carrying messages."

Golde started to interrupt.

"I know, Mama. The hair. Sometimes I had to take messages after dark, and Shimshon thought it would be too dangerous, and suspicious, for a woman to walk alone at night. I decided to cut my hair and pretend to be a boy."

"A boy!" Golde gasped.

"Do you know what the Torah says about a woman wearing a man's clothing? It says it is abhorrent to God," I said.

"Tevye," Bernice said trying to calm us. "I think God understands that this is a special circumstance."

"I checked with a rabbi before I agreed to do it, Papa. He said it was all right."

I could see Bernice had a disbelieving look on her face, but I didn't want to make an issue of it. Having a daughter who dresses and acts like a son is probably God's way of punishing me for complaining so much about having only girls.

"Really Golde, it's a necessary ruse. Nothing to worry about."

"That's fine for you to say, Bernice. She's not your daughter."

"Mama, please. It's not a big deal. I just pull a cap over my head and walk quickly. Most of the time I try to stay out of sight. When this job is finished, my hair will grow back."

"It's all your fault," Golde screamed at me.

"My fault?"

"Yes. You brought us to this place. First, our daughters live with boys, then they go to school with them, then they work with them and now, look, they're even dressing and acting like them."

I wanted to say that no one would mistake our daughter for a man, but I could see how she might pass for one if she tried to disguise herself.

Bernice started to laugh and nearly choked on her cigarette.

"What's so funny?" I yelled.

"I'm sorry," Bernice said after a moment. "We all have to make adjustments and sacrifices. Believe me, my life would be different if I'd stayed in Cleveland. The fact is Devorah's doing very important work. The Haganah is the only protection we have from the Arabs when they decide to attack us. Every man that has to be a courier is one less available to fight. Fortunately, despite their many shortcomings, the men of Palestine are willing to let women help in our struggle. They could have told me to stay at the kibbutz and cook, but our leaders, for better or worse, believe I have something to contribute to the political fight. You are contributing no less by the work you do here."

"But what are we doing?"

"As Jonathan would say, you're living Golde, living. And as long as you're here, the Arabs will be forced to accept us."

"Well, I guess it's time for me to contribute a little more," Golde said.

"What are you talking about?" I asked.

Devorah and Bernice also looked in bewilderment at Golde.

"Bernice is not the only one with a surprise to share. I have one also."

"Well?" I was waiting to hear that she had discovered a new recipe for kugel.

Golde didn't answer.

"Golde?"

"Tevye, I'm pregnant."

"I'm sure that will taste very good, but — What did you say?"

"We're going to have a baby."

The next thing I remember I was on a cot in the infirmary.

17

It's hard to complain about the weather in Palestine, considering what I left back in Russia. Still, when it rains, you'd be excused if you started building an ark. I slogged through the mud to sit in our lopsided outhouse. By the time I got from there to the stable, these boots were full of water. Of course, the minute I got inside, the rain stopped.

Now my feet are cold and clammy. My horses aren't too sympathetic, I'm sure, since they march through the mud all the time.

Working in the stable isn't so bad, especially after spending time on kitchen duty. Most of the *chaverim* don't want to do it. They prefer the fresh air of the fields. It's not that I don't like fresh air, but when one of these downpours comes, it's nice to be able to get out of the rain.

Actually, I was lucky. If this storm had hit a week ago, I would have been standing knee-deep in mud now. That's because the learned men and women of the Work Assignment Committee decided to rotate me out to the olive grove for awhile.

Maybe this too was part of a greater plan. I was reminded of Jeremiah's comparison of the Jewish people to olives. The prophet said the olive only released its oil when it is crushed and that the Jews were only prepared to serve God after they were oppressed. Perhaps I am like Jeremiah's olive, and must suffer before I can learn to observe the Lord's commandments.

I didn't mind the work, especially since you got to snack all day, but I couldn't put up with my comrades. Oren the Inventor used to stand beside me kvetching all day about how his back hurt. I reminded him of the Labor Zionist ideals of work. His response was he had no objection to working, it was bending he couldn't stand.

"Besides," he said, "if the committee had let me spend time developing my new olive picker, no one would have to break their back anymore."

"As I recall, Oren, your grape picking machine turned all the fruit to wine."

"And everyone enjoyed every drop."

"And your apple picker went haywire and started pelting people with whatever it pulled off the tree. And —"

"Tevye, you don't have to remind me. I was there, remember? Do you think great inventions just drop from the sky like manna? Someone has to think of them, then build them and test them. Do you think Edison's light bulb or Bell's telephone worked the first time they tried?"

"Well —"

"Of course not. Instead of having me waste time picking handfuls of olives, I should be fine-tuning my machine so we could all be free to do something else."

"All right, Oren," I said. "The next time it comes up before the committee, I'll give you my vote."

"Really?"

"Really."

Oren was so excited he didn't stop talking the rest of the day.

Fortunately, some new members joined the kibbutz a week later and my formidable picking skills were no longer needed. I was sent back to the stables and the barn.

I like it here. I've always loved animals and since my horses and cows take care of me, it's only fair I take care of them.

Golde says I just like a captive audience that can't talk back. Maybe. But I know they're listening. A neigh or a moo is their way of saying, "thank you, Reb Tevye. I agree, Reb Tevye. You're a righteous man, Reb Tevye."

I'm also a tired Reb Tevye. You think shoveling horse manure into a bucket isn't exhausting? It doesn't get easier to work when you get older. And, to tell you the truth, my foot is getting sore. You wouldn't believe why. Before I show you the problem, I'd better explain.

Last month, Simcha made a startling announcement at our weekly meeting.

"Since the early days," he said, "we have shared all our clothing. This has been in the best tradition of socialism, but it has had its drawbacks, as you all know." Simcha raised both his arms so we could all see the sleeves stuck around his elbows.

"You should see my underwear," Enoch shouted.

"Don't make me sick," Chana spat.

This was the type of intellectual exchange that I had come to expect at our meetings. And some people actually wondered why I held study sessions to discuss the Scriptures.

"All right. All right," Simcha interrupted. I am happy to announce that the Committee has voted to allow everyone to own their own clothes."

I think the cheer was the loudest I ever heard at the kibbutz since the committee voted to take birdseed out of the kitchen to prevent Chana from contaminating the kugel.

Well, not everyone was happy.

"What are you all applauding?" Uzi screamed over the din. What is more basic to the communal way of life than the sharing of the clothes on our backs?"

Uzi's insistence on Marxist purity had kept the kibbutz from adopting many of the conveniences being used on other kibbutzim.

"Once you begin to compromise on basic principles, you start down a path that will lead to the complete abandonment of the ideals on which our movement was founded," Uzi continued, warming up to one of his favorite topics. "Before long we will be buying and selling clothes like the petty bourgeoisie we despised in Russia. The sharing of clothes is a tradition that is no less sacred than collective labor."

Golde gave me one of her looks and I knew she could hear echoes of my words about other traditions. And I understood Uzi's argument, but I could not agree that the sharing of clothing undermined the essence of our collective existence. The truth was I wanted my own clothes.

"Believe me Uzi, we have given this very careful consideration. We understand your point and have not come to this decision easily," Simcha said. "If there are others who share Uzi's view, I would be willing to put the question to a vote of the members."

"No! No! We're with you Simcha," people shouted from around the room.

I started to stand and Golde glared at me.

"I insist on a vote," Eitan cried out, joining his ideological soul mate in open revolt.

"All right," Simcha said. "Out of respect for two of our founders, let us take a vote. All those who support the committee's decision to change our policy regarding clothing, and allow members to own their own clothes, signify by saying 'Aye.'"

"Aye!" I shouted along with seemingly everyone else in the room.

"All those opposed to the change, who wish to keep the policy as it is, say "Nay."

Uzi and Eitan stood and bellowed, "Nay."

"The change has been ratified," Simcha confirmed.

I watched Eitan and Uzi turn and storm out of the dining hall. It was one of the rare occasions when I saw the smile briefly leave Simcha's face.

As a protest, Eitan and Uzi walked around wearing ill-fitting clothes; everyone else was thrilled to have their very own peasant shirts and khaki shorts. After years of having pants that either dragged on the floor or stuck around my knees, it was nice to have a pair that was the correct size.

Of course, it is one of God's decrees that man's decisions never turn out exactly as planned. That was the case with our clothes.

The problem started when the scholars on the Work Assignment Committee decided Chana needed a change of scenery — actually everyone needed a break from her cooking — and put her in the *makhsan*. Now the laundry is probably one of the three least popular jobs on the kibbutz, along with kitchen and stable duty, so Chana was not happy.

Working in the laundry was a pretty easy job when everyone was just handed whatever clean clothes were at the top of the pile. It requires a lot more time and effort now that everything has to be sorted by owner, especially since the wise men on the committee decided, for some unexplained reason, not to let us put our names in the clothes. Instead, we were assigned numbers. I guess this was a concession to Uzi and Eitan and a way to soften the blow of the shift toward a semblance of individualism.

Well, Chana and the other laundry workers now only recognize us by our numbers. When I see her, I'll say, "*Shalom*, Chana. *Ma nishma?*" And even though we've known each other since the early days on the kibbutz, she'll still answer, "*Biseder*, 271. And you?"

So this is socialist progress. I went from Tevye, son of Reb Shneour Zalman to Tevye the dairyman to Reb Tevye to Tevye to 271.

Yesterday, we exchanged our usual pleasantries and I started to leave the laundry. Then I heard her call after me, "Wait 271. I've got some socks for you."

I went back and she dropped a handful of socks on top of my other clothes.

"And what is the occasion for this great windfall?" I asked.

"Last week I was assigned to mend old socks. Every *chaver* gets three new pairs."

"*Todah rabah*," I said, genuinely excited to get something new.

"*Bivakasha*, 271."

I should have known better and looked at what she gave me before thanking her. Let me show you this blessing that I received. Her job was to go through the old socks and cut off those that had toes or heels that were torn and sew on new toes or heels from socks that were still whole. As you can see, she got a little confused and decided to replace the worn-out heel on this sock with toes

143

she had mended. I now have a sock with toes on both ends. My toes feel fine, but my heel is killing me.

But enough about that dross. There's much more exciting things to talk about, like having a baby on the way.

Everything is easier knowing our family will grow. Maybe God finally decided to take pity on poor old Tevye to compensate for taking Shoshana from us. She can't be replaced, but at least part of the void will be filled.

It's going to be a new experience having a child here. I still haven't gotten used to the idea of children being raised in a group house, but at least I won't have to be up all night trying to stop the baby from crying.

It seems like ages since I had to worry about such things. Who would have believed Golde was still fertile at her age, and after all she's been through.

"When You said be fruitful and multiply, I never realized You didn't place a time limit on the command. I guess that's why you blessed Sarah with a child when she was ninety."

It's truly a miracle.

Having a child is something you never forget. I still can remember the birth of each one. Golde and I were so young when Tzeitl was born. We were scared to death. The delivery went fine, but neither of us knew what to do with this tiny person. I was afraid to even touch the baby for fear of somehow breaking her, but she was a strong little girl and couldn't be hurt even by my clumsiness. I used to come back from work and spend hours staring at her while she slept, amazed that I could have had anything to do with producing anything so beautiful.

When Golde was carrying Hodel, she had a lot of problems. She got sick for a while and then had difficulty moving around. She spent the last few weeks in bed, afraid to move. When it was finally time to give birth, it took hours. I had bitten my nails to the tips of my fingers and was ready to start on my toes. Hodel was no easier after birth. Golde had trouble getting her to eat or sleep. And what lungs she had. I think they could hear her screaming from Yehupetz. When she really got going, it sounded as if her whole insides were going to fly out. I spent many a night holding her and dancing around the house singing Yiddish songs my mother had sung to me. It was obvious she was not going to be a quiet child.

Our third child, on the other hand, was the quiet one. Chavaleh. I still can't bring myself to speak of her. It's too painful.

And now it's just as difficult to think about Shoshie. I guess you could say things went wrong from birth. I remember she came out backwards. Could that explain why she killed herself?

Devorah was tough, like Tzeitl. She got sick when she was an infant, but recovered quickly and grew like a weed. She would eat anything you gave her. When she got older, she wanted to spend all her time with the animals. If she found any living thing that was injured, she'd bring it home and try to nurse it to health. Golde would complain that the house was beginning to look like Noah's Ark, with all the rabbits, raccoons, squirrels, birds, frogs. She was just as gentle and sympathetic with people, so I wasn't surprised when she went to work with Dr. Susser in the infirmary here. Now, of all things, she's teaching the *chaverim* how to shoot rifles and make Molotov cocktails.

It's hard to believe my youngest, Sarah, has also become a woman. By the time she came along, I knew babies were resilient, sometimes it seemed indestructible. I could carry her with me while I worked, even though it drove Golde to distraction. She'd scream, "What are you doing milking that cow — or saddling that horse — while you're holding the baby. She might get stepped on or kicked."

But so long as Sarah was in my arms I knew she was safe. That was when I knew they were all safe. The saddest thing about children growing up is that you can't hold them to ensure they're protected.

It's funny that I think of the younger children by their Hebrew names now. Schprintze, Teibel and Beilke were such beautiful names, taken from great aunts from my side of the family. We named the first three girls after Golde's grandmothers and an aunt. When we ran out of relatives on her side, we started on mine. Now, I'm not sure what we'll do.

Deciding on a name is really the least of my concerns. After raising six children, I don't know if I'm ready to start over again, even with the help of the kibbutz. Maybe it's time to consult with a higher authority. Pardon me while I step outside for a minute.

I carried my shovel and bucket outside and looked heavenward.

"Dear Lord, I know when I was in Anatevka, I didn't ask for much, but why is that the prayer You chose to answer. I'm in Palestine now. I'm supposed to have a more direct line to You. You used to speak to the prophets and our forefathers Abraham, Isaac and Jacob. You haven't spoken to anyone in a long time — so far as I know. Don't You miss having a little conversation? Moses couldn't even speak that well and You talked to him. I know, You're afraid we won't have anything to talk about. Don't worry, we can just chat for a while, then You can go back to taking care of the rest of the universe."

"After two thousand years, we Jews are coming home and one day we will have a Jewish state like David and Solomon. You spoke to them too. Are You waiting for the new king? I know, I know. I talk too much as it is. You don't need to say anything. I'll talk enough for the two of us."

"You blessed me with six daughters and I thank You every day for them. Would it be too much to ask that the baby be a boy? He doesn't have to be really tall, but that would be nice. He doesn't have to be very strong, but that would be fine. He doesn't have to be smart, but that would be wonderful. He doesn't. . . . I would be happy no matter what You bless us with."

"Could You at least give me a hint? Don't be shy, just chime right in when You're ready."

"Are You sure You're not lonely? I am. Our family should be together, not spread across the world. What purpose does that serve? Aren't families supposed to stay together to serve You? Poor Hodel spent all those years freezing in Siberia with a man she thought was the *mashiach* and then had to endure his murder. And Tzeitl, with the nearsighted tailor. He's a good man, but I've never understood what she sees in him. And . . . well, You know who. Wherever she is, watch over her."

You see how the sky is growing darker. The thunder and lightning announce God's arrival, like it did to Moses on Sinai. This is it. God is going to speak to me at last. I knew if I had faith this time would come.

"I am ready to hear Thy word and do Thy will."

Wait, I must be on holy ground, I'd better take off my boots.

I dropped my shovel and removed my boots.

"What are you doing, Tevye?" Oren hollered.

I continued to look to the sky as the torrent began.

"Come in out of the rain before you catch cold."

"I'm waiting to hear the voice of God," I shouted back.

"What do you mean I have the voice of a clod? You're the clod, standing barefoot in the rain."

Suddenly, a bell began to chime.

This is it.

"It's time for lunch, Tevye."

The ringing stopped as the rain grew heavier. Oren gave me a disgusted wave and ran for the dining room.

I stood waiting, but heard nothing. When I looked down, I saw that my feet were ankle-deep in mud.

I picked up my shoes and shovel. Just as I was about to lift the bucket of dung, it overflowed.

I looked heavenward, "We'll talk again tomorrow."

I 8

"Tevye, what are you doing," Golde shouted as soon as I walked in the door. "How did you get so muddy?"

"I heard that mud was good for the skin, so I decided to take a mud bath."

"Dead Sea mud may be good for you; kibbutz mud just gets my clean floor dirty. Change out of those wet clothes and stop dripping."

"How can I change my clothes without dripping on the floor?"

"Run into the bedroom."

"Run into the bedroom?"

"That or change on the porch. And hurry up about it."

I ran into the bedroom with Golde sweeping after me. She continued her cleaning in the other room. I only got one arm out of my shirt before she began shouting at me.

"Tevye, you should have seen what was going on today in the kitchen. Maya caught Chana putting birdseed in the kugel again. A few of the women had been snacking and suddenly began spitting on the floor. The women who had washed the floor then started yelling at the people who were spitting. Soon everyone was screaming at Chana. What a *balagan*."

"What were you doing working today?" I yelled from the bedroom. "I told you to stay home and rest. A woman in your condition should not be working."

I had just taken all my clothes off when a thought occurred to me. I raced over to Golde.

"Did you eat any of the kugel? I'll end up with the only son who chirps instead of chants at his Bar Mitzvah."

"Don't be ridiculous Tevye. I didn't eat any kugel; besides, we might have another daughter."

"You didn't hear that," I said to the Almighty.

"Tevye, stop carrying on. I gave birth to six beautiful daughters. Would it be so terrible if we had a seventh?"

"I barely survived having six, a seventh might kill me in childbirth."

"Kill *you* in childbirth? Bite your tongue. How can you talk like that? We will have a child in the image of God and it will be what He wants us to have."

"Of course, of course, but I don't think He would want to see me trying to raise another daughter."

"Enough already, Tevye. You're worse than the women in the kitchen. Go put on some clothes already before someone comes in and sees you standing there like Adam without his fig leaf."

"I told you not to work anymore until after the baby is born."

"Tevye, we've gone through this a hundred times already. The other women worked up until the moment they gave birth and I am going to do the same. I won't have them clucking about me being a Russian peasant who can't do her share, the way they did Elisheva."

"If they keep eating Chana's kugel, they're going to cluck anyway."

"Tevye."

"Those women are putting strange ideas in your head. A woman's place is with her husband. You should be cooking for the family and not for the entire kibbutz. The way some of them eat — if

Laban gets a hold of anything before it gets to you, you end up having to lick the plate."

"What's gotten into you? After all this time on the kibbutz, you know we must all share and do our part."

"That's right, Papa," Sarah said as she walked in the door.

"Don't socialists knock anymore?" I said jumping behind a chair.

"Women have just as important a part to play on the kibbutz as men. We can do all the same jobs and do them just as well," Sarah said without the slightest embarrassment.

"Another rabbi heard from. I don't see you or your girlfriends volunteering to take my job cleaning the stables." I spoke as I moved the chair toward the bedroom and dashed inside.

"It's not such a tough job, Papa."

"That's no way to talk to your father," Golde chided.

"Don't your socialist friends believe in respecting their parents? They haven't discarded all the commandments, have they?" I hollered as I pulled on my pants.

"We believe that all people should be treated equally."

Why do I have the feeling I've heard this before? I buckled my pants and returned to face my daughter. "What is this 'we' believe?"

"I follow the teachings of the Labor Zionists who don't believe we should live in the Dark Ages anymore, the way you did back in Russia."

"Do you hear what your daughter is saying? Our traditions are from the Dark Ages and the great socialist thinkers don't like them."

"Tevye, don't raise your voice."

"Those traditions that your great thinkers want to throw away are what allowed us to survive those Dark Ages — and darker times since."

"Oh Papa, what got us through the Dark Ages won't help us in the twentieth century. It's a new world. There are new ideas to solve new problems."

"No, there are no new solutions. All you need is here," I said, shaking a Bible in front of Sarah's face.

"Tevye," Golde cried weakly, grabbing her stomach.

"There are answers to all our problems in here. You just have to look for them. You haven't looked. You don't even know where to look. You're just like your older sisters. You have no respect for tradition."

"Tevye."

As I turned around, still shaking the Bible at Sarah, I saw Golde clutching her stomach and collapse on the floor.

"Mama!" Sarah screamed.

"Golde!" I sprinted to where Golde fell. "Quick, Sarah, go and get Dr. Susser and Devorah."

Sarah raced out the door.

I sat on the ground and let Golde rest her head in my lap. For the first time in a very long while, I was scared. Childbearing was much safer in Palestine than it had been in Russia, but pregnant women had died on the kibbutz. The thought made me shudder as I stroked Golde's forehead.

"You'll be fine. The doctor will be here soon."

"Tevye."

"Yes, I'm here."

"Tevye. Will you really be disappointed if the baby is a girl?"

"Of course not. Any child is a blessing. And a daughter? What could be more precious?"

"But I have been such a terrible mother. I haven't kept the family together. Tzeitl and Hodel are in Russia. Chava married out of the faith. Schprintze is dead. My God, poor Schprintze. Why couldn't I help her?"

"Don't excite yourself. You are a wonderful mother. You have a wonderful family that loves you. Sarah and Devorah are here. You read Tzeitl's letter, Motel is saving up enough money to bring the rest of the family to Palestine. You'll see, soon we'll all be together again. And now I'm here, and I love you."

"I love you too."

Dr. Susser rushed in with Devorah and Sarah behind him.

"Mama, everything will be all right," Devorah said, taking her mother's hand.

"Let's take her into the bedroom," Dr. Susser said calmly.

The doctor and I gently lifted Golde and put her on the bed.

"Sarah, get some sheets and hot water."

I watched her run out the door toward the kitchen. My heart was racing like it was my first time, but every time is a first when it comes to the miracle of birth.

"What can I do to help?"

"Tevye," Dr. Susser said, it's been my experience that the best thing any father can do is stay out of the way. Go outside and we'll call you when we need you."

"Are you sure?"

"Get out of here!" Golde screamed.

At that moment, I knew everything was all right, so I left. As I walked out, Sarah returned with a pitcher of water and Chana brought an armful of clean sheets. Seeing the birdseed lady was not the most reassuring sight, but she was probably Golde's closest friend on the kibbutz, so it might help calm her.

"What are you doing, Tevye?" Simcha asked in his annoyingly cheerful manner.

How could a man be so happy all the time? You'd think he'd have a boil on his foot once that would make him kvetch.

"You look like an animal in a cage that's too small."

"After going through this six times already, you'd think I'd have finally learned how to pace."

"You mean?"

"What do you think I'm doing out here in front of my house, guard duty? The doctor's in there right now."

"You are truly blessed, Tevye," he said, and raised his hand to slap me. I reached up and shook his hand to spare my poor back. "You are singlehandedly helping to repopulate our homeland."

"I'm glad you appreciate my efforts, Simcha. Maybe I can be appointed to the procreation committee and give out assignments for *chaverim* to contribute to the membership drive. And I'll start with you, Mr. I'm So Happy But Still Haven't Found a Wife."

"Tevye, you're letting your old world traditions creep out again. There's no hurry for me to find a bride."

Simcha was pacing beside me at first, then gave up and stood still while I walked back and forth in front of him.

"With the restrictions on immigration the British keep imposing, work alone isn't going to make this a Jewish homeland. We need more Jews."

"Maybe I haven't found the right girl yet."

"Maybe you've been spending too much time with the sheep."

"Now, now. No need to get nasty, Tevye. Perhaps I've just been waiting for the girl of my dreams to become a woman."

"I know that tone of voice. You do have your eye on someone. Who is it?"

"What would you say if I told you it was Sarah?"

"My Sarah? Forget it. You're too old for her."

"Too old? Come on. You told me you almost let your eldest daughter marry a man your age."

"What's wrong with my age? When Tzeitl was engaged to Lazer-Wolf I wasn't my age."

"Don't get so worked up, Tevye. You'll need your strength for the baby."

"Besides, why would Sarah want to be with anyone who is so happy all the time? She needs some misery in her life, like the rest of us."

"Tevye, forgive me for saying this, but you've had enough heartache in your life for her and I combined, maybe for the whole kibbutz. It wouldn't be so bad if she didn't have to suffer, as much as I know you enjoy suffering."

"Very funny, Simcha. You just tend to your flocks and stay away from my Saraleh."

"She's almost all grown up."

"Sha! Go away and leave me to my pacing."

"Ah!"

When Golde screamed, I started for the door, but Simcha put his hand on my shoulder to stop me.

"It's okay," he said. "Let the doctor work his miracles. Dr. Susser has golden hands."

Then I heard one of the most glorious sounds in the world — the squeal of a newborn.

Sarah peeked out the door. "It's a girl, Papa."

I looked heavenward. "Thank you Lord for blessing my house. Seven daughters. You blessed Jacob with 12 sons and now you have chosen me to even things out."

"*Mazel tov*, Tevye!" Simcha said, slapping me on the back. This time I wasn't quick enough to avoid him.

"Tevye has a new baby girl," he shouted so the whole kibbutz could hear. I hadn't thought it was possible for his grin to be any wider.

I put my finger to my lips. "Quiet, they'll find out soon enough."

"Come everyone, Tevye's a papa, again."

Chaverim came running toward me shouting, "*mazel tov.*" I began to feel like the chicken served the first meal after Yom Kippur. Everyone began to sing, "*mazel tov and simen tov and mazel tov and simen tov, yehe lanu, yehe lanu, yehe lanu...*"

Then there was more wailing from inside my house. Everyone stopped singing and stared at my door.

Sarah came out holding a baby and handed it to me. When Tzeitl was born, I refused to take it for fear I would break her, but this little one I had no hesitancy to hold. What a beauty!

Devorah came backing out of the house. "It looks like I finally have a brother," she said, turning around slowly to reveal another tiny, pink infant.

"A son?" I couldn't believe my ears or my eyes. "Twins?"

"It wasn't easy for Mama. Dr. Susser's still with her. She's going to need to rest for a while, and the doctor wants her to stay off her feet for the next few days."

"See, Tevye, you *are* singlehandedly populating the country," Simcha said laughing.

I just stood there with my little daughter in one arm and my son in the other, staring first at one face then the other. The *chaverim* were singing again, more boisterously this time.

"Lord, You were testing me, weren't You? I knew it."

19

When we first came to the kibbutz, there weren't many children. Shoshana, Devorah and Sarah were not babies. Golde and I, especially Golde, were reluctant to have them live in a separate house with other children, but we told ourselves it was good for them because they would quickly make new friends. But it's different with our new son and daughter. They were allowed to stay with us at first, while Golde was nursing, but now they're here in the children's home with the *machpelet*. She's a nice lady, but we miss them. I raised all my daughters myself. All right, Golde helped — a little. Having a stranger, even a *chaver*, taking care of them now is very difficult to get used to.

We still see the twins a lot, whenever we're not working, but it never seems like enough. Golde cries all the time, "Why did they take my babies away?"

"The children belong to the whole kibbutz, just like any other possession," Eitan explains in his usual unsympathetic, dogmatic way.

"It's more efficient," Uzi declares, and goes on to explain that if each mother took care of their own children, the kibbutz would have that many fewer workers. "This way only one person is taken away from other work, and the children are still well cared for."

To my chagrin, our resident ideologists have a medical ally. "It's better for their health," Dr. Susser insists. "If children stayed in our small, dusty, drafty homes, they'd get sick more often. This way we can provide them with a reasonably sheltered environment."

Golde finds none of these arguments convincing. But we can't expect the rules to be changed just for us. All the other parents gave their children over, some with good reason, and we had to do the same. As far as I can tell, the older children have not suffered from the experience, and may have actually benefitted from not being around their parents too much.

The *machpelet* will shoo me away if I make too much noise, so I have to sneak a peek. There they are in their cribs, already starting to pull themselves up. They grow so fast. Children seem to be the only things in Palestine that grow quickly.

I don't think I felt old until the first days after their birth. Staying up all night with infants was exhausting. I'm not complaining; starting all over with babies at my age is a blessing — most of the time.

I don't think I've mentioned their names. Fortunately, we used up our relatives' names with our other daughters. So, for the first born son of Tevye, the first of our children born in Palestine, it seemed appropriate to name him after our patriarch Abraham. God promised Abraham this land and now my little Abraham will inherit that covenant. He became the ritual inheritor on his eighth day of life when he had his *brit milah*. We gave him enough wine to dull the pain, but he still screamed bloody murder. I don't think any of us ever get over having a stranger cut off part of our most precious possession. Golde couldn't bear to watch and, I must admit, I was a bit queasy.

Afterward, I came out of the house and held Abraham up for everyone to see. Then he was passed from *chaver* to *chaver*, so everyone could hold and bless him.

I pray that he grows up to be as righteous as Abraham, as just as Solomon, as strong as Samson and as wise as Rabbi Akiva. If not, maybe he can be just like his papa.

Now my daughter's name was a little more difficult to choose. I've had some practice with that problem; still, it took a great deal of thought, especially after Golde told me her name was Rachel the moment I saw her after the birth. Why Rachel instead of Leah, you may ask. Leah, after all, was Jacob's first wife and the mother of ten of the tribes of Israel. Well, Leah was the less attractive daughter of Abraham's nephew, Laban, and our little girl was a beauty from the moment she entered this world. Leah's younger sister was the beauty of her family and Jacob fell in love with her at first sight. You know the story of how Laban agreed to allow Jacob to marry Rachel on condition that he first work for him for seven years. At the wedding, Laban substituted Leah, and Jacob was forced to work another seven years before being allowed to marry Rachel. But the Good Book tells us these years of service "seemed unto him but a few days, for the love he had for her," and such is the love we feel for our Rachel. She was truly worth waiting for.

The *machpelet* isn't looking. I'll just slip in for a moment and sing them a lullaby.

Ah, come here my little Abraham, father of Israel, and Rachel, mother of Israel. You are very lucky children to be born here in Palestine. You are *sabras*. By the time you have grown up, we will have a Jewish state and you will be its first citizens. You will sit and listen to the old-timers like me tell you about the hardships of living under the British, and how we fought the Arabs for our homeland. You'll walk the grounds of the kibbutz and see trees and flowers and fruits and vegetables and animals, and never believe that when your father came most of the land was covered by swamps.

Your sisters will tell you about the distant land where they were born, where being Jewish meant being an outsider, a pariah. And you will have trouble understanding what that was like because you will be surrounded by Jews, policed by Jews, and governed by Jews.

I won't even teach you Russian. A little Yiddish maybe, so you'll know the language of your grandparents. Something like this:

Oifn pripetshik brent a fayerl,
Un in shtub iz heis.

Un der rebbe lernt kleine kinderlech Dem alef-beis.
Zet-zhe, kinderlech,
Gedenkt-zhe, tayereh,
Vos ir lernt do,
Zogt-zhe noch amol
Un takeh noch amol:
Kometz-alef: O!

"No wonder the children are all screaming," the *machpelet* said to me in a harsh whisper. "Your singing is enough to wake the dead. Get out of here."

"All right. All right. I'm going. Can I help it if they're too young to appreciate good music?"

"Don't worry, they are very good music critics. You should take their review as a hint. Now get out of here and go back to work where you belong. You'll see Abraham and Rachel later. Now shoo!"

I told you she'd shoo me away.

"Tevye! Tevye!"

Golde came running from the dining room toward me. Don't tell me she heard my singing from the kitchen. I don't think I've seen her move this fast since she found a snake in the kitchen.

"Tevye! Wonderful news!"

"Is it so wonderful, my wife that the whole kibbutz has to know?"

"Yes! Yes!"

"All right. Take it easy. Take some deep breaths before you *plotz*."

She bent over and began to breathe heavily. I was afraid she was going to have a heart attack.

"Come, sit over here on the bench."

As we sat on the bench Simcha had built for the elders of the kibbutz to rest in the garden, she pulled a sheet of paper from her skirt and held it over her head and shook it at the sky.

"Thank you Lord for Your blessings. Thank you."

"What is it that you're shaking your fist at God?"

"Who's shaking a fist? Bite your tongue. I am so grateful for God's mercy on our house."

Before I could begin to cite the litany of miseries that had befallen us in the past, she pushed the paper in my face.

"Read it. Go ahead. Such wonderful news."

She was so busy shaking the fist that held the letter I couldn't take it from her. Finally, I grabbed her wrist and pulled the sheet from her hand.

"Read it."

"If you'll be quiet for two seconds, I will."

"It's a miracle. Thank you Lord. Our family is going to be reunited."

I couldn't concentrate with her muttering in the background.

"Tzeitl and Motel have decided it is no longer safe to be in Poland. They have saved their money and they are coming here to live with us in Palestine."

She tore the letter from my hand before I could get past, "Dear Mama and Papa."

"Coming here?" I asked.

"Yes! Yes! It's a miracle, I tell you. My children are coming home."

The way she clasped her hands together and whispered heavenward, I thought maybe God had decided to speak to her instead of me. He'd have to be God to get a word in edgewise.

"And what about Hodel? What will she do?"

"She is coming also. That's why it took so long for them to save enough money to leave Poland. They needed to save enough for an extra ticket."

"Oh Lord, You work in mysterious ways," I said.

"It must be His plan." Golde put her arm around me. "But we will still not all be together."

"What do you mean?"

"Tzeitl said she got a letter from Chava and —"

"I told you never to mention that name," I shouted, jumping up.

"But she's our daughter," Golde cried as she tried to grab my hand. "And after Shoshana died you said —"

"Our daughter is dead."

"She's not dead, and she and Fyedka are going to America."

"I don't want to hear any more," I screamed, putting my hands over my ears like a child having a tantrum. As I stomped away, I could see Golde out of the corner of my eye reaching for the sky and sobbing.

20

Why is it that bad news seems to follow good news like night follows day?

At last, my eldest daughters are coming home. What could be better? But my wife had to go and spoil the joy by reminding me of another child I once had. As if I needed reminding. Each day I feel the pain of having lost my little girl. But Tevye is not a worm. Though my heart tells me she still walks the earth, my will remains unbending. She is as dead to me as my poor, sweet Shoshana.

You may ask me, "Tevye, if you had the power to bring back Shoshana, would you do it?"

And, of course, my answer would be, "faster than you can say Methuselah."

"But," you say, "it is within your power to bring your other daughter back, and yet you refuse to do so. Why?"

It is the very bedrock of our tradition. The one that has kept us alive for centuries. If we don't remain committed to our faith, above all, what will sustain us? To voluntarily do to ourselves what the Egyptians, the Assyrians, the Babylonians, the Crusaders, the Muslims and the Russians failed to do to us would be the greatest of all sins.

I cannot bring Chava back even if I wanted to, and though I have refused to speak of her, I have never given up hope that someday she can again be part of our family.

You're probably thinking, the *chaverim* are not such great examples of piety, yet Tevye does not ostracize them. Worse, you live among them.

It's true that most of my friends here would rather work than study, dance than pray, argue political ideology than Talmud, but, in their own way, they all know they're Jews. To them, living in the Promised Land and building a Jewish homeland is what it means to be a Jew. And it's not as bad as it was in the beginning. I'd like to think I've had some influence, but it was surely God's will that even our anti-religionists have begun to observe the holidays in a more traditional way and to seek me out to discuss what the Bible says about a particular problem or dispute they are having.

And, let me tell you something else. As nonobservant as kibbutzniks may be, I can't imagine one marrying outside the faith. It has never happened since we arrived and I don't believe it ever will.

I consider the *chaverim* to be my family, but still, you're right, my own flesh and blood is my greatest love. How can I explain what Golde considers my cruelty toward my own child? Perhaps God has hardened my heart as he did Pharaoh's for some greater good for our people.

"Dear Lord, why is it that Your poor servant Tevye should be treated as the evildoer? I couldn't be the liberator?"

See how the mind quickly becomes infected with negative thoughts? I can't stop them any more than my horse can stop attracting flies. It's Golde's fault. All she had to do was tell me about Tzeitl and Hodel and I would be dancing instead of *kvetching*.

My baby, Tzeitl. It has been so long since I held her in my arms. It seems she was still a child when I last saw her, and now she's a grown woman, and not so young anymore. And a mother. At last, I'll have the joy of looking at the faces of my grandchildren.

And little Rachel and Abraham will have nieces and a nephew, and learn what it means to have family. I'm even looking forward to seeing Motel. I always said he was a good man, and a hard worker, and now he's earned enough money to bring the family home. So why should I stand here complaining to the Master of the Universe for such good fortune?

I am not the only lucky one. Now Hodel can start her life over. What better place than here on our little kibbutz? Here she'll find Pertschik's utopian dream of poor *schlemiels* breaking their backs for no money. We don't have any Feferels here, but there's no shortage of blather. God willing, Hodel will find another husband among the prattlers here.

"I see you're talking to yourself for a change, Tevye," Moshe said, coming up behind me as I saddled my horse. "It's a good thing God has other things to do besides listen to you or He'd need fingers to put in His ears."

"So, you've discovered God, eh Moshe? Your friend Marx will be upset."

"He'd only be upset if I tried to talk to him in the grave. I reserve my conversations for the living."

"And who says the living make the best conversationalists?"

"Talking to you Tevye often makes me wonder."

We hugged each other. Moshe was rarely around the kibbutz anymore and it was good to see my old friend. And he was starting to look old. His muscles were beginning to sag and he no longer walked with the same military bearing of his youth. Still, he had risen in the ranks of the Haganah and was now one of the senior officers. I suspected he did more commanding than fighting, especially since he was wearing a black suit coat and long grey pants. He looked more like a banker than a soldier except for the fact the coat was several sizes too big.

"If it's not too personal, what is it you're so exorcized about?"

"Great news, Moshe. My oldest daughters are coming to join us. My son-in-law the tailor has saved enough money to bring everyone."

"*Mazel tov*," Moshe said, slapping my shoulder. "That's wonderful news. Wonderful!" He smacked me again.

"I think bad news would keep me healthier," I said, rubbing my arm. The back and shoulder slap had become the official reply to almost any *simcha.*

"So why aren't you celebrating? You look as if the *makhsan* gave you underwear two sizes too small."

"You should talk. Look at that jacket. Besides, I am happy. Ecstatic. Look at my face. Isn't this the face of a happy man?"

"It's the face of an old man. Happy, I'm not so sure."

"That's what I like about you Moshe. No matter how old and decrepit you get, you're still a *hatzuf.* What are you doing here, anyway? Shouldn't you be shooting something or somebody?"

"Tevye, I pray that I will never have to fire a weapon at anything but a decoy. Actually, I've brought some guns for the kibbutz, just in case."

"Just in case of what?" Even my horse looked startled.

"It's just a precaution. You're isolated out here. If, God forbid, anything should ever happen, it would be difficult for the Haganah to get here in time. You have to have the means to defend yourself, at least until our troops can arrive."

"Troops? Now we have troops?"

Moshe ignored me.

Many of our weekly meetings had been devoted to possible attacks on the kibbutz, but, so far, the area has been quiet. I didn't know if Sheikh Jabber was protecting us as part of my bargain with him, or if our time had not come yet.

"You're avoiding the question, Moshe. Please tell me if I should worry."

"You're on automatic worry all the time Tevye. No, for now, there's nothing new for you to be concerned about. I'm going to hide some guns here for an emergency, okay?"

"All right."

I led my horse out of the stable and walked along the dirt road toward the gate. Moshe walked beside me. For the first time, I noticed the bulge under his jacket.

"The only concern for you is a British raid. Hopefully, they won't think of searching here and, even if they do, they won't find the guns, but it's always a possibility. That's why it's important for you to be able to truthfully say you don't know anything. Do you understand?"

"Yes. But —"

"No buts. Stick to your books and leave the soldiering to me."

Moshe patted me on the cheek as though I were a child. Before I could say anything, he asked, "So, Tevye, where are you going?"

"It's a beautiful night and I thought I'd go for a ride. Outside the gates I can talk to whomever I want in peace."

"Don't worry, no one will miss hearing your monologues," Moshe chuckled, before turning serious. "But I don't think it's a very good idea. You heard what Devorah said about the Arabs' religious leaders inciting their followers to attack Jews."

Ah, my daughter the general. When Devorah returned to the kibbutz after Shoshana's death, she stayed to help Dr. Susser and train the *chaverim* to protect themselves. Golde is happy because she knows where her daughter is — and her hair has grown back. What Golde doesn't know is that Devorah periodically sneaks off to Tel Aviv or Jerusalem to do errands for the Haganah and comes back with what she calls "intelligence reports." Most recently, Devorah warned us that some of the imams are devoting their sermons to the heresies of the Jews. Arabs leaving some of those mosques, she said, have been involved in assaults against kibbutzniks working in secluded fields.

"Moshe, I thought you just said not to worry."

"I said I didn't expect the kibbutz to be attacked; that doesn't mean it's safe to go gallivanting around the countryside by yourself in the middle of the night."

"The Mufti and his henchmen are no different from the hoodlums we had in Russia."

"I know. That's what scares me."

"I'll be all right. Don't worry."

"Maybe you should take a gun."

"A gun? Me, Tevye, carry a gun? Do I look like my commando daughter? If anything ever happened I'd probably accidentally shoot my horse and then I'd have to walk home. No thank you. I'll do as you suggested before, stick to my books."

"Fine. You know best. For a minute I forgot who I was speaking to, Reb Tevye, authority on all things."

"What? I don't want to carry a gun so you insult me?"

"I'm sorry. Please don't get angry. When you get angry you start quoting from the Bible and we'll both end up standing here all night."

Before I could tell Moshe what the Bible said about quoting the Bible, he was gone, waving as he left in the backhand way he used when he was fed up with me. I've seen it from enough of the *chaverim* that I'm surprised the executive committee hasn't declared the gesture an official part of the kibbutz language to express displeasure with Tevye.

And Moshe wonders why I prefer talking to the Almighty.

As I started to ride out the gate, over the objections of the watchman, it occurred to me that Moshe was probably right about it being dangerous to go out alone at night. As I said, fortunately, up to now our neighbors have remained peaceful, but I have heard of more than one kibbutz that was attacked by its formerly passive friends.

It's a shame to have to worry about such things. Riding at night is such a heavenly experience, if you'll excuse the expression. When the sun goes down, we finally have a respite from the oppressive heat, but the breeze is warm enough that I don't feel chilled. It's like having someone blow softly on your neck in the way that makes your hair stand up just enough to tickle.

The best part is the silence that is interrupted only by the occasional buzz of a bee or whine of a hyena. I am spared the grating voices of the *chaverim* and the *hocking* of my darling Golde.

When I look back at the little oasis that we built here in the wilderness I'm amazed at our accomplishment. We have worked and we have lived, just as Jonathan said. The time has passed so quickly since the days we battled the mosquitoes day and night, and fought the wind to try to keep our tents upright with little more success.

Back then, it was hard to imagine anyone asking to join us, but now we argue all the time about whether we should accept newcomers. More *schlimazels* coming from Russia and Poland and all over Europe, who have heard of the utopian society we have built. The *vattikim*, the men who founded our settlement resist change.

They want to maintain the ideological purity of the early years and to tightly restrict any expansion. The younger people want more comrades, and they argue the kibbutz cannot survive in such small numbers. We cannot produce enough to stay financially solvent and we do not have enough men to protect the kibbutz from the attacks they believe will eventually come.

I feel strongly both ways. If we let anyone join our little family, we will quickly begin to fight among ourselves, even more than we do now. But if we don't take in more members, we will eventually die out. Even now, people are starting to leave, to find better lives in Haifa or Tel Aviv or Jerusalem. Some are getting tired of a utopia where they can own few things beyond the shirts on their backs, and are given only what a committee decides they need to exist.

As for me, I'm content. What would I do someplace else?

It's nice to let someone else worry about me for a change, even if it is a committee of *schlimazels*. Besides, I'm getting too old to change. One change per lifetime is enough, and coming here from Russia filled my quota. Life might not stay peaceful here, but it's not going to get better somewhere else, so I might as well stay. Soon the family will be together and it will be like starting all over without moving.

To think it was not so long ago that my *youngest* child was nearly full grown, and now I have two babies of my own, and soon Tzeitl's children will also be here. I had been afraid to even think of asking for the blessing of seeing my grandchildren.

"I should know better than to think You could not read my thoughts," I said, wagging my finger at the stars. "He who planted the ear, shall He not hear? He who formed the eye, shall He not see?"

It's frightening to consider that God knows everything we are thinking. Not even our greatest sages could have had pure thoughts all the time. God must balance the good and bad thoughts, and know what's in our hearts. He also watches to see how we behave. When I think about it, it's a wonder God hasn't struck me down with a thunderbolt.

Well, maybe I'm not such a bad person. God knows I try to observe His commandments.

"You also know I wasn't thinking about company," I said when I detected the sound of hoof beats. They were getting louder.

I kicked my horse and he jumped as though he'd stepped on a scorpion. The wretched beast nearly threw me, but I clung to the reins and grabbed the pommel of the saddle as I started to slip off. It must have been quite a sight to see poor Tevye with one leg over the top of the horse and the other under him while it raced down the road. I couldn't see where we were going; my eyes were pressed against the horse's neck as I vainly struggled to climb back to the saddle.

As the sound of dozens of hooves grew louder, I wasn't sure what was more frightening, the thought of falling and being trampled, or being caught by whoever was chasing me.

The fetid hot breath of an animal blew against my neck and I had a new fear, that I might be squashed between two beasts like a gnat between two human hands.

Suddenly I felt a tug against the reins and my horse began to slow. When it finally came to rest in a cloud of dust, I managed to pull myself back upright and discovered that my rescuers were a band of Arabs.

"Dear Lord, have You spared me death under hooves so that I might be slain at the hands of the children of Ishmael?"

The thought passed quickly when I recognized some of the men as members of Sheikh Jabber's clan. I just hoped he had not become less hospitable since I last saw him.

"Thank you," I said to the one whom I remembered as the leader. "I'm afraid my horse is a better runner than I am a rider."

He said nothing, but the look on his face reminded me of the Rabbi's in Anatevka when I asked him if it was permissible to have sexual relations with my wife in a barn.

Without speaking, my Arab friend began to lead my horse off toward the hills, just as he did the first time I was "invited" to meet the Sheikh. I was surrounded by the rest of the Arabs and felt a little like a Jewish Tsar with a Cossack escort. After riding over a series of rocky knolls, which had not changed throughout the years, we reached the Sheikh's tent. The silent leader beckoned me to enter. He was sitting in the same place as the last time I saw him, sucking on the end of a hookah. His son Ali was again seated next to him.

As I sat, a woman covered from head to toe in a robe and veil placed a cup of tea in front of me, while a second woman set down a plate of lamb and rice.

"*Shokran*," I said.

"Tevye, as a friend I must warn you," Ali began, speaking warmly, as though I was his closest friend in the world.

"Warn me. About what?"

"You know I have always spoken the truth to you. And from the first time we met, I told you that my people would never accept you and your fellow Jews."

It occurred to me that it was not such a blessing to be told you are hated and will be killed.

"I have always appreciated your candor, Ali."

"These are not my words," Ali interrupted. "I speak only for my father."

"Yes, of course. And I am grateful, Sheikh Jabber. It is no longer any surprise to me to hear that the Arabs want us to disappear into the sea."

"It is our land that you are stealing."

"Our land that we have returned to claim," I corrected. "And that we have bought and paid for with large sums of money — and with our blood."

"We need not argue the point. We do not see things the same way. I have not brought you here for another debate."

"Then what is the reason?"

"Tevye, I must tell you that more blood will be spilt."

"Hasn't there been enough?"

"It will continue as long as you are here."

"But why now, Sheikh Jabber? The country has been tranquil the last few years."

"Quiet yes, like the desert before the blinding sandstorm that leaves you lost and without food or drink. The hatred has only grown, bubbling beneath the surface like the lava in a volcano prior to an eruption."

"Blinding sandstorms? Volcanic eruptions? What have we done to provoke such hostility, besides building our homeland?"

"You may build it, Tevye, but you will not have the chance to live in it or enjoy it. To answer your question, yes, you have done something."

"May I ask what we have done to deserve the honor we are about to receive?" I sipped my tea and tried to pretend as though we were having a conversation about the weather.

"A few days ago a group of young Jews marched to the base of the *Haram es-Sharif* in Jerusalem."

"Harem es —"

"The Noble Enclosure, what Jews call the Temple Mount. It is where your Wailing Wall stands."

"I still don't understand."

"Our holy Al-Aqsa Mosque is there. It was a deliberate provocation. It has upset everyone, especially our more hotheaded leaders. They are sending emissaries to the countryside calling on the *fellaheen* to protect Al-Aqsa against Jewish attacks."

"But why would Jews attack a mosque?"

"Perhaps you would not. But it doesn't matter. The people will believe what they are told, and they will rise against you. I tell you as a friend to be prepared. I will have my brothers escort you back to your home. If I were you, I would not venture out alone again at night, at least until the pot stops boiling."

"Is there nothing to be done to prevent bloodshed?" I asked.

"I think you know the answer — and I know your response. From the time Ishmael was cast out by Sarah, we have been destined to compete. We claim the same land, and neither of us will accept subjugation by the other. As fellow People of the Book, we would treat the Jews well, but I know it will not satisfy you."

Ali said he spoke for his father, but I still could not tell if that was really true. The old man just sat passively sucking on his pipe, never changing expression.

"Honorable Sheikh, we have had to rely on the kindness of rulers since we were dispersed two-thousand years ago," I said, "and our health has suffered. Once the doctor has made you sicker once, you don't give him a second chance."

172

"I understand, Tevye. But you must not hold any false hopes or illusions about our will. If we defeat you, we will drive you into the sea and it will be the end of the Jews in Palestine. If you defeat us, it will only be a temporary setback. We are the many, you are the few. As I told you before, it took us two centuries to repel the Crusaders, but we succeeded. However long it takes, we will fight. How long can you hold out?"

"Ali, my friend, we share faith in the same God. He has not made the life of my people easy, but He has sustained us through famine, pestilence, pogroms and war. All those who defeated us are today gone, but we Jews are still here. As you Arabs like to say, we are a stiff-necked people. We are too stubborn to die. And you should have no illusions about our will to fight — and to win."

Ali's father stood, so the son rose as well. "Tevye, you are an honorable man. I hope that we shall find a way to avoid what I fear is inevitable," Ali said with a bow.

"*Inshallah*," I said, repeating the phrase I'd heard Arabs use so often to express their hope that God grants their wishes.

"So you have learned some Arabic after all."

"As we say in Yiddish, a *bissel.*"

"Go in peace, my friend."

"And peace to you, Sheikh Jabber. And to you Ali."

We bowed toward each other and I went to my horse. Ali's brothers had fed the old boy and given it water and now the beast did not appear anxious to leave. It looked at me as though it thought I was not worthy of riding upon its back. When the animal snorted at me, one of the Bedouins gently took the bridle and led the horse to me and helped me climb on.

I rode back in the company of Ali's brothers, who did not leave me until we were within sight of the kibbutz. I thanked them and wished them *salaam aleikum,* but they galloped away as silently as they had snuck up on me.

I sat for a moment watching them disappear over the rocky hill, the moonlight creating ghostly silhouettes. How long before they return with different intentions?

"Dear Lord, is this why You've brought us back to the Promised Land? To fight for our lives, forever? Are we to have no peace, even in our homeland?"

"Once again my house is blessed. My children finally return, escape at last from the anti-Semitism of Russia and Poland, only to come to a place where we are once again hated by our neighbors. How many more tests must we face, Lord? How many?"

21

It did not take long for the sheikh's prediction to come true. The news throughout Palestine has been terrible, like the worst days of the pogroms in Russia.

This time our kibbutz was not spared, though the damage was inflicted indirectly.

When Moshe left to rejoin his Haganah unit, Jonathan left with him. I teased Jonathan about being too old to fight.

"Tevye," he bellowed, "the defense of liberty knows no age limit."

Jonathan was very serious. He still worked as hard as anyone on the kibbutz and whenever trouble was reported in the country, he would go to see what he could do to help. Usually, he came back quickly, because he was too well known in Palestine to work with the underground Jewish army, but Devorah told me Jonathan was a great inspiration to the younger men, and had taught the Haganah a great deal about strategy.

I hadn't given his departure another thought. Then, while I was working in the barn, Shmuel rang the bell frantically. I wasn't sure what it meant because the sound was far more urgent than the typical alarm he'd drilled us to expect.

Everyone came rushing to the dining room. When we got there, Moshe was on his knees wailing over a blanket covering something on the ground. Simcha, the man who never frowns, was holding Moshe, trying to comfort him. Both of them were sobbing.

Shmuel was still ringing the bell. If it were not for the tears streaming down his cheeks, I would have thought he was in a trance. Oren finally pried the clapper from his hand.

"What's happened?" I asked.

The *chaverim* were just standing silently, unsure of what to do.

Finally, Simcha spoke. "Jonathan is dead."

"What?" I said.

Simcha slowly pulled back the top of the blanket to reveal Jonathan's blood-streaked face.

One great shriek seemed to emanate from everyone's throat simultaneously. People fell on the ground, others just collapsed in the arms of those around them.

I looked for Golde. She, Sarah and Devorah were sitting on the ground holding each other, weeping uncontrollably.

My knees suddenly gave out and I found myself beside Moshe and Simcha. They looked at me and then we embraced each other.

Moshe choked back his tears for a moment and muttered, "There was nothing we could do. We got there too late. So many bodies."

"What happened? Where, Moshe?" I asked.

"It was in Hebron. Friday night a group of Arabs had started throwing rocks at the students going to the yeshiva. On Sabbath morning, a mob of Arabs came and attacked Jews with knives and clubs and axes. They killed Rabbi Slonim."

"No!" Tevye cried.

"He was not the only one. Dozens were murdered. A few Arabs tried to help Jews, but thousands of Arabs came shouting 'Kill the Jews.' Finally, a policeman escorted some of us out of the city. We came here, but most of the Jews who got away were heading for Jerusalem. No Jews are left in Hebron."

Moshe put his head on Jonathan's chest.

Simcha and I just looked at each other. Moshe sat up again, and composed himself enough to whisper, "A sniper fired from a roof and hit Jonathan in the back. There was nothing we could do for him. Before Jonathan lost consciousness, he said, 'Trumpeldor was right. It *is* good to die for one's country.'"

Moshe broke down again. The three of us just stayed on the ground, holding each other.

The whole kibbutz was in shock after Jonathan's death. Bernice came from Jerusalem for the funeral. She had been as close to Jonathan as any of us, but she hid her grief. I think she thought someone had to maintain enough composure to think about what had to be done to ensure no one else died.

A meeting was called for the entire kibbutz. This time Shmuel rang the bell in a way that was barely recognizable as the call to a meeting. I looked at him as I entered the dining room. He leaned against the post supporting the bell as if it was holding him up as well. Shmuel's face was so pale and his eyes so glassy, he seemed barely alive. He reminded me of a seashell whose owner had moved.

As sad as the *chaverim* were over the death of my Shoshana, that anguish was nothing like the devastation everyone felt now. You could hear sniffling throughout the room. People slouched in their chairs. Natan and some of the others from my study group mumbled prayers for the dead. Golde held a handkerchief to her face and leaned against me. Devorah and Sarah sat beside me holding hands.

Bernice strode up to the podium like a general addressing the troops. Without any preamble, she began.

"We have all suffered a terrible, terrible loss. Jonathan can never be replaced, but we must carry on in his stead. Tonight, many Jewish families are grieving. They grieve for us and we grieve for them."

She spoke with strength and emotion. I felt myself straighten up. Others did the same. Bernice had a gift for inspiring others.

"The Mufti incited the Arabs in Jerusalem and they attacked the Jewish Quarter in the Old City. Later, marauders went to Hebron, the site of the Cave of Machpelah, where our forebears, Abraham and Sarah, Isaac and Rebecca, and Jacob and Leah are buried. The Arabs massacred men, women and children. Villages around the country were also attacked. Even Tel Aviv was not spared. I don't know how many casualties we suffered, but the number of dead might number more than one-hundred."

The audience groaned and the sniffling turned to wailing.

"Kill the Arabs!" someone yelled from the back of the room. Then others joined in chanting, "Kill the Arabs! Kill the Arabs!"

I couldn't believe my ears. My friends, these peaceful farmers were in such a frenzy they were prepared to commit murder.

Bernice held up her hands and shouted, "No, that is not what we will do! We will bury our dead, and we will mourn for them. But the one thing we will not do is dishonor their memories."

The chanting faded.

"We *will* avenge these murders!"

The crowd cheered.

"Oh yes, we will have our revenge. But our retribution will come the way Jonathan would have wanted. Not by violence."

"How? How?" several voices asked.

"By living! Living here on our kibbutz in our homeland, the land God promised the Jewish people. We must live and we must continue to build. The creation of an independent Jewish state is the best revenge for what the Arabs have done. Because when we have our state, no Jew anywhere in the world will have to live in fear again."

Bernice was right. That is exactly what Jonathan would have said.

"No one will hand us our independence. Not the British, not the Americans, not the League of Nations. We must be prepared to fight for it. I am not speaking about blind rage to avenge the deaths of our loved ones, I'm talking about using all our resources — our brains, our money, our negotiating skills and, if necessary, our arms — to achieve our goal."

By the time Bernice had finished her speech, you couldn't hear a sniffle. People who practically crawled into their seats, strode out with their heads held high, determined to fulfill Jonathan's mission. Others swarmed around Bernice, asking her what they could do.

"Bernice is quite a woman," Golde said, sitting more upright herself.

"She's a great leader," Devorah said. "Someday, she will lead our whole people."

"A woman?"

"Don't start, Papa."

I had to admit, at least to myself, that Devorah was right. Bernice is a great leader and I will follow her wherever she asks me to go.

After her inspirational talk, Bernice met with a smaller group of us to talk about more practical matters. The first thing she did was light a cigarette.

"We have to strengthen our defenses. So far we've been lucky that we haven't been attacked. I'm not sure how much longer that will last. Many of the kibbutzim in this area are now targets of Arab raids."

"What should we do?" I asked.

"First, we build our fence higher and post more guards. Second, no one should be allowed to travel outside the kibbutz alone. Third, I will look into ways for us to obtain more weapons."

It was good that Moshe had the foresight to create a cache of guns on the kibbutz, and that Devorah had trained everyone old enough to hold a rifle how to use them.

"I will go to the Haganah to ask for more arms," Devorah said.

I was proud that my daughter was the one who stood up to help defend our kibbutz, but I was also scared that she was again placing herself in harm's way.

"That won't be necessary, Devorah," Bernice said. "Moshe can do that for us. Thank you for volunteering. I have another job in mind for you."

"Really? What?"

"Later."

I don't know who was more curious about what Bernice was thinking, Devorah or me.

"So Bernice, what are our good friends the British doing about the Arabs?" Laban asked.

She laughed in between puffs from her cigarette. "The British are worse than no help at all. After the Arabs are allowed to go on a rampage for a few days and murder scores of Jews, they show up with sufficient force to stop the violence. God forbid, they should intervene during the initial attacks or, horror of horrors, prevent them in the first place. Usually, they end up arresting more Jews than Arabs."

"But surely they see that we are innocent victims who need protection."

"Hah," she spat. "Tevye, you have a lot to learn about politics. The British fined the Arab villages, but the Mufti protested the Chancellor's 'brutality.' So, what did the honorable Chancellor do? He announced an inquiry into the conduct of *both* the Jews and Arabs. Can you imagine that we, the victims, should be equated with the murderers? That's politics, Tevye."

Bernice hardly looked like the political powerhouse she had become, sitting in her flower patterned dress, wooden shoes with unkempt auburn hair, which she continually brushed from her large darting eyes. The cigarettes she pumped in and out of her mouth were the main distraction from her bulbous nose, which reminded me of a knot on the trunk of a tree.

"So, what will happen next?" I asked.

"Can I see into the future? If you're asking me —"

"You're the only one here," I said and received an icy stare through the haze of smoke.

"The British will hold an inquiry and they will find that the Arab violence is caused by Jewish immigration. The gates will then be pulled more tightly shut. And do you think that will satisfy the Arabs? Of course not! They'll stay quiet for several weeks, maybe even a few years, and then the attacks will begin anew. And they won't stop until we have been driven into the Mediterranean."

Bernice saw me nodding.

"You agree, Tevye?"

"I have always hoped we could find a way to live in peace with our neighbors, but my friend Sheikh Jabber said the same thing. In fact, he warned me about the violence. He said the Mufti's men were claiming the Jews were trying to destroy Al-Aqsa Mosque. He said the *fellaheen* would listen and rise against us."

"Your friend is a prophet — a prophet of doom."

"There's more, Bernice. He also said the war would continue until we were driven into the sea. Even if we repelled them in the short-run, he said they would continue to fight us for as long as it took to destroy us."

"It doesn't take a prophet to know that, Tevye," Bernice said, waving her cigarette. "It's what I've been trying to tell the Executive Committee, but many of the members still want to talk; they believe we can reach an understanding with the Arabs if they understand we mean them no harm. It's *tepshee*, absurd. They will never accept a Jewish state in Palestine."

"So, what do we do?"

"Well, the politicians will continue to negotiate with the British in London. Weizmann still has some influence. But we will have to be better prepared to defend ourselves and, if necessary, ready to go to war to liberate our homeland. Right now, we are far too weak."

"But," I interrupted, "Moshe said we have troops."

"Troops? Hah! We've got boys with a handful of pistols and old World War One Enfield rifles. Our priority must continue to be *aliyah*. We must bring as many Jews as possible to Palestine. In fact, that is one reason, I've come. I need to talk to you alone for a minute, Tevye. Excuse us, please."

Bernice got up from the table in the dining room and walked outside with me following. She stood so close to me, I felt like I was smoking the cigarette with her.

"I want to talk to Devorah about a special mission."

"My Devorah."

"No King David's Devorah. Or course your Devorah. She is fearless and already has done work with the Haganah. We're going to be increasing our efforts to bring in illegal immigrants and I would like her to be involved. We can use a nurse. There's a new plan to try to smuggle the immigrants in by sea, but I'm told the ships are floating death traps. Most aren't seaworthy, and we're afraid the long days at sea with little food or water will kill the weaker passengers. Even the strong ones will come down with diseases, and some bring their illnesses with them here. We've got enough problems without importing foreign germs.

"This sounds too dangerous Bernice. Why can't a man do it?"

"I see you haven't left your old world ideas completely behind yet. You've seen women do all the jobs of the men here on the kibbutz."

"Almost all."

"Not for lack of trying. Anyway, we have men involved, but we need her skills as a nurse. I'm sure if the Haganah asked her, she would do it, and you probably would never know she was involved. But I feel that you are like family Tevye, and I wanted you to know the sacrifice we will be asking of her — and of you."

I could almost feel Bernice's eyes on my face. She stared at me without blinking, looking determined to have my assent. It was never easy to say no to Bernice. But is she asking too much this time? Four of my daughters are separated from the family. One is already dead.

Damn Chaim for what he did to my Shoshie!

How can Bernice expect me to put one of my children in danger? Golde will be heartsick and it will give her something new to worry about all the time, as if she needed an excuse to suffer.

On the other hand, it is an honor to be asked to serve your people, and a tribute to Devorah that she is so respected and needed. How can I stand in the way of her fulfilling her duty to the *yishuv?* Then again, what choice do I have? No more than when she ran off to join the Haganah in the first place. She will want the responsibility and I will be powerless to stop her from doing whatever is asked of her. Maybe God put the name Devorah into my mind when she was born so that my daughter would follow in the footsteps of her biblical namesake.

"You're right, Bernice. Devorah is a brave girl. And a stubborn one. I'm sure she will do it, whether I approve or not. As it happens, I approve."

"Good."

I watched Bernice take a long last drag on the cigarette before stomping on the meager remains with her shoe.

"Tevye, you know as well as anyone what it required to build the little corner of Eden that we have here among the mosquitoes and bees and wind and rain and mud. That struggle is nothing compared to what is ahead. It will take more than shovels and hoes and plows to create a state. Everyone will have to do their part. We are so few that we cannot afford to have anyone watch from a safe distance. Each of us, young and old, men and women, must contribute in some way to fight for our homeland."

"You talk like a Prime Minister. Perhaps that will be your destiny in our Jewish state."

Bernice laughed and then began to cough.

"No Tevye. I don't want to be involved in politics. I am doing my part now to win the war, but after we've won — and I have no doubt we will win — and we have our state, I want to come back here and live out my days watching our children and grandchildren grow old. That is the reward I crave."

She put her hand on my cheek and smiled. For a moment, I felt like her child and was grateful for the comforting words she had spoken.

"And speaking of grandchildren, I understand you will finally get to see yours. *Mazel tov.* You must be very excited."

She switched subjects so abruptly I was dumbstruck. It was one of Bernice's incomparable skills, the ability to speak as comfortably about world affairs as personal ones.

"You are excited, aren't you?"

"I feel like Noah when he saw the rainbow from the ark," I said, recovering my balance.

"That's wonderful. I can hardly wait to meet your daughters. You know everyone in the movement knows about Hodel. She's a heroine."

"My Hodel, a heroine? I don't understand."

"Pertschik was very well known, and apparently liked, by our leaders in Russia. He was one of the people who had the courage to speak out against the Tsar and to denounce the Communists early on as hypocrites. Even in prison, he was organizing the resistance and preaching the need for Jews to find a homeland where they could enjoy the fruit of their labors."

"Pertschik was quite a man." I said, suddenly realizing Feferel had been more influential than I'd ever imagined.

"Yes, he was, Tevye. Did you know that Jonathan tried to visit him in prison?"

"No. He never told me."

Bernice lit another cigarette.

"He might not have realized Pertschik was your son-in-law at the time. In the end, Jonathan couldn't reach him. But he knew of his work, and his courage. And much of what we learned about Pertschik came from his wife, your daughter. She would write down Pertschik's thoughts and have them printed and smuggled out of Siberia. She tried to carry on his work after he was executed, but the authorities came to arrest her. We think she was captured and escaped. She fled and apparently hid for a while in small towns in the Pale. I think that was about the time you lost track of her."

I remembered how worried we were when her letters stopped coming. We feared the worst.

"Yes, there was a time when Tzeitl didn't know where she was. We were so worried; I think the uncertainty contributed to Golde's sickness."

"Well, from what I've heard, she continued to organize even while she was on the run. I have a feeling that before she reached Tzeitl, Hodel had to leave Russia or face her husband's fate. I don't know if she convinced Tzeitl to leave Poland, or it was the other way around, but I understand from our contacts in Warsaw they left about a week ago. They are supposed to board one of our ships sometime next month."

"They're on their way?" I said. It was too good to be true.

"Tevye, I have to be honest. Even if they make it safely to the ship, I'm afraid there's no guarantee they'll make it to Palestine. With new restrictions on immigration sure to follow this last round of violence, the British are liable to turn the ship around. That's why I'd like Devorah to go and help smuggle them out."

So Bernice had another card to play if I hadn't agreed to let Devorah be part of the mission. It was easy to see why she was an effective politician.

"I thought you said you just needed her to be a nurse."

"Yes, on our ships carrying illegal immigrants, like the one that Tzeitl and Hodel will have to use."

"Three of my daughters on the same ship, in danger. I don't think that I can take it. I know the anxiety will kill Golde."

"That's why we aren't going to tell her."

"But —"

"Are we?" Bernice repeated, looking at me with the same steely stare she used when she asked me to let Devorah go with her.

I closed my eyes. My temples throbbed. It felt like all my sayings from the Bible were trying to burst out of my head at once.

"Tevye?"

"I won't say a word."

"Good. God-willing, we will see all of them here in a few weeks."

"*Inshallah,*" I muttered.

"What's that?"

"Oh, just a saying I've picked up from the Arabs."

22

It's amazing how cold it can get here at night. I'm freezing to death even though I'm wearing everything I own. I wrapped myself in burlap and stuffed my socks with newspaper and it still feels like icicles are forming on my ribs and toes.

Of course it doesn't help that I'm doing nothing but lying here on my stomach in the mud. I'm right under a beautiful apple tree, but I can't even grab a snack because they're not ripe yet.

I don't know what's scarier, holding a rifle or the thought of having to use it. After Bernice left, the Defense Committee made sure all the men and women were properly trained to fire the weapons. It's difficult to feel too confident with our marksmanship, since we didn't have enough ammunition to take more than a couple of shots at stationary targets. And, as Moshe explained, shooting a tin can and a human are two completely different things.

Every few minutes, I hear a noise and strain to see through the darkness. The whistling of the wind, the rustling of a lizard, the humming of a mosquito, any sound or movement puts me on the edge of panic. At first I didn't want to lie on my back for fear of falling asleep, but I needn't have worried. Even without this flask of coffee, I don't think I could relax long enough to doze off.

I thought I was being clever by choosing guard duty here, where I wouldn't have to spend all night walking. I should have been suspicious when Timur and Enoch volunteered to patrol the fences. Their feet may get tired, but at least they'll stay warm and dry while they're moving.

It could be worse, a lot worse. It might start to rain or I could have gotten stuck laying here with Natan. Fortunately, he was assigned to a different orchard and I was allowed to stay here by myself. The person I really feel sorry for is whoever was given the joyous task of accompanying Faiga. She doesn't need to carry a gun; she can simply talk the Arabs to death.

You might be wondering why a woman was given sentry duty; well, the decision was not made easily. We actually had quite a row. Most of the men said it was too dangerous. A few said lying on their stomachs all night was too difficult. Others suggested the women couldn't shoot as accurately. You should have heard the tumult. The women finally said they would not do any work for the kibbutz — no cooking, cleaning, sewing, nothing — unless they were allowed to contribute to the defense of the community.

Reluctantly, the men agreed to allow women to patrol the inside perimeter and to act as messengers. Some men and women protested, but the majority accepted this compromise.

So Faiga is walking around the houses sharing the news of the world, and I am sitting here shivering, trying to keep from shooting the first leaf the wind blows in my direction.

Bernice was right about the British reaction to the Arab riots. A Royal Commission was sent to visit our happy little homeland. I'm beginning to think the British and their commissions are the eleventh plague.

Anyway, no one was too surprised when the honorable representatives of His Majesty's Government concluded that the Mandatory government and police were not to blame for the violence. We expected them to find the Arabs responsible for the attacks on us, but what shocked everyone was the Commission's explanation.

The honorable group said the Arabs did not plan the attacks and suggested they were justified because of the Arabs' hostility toward the Jews and fear for their economic future. So rather than punish the Arabs, or take steps to protect the *yishuv*, the commissioners recommended that Jewish immigration be restricted, that Arabs be protected from being evicted by Jewish land buyers and that the Jewish Agency be told that it would have no role in governing Palestine!

The Arabs discovered a formula to prevent us from rebuilding our homeland: Attack and kill us and then the British will blame the Jews and prevent any more from coming to Palestine. It's as if God has reversed the order in the universe.

I was afraid to tell Golde the news. Her mood has changed so dramatically from the dark days after Shoshana's death. The birth of the twins was like a renaissance for her. Her face sparkles like the sea at sunrise whenever she is with them. When they were in the dormitory, she talked about the children nonstop. Abraham and Rachel are walking, talking, jumping, laughing. Whatever they do is cause for a blessing and a minute by minute description.

I think some of Golde's coworkers are getting a little tired of hearing about the miracles our children are performing each day. God, after all, spent less time describing the creation of the world than Golde does talking about Abraham dressing himself or Rachel going to the potty.

The news that Tzeitl, Motel and Hodel were coming to join us made her feel like the Israelites seeing the Promised Land for the first time after wandering forty years in the desert. Now I was afraid the British would leave us, like Moses, standing within view of what we longed for, but not allowed to enjoy it.

Don't get me wrong; I'm thrilled by the thought that the family will be together again, but, given all that has happened, I try not to get too excited for fear of being let down. If it is the Almighty's will that we are reunited, we will be reunited. If not, well, perhaps in another world. That is my attitude, but I don't think Golde can take more disappointment.

The crackle of leaves made me jump. I looked from side to side, but couldn't see anything but trees and rocks and dirt — and a figure dressed in dark clothes with a hat pulled over their face.

I nervously pulled back the hammer on the rifle and stared down the barrel, just as Moshe had taught me.

"Who's there? What's the password?"

"New York Yankees," said a familiar voice.

I rolled over and nearly fainted. Bernice suggested a bunch of American code words before she left, thinking the Arabs could never discover or fake them. I had no idea what Yankees were; all that mattered was that a friend was approaching. The hooded man bent down and pulled off his stocking cap.

"It's freezing," Simcha said, his smile frozen as always. "Reminds me of the old days in Russia. Here, I brought you some more coffee."

My hand was shaking so much, Simcha took my flask and poured for me.

"What's the matter, old friend? Tough night defending the apples?"

"Simcha, you nearly scared me to death."

"I'm sorry, if you'd rather I leave."

Simcha started to get up. I grabbed his arm.

"No. I'm just not cut out for this sort of thing. I don't have the nerves for it."

"To tell you the truth Tevye, neither do I." We both took sips of coffee. "Moshe is the one who seems to enjoy the danger. It excites him in a perverse kind of way."

"Any more excitement and I think I'll go to the bathroom in my pants," I said.

Simcha laughed. Sometimes I wondered if bugs flew into his mouth between the gap in his front teeth.

"So, Tevye, other than ghosts, I take it things have been quiet."

"Yes. Thank God."

"Let's pray that it lasts."

"I do every day."

"I'm sure you do, Tevye."

The coffee tasted awful, but at least it was warm. I wished Simcha had also brought me something to eat. I was beginning to fantasize about chocolate cake and apple pie.

As if reading my mind, Simcha reached inside his jacket and pulled out a bag. "Golde thought you might be hungry."

He handed over the bag and I stuck my face into the opening. "Sunflower seeds?"

"She said you need to lose weight."

It was a good thing I was sitting or my face might have fallen so hard I would've hurt my chin. Simcha had an unusually stupid grin on his face. He was biting his lower lip as if he was trying to keep from laughing.

"What?"

Finally, he burst out laughing. He could have scared hyenas away.

"Golde figured you would have that reaction. She imitated your face exactly."

"Ha, ha. Very funny."

"Here, she also sent you this," Simcha said, pulling another bag from his jacket pocket.

I grabbed it away from him. He was still laughing.

"This is more like it," I said, and took a bite from the piece of apple strudel. "And you can't have any," I mumbled with crumbs falling out of my mouth.

"*Biteavon.*"

I polished off the desert and licked my fingers. "So, what is new from the exciting world of the committees? Without Faiga here, I'm afraid I'm out of touch."

Simcha took a handful of sunflower seeds from the other bag and shook them in his palm. "The Economic Committee says we should have a record crop this year. We might even be able to afford a new tractor."

"The machine that does the work of horses and oxen."

"Yes, Tevye. You just sit and ride around. You don't have to feed it or whip it. It won't get tired or decide to stop working."

"I wouldn't be so sure about that if I were you. Mechanical beasts also have minds of their own."

"I'll take my chances," Simcha said.

"Are you sure that it's still work? The committee might decide you're losing touch with the land."

Simcha chuckled. With him, sometimes it was hard to tell if you were really funny or he just laughed at everything.

"Tevye, you forget. I am the chairman of the committee now. I think the purchase will be approved. Besides, I'm getting too old to bend over all day."

"Old. You? Please. Raise eight children and then tell me about getting old."

"What are you complaining about?" he said, spitting a shell through the gap in his teeth. "I've seen you chasing those twins around the kibbutz. You've still got plenty of energy."

"And what choice do I have? If I didn't chase them, they'd chase me, and I don't think I can outrun them."

"Well, little Abraham looks just like you. A tough break, but I suppose he'll learn to live with it."

"Very funny."

"Fortunately Rachel inherited Golde's looks. When she gets older, her father will not be the only one chasing her."

"Well, Tevye's daughters are all known for their beauty — and their intelligence."

The wind kicked up and I shivered. Simcha poured some more coffee for me.

"Yes, yes. I know. You've told me two or three hundred times. And, I have to admit, you were not lying about Shoshana, Devorah or Sarah."

"Speaking of Saraleh," I interrupted. "When are you going to get married?"

The question was more on Golde's mind than mine. Sarah and Simcha had been spending a lot of time together over the past few years and Golde didn't think it was proper. She was anxious to have a real wedding, despite our less than happy experiences in the past.

"Married? We're just good friends who enjoy each other's company."

"Friends, hah! I told you that you were too old for her."

"Give it a rest, Tevye."

"Okay, but my daughters are not known for waiting for men to ask them."

"Well, maybe I want to see if your daughters in Poland are also such beauties."

If he were not such a good friend, I would have punched Simcha. "Why, do you think my family is like a market, that you can go shopping?"

"Take it easy, Tevye. I'm joking. You're the one who started it with all the marriage talk. I just wanted to ask if you think Tzeitl and Hodel will be able to get here now that the British have reduced the quota again."

Simcha may be happy, but that doesn't make him funny. I calmed down anyway and repeated what Bernice told me.

"God alone knows when they will arrive. Bernice said the Haganah is buying ships to smuggle more immigrants into the country, but it is very dangerous. The ships aren't always the most seaworthy. Even if they make it to the coast, they may not be able to evade the British naval blockade. They could end up being sent back or imprisoned."

My face must have betrayed my concern because Simcha grabbed my arm and squeezed it reassuringly.

"Was it so much different for us, Tevye? Our trip wasn't exactly a luxury cruise. The dream of reaching the Promised Land will keep them going, just as it did for us. We will bring them home. You'll see."

Simcha put his arm around me. I wanted to share his optimism, but I was scared.

"Tevye, there's something else. What is it?"

"Devorah is involved. I can't tell Golde because she will worry herself to death."

"What does Golde think Devorah is doing?"

"Bernice told her she's doing courier work again for the Haganah in Tel Aviv. That makes her anxious enough, believe me."

"And you're worried too?"

"Of course. My little girl doesn't know anything about boats. She doesn't even know how to swim. What will she do if something happens to the ship? What if the British arrest her?"

The image of Devorah floundering in the water helplessly, surrounded by sharks, while English soldiers watch her drown has been a recurring nightmare.

"I've known Devorah since she was a little girl, Tevye. And she's not a child anymore. She's a grown woman and as tough as nails. She's been working for the Haganah for a long time, and there's always been an element of danger. To tell you the truth, I think she likes taking risks. There's something about putting your life on the line that makes you feel more alive. That's the way Moshe feels."

"Only a fool seeks danger."

"Everything about living here is a risk. You know that Tevye. Devorah's in no more danger than the rest of us."

"I wish I could believe that."

"Tevye, she's not going to be the captain of the ship. She's a nurse. And, if it will make you feel any better, I taught her how to swim."

"What? When?" I nearly spilled coffee on myself.

"Before the troubles with the Arabs made it too dangerous, I used to take some of the kids for hikes and field trips. Sometimes we went to the Kinneret and I taught the kids to swim. Devorah was one of the fastest learners."

I didn't even know my daughter could swim. I wondered how many other secrets my family kept from me.

"And how, may I ask, did you learn to swim?"

"My father taught me in Russia."

"Maybe you can teach me sometime."

"I don't know, Tevye. You're awfully old, especially after raising eight children."

"*Hatzuf*," I said, slapping Simcha's shoulder.

"And speaking of your children, you should have heard all the commotion coming from your house. I'm surprised you can't hear them all the way out here. The kids are shouting and Golde's voice is booming above theirs."

What a surprise.

"Tevye, why don't you go on home? I'll stay here for the rest of your watch."

"Thank you," I said, handing Simcha my rifle. I felt immediately relieved to be rid of it. "I'd better go and find out what's going on. *Shalom*, Simcha."

"*Shalom*. Tevye. And don't worry. You'll be introducing me to those beautiful daughters of yours before you know it."

I watched Simcha walk toward another part of the orchard in the loping gait he had that reflected his always cheerful manner. He plopped himself down under a tree and aimed the rifle at the darkness.

No creature had ever been more aptly named. Simcha truly was a joy and he had eased my worries. But I still wasn't going to say anything to Golde about Devorah.

I was barely within sight of the house when the clamor began to hurt my ears.

"What's this?" I shouted, entering the house and seeing Rachel and Abraham having a tug of war with a sapling.

The room instantly grew silent.

"What's going on here?"

"They're fighting over who will plant the tree," Golde said.

"Children, come here." The twins ran over and hugged me. Abraham kept a tight grip on the tree.

"I'm glad that you are so excited about planting a new tree for Tu b'Shevat. I'm sorry that we only have one, but the committee said we could only afford one per family. Now, I could choose who will plant the tree, but I would rather that you decide."

"I should get to plant it, Abba, because I can dig the hole. Rachel's too weak to shovel."

"I am not weak."

Rachel started to swing her fist at Abraham and I caught it before it reached its target.

"None of that," I said, taking the seedling from Abraham. "Why do you think you should be the one to plant the tree, Rachel?"

She looked up at me with her big green eyes that she knew could get almost anything she wanted from me.

"I think we should take turns. This year I get to plant the tree and next year Abraham does. That would be the fair thing to do."

Golde was sitting silently, apparently content to let me resolve the dispute. She knew how her daughter's mind worked. Golde told me more than once — she tells me everything more than once — how Rachel reminded her of herself as a little girl.

"Rachel, do you think you'll remember that it's Abraham's turn next year and let him plant a tree without making a fuss?"

"You could write it down to be sure."

"Well, that sounds reasonable. What do you think Abraham?"

"No way. She'll forget all about it and start fighting all over again. Besides, why should I have to wait a whole year before I get my turn? Why can't I go first and she can plant it next year?"

"Rachel?"

"I want to go first. He always gets his way because he's a boy."

"Now Rachel that's not true."

"It is." She broke into tears and ran to Golde.

"*Abba*, she always starts crying when she doesn't get what she wants. Maybe I should cry too."

I watched Abraham try to force himself to cry, but all he could do was make tearless sobbing sounds.

"All right. Stop crying, both of you. Rachel, come here."

Rachel wiped her face with her sleeve and slowly came over to me, whimpering softly and looking unsure if she had succeeded in making me feel badly enough to give in to her.

"Children, what do you think King Solomon would decide?"

Abraham scratched his chin as though he had a beard. "He would probably say we should cut the tree in half and each plant part."

"I want the top half, the pretty part," Rachel shouted.

"No, I want the part with the leaves," Abraham said, making a grab for the tree, but I pulled it out of his reach.

"Well," I asked, "what happened in the story of Solomon and the child who was claimed by two mothers?"

"One mother agreed to split the child, but the other wouldn't because it would have killed the baby," Rachel answered.

"Right. So King Solomon knew the real mother was the woman who would rather give up the child than see it harmed."

"But the tree isn't a baby, *Abba*," Abraham protested.

"Isn't it?"

"I understand, *Abba*," Rachel said. "It's a baby tree and if we split it in half it will die. So I prefer that we don't cut it in half. That makes me the person who should get it, right?"

"You are right that the tree would die if we cut it in half, but that doesn't mean it's yours. You know what I think Solomon would do in this case? I believe he would say that one person should dig the hole for the tree and the other should plant it. And since Abraham said he was the strongest, I suggest that he dig and Rachel will plant. Is that all right?"

I could see them both considering the solution. Abraham opened his mouth to protest. I raised my eyebrow.

"I think that's fair," Abraham said.

"Me too," said Rachel.

"Good. Come and give me a kiss."

The children kissed me. Out of the corner of my eye, I saw Golde smiling.

23

"Tevye, wake up," Golde said, elbowing me. "The meeting's about to begin."

I could barely keep my head up. Golde elbowed me harder in the ribs.

"Enough woman. My hearing isn't improved by hitting me."

"I don't care about whether you can hear. I just don't want to have to listen to your snoring."

As soon as I lifted my head off the pillow, I could clearly hear Shmuel's ding-ding, dong-dong, ding-ding, dong-dong, echoing through the kibbutz. More than one *chaver* had threatened to beat him to a pulp with his clapper.

"A meeting at midnight? I think I'll skip it tonight. I'm beat."

"You're not skipping anything," she said, pulling the blanket off me. "You can sleep afterward."

"Or during," I mumbled.

The *chaverim* assembled with their usual lack of late night enthusiasm. The dining hall was beginning to look its age, with paint chipping and walls cracking. When it rained, we had to spread pots around the floor to catch the runoff from all the leaks. The good news was that it meant we didn't have to go to the well for drinking water. At meals, some *chaverim* just reached down and drank out of the pots.

Tonight, we didn't have to worry about a deluge through the ceiling. We just had to cover ourselves with blankets to stay warm.

Meanwhile, sitting in the front of the room looking unaffected, as usual, was my good friend Simcha. He sat smiling, patiently waiting for everyone to arrive, looking as fresh as he did when he awoke in the morning.

"I'll never understand why we have to meet so late at night. It's Simcha's only obnoxious habit. But, look at him. Even at this time of night, when the rest of us can barely keep our eyes open, he looks as alert and cheerful as ever."

"Shush already," Golde said. "He's about to start."

I looked around the room. Nothing had changed in all the years of meeting to discuss the kibbutz's affairs. The apathetic members always slouched in the back and tried to sleep through the meeting, while the politicians sat stiffly in front, looking as though they'd slept all day to prepare for the evening's debate. Then there were those like me who were genuinely interested in the discussion — at least part of it — but felt too exhausted to pay much attention. Fortunately, I have my own alarm clock.

"Quiet," Golde said as she poked me again.

See what I mean.

"*Shalom chaverim,*" Simcha said brightly, with no hint of an apology for the lateness of the meeting. "As you know, the Royal Commission issued its report and the Mandatory Government is carrying out its recommendations, the worst of which is that immigration will again be curtailed. This will create problems for our brothers and sisters who are trying to reach Palestine, but efforts are being made to help them."

"The good news is the report appears to have appeased the Arabs for the moment. I don't expect it to last. While it does, however, we have to take advantage of the opportunity to do as much as possible to expand all of our industries. I want us to also begin to carry out the rest of Bernice's recommendations, fortify the kibbutz more heavily, acquire as many weapons as possible and train our young people to shoot."

Murmuring grew louder and louder before Natan stood up and asked, "Simcha, is there something you're not telling us? Do you expect us to be attacked?"

"No Natan. As I said, for the moment, the violence has abated, but I don't believe the Arabs have changed their view toward Zionism. The time will come, I'm afraid, when we'll have to defend ourselves. I want us to be ready."

Eitan was usually one of the people who slept in the rear, but he was roused by the unusual hubbub and stood. "Where will we get weapons, and who will train us now that Moshe and Devorah are gone?"

"Don't worry. That is being taken care of. I just wanted to let everyone know what to expect."

The words hardly registered in my brain. It was not so much that I was half asleep, I just found myself staring at Simcha, remembering the young man who had stopped me on the road from Anatevka ranting about the marvels of the Holy Land. From the day we arrived, he had been one of the hardest workers, and it was only fitting after so many years, and Jonathan's death, that he had become the acknowledged leader of the kibbutz. It was the young idealists like him, more than old cockers like me, who had made so much progress toward building our state, from draining the marshes to planting the fields to administering the finances. Simcha, Moshe and others like them had done it all. I felt a surge of pride, as though he were my own son.

"I would like to congratulate the construction team on the completion of the new bathroom."

"Now that's good news!" I jumped up and shouted as the *chaverim* applauded wildly.

"Sit down, Tevye," Golde said, tugging my shirt.

"You wanted me to wake up and now I'm up."

"You can stay awake sitting down."

Simcha held up his hands to quiet the room. "I've been asked to warn you all that some of the wood and tools are still lying about, so please be careful when you go out at night."

"I'd hate to come back with more than I left with," I said, provoking laughter among the members and another shot in the ribs from Golde.

"I've also been asked," Simcha said, losing the battle to control his own laughter. "I've also been asked to remind everyone that tomorrow evening the poetry group will be meeting to discuss Bialik's latest work. And, on a more serious note."

"More serious than Bialik?" Natan interrupted.

"Well, maybe not that serious, Natan. The Committee has been alerted that we are having some problems at the *makhsan*. When we agreed to allow the membership to own their own clothes, we did not anticipate that anyone would remove clothes from the laundry that do not belong to them. I'm sure this has occurred accidentally from time to time. A greater concern is the discovery that the numbers on some garments have been sewed over."

I looked around the room and saw that everyone was looking at each other suspiciously. I got the feeling more than one person was guilty.

"Anyone who is caught committing such a crime," Simcha continued, "will be publicly denounced and suffer the appropriate punishment. The removals must stop."

The smile never left Simcha's face, but his tone left no doubt that he was concerned and angry. The *chaverim* put their heads down and slumped in their seats like children who had just been chastised by their parents.

"I have one more announcement. And this one I am happy to make. The Economic Committee has decided to purchase a new tractor, which should increase our productivity and relieve some of the burden from our animals, not to mention our backs. The committee will be issuing new job assignments to many of you in the next week."

"And who will have the privilege of driving our new tractor?" Natan shouted.

Natan did not only pester me with his questions about the Bible. He annoyed everyone. If it wasn't for his interruptions, our meetings would probably take half the time.

I was so intent on Natan's question that I almost missed the answer.

Simcha looked in my direction and had a particularly wide grin that meant he was not just happy but pleased with himself.

"Tevye will be our new tractor driver," he proclaimed.

"Tevye?" Timur blurted from the back of the room, and then began laughing. Soon others joined in. Even Golde was laughing.

I rose and shouted, "And what is so funny?"

"It's just that you are the person that we least associate with anything new or modern," Timur replied. "You're still driving your little milk cart and practicing your *shtetl* rituals. It's like introducing a car to a Philistine." Timur laughed so hard he began snorting.

"You're playing a joke on me, Simcha. Very funny."

Simcha never joined in the laughter. "It's no joke, Tevye. The world is changing, and the kibbutz will have to change with it. That's progress. I'm afraid the situation with the Arabs makes it unsafe for you to make your deliveries to the villages and other kibbutzim. I want you to have a new job here. I think this will suit you."

"Yea, another chance for Tevye to spend all his time on his *tuchis*," Enoch shouted, causing Timur to laugh so hard he began choking.

Before the laughter had died down, the doors burst open. The room fell silent and everyone turned around anxiously.

I was waving my finger at Simcha, about to quote from the Bible about injustice when I turned to see the cause of the disturbance.

I couldn't believe my eyes. The first person I saw was my Devorah in khaki shorts and shirt with a rifle slung over her shoulder. Her hair had grown back and was longer than ever, falling down her back in a ponytail.

Two boys in green uniforms, who looked younger than Devorah, followed her through the door carrying a large crate. They reminded me of the two boys who had come to the kibbutz years earlier with an injured soldier. Yossi and Shimshon were no longer boys. Devorah had told me on her last visit that they were now senior commanders. The young recruits pried open the crate and began passing out rifles.

As Devorah made her way to the front of the room, Golde pushed toward her. I was still staring at the doorway when slowly, reluctantly, a group of children entered. They were followed by a small band of disheveled men and women.

One tall skinny man with a stovepipe hat stood above the rest. A woman was just behind him holding the hands of two little girls, with a small boy clinging to her skirt. It was Motel and Tzeitl. I nearly ran over Chana and Laban to get to them. I didn't even look at Motel's face before embracing him.

"Papa," Tzeitl cried, and hugged me as soon as I released Motel.

I never used to act like an old woman before I came to Palestine, but now I seem to quite often. I couldn't help myself. Tears flowed like the waters of the Banyias.

"Thank God!" I heard Golde shout behind me as she too raced over to hug her family.

The four of us stood holding each other and the room burst into applause. I saw Devorah out of the corner of my eye. She was wiping away tears. I held out my hand to her and she joined our embrace.

"Mama, Papa," Tzeitl sniffled. "Would you like to meet your grandchildren?"

"We gave them all Hebrew names because we always knew we would join you in Palestine," Motel said.

I patted Motel on the back, then bent down to see three of the most beautiful faces I have ever seen in my life.

"Papa, this is my eldest, Rebecca."

"*Shalom Zeyde*," Rebecca said and came over and put her arms around my neck.

"*Shalom* Rebecca," I said trying to keep from breaking into tears again at the sight of a freckled face that looked like Tzeitl's when she was that age.

"And this is Leah."

"Look at the flower I found outside *Zeyde*," she said, handing me one of the newly bloomed roses. I could just imagine the fit Maya and her Flower Committee would throw when they realized one of their plants had been touched.

"Thank you, Leah. It's beautiful. And so are you. You are the prettiest girl in all of Palestine." I gave her a hug and kissed her cheek, but she ran behind Tzeitl's skirt.

"Grr," the little boy growled, holding his hands up with his fingers bent like claws.

"And this ferocious beast," Tzeitl said, "is Aryeh."

"Aryeh, my little lion. You are very scary, and so big," I said, lifting him up over my head.

"Tevye, what are you doing?" Golde shouted. "He's a boy, not a sack of flour."

"You're wrong, Golde. He's an angel sent by God. They're all angels."

I put Aryeh down and knelt on the floor to hug all three of my grandchildren.

"Do you think I might join you?" a voice cried out from the doorway.

When I looked up, I couldn't believe my eyes. I had to rub them to be sure I wasn't hallucinating.

There stood my Hodel. I couldn't even speak when I tried to call her name. Golde just put her hand to her mouth.

"Mama! Papa!" she shouted as she ran to us and jumped into my arms.

"Dear Lord, I don't know if I have enjoyed a more blessed day. Thank you."

24

It's hard to sleep. I'm so excited I've just been lying here staring at the ceiling.

Golde's reaction was the opposite. She finally felt relaxed enough to pass out the minute her head hit the pillow. Now she's snoring so loud, the Jews in Haifa are closing their windows.

How can I describe my joy at having my family reunited? I always believed we would be together one day, but the years passed and it seemed as though I would miss their whole lives. My little girls are all grown up. Skinny little Tzeitl has filled out and now she's the mother of three beautiful children. I am amazed at how much she looks like Golde when she was a young mother. Her hair is combed the same, she speaks to her children the way Golde spoke to ours, she even has some of the same gestures, like throwing her hands up in exasperation at Motel, and looking heavenward to make a remark to the Almighty.

My thoughts of her and Motel have been haunted by the memory of their wedding being interrupted by the Russian hooligans.

It was difficult to imagine her happily married, even with the man of her own choosing, but, despite the hardships, she says her life has been wonderful.

Motel is still thin and looks sickly. Something has changed though. He walks upright instead of slouching. When he speaks, it is not with the stuttering uncertainty of his youth, but with confidence and authority. He used to nervously polish his glasses all the time, now when he does it he looks thoughtful. I always believed he was a good man, even if he was penniless, because he had an inner strength. And that strength is what must have allowed him to survive in Poland, and to feed his family.

And what a family. Those children are like the pearls of an oyster. When I first laid eyes on Rebecca, I couldn't help thinking I was seeing Tzeitl. Not only does she have her looks, but I've already discovered she shares her mother's willfulness. You can't tell her anything without getting an argument.

"Rebecca, why don't you comb your hair?"

"I like it the way it is."

"But it's a mess."

"No, it's stylish."

"But your eyes are covered."

"I can see fine."

Most conversations with her go the same way. Tzeitl insists Rebecca is going through a stage. Wait till she finds out how long it lasts.

Leah has more of her father's looks. Hopefully, she'll grow out of it. But she couldn't be smarter if she'd eaten from the Tree of Knowledge. Whatever you ask her, she has an answer. And, if she doesn't have an answer, she asks questions to help her find one.

My grandson will be like me. Handsome, smart, agreeable, a friend to man and beast. For now, Aryeh loves to build. He takes pieces of wood and turns them into a stable or a cabin or a birdhouse. To his mother's chagrin, his favorite game is what he calls "army." He builds a fortress and pretends to have battles with little toy soldiers.

Tzeitl and the children are having a difficult time adjusting to the separation imposed by the kibbutz. She is working with Golde in the kitchen and cries all day. It will take time, but she'll get used to our lifestyle.

It's been easier for Motel. The geniuses on the Work Committee originally assigned him to the barn. It didn't take long for them to figure out he didn't know which end of the cow to milk. After great deliberation, they decided his talents could best be used in the clothing department, especially now that the *chaverim* are allowed to own their own clothes. The biggest problem then became Motel's desire to show off his talent. He had to be told we want things simple, the plainer the better. The last thing the elders wanted was to let people have clothes of their own that would arouse envy.

"You mean you want me to purposely make peasant garments?" Motel asked, with his eyes peering over the top of his glasses like a tortoise peeking out of its shell.

"That's right," I told him. "We want you to use all your talent and creativity to design the drabbest clothing you can imagine."

I have to give him credit. He has done just that. When I put on his clothes, I feel like I should be sitting on a street corner in town asking for alms. I think I was better off in the clothes that didn't fit.

The changes in Motel and Tzeitl all have been for the best, but how can I explain what has happened to Hodel? The years in Siberia took a toll on her physically. She was always pale, but now her skin is ashen and wrinkled. Her hands are more worn than mine. She walks with a slight limp, but refuses to explain what caused it. Tzeitl was born almost two years earlier, and certainly has not had an easy life, but Hodel looks ten years older than her sister. Her hair has already turned gray and some has fallen out.

But the most disturbing thing about her appearance is in her face. The bright smile that she used to have whenever I read to her, or took her with me on my rounds, is long gone. Even the night she arrived, Hodel looked as though it was a strain to grin. I know that she was happy to see me, but it was as if she could not feel joy.

The emptiness is in her eyes also. The sparkle is gone, replaced by a lifelessness that frightens me. It was the look Shoshana had after the "wedding." I know that Hodel will not do anything rash, though, because she is strong, maybe stronger than any of us. She has survived Pertschik's murder and pursuit by his killers. She has reached the Promised Land. Now Hodel has an opportunity to fulfill Pertschik's dream of living in a worker's paradise.

Until Bernice told me about Jonathan's attempt to visit Pertschik, I had no idea my daughter was considered a living legend. The young *chaverim* never said anything to me, but it turned out they had all heard of Pertschik and the woman who stood by him during all his years in prison. They welcomed her as a hero.

Such praise was heaped on my Hodel that I was filled with pride. No one would have blamed her if she had basked in the adoration like David after he felled Goliath, but she was totally unaffected by it all. The mask that now hid the face I had loved since birth was frozen in pain from events in another place and another time.

Hodel reluctantly accepted the nomination to the Executive Committee, but I'm told she has said nothing at the meetings so far. She has thrown herself into her work, demanding the opportunity to work on the crew building the road from our kibbutz to the others farther north. I have tried to talk to her, but she says nothing about the past. I asked Tzeitl, but Hodel would not even share whatever dark secrets she keeps with her sister.

"Dear Lord, what did the Russians do to my baby to wound her so deeply? I know they murdered her husband, but I think there's more. Can You ease her burden? I would gladly take it upon myself."

Perhaps after Hodel's been here longer, and realizes she has the chance to complete Pertschik's mission, the spell will be broken.

We've been so overjoyed by Tzeitl and Hodel's return, I must confess we've neglected the other children. The twins grow like the cypress trees we planted at the entrance of the kibbutz, tall, thin and strong. They spend most of their day at school, but they're gradually being introduced to the work that needs to be done, peeling potatoes, sorting peas and beans. They have their own miniature farm where they can feed chickens and ducks.

Abraham likes to have me read to him, but the minute I finish, he says, "*Abba*, can I go out and play now?" I want to teach him Torah, but what he enjoys most is playing soccer and racing with his friends through the kibbutz. He is the fastest and most skilled of the group. I'd prefer that he be the most learned. He also has inherited the family stubborn streak, so it does no good to try to force him to study. He just sits and pouts until I let him go to be with his friends.

Little Rachel is happy to play by herself. She dresses up her dolls and sits them in front of her while she performs. She sings, dances, puts on little plays. Bernice used to tell her stories about America, especially about Hollywood. Since then, all Rachel's talked about is wanting to be an actress. She says one day she will move to California and become a movie star with fancy clothes and a big car.

Abraham teases Rachel mercilessly, and says she will never be more than a farmhand, performing for goats and sheep. That's about the time I have to step in to prevent any bloodletting.

For all their bickering, the twins are closer than any two people could be. They seem to know what each other thinks and feels. When one gets hurt, the other says they have the same pain. You can see past the natural sibling jealousies to a bond that is unique. They may goad each other, but they are very protective and neither will allow anyone to molest the other. Abraham, in particular, has gotten into trouble more than once for hitting another child who he thought was picking on his sister.

The twins both look up to, and adore their sister. Sarah had grown accustomed to being the oldest child. After being the youngest her whole life, I think she really enjoyed the idea of giving orders to siblings instead of just taking them. More often, though, she acted like a doting aunt.

Sarah is working now in the chicken house. She says Simcha is the one who should be in the coop because he has been afraid to marry her. I don't know who is more frustrated, Sarah or Golde. I take that back – of course I know.

Now that the family is reunited, poor Golde worries almost full time about potential grooms. She has already started complaining again that the kibbutz has no matchmaker, as if one of Tevye's daughters would ever allow someone else to choose their husband. To tell you the truth, I don't miss having the responsibility for the happiness of my daughters. How could I find anyone learned enough for my angels? All right, maybe a rabbi would qualify, but Golde would insist on a rich rabbi and those are a lot harder to find.

It's difficult to believe I almost chose to give my Tzeitl to the butcher Lazer-Wolf. A butcher! And one old enough to be her papa. I'm glad I thought better of it. Motel certainly turned out to be a good husband and provider.

You see how quickly my thoughts go back to my eldest? Devorah hardly stayed long enough for me to have a thought about her. Golde tried to ask her what she'd been doing, and why she was with the newcomers, but all Devorah would say is that she was doing God's work.

When Golde was not in the room, Devorah did tell me the Haganah had agents all over Europe buying anything that would float. Many of the boats are old, rusty and unsuited for carrying people, she said, but the immigrants don't care. They want so desperately to come to Palestine. At first she didn't think the Haganah needed her, but when she saw the condition of many of the people fleeing Europe, especially after weeks on the sometimes stormy seas, she felt like the most important member of the army.

Devorah said the whole world was contained in those little ships, mothers, fathers, children, everyone with a tale to tell. Women giving birth, old men dying, the cycle of life unfolds each day before her eyes. And after surviving everything else, and coming within sight of the Promised Land, the British can swoop in like an ill wind waking you from the most pleasant dream. If they are caught, the Jews are sent back and the Haganah fighters are arrested.

"You could drown in a shipwreck, catch a disease or be arrested. Aren't you scared?" I asked.

Do you know what Devorah said? This child of the kibbutz's school of socialists and atheists? She said, "Papa, the Talmud teaches us that to save one life is as if you saved the whole world."

Can you believe my daughter is quoting the Talmud to me? And you do not believe I am blessed?

I asked her where the children had come from that had arrived along with the rest of our family. They were all alone.

Devorah explained that they had come from Germany. The Chancellor, a fellow named Hitler, is a pathological anti-Semite. When he first took power, she said, Jews began to lose their jobs. The situation has grown steadily worse and many Jews are so afraid of what may happen they've begun to send their children out of the country. Devorah explained that the Haganah is bringing as many as it can to Palestine. The kibbutzim have offered to take them in.

She barely finished her explanation before she had to leave again. She was returning to her job of saving the whole world.

25

Can you hear me over the racket this tractor is making? No? I didn't think so. I don't even think God can hear when this confounded machine is on. Let me give the engine and my ears a rest.

My good friend Simcha thought he was doing me a favor by letting me ride this four-wheeled *grogger* around the fields instead of having to whip my obstinate horse to pull my wagon.

"You can just sit and relax and let the tractor do all the work for you," he said. "You'll look like a chauffeur."

Well, it certainly saves a lot of time working in the field, but this noise is enough to drive me insane. I enjoyed the slow, *quiet* life with my horse and wagon. I could think. I could sing. I could talk to the Almighty. But now?

I complained to Simcha and he said he would take it up with the Assignment Committee. I hate to tell you how long ago that was. I think they call their decision process "due deliberation." God created the entire world in less time than it takes them to determine who should do the laundry.

At least it's been quiet outside the kibbutz. You remember the Royal Commission the British convened after the riots? The one that recommended Jewish immigration be curtailed? Well, the High Commissioner took the advice and imposed a quota over the objections of Bernice and the other Agency politicians. During these long years the Committee has been considering my request for a new job, the Arabs have acted as though they were satisfied with the British actions.

My friend Sheikh Jabber and his son Ali warned me not to be misled, that the Arabs were still seething. The Arabs, they said, will not be content with preventing more Jews from coming to Palestine; they want to expel those who are already here.

The kibbutz is taking new precautions to fortify our defense. If you look toward the gate, you'll see Moshe's latest brainchild. He calls it the stockade and tower. You see that line of women stretching back to the center of the kibbutz? They're passing baskets and pails of stone and gravel to the builders. Our carpenters have been working night and day to finish it before the rainy season. When they're finished, it will be thirty feet tall. It's going to have a searchlight to help us see beyond the perimeter and allow us to send signals to other kibbutzim.

You can't see it from here, but beyond the fence, we've also added rows of barbed wire, so a visitor would be excused if they thought they were entering a military encampment instead of a farm. I think Moshe spent too much time visiting ancient fortresses in Palestine and decided to turn our kibbutz into one.

The fear of violence has grown to the point that the *chaverim* spend very little time outside the kibbutz. Moshe and other Haganah officers come here periodically to give us additional training. They also send some of their troops here to practice beyond the eyes and ears of English spies.

Workers in the fields now usually carry weapons. Even I take a rifle with me, though I can't imagine how I'd shoot it while riding this tractor. I'd probably end up falling off the tractor and being run over before any Arab could reach me.

Carrying a rifle hasn't made me any more comfortable with guns. I still feel allergic toward them. And the idea of killing a human being, even in self-defense, is something I find too horrible to contemplate. I know that it's permitted, and the Jewish people have fought many wars through the years, but I have always wanted to fight my battles with my mind and the words of the sages. From talking to the Sheikh, I know that my way will not suffice. So I take my turn as a watchman and pray that no one approaches. So far, thankfully, those prayers have been answered.

But I don't know how much longer God will spare me. Ali says the situation is growing tenser and that violence could flare again at any moment. The limitations on immigration the British imposed immediately after the riots have gradually been relaxed in the last couple of years and more Jews than ever before are rushing to Palestine. Ali says it is making his people very angry.

I tried to explain that many of the Jews who are coming are trying to escape persecution. Now the problem is not so much in Russia as in Germany. Bernice tells us Jews are being stripped of citizenship and she fears the situation will grow much worse. She said Devorah and the Haganah were beginning to focus more attention on helping German Jews escape to Palestine.

Ali wasn't interested in the problems of the Jews. All that concerned him was that they were coming to Palestine instead of leaving.

Meanwhile, here, my family goes on living. Motel still works in the clothing shop, but now he is allowed to make something other than peasant clothes. He's begun to design more attractive clothes, and even use a few bright colors, which the kibbutz now sells.

Tzeitl was slower to adjust, mainly because she had difficulty getting used to being separated from her children. But now that the kids are older, and have their aunts and uncles to be with, she is more comfortable.

The person who has changed the most is Hodel. I told you that she was welcomed as a heroine because of what she had done in Russia. Well, she was immediately put on the Executive Planning Committee and, after several months of silent participation, she threw herself into the business of running the kibbutz. When Hodel realized all we had accomplished, and then became part of the growth of the kibbutz herself, she began to come alive again. She spoke at the group meetings and gave passionate speeches that reminded me of Pertschik. And that's not just a father's boast. When I looked around the room at the reaction of the others, I could see the members were moved by her, and believed what she said.

Sometimes Hodel gets into arguments with Eitan and Uzi, but I think it has less to do with differences in opinion than the fact that they see themselves being replaced as the kibbutz ideologues. To her credit, Hodel is very careful to be respectful toward them. She always acknowledges their contributions as founders of the kibbutz, and credits their devotion to socialist ideals with guiding us in the proper direction. Tactfully, she explains her desire is only to reinforce those principles and make sure the kibbutz continues on the path they have set.

My heart fills with pride each time I hear her shout from the lectern, "We must remember what Jonathan fought and died for, to build this land that has been promised to the Jewish people by God Almighty. We will have a state of our own, but we must build it with our own hands and not let anyone, the Arabs, the British, the capitalists or anyone stop us from accomplishing our divine purpose."

The talk about God's role drives Eitan and Uzi nuts. They're still devoted atheists. But, thank God, my Hodel never forgot the lessons I taught her, not even in the Siberian wasteland. She knows there is a God and that His hand guides our work.

As much as she enjoys having the respect of the *chaverim*, and being a leader of the kibbutz, the smile did not return to her face until she attracted the attention of one particular *chaver*. Old Simcha himself has fallen for my Hodel. I think he was smitten the day she arrived.

Hodel remained fiercely loyal to Pertschik for a long time. Simcha understood and never pressured her. It took all these years before she allowed herself to accept his love. Now, at last, we may see a truly happy wedding.

Of course, such a wonderful development had to be accompanied by at least a little *tsouris*. You see, Simcha had the awkward task of separating himself from Hodel's younger sister.

It had become clear to everyone but Sarah that Simcha had no intention of marrying her. We all thought Simcha was married to the kibbutz, like his mentor Jonathan. Sarah refused to believe that. She was convinced it was just a matter of time. When Hodel arrived, the relationship began to change. Slowly, Simcha reduced the amount of time he spent with Sarah and increased his activities with Hodel. It happened so gradually I'm not sure it has fully hit Sarah.

The end of her relationship with Simcha was the culmination of a series of blows Sarah felt since the return of Tzeitl and Hodel. Sarah had enjoyed being the older sister, and getting a lot of attention from Golde and me, not to mention other *chaverim.* That is no longer the case.

It soon became clear that Sarah was jealous of her older sister, both for winning Simcha's affection and for being the subject of such adoration from other members. Whenever they were together, Sarah tried to pick a fight. Hodel was too wise to take the bait, which only angered Sarah more. I'm not sure what to do about it. I just hope it will all blow over after the wedding.

At least Golde's happy — well as happy as a constantly suffering mother can be — since our daughters returned. She's waited and dreamed and prayed for this day since we left Anatevka. She still worries, of course, about Devorah's safety, and whether Sarah will ever get married, but she now goes around the house humming gaily and isn't even bothered when I answer her questions with quotes from the Bible.

Her greatest joy is spending time with the young children. The twins and the grandchildren have given her a renewed sense of purpose. They are the future of our people, and Golde is determined to do what she can to mold them in her image.

I feel the same way. I spend every free moment I can with little Abraham and Rachel. Actually, they're not so small anymore. We read together from the Scriptures and I tell them stories about our life in Russia. They sit in my lap, one on each side, listening to every word as though it were coming from Moses himself. I must admit, it's a nice feeling.

Rachel is like a sponge. She remembers everything I say and can recite from the Talmud like a yeshiva student. Of course, she turns every lesson into a production, choosing to act out the parts of the different rabbis. She portrays Rav Eliezer as a finger-wagging boor. Rav Gamliel is always half asleep, coming alive when a point is disputed. Hillel is quiet and thoughtful. Everyone becomes a character in her play. Golde finds her acting entertaining, but it drives me to distraction when I'm trying to explain the meaning of the words she's parroting.

Abraham is equally capable of absorbing the information, but he still doesn't want to spend the time or the energy. Sometimes I think he just wants to spite me, but, most of the time, I think he just has his mind elsewhere, either on soccer or his older sister. He adores Devorah. Whenever she comes to visit, he sits with her listening to stories about the Haganah. He talks a lot about fighting, and one day I caught him trying to sneak into the field with my rifle to practice shooting.

Golde is mortified by his interest in the Haganah and yells at Devorah not to fill his head with stories about the danger and adventure of her work. I would prefer that he focus on his studies, but — and I can't say this to Golde — I fear that he will need to know how to fight. By the time he is an adult, the deciding battle for Palestine that Sheikh Jabber predicts may be upon us.

I don't know whether to wish for that climactic battle or not. We have created a nice life for ourselves here in our homeland. Will it make so much of a difference if we have a state or not? Bernice says it will.

"Unless we can control our own destiny, we will never be safe, nor will Jews in the diaspora," she lectured me. "Look at the Jews in Germany, Tevye. No country wants them. Where will they go if not Palestine? And if we do not control immigration, how can we ensure they will be allowed in?"

We are lucky to have Bernice working for the Jewish Agency. She looks like such a mild-mannered lady, but she is as tough as a camel is mean. She understands politics far better than I, and what must be done to guarantee our independence.

It's time to head in, so I have to start this blasted tractor again. Look at the starlings. They dive for the grubs exposed by the plow.

The noise will scare them away. I wish it had the same effect on the Arabs.

As I drove into the shed, I saw Motel in an animated conversation. I put the tractor away and came outside to hear my son-in-law shouting. I remember when he was afraid of his own shadow. Now he debates the *chaverim* like a *sabra*.

"What do you know? You've only been here a short time. We've gotten along with our neighbors for years," the son of Laban the Miser said.

"Udi, I'm telling you," said Motel, "when I went to the village to buy some cloth I overheard some of the men talking about an attack."

"And since when do you speak Arabic?" asked Rafi, the know-it-all son of Timur.

"I've learned so I could deal with the Arabs in the market."

"The only way we'll have peace is if we trust each other," said Udi.

"The way the Jews in Hebron trusted them?" chimed in Benny, who had taken his father Enoch's place as bee keeper.

"That was years ago," Rafi protested.

Benny held his fingers in front of Rafi's face. "We cannot even go to pray at the Western Wall in Jerusalem anymore because our friends complained to the British about our holiday observances."

"Listen to me, all of you," shouted Motel. "We can't afford to take any chances. We must be prepared for an attack. If one comes, we will be ready for them; if it does not, so much the better. We will have lost nothing."

My Motel, a leader, a fighter? I have to admit, he was inspiring me a little bit. I walked to his side and patted him on the shoulder.

"Motel's right. We never thought our village in Russia would be the scene of a pogrom, that the neighbors we had lived with peacefully for years would turn on us, but we were wrong. There we were a tiny minority and could do nothing to protect ourselves. Here, here in our homeland, it is different. Here we can defend ourselves. We must!"

"But the Bible says to love your neighbor as yourself," said Rafi.

"All of a sudden the socialists are quoting the Bible to me? The Good Book also says that if a man comes at you with a sword, you should kiss him with the steel of your sword."

"It does?"

"Rafi, do you remember how Moses killed the Egyptian who was beating a slave?" Motel asked. "The Rambam says every Jew is obligated to rescue any victim of violence from the pursuer, even at the possible expense of the pursuer's life."

"Excuse me, but are you expecting trouble," a British officer said from behind me. Soldiers were fanning out behind him, picking at the dirt with the ends of their rifles.

"Motel was in the Arab village today and says he heard the Arabs are planning an attack," replied Udi.

"Really? I've heard of no such plan. You should know that there is really nothing to worry about. My men will protect you from any harm."

"The way you protected the Jews in Hebron?" said Benny.

"There was nothing we could do in Hebron. By the time we got there the Arabs had left."

"And why did you disarm the Jews who tried to defend the city?"

Benny had not learned to speak to officials with the proper deference. In Russia, challenging a soldier in such a manner would be grounds for arrest, if not execution. I was surprised by the Englishman's calm demeanor.

"Now you all know it's illegal to carry weapons. We were simply doing our duty. How can you expect the Arabs to accept you if they are afraid you will attack them?"

"Attack them?" I said.

"Yes, that's what they fear. As the mandatory power in Palestine, it is our duty to keep the peace, so I will have to insist that you make no effort to obtain weapons; otherwise, we will have to confiscate them. If you don't mind, I have orders to search the kibbutz. Good day, gentlemen."

"Good day," we answered politely, helplessly watching the soldiers enter our homes.

"You might as well follow them. You're probably going to have a big mess to clean up after they leave," I said to the other *chaverim.*

As they left, I shook Motel's hand. He had a surprised look on his face. "What's wrong?" I asked.

"Well, it's just that I never felt such warmth from you before, Papa. You know, when I wanted to marry Tzeitl, you were not exactly thrilled."

"Could you blame me? You made your own match! Whoever heard of such a thing back then? Now, well, now the papa is lucky if he gets invited to the wedding, let alone have a say in the partners for their children. I wanted a scholar, and Golde dreamed of a wealthy man to marry our daughter and you, forgive me for saying it, were neither."

"I know, but I promised your daughter would not starve and I kept that vow."

"Yes you did. And you did more, much more. You are rich in spirit. Don't tell anyone I said this, because I'll deny it, but you have made me very proud. I'm glad that you married Tzeitl."

"Thank you, Reb Tevye," Motel said, kissing me hard on both cheeks. "You don't know how much it means to me to hear you say that."

"Remember, you didn't hear it from me," I said, and slapped him on the back the way Moshe and Simcha did to me. "Now go home to my daughter and grandchildren. Enjoy them. They are treasures."

"I will," he said and ran off.

He looked back at me with a smile to rival Simcha's and then tripped over a flower pot. He shakily got to his feet and shrugged his shoulders before turning and racing to his house as if it were on fire.

Well, he hasn't changed completely.

"You work in mysterious ways, Lord."

Later that evening, when I got back to my room and climbed in bed with Golde, I was still thinking about the discussion among the *chaverim*.

"You know," I said, "that Motel has turned out to be quite a man."

"Motel? Tzeitl's Motel? The tailor Motel?"

"Yes, Motel, Tzeitl's Motel, the tailor Motel. Do you know any other Motels?"

"I've always thought he was a nice boy, a little thin maybe, and not such a scholar and —"

"Not so rich. I know. But he has grown and matured. You should have heard him today talking about standing up to the Arabs and protecting the kibbutz. Whoops."

"What do you mean protect the kibbutz?"

"Did I say protect? I meant project. The new project on the kibbutz."

"Tevye."

"All right, all right. You know I can't lie to you. We are building a new fence around the kibbutz in preparation for Hodel's wedding. Motel said some of the women were complaining that the Arab men from the village come to watch our weddings and stare at them."

"Oh. You're right. *My* Motel has become a good man. Not many would show such concern for the feelings of women. You wouldn't."

"How can you say that?"

"I've known you a long time."

26

Our British friends searched the kibbutz and originally found nothing. For some reason, though, they returned the next day and seemed to know exactly where to go to find a cache of small arms Moshe had hidden in the garden behind the dining hall.

"We warned you against building private arsenals," the British commander said as he supervised the confiscation of the weapons.

To everyone's surprise, he then pointed at Simcha. "Cuff that man. He's coming with us."

"What?" Hodel screamed.

I was in shock. Another of my daughter's loves being carted off to jail. How do they have such luck?

"There must be some mistake," I said. Everyone knew Simcha was about the most peaceful soul on earth, but I knew I couldn't explain that to the police. I certainly couldn't tell them that Moshe was the one who had brought the guns. Fortunately, Moshe was back in Tel Aviv with his Haganah unit.

"Yes, there has been a mistake," the Englishman answered. "And you all made it by hiding these guns. Someone must be held accountable and I'm told this man is your leader."

"We have no leader. We all share in the responsibility for the kibbutz," Hodel said, pushing her way to stand directly in front of the commander.

"Would you prefer that we arrest everyone?"

"Yes," Hodel answered.

The officer considered that for a moment. Then probably realized the British didn't need the bad publicity that would come from putting the membership of an entire kibbutz in jail.

"That won't be necessary."

"Then take me," Hodel said.

Golde gasped.

"What are you doing?" I whispered and gestured for Hodel to step back.

The commander stared at my daughter warily. "It's commendable that you are willing to stand up for your friends."

"It is my duty, just as it is the *kevutzah's* obligation to obtain the means to defend ourselves."

"All right," the Englishman said, waving his finger at her almost dismissively. "Take her too."

One of his men started to put handcuffs on Hodel. Golde dug her fingernails into my arm so hard I thought blood would spurt out.

"That won't be necessary," the commander said, and the soldier put the handcuffs away.

Then the soldiers took Hodel and Simcha to a car and put them in the backseat. A few minutes later they were gone.

Golde started sobbing.

"What should we do?" Eitan asked.

"First, we'll contact Moshe," Motel said, suddenly taking charge. "He'll know what to do. It won't do us any good to worry in the meantime. The good news is they didn't find most of our weapons. I just don't understand how they knew to look in the garden."

Everyone had the same thought, that someone had betrayed us, but no one could bring themselves to utter the words aloud.

"All right, everyone go back to their work," Motel ordered, sounding every bit as forceful as Jonathan when he was our unquestioned leader. "We'll meet tonight to discuss what needs to be done. I'll try to reach Moshe."

Everyone shuffled back to their jobs, mumbling amongst themselves, wondering who could have done such a terrible thing.

As Golde and I walked back to our room, I thought that our family had been cursed and I vowed never to agree to any more weddings. I wonder if Hodel noticed the tendency for her mates to land in jail. Knowing Hodel, she'll probably arrange to marry Simcha in prison.

I went into the bedroom to change clothes. Golde just sat in a chair staring out the window and wringing her hands.

Sarah suddenly burst in, shouting, "Oh Mama!"

When I came to see what was the matter I found Sarah crying hysterically. She was kneeling at Golde's feet.

"What have I done? What have I done? Oh Mama, what have I done?"

"What's wrong, Saraleh?" Golde said, stroking her head. "Hodel will be home soon. I'm sure the British won't put her in prison."

"That's not it," she sobbed, shaking her head as though she didn't want to be comforted.

"Then what?" Golde asked.

"I was the one who betrayed the kibbutz."

"What?" I was so shocked I could barely speak.

"I did it, Papa," Sarah said, crawling to put her arms around my knees. "Oh, I'm so ashamed." She choked back the tears for a moment. "I told the British officer where the guns were hidden and that Simcha was responsible."

Golde gasped.

"But why? You know we need those guns to protect ourselves. And turning in Simcha?"

"Forgive me, Papa. Please, forgive me. I was so jealous of Hodel. Ever since she came, everyone has done nothing but talk about how brave my sister is, how smart, how this, how that. And then Simcha rejected me and chose Hodel. After all those years of waiting for him. I was angry. I was hurt. I —"

"You've done a terrible thing, Sarah. In your desire to hurt your sister, you've endangered the whole kibbutz."

"But I didn't tell them where the rest of our guns are hidden."

"It doesn't matter," I said. "And to bear false witness? You have falsely accused Simcha and he may now be sent to prison."

"I know, Papa, I know. I'll go to the police. I'll tell them that I smuggled the guns to the kibbutz. I'll say they should arrest me instead."

Golde came over and drew Sarah to her breast.

"There, there child. You'll do nothing of the kind. We will find a solution. Don't worry."

Golde was looking up at me over Sarah's shoulder with an expression of hopefulness.

How could my own daughter have done such a thing? I knew she was upset by the attention Hodel was receiving, but who could imagine this would be her reaction?

"Oh Papa, forgive me. Please, forgive me," Sarah said, dropping to the floor and grabbing my legs again.

"It's all right," I said, bending down to take her arms and lift her off the ground. "As your mother said, we will find an answer. But it is not I that must forgive you. You must ask forgiveness from the entire kibbutz and, most importantly, from Hodel and Simcha."

"But I'm so ashamed. How can I face any of them again?"

I lifted her chin with my fingers and gazed into the cloudy green eyes. "Repentance is not supposed to be easy. You have done a terrible thing, and the punishment should be much worse than to simply apologize. To tell you the truth, I don't know how the *chaverim* will react. They might decide to expel you from the kibbutz."

"No!" Golde yelled. "Not after we've finally got our family together."

"Like everything else, it will be up to the committee," I said, scared of how the membership might react.

Sarah swallowed hard. "All right, Papa. I'll do it. Tonight, when Motel calls the meeting."

She started to walk away. I pulled her back and hugged her tightly.

"It will be okay, Sarah. As the rabbi said, 'If her mouth had spoken falsehood, let it now be opened in wisdom.'"

That evening Shmuel rang the bell for our meeting. We all filed into the dining hall. Golde and I sat in the front, with our family beside us — all of us, that is, except for Sarah.

I was once again impressed by Motel's assertion of authority as he stood behind the podium and held his hands up asking for quiet.

"*Chaverim*! Please! Please!"

The room slowly grew silent.

"I was unable to get in touch with Moshe. I'm afraid he is on a mission and can't be reached at the moment."

People groaned.

"But I did contact Bernice. She was outraged by the British actions and said she would immediately lead a delegation from the Agency to complain to the High Commissioner."

The groans turned to cheers. The American had long ago earned everyone's respect for her political skills.

"Until we hear from her —"

"Wait, I must speak!" Sarah shouted from the doorway.

"Sarah, we're in the middle —"

"I know Motel and what I have to say must be said here and now to everyone."

I don't think pride is the right word to express what I felt as Sarah strode to the podium, but it was certainly a good feeling knowing she was doing the right thing, despite the embarrassment.

"My friends and family, I have something to tell you," Sarah began. "The reason the British came here today and found the guns in the flowerbed is that I told them they were there."

Some people gasped, others shouted, "What!" or "Why?"

"There is more. I also told them Simcha was responsible."

There was near bedlam in the room as people began yelling and cursing.

"Quiet! Quiet!" Motel screamed, trying to be heard over the tumult. "I said quiet!"

When the room was still, Sarah continued. "I know you are wondering why I would do such a horrible thing. I have no excuse. If it is your will, I am prepared to leave the kibbutz as punishment."

Golde bit her knuckles. Tears covered her face. I sat and chewed my lip.

"But first I wanted to stand before you and beg for your forgiveness. Please, forgive a foolish woman for letting jealousy blind her."

"Forgive? How can we forgive such treason?" Laban shouted. "What you've done is indefensible. I move that Sarah be immediately expelled from the kibbutz."

"I second the motion," Timur said quickly.

The room was again erupting in chaos.

"She's my daughter. I take responsibility," I said, jumping from my seat.

Now people who I had called family for years suddenly began calling for my expulsion.

"No, Papa. I am old enough to be accountable for my actions," Sarah yelled.

"Stop! Everyone stop!" Motel was screaming and banging his fist on the podium. "Stop!"

"You should not talk, Motel, you're related," Laban said.

"We are all related!" Motel shot back angrily. "We are all family. And what does a family do when one of its members commits a sin, even a grievous one? Does it banish that person? Does it cease loving them?"

I listened to Motel and my thoughts immediately went from one daughter to another, one who I had indeed banished.

"No! That is not what our sages teach us. We believe in *teshuva*, repentance. If God can absolve us of our sins against Him, how can we be any less forgiving?"

"That's my Motel," I whispered, elbowing Golde in the ribs.

"Our tradition says that a sinner must recognize her sin. Sarah has done that. She must also show remorse. I believe that coming here, in front of all of us, is an honest sign of contrition. But this is not enough. She must resolve never to commit this sin again. Sarah?"

"I will never do anything to harm anyone on the kibbutz again. I swear."

"That is still not sufficient. The sinner must also undo the damage. To tell you the truth," Motel said, turning to his sister-in-law, "I'm not sure how you can do that Sarah."

"I still say we should expel her," Timur shouted. "Let's vote."

"I will go with Bernice to see the High Commissioner," Sarah shouted. "And I will see that the guns that were confiscated are replaced."

"How will you do that?" Laban asked.

"Don't worry. I will do it."

"Let's vote," Timur said again. "The motion for expulsion has been made and seconded."

"All right," Motel said. "We will vote. But this will not be a secret ballot. If you are going to vote to expel a member of the family, you must do it publicly. One more thing. Before we vote, I want to remind everyone that withholding forgiveness is cruel and is considered a sin by God."

Sarah just stood beside Motel staring at her feet. I looked around the room. Other than Laban and Timur, who seemed determined to evict my daughter, I could not read the faces of the others. Sarah's sisters were all holding hands and praying under their breath. Golde had stopped crying and wiped her eyes.

"All right, all those who believe we should forgive Sarah and allow her to stay on the kibbutz, raise your hands."

I raised my hand as did the rest of the family. I slowly turned, afraid to see what the rest of the *chaverim* were doing. No one else had their hand up. These were our friends, our family, since we arrived in Palestine. They might as well drive a stake through my heart.

Chana slowly raised her hand. Then Oren. Then Enoch. The few hands that went up slowly were suddenly matched by others. Now it seemed that everyone was raising their hands without hesitating.

I strained to see through the sea of arms. Timur and Laban had their hands in their laps. They looked at each other, and then raised their hands.

"I don't think we need to consider the alternative," Motel said. "Sarah may stay."

"Thank you, thank you," Sarah said in a barely audible whisper through her tears.

"You know something, Tevye." Golde said. "That Motel *is* a person."

27

The kibbutz forgave Sarah for what she did, but the *chaverim* will never forget. Most behaved coldly toward her after the apology. Timur, Laban and a few others treated her like a pariah. Fortunately, most of the people who were close to Sarah remained her friends.

Sarah also kept her word about replacing the guns we had lost. A few days after her admission, she came back with Yossi, Dr. Susser's son, who was now one of the top-ranking officers in the Haganah. Yossi brought twice as many guns as the British had confiscated.

As it turned out, she didn't need to do anything for Hodel. The British released her the next day. It was a little tougher to extricate Simcha. Bernice didn't want Sarah admitting anything or trying to take the blame. Instead, the American used her charm on the High Commissioner and explained that she lived for many years on the same kibbutz and could vouch for Simcha's character. The Englishman wanted to make an example of Simcha, but could see that Bernice would never give him a moment's peace, so he agreed to reduce his sentence.

Sarah was allowed to visit Simcha and apologized for what she'd done. Not surprisingly, he forgave her. I was less sure of Hodel's reaction. She had a military bearing from her days with Pertschik and, afterwards, organizing resistance to Lenin, so I feared she might see Sarah's acts as treasonous, the way Laban and Timur viewed them.

I needn't have worried. Hodel knew what it was like to be jealous of a sister. When she was a child, she had resented what she saw as the favoritism we showed toward Tzeitl. All the years of being separated from her family also made her determined never to allow anything to come between her and her sisters and parents again. Hodel was only upset about the effect of the affair on the morale of the kibbutz, but now she saw a new challenge, rebuilding the camaraderie and preparing everyone for the fight we all felt was coming.

One thing that helped everyone emerge from the gloom that had fallen over the kibbutz since Hodel and Simcha's arrest was the arrival of one of our most joyous holidays, Chanukah, which commemorates the victory of the Maccabees over the Syrian emperor Antiochus. Recalling the story of how a small group of revolutionaries — led by a Jew named Mattathias and his son Judah — defeated an enemy who was trying to destroy them, reminded all of us that we could prevail over the Arabs.

According to our tradition, when the Maccabees recaptured the Temple, they found that Antiochus had desecrated it. They needed oil to purify the Temple, but found only enough to burn for one night. Miraculously, it burned for eight, so we celebrate the holiday for eight days.

We have always kindled candles, one for each night, plus a *shamash* used for lighting, and placed them in a *menorah*. On the kibbutz we have another tradition. At night, bonfires are ignited in the fields with a torch that is passed from one *chaver* to another. This was the way Jews once celebrated victory in battle and spread the news throughout the country.

After the fires were all ablaze, the children began a procession, carrying their own torches. Our little kibbutz band played from a stage we'd constructed for a production my Rachel had written about the Maccabees. She'd been so excited all week, I could barely talk to her. Abraham was excited too, because his sister asked him to play Judah Maccabee.

I remember, during our first years on the kibbutz, worrying how our children would know what it means to be Jewish, growing up without prayers three times a day or hours of study. How would the use of a hoe or an ax or a plough provide a moral guide for their lives? But they could not escape their heritage, not here in our homeland. So even though little Abraham will not have the education that I had, I am not concerned. He will understand what it means to be a Jew, as will Rachel.

I've learned that, even here, on the kibbutz, we are infused with the spirit of the Lord. Rav Kook was correct when he said the spirit of Israel is so closely linked to the spirit of God that even the most secular nationalist is imbued with the divine spirit, even against his own will. Here in this land that God promised us, He is everywhere. He is in the soil that runs through our fingers, the water that we drink, the food that we eat and the air that we breathe.

And maybe because my comrades realize this too, they have taken a greater interest in studying. In the beginning, I often studied alone. When more people joined me, the sessions became so contentious Jonathan told me to stop them. Slowly I began to invite selected *chaverim* to study with me. Now, sometimes the entire kibbutz, all right, everyone but Uzi and Eitan, will sit together to study the *parsha*. Yes, even the women will join us, God forgive me.

Now that we have firmly established ourselves in our homeland, I've noticed a greater thirst for the wisdom of the sages, a desire for a better understanding for what brought us to this place. Celebrating holidays like this helps.

I watched the youngest children march past the adults first singing, *Am Yisrael Chai*, "The Jewish people lives." They are the hope of the future, the ones who will carry the torch for our people.

The older children are coming now. They look like a small army in matching, well nearly matching, khaki shorts and shirts, with white socks and blue hats. Rachel is staring straight ahead. I think she's too nervous to look over here. Abraham is in his costume. As he passed, he waved his wooden sword.

Slowly all the children made their way to the stage. Now there are so many! We've certainly done our share to be fruitful and multiply, but a lot of the kids came with Devorah from Germany. It broke my heart to know that their parents had sent them to Palestine knowing they might never see them again. These little angels are now as close to their kibbutz families as the ones they left behind. None of us want to think about their parents' fate, but we are very concerned by reports that Hitler is imposing new hardships on the Jews.

But this is too happy a moment to dwell on such things. We have enough time for evil tidings after the *chag*.

I was waiting for the children on stage to begin singing the songs they'd rehearsed when Natan pointed to where the children had come from and shouted, "Look!"

Everyone turned. A flickering glow could be seen moving through the darkness. Rafi and Benny took their rifles off their backs and aimed them in the direction of the light.

I held my breath. We all did.

Then I raced over to Rafi and Benny and pushed the barrels of their guns toward the ground.

A man came out of the darkness holding a torch. He was smiling.

"Did I miss anything?" Simcha asked.

"I guess we had our own miracle this year," I said.

28

Miracles don't last forever. The Red Sea closed, manna stopped falling from the heavens, and the Temple was destroyed.

Once again, my friend Sheikh Jabber proved prophetic when he predicted it would only be a matter of time before the Arabs exploded again. We had been lulled into a false sense of security by the tranquility of the past several years, and emboldened by the arrival of thousands of Jews from Germany and other lands. Despite the continued duplicity of the British, Bernice said the prospect of independence was on the horizon.

Then Arab bandits stopped a bus and killed two Jews. Violence soon spread. Jews were attacked in Jaffa, Beit She'an, and Hebron. Thousands fled their homes. The British imposed a curfew on the cities. The Mufti responded by calling for an Arab strike, which paralyzed the government.

Strangely enough, the Jews have benefitted from the strike. In many places, Jews had hired cheap Arab labor to do their work in the fields and orchards. For those Jews, evading work was more important than becoming one with the land. The Arab boycott has forced them to do their own planting and harvesting.

It soon became clear the strike was not having any impact on British immigration policy — Jews were still arriving in Palestine — so the Mufti's henchmen returned to violence. Our little kibbutz became an island fortress that we rarely left.

So here I am again, sweltering in the field. Simcha finally agreed that I am getting too old to ride a tractor and promised to move me to another job, but, as usual, the wheels of the kibbutz bureaucracy turn slowly and nothing has changed.

My darling twins are playing soccer in a fallow area just beyond the edge of this field. They're waving to me. I waved back and nearly fell off the tractor. I could see they were laughing and shouting, but the sound was drowned out by the tractor. I probably wouldn't have heard them anyway, since I've started plugging my ears with cotton to try to prevent the engine noise from driving me insane.

As I turned away from them to plow the other direction, I saw Abraham kick the ball so hard it flew past Rachel's head and over the kibbutz fence. I didn't think anything of it and rode off toward the far end of the field.

I'm not exactly sure what happened next. We've pieced it together and have a pretty good idea, but I have trouble talking about it. I've prayed for God to blot if from my memory, but it is the curse of the living to remember our nightmares and to forget too easily the joyous moments.

Apparently Rachel slipped through a gap in the fence to look for the ball. It had rolled down the hill, behind some rocks and into the weeds. She was gone for a long time and didn't respond when Abraham made jokes about her getting lost. When Rachel didn't answer when he called to her, Abraham finally became concerned and went after her.

When he got down the hill . . .

"Please God, don't make me repeat it. Don't even let me think it."

I can't make the memory go away. When Abraham came out from behind one of the rocks, he saw two Arabs holding Rachel down on the ground. One had his hand over her mouth. Her shorts were ripped and a third Arab was between her legs.

The Arabs were much older and bigger than Abraham, but he acted on impulse and charged the boy on top of Rachel. Before the Arab knew what was happening, Abraham had knocked him to the ground and was punching him with all his might. The other two Arabs came to their friend's rescue and pulled Abraham away. My son screamed, "Papa! Papa!" but God closed my ears to his cries. "Forgive me, Lord," but I could not hear anything over the roar of the tractor.

Abraham fought the two boys like a lion, but they were too strong for him and finally knocked him unconscious with a rock. One was about to stab him with a knife when Udi raced to the scene. He was on guard duty along the perimeter and heard my son shrieking for help.

Udi dashed down the hill and fired his rifle at the Arabs. The shot missed, but it sent them into a panic. The two boys who had beaten Abraham picked up their fallen comrade and dragged him off. By the time Udi reached my children, the Arabs had escaped.

The shot was loud enough to penetrate my ear plugs. I turned off the tractor and listened. Then I heard Udi shouting for help and saw him appear on the other side of the fence. He was shooting his rifle in the air like a madman.

I looked around for Abraham and Rachel and realized immediately that the worst had happened. I jumped down from the tractor and twisted my ankle. The pain was excruciating, but I ran as I had never done before toward the fence.

Udi fired two more shots in the air. In the distance, Shmuel began to ring the alarm.

When I reached the fence, I started to climb, but Udi pointed to the opening the children had crawled through and I got on my stomach, held my breath and slithered through. He led me down the hill. The sight that greeted me was the most horrible I think I have ever seen. If *gehenna* exists, I can't imagine it being any worse than the place I was standing.

Beside one rock was my beloved Rachel, her blouse torn and her pants ripped off. I could see her eyes were open, but wasn't sure if she was breathing. She just lay on the ground lifelessly. A few feet away, my only son was sprawled in the weeds, his head bleeding and looking no more alive than his sister.

I was paralyzed with fear, guilt and indecision. I had turned away and not seen them leave the safety of the kibbutz. Now, because I had failed to warn them against going outside the fence, they could be dead. I looked from one to the other, unable to move. They were both my children and I didn't know who to go to first.

"Check on Abraham!" Udi screamed.

He had to say it twice before I realized he was talking to me. By then he was leaning over Rachel and helping her to sit up. I could see that she was alive, but she looked at me as if I wasn't there.

"Tevye!" Udi shouted again. "Put something around his head to stop the bleeding."

I ran over to my son, pulling my handkerchief out as I knelt beside him. My heart nearly leapt out of my throat when I saw his chest move. I wrapped the handkerchief around his head.

"Abraham, Abraham," I said softly. "Speak to me, Abraham."

He didn't answer.

A few moments later, we were surrounded. Rafi helped me to my feet as several other *chaverim* lifted Abraham. I saw others doing the same for Rachel.

"They'll be all right," I heard someone say, but the words just floated through the air and past me like desert sand in the wind.

I followed my friends as they carried the limp bodies of my children toward the infirmary as though I was in a daze.

"What's happened?" Simcha shouted, sprinting over to me. "Oh no," he said when he saw the children.

Simcha saw me, but I didn't see him.

"Tevye, Tevye." He put his arm around me and I started to collapse. "Come, my friend. You have shouldered the burdens of the kibbutz for many years, let me carry you."

Then with strength I didn't know he possessed, Simcha lifted me onto his back and carried me to the infirmary.

By the time we reached it, the whole kibbutz was in the court-yard. I was aware of bodies encircling me, but their faces were a blur. Then I heard a scream.

"Rachel! Abraham!" Golde came running. "Oh God of Abraham, Isaac and Jacob, what has happened to my babies?"

"They'll be all right," I heard a voice say.

"Tevye. What's happened? Are you all right?"

This I heard clearly, because Golde shouted directly into my ear. I was able to stand and Simcha let me down. I saw that Tzeitl, Hodel, Sarah and Motel were behind Golde staring at me. Tears were running down their faces.

"What happened to the children, Tevye?"

I started to speak, but no words left my mouth.

"Come Golde," Simcha said, let's wait outside the infirmary while Dr. Susser works his magic.

I felt Simcha's arm around my back carrying me along. His other arm was around Golde. The next thing I knew we were all sitting on the porch of the infirmary. Golde jumped up immediately and started to go inside, but Simcha put his hand up.

"But they're my children," she sobbed.

"It's okay, Mama," Tzeitl said, embracing Golde. "We can't do anything for them inside. Let's stay here and pray."

"Oh Merciful God," Motel said, "You have blessed this family with these beautiful children. Do not take them from us before their time. They have not yet begun to serve You."

I looked at Motel and somehow knew that God was listening to him.

"You have reunited our family here in the land You promised to our people. You have watched over us all these years. Do not forsake us now."

"Amen," dozens of voices said in unison.

Only then did I realize virtually the entire kibbutz, from Simcha to Chana to the atheists Eitan and Uzi were standing outside the infirmary praying with us. I don't know if it was the power of that collective prayer, of if they had been written into the Book of Life at Yom Kippur, but God spared my children and for that I will be eternally grateful.

It seemed like days, but it was only a few hours before Dr. Susser came out. "They'll be all right," he shouted to the crowd.

Some people applauded, others just sighed with relief. I heard voices saying, "Praise the Lord."

"Tevye, you and Golde can come in, but I'd like the rest of you to wait a little longer," Dr. Susser said.

Hodel started to protest, but he just put his finger to his lips and she kept silent.

Golde and I followed the doctor. When we were just inside the door, he pulled us aside.

"What's wrong?" Golde said, panicking instantly.

"I just want to explain their condition before you see them. I think Abraham will be fine. He was hit pretty hard on the head, but, fortunately, like his father, that's the hardest part of his body. I stitched up the gash and put a bandage around his head. I think he's got a concussion and I'd like to keep him here for a couple of days so I can keep an eye on him, just to be safe. He'll probably be out running around like before by the end of the week."

A sense of relief shot through me like a thunder bolt, but I sensed the news was not as good for Rachel.

"Rachel was not seriously injured. She suffered some cuts and bruises from being thrown on the ground and struggling." He stopped speaking and looked at the ground. "I don't know how to tell you."

"I know," I interrupted.

"You know what?" Golde said. Her eyes looked like they would burst from their sockets.

"The Arabs who did this," I stuttered. "They —"

"Oh my God!" she put her hand over her mouth. "Oh my God!" She fell on the floor and started crying hysterically, "No, no, no, no."

I sat on the floor and cradled her in my arms. She continued to wail "no, no, no, no. Not my baby. Not my baby."

"Physically, she will be all right," Dr. Susser said gently. "Psychologically, she's still in shock. Even when she's feeling up to leaving the infirmary, Rachel is going to need a lot of attention, and a lot of love. I'm not sure how someone gets over something like this, but I do know the mind is an amazing instrument and, with help, any trauma can be overcome. But it will not do her any good if you go to pieces. She needs you to be strong and loving. You saw all the *chaverim* out there tonight with you; they will stand by you, and by Rachel, through her recovery. She is not alone, and you are not alone. Remember that."

I kissed Golde's head and looked up at the doctor. I felt tears dripping off my cheeks. "Can we see them?"

"Yes, of course. But don't expect them to speak. Abraham is sleeping and —"

"And what?"

"And I don't think Rachel is ready to talk yet. Give her time."

"Come Golde," I said, and helped her stand.

We both wiped the tears from our faces and walked to the beds where our children lay still, the only sign of life was the movement of the blankets covering chests as they breathed.

My son, my only son, Abraham, had a bandage around his head. He could have run and left his sister, or yelled for help, but he stood and fought like Judah Maccabee to protect Rachel. I couldn't think of a more courageous act. I have been truly blessed.

Golde sat on the side of the bed and stroked his face. "Abraham, this is your Mama. You did a brave thing today, and God will reward you. And so will I. When you come home, I'll bake something special for you, cookies with carob chips, your favorite." She leaned over and kissed his cheek.

I bent down and kissed his head.

We moved over to Rachel's bed. We expected her to also be sleeping, but her eyes were open.

"Rachel? Rachel, are you in pain?" Golde asked.

My daughter just stared straight ahead and gave no indication she heard Golde.

I knelt beside her bed and spoke softly into her ear. "Rachel, it's Papa. I have a new book that I think that you will like. It's a collection of Bialik's poems. Maybe I can bring it later and read them to you. Would you like that?"

She remained motionless. Her lifeless eyes gazing at the ceiling scared me.

"What's wrong with her eyes?" I whispered to Dr. Susser.

"She's awake, but as I told you she's in shock. What happened to her was such a trauma that her mind has shut down so she doesn't have to think about it."

"But how can she live that way?"

"As I said, physically, she's all right. Her brain is fine. It's just going to take awhile for her to recover."

"How long?" Golde asked.

"You're going to have to be patient. I can't tell you."

"Hours? Days?"

Dr. Susser looked at his shoes again and took a deep breath.

"Longer?"

"I just don't know. No one does, except God."

"Oh Tevye," Golde broke down again and fell against me.

I stared at Dr. Susser, but he just looked at me helplessly. Then I turned to my bruised and bandaged children and began a silent prayer.

29

"Dear Lord, why have You chosen to torment me? Have I failed You in some way? If so, why don't You put out my eyes, or cut out my tongue or take one of my limbs? Why must You take Your wrath out on my poor children? Wasn't it enough to take Pertschik from us? Did You have to also lead Chava astray? Was it necessary to Your great plan that You should torture poor Shoshana to the point she took her own life? *Dayenu!* It should have been enough! Couldn't You have spared the twins — my only son and precious daughter?"

"Who am I to question Your wisdom, Your plan? Forgive me Lord for being but a simple man who wishes to be Your servant, but I cannot understand why You have chosen to afflict my family with plagues like those you brought upon Pharaoh. Why, oh Lord? Why?"

Here I am, standing in a field in the middle of the night shouting at the Master of the Universe. No matter how loudly I scream, He refuses to answer.

I'm afraid that God has not meant for Tevye and his family to find happiness for more than a few moments at a time. Every time it looks as though we have overcome one tragedy, the Almighty sends us a message that we should not be as foolish as to take for granted His good favor.

No one can bear to speak about what happened to the twins, so it is simply referred to as "the incident." I wish that I could report that the passage of months and years has blotted out the memory, but it has not. Who can forget when I see my dear Rachel each day, sitting in the corner staring out the same window? I don't know what she sees, or if she can see anything at all. Oh, Dr. Susser tells us her eyesight is fine, but the blank look on her face makes her appear blind.

Golde sits by her side, stroking her hand for hours and reciting the twenty-third psalm. Sometimes Sarah combs her hair and Tzeitl's children read to her. We can't tell if she hears any more than she sees. Not even sudden loud noises seem to affect her.

This was a child who laughed and played as though the kibbutz was nothing more than a playground for her amusement. I can still see her dancing and singing, telling us how someday she would move to Hollywood and become a famous movie actress. She would talk nonstop about the glamorous life she would lead, and the things she would buy. Abraham used to tease her about being bourgeoisie and failing to live up to the ideals of the kibbutz. But she never backed down. She'd tell him that God could be served in many ways, and hers would be to bring joy to millions through her acting.

My twittering little bird could not be discouraged, but now she has been silenced. The light that shone from within her was snuffed out by the incident. She has not spoken a word since that day and Dr. Susser now admits she may never speak again.

Whenever I thought about what happened to Rachel, I would cry. For months I couldn't sleep and did everything I knew to try to communicate with my precious little girl. Nothing worked. I feel so wracked with guilt, knowing that if I'd been paying closer attention, or heard their cries, I might have prevented it all. I can rage at Chaim and his father, and blame them for the death of

Shoshana, but I blame only myself for what has happened to little Rachel.

I know there is no perfect happiness in this world, that even our father Abraham had to suffer. After God spared his son Isaac, Abraham returned to find his wife Sarah dead. Why don't I find comfort in this knowledge?

"I try, Lord I try, not to lose faith, but this time I wonder if You have finally found a test for me that I cannot pass. How could You allow such a thing to happen to an innocent girl? How? Forgive me for questioning You, the Creator of the Universe, but after all that my family has gone through, surely I deserve to ask how Your divine plan is served by heaping misery on poor Tevye and his children. Were the few years of happiness and tranquility we enjoyed after You reunited our family all we are to be permitted?"

Do I sound bitter toward God? You're right, I should not be. It was not God who raped my daughter, it was men, despicable men who deserve a hundred times the torment they have inflicted upon Rachel. How can we share this land with such people? There must be a way for us to live together or we will be doomed to fight for an eternity.

I am not ready to give up yet, not even after the incident. I still have hope.

The incident did not leave any lasting physical scars on Abraham, thank God, but it did something perhaps worse, it seared his heart with hatred. When he explained what had happened to Rachel, he did not cry or show grief, he only expressed anger. I could see the blood rush to his face and his fists and teeth clench as he recalled the horrible scene.

"I will have my revenge," he said coldly, "if I have to kill every Arab in Palestine."

I tried to talk to him, to convince him that violence is not the answer, that God will render judgment on the rapists. He would not even listen. Instead, he would say the Arabs were beasts who should be hunted like other wild animals. As the Arab revolt escalated, it was impossible to change his mind. Jews were being killed around the country, the railroad was paralyzed, even the Old City of Jerusalem was in danger of being lost.

One day, Abraham announced he was leaving to join his sister in the Haganah. Golde pleaded with him to stay. I thought he was too young to fight, but I knew better than to say anything. I tried to convince him he could be more helpful defending the kibbutz, but he said he wasn't interested in sitting back and waiting for the Arabs to attack. He wanted to go on the offensive. He said he'd heard of a British officer who was training Jews to carry out raids on the Arabs and to take the battle to them, even going so far as to cross into Lebanon and Syria.

"For every day of my sister's pain, I will inflict a hundredfold agony on the Arabs," he said.

What could I say to ease his bitterness?

"Abraham, the Bible says, 'Do not say, I will repay evil; but wait on the Lord, and he shall save you.'"

Abraham came to me and said, "I'm sorry, Papa. I must go. If there was any purpose in what happened, it was to direct me to fight for our people to ensure that no other Jewish girl has to endure what Rachel has suffered."

He hugged everyone in the family before going over to Rachel. She was sitting in her usual place beside the window, eyes transfixed on some point known only to her. Abraham got down on his knees and took her hands in his. She did not look at him or change expression.

"Rachel," he said softly. "I am going away now, but I'll come back. Even while I'm gone, know that I will be with you in here and here." He gently put his finger on her heart and head. "We are one, in mind, body and spirit, now and forever."

Abraham stood and put his arms around her stiff body and then kissed her on both cheeks. Then my only son turned and walked out of the house.

Once again, a child of Tevye goes his own way. I can only pray that God watches over him and returns him safely to us. I put my arm around Golde. I didn't think she could take it, but she watched him leave without shedding a tear. Maybe she has also cried herself out.

As it happened, whatever revenge Abraham exacts, it will not be on the criminals responsible for the incident. On one of my rare trips outside the kibbutz, I was summoned in the usual way by my friend Sheikh Jabber. When I sat to break bread with him, one of his sons brought out a covered tray. I expected to be served a new Bedouin delicacy; instead, the cover was lifted and what I saw caused me to choke back vomit. The platter held the male organs of three men.

"Nothing can erase the pain inflicted upon your daughter," Ali said for his father, "but we have imposed our punishment for the crime. You should know that we are not all barbarians, and the actions of a few should not make you misunderstand my people."

I was too shocked to speak.

30

You're never too old to work. That's the philosophy here, so even though I don't get around as well as I used to, the Committee still finds some use for me. As the Psalm says, "Cast me not off in the time of old age; forsake me not when my strength fails."

For now, my job is tending the gardens. In Anatevka, I didn't know a weed from a flower, but, slowly, I'm learning. Of course, I've got enough teachers. Maya and her Flower Committee stand over me as though I were handling diamonds instead of dirt.

That's too much water. Not enough water. Clip the bud here, there, everywhere. I may ride the tractor around the garden just to drown them out.

The good news is I can sit here in the shade and relax and no one will look askance, the way they would if a field worker took a break before the scheduled rest. The better news is that I don't have to work as long as I once did, and I finally have the time that I've always dreamed of to study and pray. And I've done a lot of praying since the incident with the twins.

You hope that time will ease the pain, but it doesn't. I can tell you because of the emptiness that's still in my heart even though many years have passed since losing Chava and Shoshana. I try to block out Golde's words about Chavaleh, but I can't ignore them completely. I know she's living in America. At least she is healthy. Poor Shoshana had so little time to enjoy life. From time to time I even wonder what happened to Chaim, may his name be cursed, and his pot-bellied, cigar-smoking father.

It's funny how quickly the days and weeks pass. I look at the cypress trees along the road from the gate to the dining room. I can remember when we planted the saplings and now, now they are towering sources of shade.

Russia seems almost like a childhood memory. We've lived in Palestine nearly twenty years and I can still hardly believe what we've built from the wasteland that was here when we arrived. Our little kibbutz was little more than an oasis at first; today, it is like a small village with wooden homes where there were once tents, gardens and groves where swamps had previously been. The soil has yielded to our backbreaking efforts and now sprouts fruits and vegetables instead of weeds.

Sometimes I feel that I am of little use anymore, but Simcha and the other *vattikim* assure me that in my old age I have an important role to play as teacher. Now I spend most of my time with the young people, sharing what little I know of the Holy Scriptures.

I am ashamed to admit the words do not have the same meaning they did before the incident. Each day I look at poor Rachel, growing older yet never changing. She eats, sleeps, drinks and goes to the bathroom but otherwise shows no signs of life. Our routine has hardly changed. Golde sits and reads or talks to her, and the other children groom her and tell her about what they have done that day. God forgive me, but I have begun to lose hope. I have spent less and less time with her, because I cannot endure the pain of seeing her this way, especially knowing that it is my fault.

As bad as I feel about Rachel, and my behavior toward her, it is at least comforting to know where she is and what she is doing. We have no such reassurance about Devorah and Abraham.

The last we heard, Devorah was still working with the Haganah to smuggle in refugees. The British have become more determined to seal the gates to Palestine, so the work is growing more dangerous.

We are not sure where Abraham is now. From time to time, news reached us about a daring raid the Special Night Squad launched against the Arabs. Apparently, they became too successful for the tastes of His Majesty's Government, and Orde Wingate, the British officer who was training the Jews, was recalled to England.

Next we learned that Abraham was trying to join an elite unit of the Haganah, but that he was also talking to people who formed a new armed group that is more extreme, and wants to more aggressively attack both the British and the Arabs. Already, we have heard this new organization has blown up government buildings in Tel Aviv and Jerusalem and sabotaged the railroad lines.

I'm not sure what these Jewish wild men hope to accomplish by attacking the British. The prime minister poured troops into Palestine to end the Arab revolt, and surely will crush any attempt by the Jews to undermine his authority.

At least most of the violence by the Arabs has subsided, but not before they imposed a heavy price on the *yishuv*. One kibbutz was under almost constant sniper fire and had to repulse an attack by an armed band. Most of the women and children were evacuated and only recently returned. The worst episode, though, was a massacre near Tiberias where nineteen people, including eleven children were killed. Maybe this momentary peace we are now experiencing is just a lull before the real storm.

"Tevye, didn't you hear the bell?" Golde shouted. "It's time for the meeting."

I confess my hearing is not as good as it used to be, but I can still hear that confounded bell when it rings. Of course, it's not the same since Shmuel died. He was buried near his friend Jonathan in the kibbutz cemetery. The bell he had rung for so many years was placed on top of his grave. Now old Laban the Miser has the job and, let me tell you, when it comes to ringing a bell with conviction, he's no Shmuel.

"Come already."

"Golde, what's your hurry?"

"I want to get a good seat. Bernice has come to give us a report."

"Bernice is here?"

"Yes, yes, didn't you hear me? Let's go."

Now that Golde spends less time in the kitchen, she's become a great lover of meetings. She likes to sit in the front row and always asks questions. Not even Natan the Nudnik asks so many questions.

We don't move so quickly anymore, so by the time we reached the dining room it was already nearly full. Our membership has doubled in the last few years and the Membership Committee finally decided to build a new dining room so we don't have to eat in shifts or on top of each other. For the moment, we still have to cram ourselves into what now seems like a closet to hold our meetings.

I saw Bernice follow Simcha up to the microphone. She was wearing another one of her famous flower-patterned dresses, the style that had once caused a furor on the kibbutz because it was a departure from the normal drab peasant clothing. It had been some time since she'd visited. I assumed she was too busy with politics and negotiations and other important matters in the diplomatic battlefield to establish our state. She had put on a great deal of weight and her hair was turning prematurely gray. Like the rest of us, the daily struggle in Palestine was making her age beyond her years.

As Simcha held up his hands for quiet, the people still determined to talk began to mumble, which provoked another group, the shushers, to begin hissing like snakes. Between the mumblers and the shushers, it was impossible to hear anything.

Finally, Eitan stood up and shouted, "*Sheket!*"

That didn't work immediately, so he began banging his cane on the floor while screaming louder, "Quiet!"

I'm not sure if it was his yelling or the fear of the *chaverim* that Eitan might have a heart attack if he had to keep shouting that brought the group to order, but the room fell silent.

"As you can see," Simcha began, "Bernice has returned to give us the latest news from the political front. We will save our other business for next week so she can have our undivided attention for as long as necessary."

He turned to the woman who had become the most powerful and best known female in Palestine. Bernice strode to the microphone and began to speak with the self-assurance and authority that had earned her that fame and influence.

"My friends, my heart is overflowing with joy to be with you tonight. You don't know how much I miss the life I led here, and the opportunity to join you in building our state from the ground up. I hope that in my own small way I am also making a contribution, but for now, I am sorry to say, most of the news is not good."

I looked around the room. Everyone was sitting up, straining to hear Bernice's every word. For many years now, she's been the closest thing we've had to Moses. And like Moses, the reports she brings are rarely all good.

"Since I've been away, I'm not sure how much of the news from Germany has reached you. It is heartbreaking and alarming. Thousands of synagogues have been burned, Jewish businesses have been looted and confiscated, cemeteries have been desecrated and thousands, tens of thousands of Jews have been arrested and sent to prison camps."

The breath caught in my throat and a loud gasp came from the audience. A few people began to weep softly. Over the years, we'd taken in quite a few immigrants from Germany, mostly children, and I could only imagine their fears. I looked over at Golde; she was squeezing her hands together so hard her they were turning red.

"We're trying to get people out, but it's growing more difficult. Other countries are turning a blind eye to what Hitler is doing to the Jews. Even Roosevelt has been silent. And few places are allowing in the Jews who escape. Not even the United States. Now that Germany has invaded Poland, while the world looked the other way, I fear the situation will only grow worse."

People seemed to sink in their seats. I don't think I have seen such looks of despair on the faces of my friends since Jonathan was murdered. After hearing what was happening to our brothers and sisters in Germany, I began to feel ashamed for only thinking about my troubles.

Bernice wasn't finished.

"We had a chance to bring 10,000 children to Palestine and the British refused to give them entry visas. And this, my friends, is why we must have our state! We can count on no one but ourselves. If we can't control immigration and welcome every Jew in the world to their homeland, we will always be subject to the whims of others, and the anti-Semitism of tsars and dictators."

She paused and looked at us with the blazing eyes of a prophet.

"Friends, we have come home and we will build a state," she said, pounding the lectern. "And we *will* welcome every Jew. And we will control our own fate in our own land!"

The room erupted in applause as the members began to sit up straight again, some stood and whistled.

Bernice held up her hands for quiet.

"But," she waited for the noise to die down. "But, it will not be easy, my friends. We have reclaimed our land and we have once again made it flow with milk and honey. We have fought and we have worked and we have built the framework of a nation. But we are still at the mercy of the British and I'm afraid the news is not good on that front either."

People again began to sink in their seats. Our emotions were rising and falling like the Israelites after they were freed from slavery, only to discover Pharaoh' s charioteers were pursuing them into the desert. I was beginning to wonder if it was better not to be aware of what was happening.

"As you know, the Peel Commission suggested partitioning Palestine. According to the plan, the Jews and Arabs would each have states and Jerusalem would remain under British control. Even though the Arabs would be allotted a much larger area, they rejected the proposal. We were not happy with the borders drawn for our state; it would leave us with a tiny fraction of Palestine, especially after the British gave nearly four-fifths of our homeland away to Abdullah. Still, we are willing to negotiate. The Arab position remains that Jewish immigration must be halted and that they be granted independence in all of Palestine."

"Never!" Natan shouted. Others joined in.

Bernice held up her hands again. "Do not worry my friends; we all share your sentiment. The Agency will never accept such an outcome. But I'm afraid the situation is still worse. Our good friend Churchill has now decided the British Government will no longer support the creation of a Jewish state. He has caved into the Arabs and imposed a ceiling of seventy-five thousand immigrants over the next five years. After that, we will require Arab permission before any more Jews will be allowed into Palestine."

"So, what are we going to do about it?" Eitan said. "Is the Agency going to crawl to London and beg for a change in policy? Will Weizmann go to more cocktail parties to ask for a new slap in the face?"

"No one is going to beg for anything!" Bernice said with the kind of controlled fury that allowed her to engage in diplomacy. "I'm told that no one had ever seen Weizmann as angry as when he found out about the new White Paper. Ben-Gurion has said that we will never accept it. We will fight rather than submit to Arab rule, and Ben-Gurion has warned the British that repressing a Jewish rebellion will be as unpleasant a task as the repression of the Arab revolt."

We all started to clap and hoot.

"Ben-Gurion asked me to give you a message. He said, 'We shall fight against Germany as if there were no White Paper, and we shall fight against the White Paper as if there were no war against Germany!'"

She paused to let us applaud again, then continued in a soft, calming voice.

"It will not be an easy battle, my friends. Besides perhaps America, England is the most powerful country in the world and Churchill will not bend unless we force him to. Already, the Colonial Office is retaliating for our smuggling efforts by refusing to grant even the immigration visas provided by the quota. They have become more aggressive in their campaign to disarm our men and to arrest members of the Haganah."

Living in relative isolation on the kibbutz, I had never paid that much attention to our British overseers. I had not bothered them and, except for confiscating some weapons, they had not bothered me. But now, for the first time, I began to grow angry. The more Bernice said, the more I filled with rage.

"We will not be intimidated," she continued, raising her voice again. "As the Bible says, we are a stiff-necked people. We did not let the swamps or the malaria stop us from planting our fields or building our homes. We have not allowed the Arabs to push us off our land and we will not give in to British efforts to prevent the establishment of a Jewish state in our homeland!"

The *chaverim* were in a frenzy now. Bernice really knew how to work a crowd. She let us scream and shout and whistle. All the time, she stood ramrod straight with a determined look on her face and no trace of a smile.

Over the years, I had found Bernice to be one of the warmest human beings I'd ever known, but when she shifted into her politician's mode, she became a different person. That sweet exterior and congenial demeanor changed to razor sharp steel. The feeling of resolve she conveyed gave us all confidence that she spoke the truth. She wasn't finished yet.

"The Haganah is registering all men and women between the ages of eighteen and thirty-five. The time has begun to build a Jewish army and to fight the British policy."

The young people were particularly excited and were jumping up and down even as Bernice continued to speak.

"More than 150 years ago, the American colonists were in a similar position. One small state, not much bigger than Palestine, adopted the motto, 'Live Free or Die.' That will be our credo as well."

"Like most of you, I am not a religious person, but I truly believe that God has promised this land to us and that He will be with us in our fight. And, like that small band of American freedom fighters, we will defeat English tyranny and build an independent nation!"

3 1

I have lived in Palestine many years, but I am beginning to feel the end of my days is nearing. As a rabbi once said, "In youth we run into difficulties; in age, difficulties run into us."

I have reached the point in my life when you begin to need spare parts for things that can't be fixed. My hands are growing stiff and I have trouble holding onto things. The years of doing my horse's work finally have taken a toll on my back. Even my feet hurt. I know this is the way of all things, to wear out eventually, but it would be nice if it didn't happen all at once.

If, as the old Yiddish proverb says, "a man is as old as his wife looks," I may be aging rapidly.

The years have exacted a different price from Golde, more psychological than physical. The emotional weight has worn her down. First Hodel followed Pertschik to Siberia; then Chava abandoned the faith; our family was expelled from our home and was separated; Shoshana passed away; Devorah joined the Haganah; "the incident" snuffed the life from Rachel and turned Abraham into a rabid Arab-hater. On top of all that has happened to our family, we hear frightening stories from Germany and, right here, discover the British are reneging on the Balfour Declaration. The list of torments seems endless. Now Golde never smiles. She eats so little I fear she will wither and blow away in the next *khamsin*. And each night she cries herself to sleep.

"Dear Lord, why can't You ease her pain, or give me the strength to do so? All these years of prayers and so little of what I've said seems to have reached Your ears. I'm not complaining; after all, You have blessed me with a wonderful family and granted me the honor You denied even Moses, to live in the land You promised to our people. Still, why must every blessing be balanced by a curse, each moment of joy by sorrow and grief?"

"Will You allow Your people to live in this land, or will the Arabs drive us out as the Assyrians once did? Are we being punished for the lack of belief of some of my friends, whose God is the apostate Marx? What sin have the Jews of Germany committed that You have brought a new Pharaoh to torment them?"

"All of my life I've strived to understand Your words and Your plan. Is this arrogance?"

"Is there nothing You can do to help my poor Rachel?"

I fell to my knees as we normally do before God only on Yom Kippur. As I lay on the ground, I suddenly felt a shiver run through my entire body. I don't know if God put the image in my mind, but I immediately knew what I had to do. It was a dream I had expected to fulfill as soon as I arrived in Palestine, but for all these years have never managed. I felt that I was being drawn to Jerusalem, to the place where God's temple once stood.

When I went to tell Golde what I planned to do, she became hysterical.

"Now, after all these years, you decide to go to Jerusalem," she said, wringing her hands. "Between the Arabs and the crazy Jews and the British police, there's no telling what could happen to you."

"Golde, how can I explain it to you? I feel compelled to go."

"Compelled? After all your private conversations with God, now you're going to start believing He's answering you?"

"Golde, I'm an old man. God alone knows how long I have left in this life. Before I die, I would like to see Jerusalem."

Golde started to object, but stopped herself. She clasped her hands together and closed her eyes. In all our years of marriage, I've never known her to give in so quickly during an argument.

"All right," she said a moment later. "You can go."

"Thank you," I said, and started to hug her.

"On one condition."

"Uh-oh. Here it comes," I mumbled, backing away to prepare for the blow.

"You can go to Jerusalem, but only if you take me with you."

"What? But you just said —"

"I know what I said. And if anything happened to you, I could not live with my guilt. I would rather that we face whatever danger is out there together, as we have on the kibbutz."

Before I could respond, she said, "That's it. I won't argue with you. I'm going."

I looked at her standing with her hands on her hips and a sense of purpose I hadn't seen since the days she tried to find husbands for our daughters. I even thought I saw a glint of happiness in her eyes, though her face remained a melancholy mask.

"It would be a pleasure to have you join me."

And so the next day we left the safety of our kibbutz for the place Jews have directed their prayers for thousands of years — Jerusalem.

We sat beside each other on the bus. The windows were covered with thick nets to protect passengers from rocks thrown by Arabs in villages along the road.

Golde was silent for an unusually long time. Finally, she asked, "Tevye, do you really think God spoke to you?"

"To tell you the truth, I don't know. I didn't see a burning bush, if that's what you mean."

"No, that's not it."

She was looking at me strangely. Suddenly, she took my hand and held it between hers.

"You know I've never told you this, Tevye, but your faith has helped me stay sane all these years. Somehow, despite everything, you have never lost your belief in God's mercifulness. I've prayed and hoped God would explain why we have had to suffer such pain, but He's never answered me. But, in some way, God seems to communicate with you, to give you the will to go on. With all that has happened to our family, I don't know what I would have done without you."

I looked at her and saw a tear snake its way down her cheek. I brushed it aside with the back of my free hand.

"I believe God has a plan for all of us, and that all that has happened was for a reason. Rabbi Jonathan said a potter does not test a weak utensil. If he hits it just once, it will break. So he tests only the strong ones, for even if it is hit over and over it will not break. So God does not test the wicked, but only the good ones."

"My strength is waning, Tevye."

I moved closer and whispered in Golde's ear. "Do you know the real reason I have never lost faith?"

Golde shook her head.

"Because God brought a woman into my life who bore eight wonderful children, raised them to be *tzaddikim*, and loved and took care of a disagreeable old man like me. I believe in God because I believe in you. As the Good Book says, 'Whoever finds a wife finds a good thing, and obtains favor from the Lord.'"

Golde smiled and, for the first time, we kissed in public.

32

Golde and I fell asleep in each other's arms. When we awoke, the bus was weaving through the hills to the outskirts of Jerusalem.

Few of our friends had left the kibbutz over the years, so we did not know anyone who lived in Jerusalem, except Bernice. We were reluctant to visit her because we knew how busy she was with politics, but Golde insisted, telling me it would not be polite to come so far and not to drop in on a member of the family.

Golde was right. Though the amount of time she actually spent living with us was short, Bernice had become a sister to us both, and an aunt to our children. We felt closer to her than the *chaverim* who we'd seen day in and day out since we'd arrived in Palestine. Bernice was also the one who watched over Devorah like she was her own daughter, and always made a point of letting us know Devorah was all right whenever she came to the kibbutz.

Although Bernice was born in Russia, the time she'd spent growing up in the United States had made her as different from Golde as I am from Roosevelt. Still, the two of them became friends from the first day they worked together in the kitchen. I think my wife appreciated the fact that Bernice did not resent the assignment the way so many other women did. At the same time, Bernice didn't hesitate to assert herself. She was the person who had brought in different types of food, and made an effort to give even our original crude dining room the feel of a real home. Bernice was also the one who had horrified everyone by wearing colorful, flowery dresses instead of the drab peasant clothes the ideological purists preferred.

If the kingdom of Israel were to be resurrected, Bernice would make an excellent queen. She wasn't exactly the physical image of a monarch, with her bulbous nose, bushy eyebrows and stringy hair pulled back behind her head like a bird's nest, but her motherly passion, unbridled determination, intelligence and basic goodness endeared her to everyone.

Golde didn't like my description of her looks, but she agreed about Bernice's qualities and said, with Bernice for a queen, we wouldn't need a king.

As we knocked on the door of Bernice's small stone house, I pictured her sitting on a throne, wearing a magnificent robe and golden crown, and holding a bejeweled scepter.

She answered the door wearing a housecoat and slippers.

"Welcome to Jerusalem. Come in, please," Bernice said, beckoning us into her tiny kitchen. "Sit, sit. I already have some coffee ready."

We sat at a small wooden table in a corner. My feet were halfway into the living room.

"Wait, I've just made this honey cake. I think you'll like it." She put down the plate and hurriedly returned to the sink to pour the coffee.

I reached for the biggest piece of cake. Golde slapped my hand and gave me her "tut tut" look. I took a smaller piece and bit into it. As I did Bernice said, "I got the recipe from Chana."

I spit the cake halfway across the room. Golde's eyes nearly popped out of head, but Bernice had her back to me and pretended, at least, not to notice.

"Actually, Chana gave it to me years ago, before her accident with the birdseed. I don't think I ever trusted her recipes after that first kugel."

Bernice brought over two cups of coffee and sat next to us. She ate a few crumbs from the plate of cake and then lit a cigarette. The ashtray was already full of butts.

"So, Tevye, you've finally come to visit after all these years. I should ask what took you so long, but it doesn't matter. What's important is that you are here."

"Well, you know what life is like on the kibbutz, Bernice. I'm getting old and I was afraid my chances of seeing Jerusalem were running short."

"I'm so glad you came too, Golde," Bernice said, patting her on the hand. "I miss you and the other *chaverim*. When all this is over, and we have our state, I'm coming back to live with you for good."

"Somehow, I doubt that Bernice," I said. "You like all this political intrigue too much. And you seem to be good at it."

"Not because it's what I want, Tevye. Strangely enough, as Eitan might say, this is the task suited to my abilities. We all have a role to play in building the state, and this is mine at the moment. But I won't always be needed."

"I'm not so sure."

"It's nice of you to say, but I don't think I'd miss dealing with anti-Semites and aristocrats and diplomats and even some of my colleagues at the Agency. The only thing I'd regret if I moved back to the kibbutz would be living in Jerusalem. This is truly a beautiful and magical place."

When Bernice talked about the city, she had the starry-eyed look Rachel would get when she talked about Hollywood. My face must have dropped at the thought.

"What's wrong, Tevye? Is something wrong with the cake?"

"No, no. Of course not, Bernice."

"Do you realize how improbable it is for me to be here? For any of us to be here?" Bernice said excitedly. My father was a shopkeeper in Minsk. My mother had three children who died before I was born. Can you imagine?" Bernice saw the pained look on Golde's face. "I'm sorry, Golde. You probably know better than anyone what I'm talking about."

"It's all right."

"And then for my family to move to America, and for me to grow up in Cleveland, Ohio, of all places. Who would have dreamed that one day I would be sitting in holy Jerusalem drinking coffee in my very own house? When I think about it, I feel like miracles do happen."

"Maybe I've had some influence on you after all."

"More than you know, Tevye. More than you know. This was King David's capital and one day, despite the British and the Arabs, it will be again. I believe that is God's plan." She leaned over toward me. "Can I tell you a secret? We may have to surrender Jerusalem to secure our state in a sliver of Palestine, but, mark my words, a prime minister will eventually stand near where we are sitting and welcome the leaders of the world to Jerusalem, the capital of the Jewish State."

"Bernice, you know I'm not a political person, and would be the last one to question your wisdom in such affairs, but how can you even consider giving up Jerusalem, even for a state elsewhere? It's like trying to cut out your heart to save your arms and legs."

"I know it's difficult for a spiritual man like you to understand; it's not so easy for me to stomach either, but the reality is our political position is still very weak. We have brought thousands of Jews here, but we are still vastly outnumbered, and the British are much more interested in currying favor with the Arabs than with us."

"Why?" Golde asked.

"One reason is there are more of them than us. They are the majority throughout the Near East and North Africa. This region used to be little more than a sandlot separating Asia and Africa, but since oil was discovered, it's become much more important to all the great powers. A Jewish state in Palestine doesn't serve any of England's national interests."

Bernice crushed out her cigarette and immediately lit another. My eyes had already begun to water.

"Now that the war is spreading, and the Nazis are threatening all of Europe, our little problems don't seem that important to the Allies. But to us, it's never been more vital to reach our goal. I don't know how much you've heard, but Jews in Nazi-occupied lands are being arrested and deported to God-knows-what kinds of prisons. I fear the fate of all of European Jewry may depend on whether we are successful, because we are the only ones who will open our arms and welcome our brothers and sisters."

"Is it really that serious?" Golde asked.

"Yes, I'm afraid it is. Unfortunately, the British have tied our hands. Since the Churchill White Paper, they have slammed the gates of Palestine shut. Only a fraction of our quota is being allowed in, and the numbers we are able to smuggle past the blockade are tiny. We are trying to carry out Ben-Gurion's vow to fight the Germans and the British, but we are losing both battles at the moment."

"Perhaps you need more spiritual men in the Agency Executive."

Bernice laughed. "Maybe you're right, Tevye. But enough depressing talk. Let's go to the *Kotel* and we can all pray for guidance."

"*Kotel?*"

"Actually, it's *Kotel ha-Ma'aravi.* That's what we call the Western Wall. The *goyim* usually refer to it as the Wailing Wall because they say Jews are always weeping in front of it."

I took one last piece of cake before Golde could slap my hand. Bernice crushed her cigarette in the ashtray and placed our dishes in the sink.

"Just let me put on some shoes and fresh clothes and then I'll show you Jerusalem."

Golde and I sat in Bernice's living room while she changed. Instead of furniture made of *pachim*, she owned real wood couches, and chairs with soft cushions. Flowers were neatly arranged in vases around the room. I felt nostalgia for our house in Russia, when we had bedrooms for the children and our own kitchen.

"Sit down, Tevye. Stop snooping around."

I gestured for Golde to be quiet while I looked at the pictures on the wall. Photographs of her family in America hung beside portraits of Herzl and Weizmann and a shot of her in the kitchen at the kibbutz tasting something from a spoon over a pot.

"Come and look at this, Golde." I said pointing to one grainy picture.

"No, you come back and sit down."

I had never seen this photograph before. A group of men was standing in a field. Jonathan, Moshe, Simcha, Eitan and Uzi were standing barefoot in the mud with shovels in their hands. They were all wearing shorts, sleeveless shirts and Russian workers' caps. Bernice stood in front of the group with a pail. She was also barefoot, but wearing a skirt and long-sleeve shirt.

"Recognize everyone?" Bernice said, coming out of the bedroom and standing beside me.

"We were all so young. Look at that guy between Simcha and Moshe."

The bearded man she was pointing at was dressed much differently from the rest. He had on a hat that looked too small for his head, long pants, boots, a shirt with the sleeves rolled up to just below the elbows, with a prayer shawl over the top. He was smiling.

"If you don't mind me saying so, Golde, Tevye was a handsome young man."

"What do you mean, was?" Golde said.

Bernice stared at me for a second. "You know, you're right. Come on, let's go."

We left Bernice's house and walked all around the city. It was a glorious day. The sky was cloudless and a gentle breeze made it feel comfortably warm.

I was surprised by how steep some streets were; I hadn't realized the city had so many hills. I felt myself getting tired quickly.

"What's that tower up ahead?" Golde asked.

"That's the YMCA. It was built in the early thirties."

"What is it?"

"The letters stand for Young Men's Christian Association. It's a place with all sorts of activities for Jews, Muslims, and Christians. They still believe everyone can learn to live together in peace."

"Leave it to the *goyim*," Golde said.

"The bell tower is more than one-hundred fifty feet tall. I'll bet Shmuel would have loved to be up there."

"And this building with all the soldiers?" I asked, pointing to the building across from the YMCA.

"That's the King David Hotel. It was built around the same time as the Y. It is supposed to be one of the most elegant hotels in the entire region. The British use one wing for offices. Their Criminal Investigation Division is there."

"Tevye, look at that!" Golde shouted.

"What?"

"The big tower with the arms."

"You've never seen one, Golde?" Bernice asked.

"No, what is it?"

"A windmill. Montefiore's windmill to be more precise."

"Who's Montefeefor?" Golde asked.

"Sir Moses Montefiore. He was an English philanthropist who gave money to build houses to help relieve the congestion in the Old City. We call the area Mishkenot Sha'ananim, Dwelling of Tranquility. The windmill was built about eighty years ago to provide work for needy Jews and reduce the price of flour."

"There it is!" Golde shouted excitedly.

When we came around the big square building Bernice called the King David, we saw the walls of the Old City. It was so exciting the weariness and soreness I felt from walking disappeared.

"The view is wonderful, isn't it?" Bernice said, lighting another cigarette.

"It's beautiful," Golde said.

I don't think I knew quite what to expect, but Golde was right, it was magnificent. An old stone walled city within the new city.

"Hard to imagine, isn't it, that such a small place could be the scene of centuries of fighting between Jews, Muslims and Christians. During the first crusade, the Christian soldiers massacred every Jew in the city. Now, I fear, the Muslims may do the same."

Golde and I looked at each other, surprised by Bernice's matter-of-fact tone.

"You see the opening to the left, where the people are entering?"

"Yes," I said, feeling the excitement of a child with a new toy.

"That's Jaffa Gate. The Arabs call it *Bab ul Khalil*, the Gate of the Friend. That breech in the wall where cars are entering was made after the Germans conquered the city in the nineteenth century, so Emperor Wilhelm could ride in on horseback in a grand procession. There are seven other gates, though one, the Golden Gate, is sealed up."

"That's the gate through which the *mashiach* is supposed to enter the city."

"Very good, Tevye. The Muslims sealed it up centuries ago. They thought that would keep the Messiah from coming."

"Nothing will stop the Messiah from coming," I said.

"The tower sticking up to the right of the gate is the Citadel; some people call it David's Tower. It was actually a minaret built by the Turks. There's another tower nearby that was built by Herod two-thousand years ago."

"You're quite a historian, Bernice."

"You're drawn to it when you live here. You want to know everything about the history of the city, and there's so much to know, going back millennia. Civilizations have been built on top of civilizations here. Take the wall itself. It's not the original wall of the city. This one was actually built by Suleiman the Magnificent in the sixteenth century. Come, I don't want to bore you with details. It's more impressive from inside."

We walked down a path that took us past the windmill.

"As you can see, the windmill isn't used anymore," Bernice said. "It became obsolete when steam-powered flour mills were built. This neighborhood, by the way, is called Yemin Moshe. You see how the houses all look similar. Almost everything is built from Jerusalem stone from the Judean Hills."

We walked down a steep hill to an empty, rocky area that separated the newer part of the city from the walled one.

"This is called Sultan's Pool," Bernice said. "It was used to sell camels at the turn of the century. If you'd like, we can go through Jaffa Gate and pass through the Arab *souk* on the way to the Jewish Quarter. It's interesting. You can find jewelers, silversmiths, fruit and vegetable stores, leather goods, you name it. To tell you the truth, though, it's not the safest place these days."

The hint of danger was enough for Golde. "No, I'd rather go directly to the *Kotel.*"

"As the Good Book says, 'Trouble will find you, there's no need to go looking for it.'"

"You're always good for a Biblical reference Tevye. I think you'll find more than a few people here who share your passion."

"It's so big. I've never seen anything like it," Golde said, once we reached the foot of the outer wall of the Old City.

I rubbed my hands against the stones. They were surprisingly smooth. "I should say a blessing."

"Wait," Bernice said. "This is nothing."

We walked along the wall. A monastery was on the other side. A huge stone gate was before us.

"This is Zion Gate," Bernice explained. "Believe it or not, a leper colony was once located nearby."

The image made me quiver.

"Why can't you walk straight in?" Golde asked.

"That's a good question. It was built when armies rode on horseback. If the gate led directly into the city, an army could charge straight through, By making the opening at an angle like this, it prevented horses from being able to gallop full speed into the city — or so I'm told."

I kissed the giant *mezuzah* as we passed through the gate. We kept walking. Golde and I didn't know where to look first. The area was bustling with life. Sephardic Jews dressed in abas with funny little red hats on their heads, dark-skinned Arabs in long jellabas and *kaffiyehs*, British soldiers in uniform and Americans in stylish suits. We walked through a narrow cobblestone passageway. On either side were buildings with small apartments, all made of the same Jerusalem stone. The serpentine paths were like a maze, and I wondered how visitors kept from getting lost.

I squeezed Golde's hand. She looked at me with the kind of excited look she usually reserved for wedding announcements.

The only unpleasant thought I had was that the streets were filthy.

"How could the holy city be kept in such a state, Bernice?" I asked.

"What, you mean the dirt? I don't know. All I can tell you is it apparently used to be much worse. The gate closest to the *Kotel* is called the Dung Gate because it used to be a garbage dump."

"I can't believe it," Golde said.

"It's true. When the German Jews came here they built over it."

As we reached a kind of courtyard, Jews in black coats with long *payos* hanging under streimels were seemingly everywhere.

Women in long skirts and heavy blouses, with kerchiefs covering their heads, were pushing baby carriages through the area, periodically shouting at older children who were dashing about. The men were scurrying around like ants heading back to the nest. They disappeared into different buildings.

"We're now entering the Jewish Quarter," Bernice said. "See that building over there, the one that big group of men is entering? It's probably the oldest synagogue in the city. It was built by the Ramban in the thirteenth century."

"The Ramban," I repeated, unable to believe I was walking in his footsteps.

"The building with the arch is the Hurva Synagogue. It's only about eighty years old."

A group of Hasidim brushed past us.

"I fear for these people," Bernice said once they'd passed. "They're so isolated within these walls, the Arabs can cut them off from the rest of the *yishuv*."

"Can't the Haganah protect them?" Golde asked.

"I doubt it. They're surrounded by areas controlled by the British or Arabs. We know the British won't help us; I only hope they don't do anything to make it easier for the Arabs to strangle the Old City."

"You don't think the Jews should abandon their homes, do you?" I asked.

"Of course not. We've been living here for thousands of years, and no one is going to drive us out of the heart of our homeland."

"I'm glad to hear you say that, Bernice."

"Tevye, we'll defend Jerusalem to the last Jew. Say, this is interesting. Down there in that apartment is another synagogue. Many centuries ago, when only a remnant of Jews lived in Jerusalem, they had to meet secretly to conduct services. One Sabbath only nine Jews were present and they couldn't find a tenth for the *minyan*. Suddenly, a stranger appeared. After the service, he just as mysteriously vanished. The legend is that it was the Prophet Elijah, so this place is called the Synagogue of Elijah."

"It's amazing. Everywhere you look is another story," I said.

"You are literally walking in the footsteps of history, Tevye. Here, down this way is the *Kotel*."

"In this narrow alley?" Golde asked.

Neither Golde nor I could believe we were standing in front of the last remnant of the wall supporting the structure where the Second Temple stood. We were also shocked to see this holy place, which Jews pray toward every day, was wedged into a passageway that was narrower than the kibbutz dining room.

We walked into the alley. Beggars were all along the way. I reached into my pocket and gave the first one a fistful of piasters.

"I know it's a *mitzvah*, Tevye, but you probably shouldn't give them money. It just encourages them to stay here and block passage to the *Kotel*."

"Bernice, how can I deny alms to the poor, especially on such a blessed day?"

"All right, Tevye. I just hope you have some money left to get home."

As I put coins in outstretched hands, a crowd of beggars swarmed around me.

"*Mitzvah. Mitzvah,*" they mumbled.

I heard Bernice say to Golde, "I warned him."

When I broke free of the disheveled mob, Bernice continued her narrative.

"Up above is the Temple Mount. The Muslims have two of their most sacred sites up there. The one we saw before with the silver dome is Al-Aqsa Mosque. The beautiful blue tiled building with the golden roof is referred to as the Dome of the Rock. It's called that because it is built over the rock where Abraham is believed to have tied Isaac when God asked him to sacrifice his son. The Muslims believe Allah ascended to heaven from that spot. I've never been inside, but I'm told it's quite beautiful."

By the time Bernice finished talking, we found ourselves in front of the Western Wall. I had dreamed of this moment all my life, but still couldn't believe it was before me. All you could see were yellowish granite rocks towering above us. Caper plants were growing between many of the stones. I just stared, wide-eyed with awe.

"The wall is about sixty feet high and those stones weigh a couple of tons each. Can you imagine?" Bernice said, stamping out her cigarette under her heel.

"I never thought I would see this," I said.

Golde couldn't speak. She just began to cry.

"Thank you, Lord, for allowing me to live to this day," I said aloud.

I noticed Bernice was staring at the Wall with an expression of longing, like a person seeing a loved one off at a train station.

"Already earth begins to hear old prophet tones with interest new, and long foretold events appear. Swiftly unfolding to the view; And Zion's hope, so long deferred hastes to its glad fulfillment when, according to His faithful word, God will remember her again."

"Is that from the Bible, Bernice?" Golde asked. "I've never heard it."

"No," she replied, returning from the far off place she had seemed to be speaking from. "It's just a poem someone here taught me. Listen, if you want to give a prayer of thanks, Tevye, you can go right up to the wall itself. You can touch the stones if you like. Some people kiss the wall. See those men."

I watched the men in long black coats and hats *shuckling* as they prayed, some moving back and forth so quickly they looked like black blurs. The men closest to the Wall pressed themselves against the stones. Some were indeed kissing them.

"Where are those people going?" Golde asked, pointing to a gate at the far end of the Wall where some men were passing in and out.

"That's a garden where you can also see part of the wall. The owners let Jews who can't find space here in front of the wall inside their yard — for a fee."

It was hard to believe Jews were being forced to pay for the honor of praying at our own temple.

"There's also a tradition that you can write your prayer on a little slip of paper and stuff it between the stones. Here, I brought a pen and some scraps of paper — we call them *kvitlach* — for you to write what you like."

Golde and I both took the paper from Bernice and took turns writing our prayers. Can you imagine writing petitions to God? This is His place. I felt like Moses at Sinai again and wondered if I should take off my shoes because I was on holy ground, but no one else was doing so.

"Come Golde, we have to *daven* on this side of the Wall. Tevye, we'll meet you back here. Take as much time as you want. None of us know when we will return, so let's make the most of this opportunity to thank God and ask for His blessing."

I watched for a moment as Bernice led my wife to the Wall. They stood right next to it. Hesitantly, Golde put her hands on the stones and then rested her head against them.

The Good Book says the Temple was the sight of many miraculous things. The ritual sacrifices did not smell, flies never entered, the ashes from the fires were swallowed up and no matter how many people worshiped inside, space could always be found to prostrate themselves before God. And now I am standing near the place where such miracles occurred.

I walked to the other side of the *mechitza*, where many more men were praying. Most were dressed in long black coats and fur hats. The older ones had long gray beards and side curls. Different groups seemed to be praying together, but a few individuals stood on their own in silent contemplation. I went over to join a group that was praying aloud.

"Because of the palace which is deserted," the reader said.

"We sit alone and weep," the rest answered.

"Because of the Temple which is destroyed."

"We sit alone and weep."

"Because of the walls which are broken down."

"We sit alone and weep."

"Because of our greatness which has departed."

"We sit alone and weep."

"Because of the precious stones of the Temple ground to powder."

"We sit alone and weep," I repeated with the others.

"Because of our priests who have erred and gone astray."

"We sit alone and weep."

"Because of our kings who have condemned God."

"We sit alone and weep."

"Amen," I said.

The group began to break up. I walked to an empty space against the Wall and looked straight up. The size of the stones and the height of the Wall made me feel small and insignificant, like a fish in the ocean. That's as it should be in the presence of the Almighty.

Standing so close, I could now see the textured surface of the stones, which were worn and damaged from nearly two-thousand years of abuse from rain and wind. Dozens of scraps of paper were crammed into every crevice within reach. I took my *kvitel* and reached as high as I could, then used my middle finger to wedge it into a space where the mortar had eroded.

I gently rubbed my hand over the stone in front of me and felt its striations. Then I kissed it. I'm not sure why, but I was overcome by a feeling of love for what the stone represented. I put my forearms on the Wall so I could rest my head against it. Perhaps it was my imagination, or just wishful thinking, but I felt something. I don't know quite how to describe it without sounding crazy. It was as if the stone was pulsing with life. God is here.

"I have spoken to You all my life and sometimes wondered if You heard my prayers," I whispered.

"You have blessed me with more than my share of joys and miseries. Perhaps now that I am standing at the Wall of Your house, I will be close enough for You to hear me."

"I am thankful for many things. For my beautiful and loving wife, my wonderful children, grandchildren and friends, for the opportunity to stand here in this spot."

"I have tried to serve You in the best way I know how, to study and to teach, to observe Your commandments and to raise my family to do the same. Now, I ask only that You keep my family together, and protect them. You have brought Tzeitl and Hodel back to us, but Devorah and Abraham are gone, and in constant danger. Please watch over them. I know that Shoshana is with You. I miss her terribly and not a day goes by when I do not think of her. You will not bring Shoshana back until the *mashiach* comes, but my youngest daughter is not yet in Your care. My little Rachel did not deserve her fate. Surely, You did not mean for her to be silent for the rest of her days. I would gladly give my tongue if it would bring back her voice. I beseech thee oh Lord, Master of the Universe, bring my little girl back to me."

My emotions overwhelmed me. I wiped tears from my eyes with my sleeve. I didn't want the thought to enter my head, but it did the way a mosquito can always find a hole in a net, and then it would not leave. It did not seem right to ask, but if it was in my mind, then surely God already knew what I was thinking.

"Your commandments are clear, as are the consequences for violating them, but I still must ask that You look after the child I turned my back on for so many years. Watch over Chava and, if it is Your will, bring her back to us, to our people."

I started to leave the Wall and thought of something else.

"Dear Lord, I hope You will not think me greedy if I ask one more favor. I waited all my life for this moment, and, as Bernice said, I don't know if I will have this chance again. You have brought Your people to the land that You promised Abraham. We have worked hard to restore its beauty. Please do not allow the Arabs to do what the Amalekites and so many others did to us in the past. We have wandered for far more than two-thousand years in the deserts of the world, from Russia to America to England. Let us find peace in our homeland."

"Thank you, Lord, for blessing my house and hearing my prayers."

After I finished, I stood still for a long time, waiting for an answer. If God was ever to speak to me, surely this would be the time.

I heard nothing. The stones did not move, or suddenly sprout water. The weeds did not burn. The clouds did not open. All I felt was a sudden chill wind that made the hairs on the back of my neck stand up. I shivered but did not feel as though I'd received a divine reply.

I turned and saw that Golde and Bernice were waiting for me, so I started to leave the Wall, backing away as I'd seen others do, as a show of respect to avoid turning one's back on God. My eyes remained fixed on the spot where I had stood. Another gust of wind nearly blew my hat off. I grabbed it just as it started to fly away. Just then, I saw my *kvitel* blown out of its resting place. I started to go after it, but it was gone before I had the chance.

33

The trip to Jerusalem was wonderful, like a visit to the Garden of Eden. If nothing else, it strengthened my faith and gave me the will to go on trying to build our state.

Of course nothing with Tevye can be all good. Before we boarded the bus to return to the kibbutz, Bernice took me aside and told me she was worried about Abraham.

"Why?" I asked. "He's part of the Haganah, just like Devorah. He's helping to protect the *yishuv*."

"Not exactly, Tevye," Bernice said.

She had a very serious tone and was smoking more rapidly, the way she did when she was especially worried.

"I don't understand."

"I didn't want to say this in front of Golde, because I know it would upset her. The truth is Abraham is not in the Haganah."

"What?"

"He joined a splinter group, the Irgun Z'vai Leumi. It's a militaristic group of Jabotinsky's followers. Instead of just defending the *yishuv*, they actively seek out Arabs to attack. But they don't only kill Arabs; they're also increasingly targeting the British. It's making the Agency's life hell. We keep telling the British we're ready to govern ourselves and then the Irgun, or the Lehi, which is an even more radical group, go and blow something or someone up. Jabotinsky taught his followers that only Jewish armed force would ensure the creation of a Jewish state and now they are trying to accomplish that goal. It's madness! The British have thousands of troops in the country and the Irgun has, at most, several hundred members. All they do is make negotiations tougher for us. The British want to take away the Haganah's weapons and to lock up the leaders of the Agency as retribution for the Irgun's behavior."

"Abraham has killed people?"

"Tevye, I don't mean to unsettle you. I don't know that he has done anything wrong. Let's just say he's running around with the wrong crowd. If the British capture him, they'll throw him in prison. A couple of years ago, they executed one of the Irgun's men. I don't want anything to happen to him. He's family to me. But I can't reach him."

"What can I do? I haven't seen him. I didn't even know about what you've just told me."

"I know. I know. They're very secretive. But Abraham might come to visit or contact you at some point. God knows when. If he does, try to talk him into staying at the kibbutz to help with the defense there, or to join the Haganah."

"I hope that I have the chance."

"Me too," Bernice said, giving me one last hug.

"So, what did Bernice want?" Golde asked when I returned.

"She just wanted me to give Simcha a message."

"About what?"

"If she had wanted you to know, she would have told you."

"Such a man!" Golde turned her back on me.

I guess the glow of our visit was wearing off already. I wish Bernice would have told me about my son before we went to the Wall, so I could have added to my petition. Well, I guess it's never too late. I tried to whisper.

"Dear Lord, I know I've asked for a lot, and I'm not at the Temple Wall anymore, but could you watch over Abraham and help him see that he has chosen the wrong path to bring about the redemption of our homeland."

"What's the matter with him?" I heard someone pointing in my direction ask his companion.

"Probably Jerusalem Syndrome."

"What's that?"

"People come to Jerusalem and suddenly think they're the Messiah and can talk to God. Happens all the time."

"I spoke to God long before I came to Jerusalem," I shouted.

The two men just laughed and walked away.

"What are you shouting about Tevye?"

"Nothing Golde."

It must have been the combination of the excitement and the length of the journey, but Golde and I both slept the entire way home. With Golde resting her head against my shoulder, I was reminded, again, how much we relied upon each other. The trip made me feel closer than ever to her.

"Tevye! Tevye!"

I had hardly stepped inside the kibbutz gate when Natan came running. Just what I need now, a grilling from Natan the Nudnick.

"Tevye!"

"Stop yelling already, Natan. I'm right here. What is it? Do you have a question about this week's *parsha*?"

"Yes, I do, but that's not what I came to tell you."

"Good, then I have something to look forward to. Now, if you'll excuse me, I've had a long trip back from Jerusalem and I'd like to get some rest."

"But Tevye, haven't you heard the news?"

"News? What news?"

"The *Struma* exploded."

"That's very upsetting news Natan. Now what is a *Struma*?"

"It was a transport ship carrying hundreds of Jewish refugees from Romania. The British refused to let it come to Palestine and when the ship's engines died it docked in Istanbul."   "Turkey? Why didn't they get off the ship there?"

"The Turks wouldn't let them."

"I don't understand Natan. If the ship was broken, why didn't it stay in port?"

"After the British refused to accept the refugees, the Turks decided to tow it out to sea. They just left it floating in the Black Sea."

"So you're telling me a ship full of Jews trying to escape from Hitler was just set adrift in the sea?"

"Yes Tevye. And then it was hit by a Soviet torpedo."

"Devorah!"

The fear was always lurking in the back of my mind that something could happen to Devorah during one of her missions of mercy. We usually did not hear anything from her, or about her, for months at a time. But this is the first time something like this has happened, where we know she could have been arrested or killed. Please God let her be all right.

"What happened to the Jews on the ship?" I asked, dreading what the answer might be.

"The report we got was that there was only one survivor who was picked up by the Turks. The British let him into Palestine and he told the story to the Haganah. He said there were more than 700 people on board, including about 100 children."

Natan was still standing inches from my face. I don't know what he expected me to say. There was nothing new about Russians killing Jews. I was heartbroken for all the people who died, but my biggest concern was whether Devorah was on board.

"Thanks Natan," I said finally. "Talking to you is always a comfort."

"I thought you'd want to know."

Simcha came over just as Natan was leaving.

"I see the messenger of doom has spoken to you. Tevye, the chances of Devorah being on the ship are remote. Don't worry, and don't say anything to Golde. I'll get in touch with Bernice and find out what really happened, as opposed to what the radio says, and have her send word about Devorah. All right, my friend?"

He put his arm around me and flashed his most reassuring smile. It didn't help. I felt as though this was God's answer to my prayers, to bring yet more misery upon me. Perhaps it is a punishment for asking for too much, for not being grateful for what I have.

Simcha still had his arm around me with a grin on his face. Just as I was feeling a new sense of despair, I was staring at what looked like the happiest man in the world.

"What aren't you telling me, Simcha?"

"Tevye, you of all people knows that God always balances the bad with the good."

"I'm not so sure about that."

"Well, then, let me reassure you. Hodel and I are getting married. We've decided with all the turmoil in the land, we can't afford to wait any longer. The wedding will be next Sunday."

Wedding, next Sunday. I was too dumbstruck to speak.

"Aren't you going to wish me mazel tov?"

I opened my mouth but nothing came out. Simcha slapped me on the shoulder and that roused me from the shock. "Of course, I'm going to wish you mazel tov!" I grabbed him by the shoulders and hugged him and kissed him on each cheek. You know we all thought you were married to the kibbutz."

"I was until I found the most wonderful woman. Hodel is quite special and I expect to spend the rest of my days making her happy."

"Amen! I can't wait to tell Golde."

Needless to say, Golde was ecstatic. She was not happy that she would not have weeks to plan the wedding, but I explained to her that Hodel and Simcha wanted a very simple wedding because they did not feel it was right to have a big celebration with all of the violence in the land.

Golde thought this was precisely the time to have a real *simcha*, but Hodel didn't think it was appropriate after what had happened to Pertschik and her mother understood.

34

⊂≈⊱χ⊰≈⊃

"Rachel, my darling Rachel. You sit here staring out the window and I want nothing more than to hear you speak. Papa. Mama. Bird. Flower. Anything."

I knelt beside her and took her hand.

"I know the words are trapped inside you. If only God would show me the way to unlock you from this prison, I would gladly change places with you."

"Once again God has challenged me to see that what has happened to you is somehow for the best. Maybe you are better off because you get to look out at the same beautiful scene each day from this window. You see the birds and the trees and the flowers, but are shielded from all the horrors that lie beyond this view."

"Your sister Hodel had a lovely wedding. She married Simcha. At first I thought he was too old for her, but he is so in love with her and Hodel finally found a man who could take Pertschik's place in her heart – or maybe share a piece of it. You can only

285

imagine how happy the wedding made your mother. She's kvelling like the day you first said *eema.*"

"I wish the news about your brother Abraham was as joyous. He is still trying to avenge what was done to you. Knowing that he could not prevent it is his own private *gehenna.* I haven't seen him since he ran off to fight the Arabs. Bernice says he's gotten mixed up with terrorists who are doing terrible things and threatening everything we've worked so hard to attain. They have become more militant since the *Struma* was sunk. They are now determined to drive the British out of Palestine. Abraham is following the path that God has set for him. If the Lord wants us to live in this land, I am sure your brother is doing the Lord's work."

"Still, your mother and I worry. When we're not thinking about Abraham, we're having nightmares about Devorah. Natan scared me to death when he brought me the news about the *Struma* sinking. When we heard only one person survived I thought I'd go crazy. Luckily, Bernice quickly found out your sister was not on the ship. But every time an illegal immigrant ship was stopped, we held our breath waiting to hear from Bernice. Before the *Struma,* we had sleepless nights waiting to hear if Devorah was on the *Pencho,* or the *Salvador* or the *Patria.* From what we hear, things have gotten so much worse in Europe that I'm afraid we will soon be hearing about more ships being captured and sunk."

"Maybe I shouldn't be telling you all this. Why spoil the beautiful view with such ugliness?"

"You know your sister Hodel doesn't want children because she doesn't want to bring kids into such a world. Can you imagine giving up the opportunity to have a gift from God like you? I tried to tell her that God commanded us to be fruitful and multiply, but she won't listen. Maybe after we have our state, she'll change her mind."

I kissed Rachel on top of the head and then heard Laban ringing the bell for dinner.

"Come Rachel, it's time to eat," I said, and lifted her gently from the chair and began to lead her across the courtyard to the dining hall.

As we walked, I thought about how difficult it was to be a father. When I was young, I didn't have the strength to fight my daughters. Now that I am old, I can only give them advice and hope they will respect the wisdom of my years. Hodel always said she'd seen too much evil in her lifetime and didn't want to inflict it upon a helpless child. Everything that is happening now just justifies the decision in her eyes.

But who will change the world, if not the children? When I see my grandchildren, I am hopeful. Tzeitl and Motel are good parents, better than me and Golde. Rebecca has grown as beautiful as her mother and works beside her and Golde in the kitchen. Leah idolizes her aunt Devorah and has learned to be a nurse. When Dr. Susser died, she was the only one who could care for the sick before Dr. Riesman arrived from Germany. Aryeh, of course, wanted to join the Haganah, but we convinced him to stay here, and now he is organizing the kibbutz defenses. He inherited his father's skill with his hands and has built a machine shop to secretly manufacture arms.

Here, within our little village, I worry only about Sarah. She has still not married and I fear she will never find a husband. Golde has done everything to make her a match, but she just says her love is the kibbutz and her family. She's known most of the men her age since they were all children and she prefers to be "just friends" with all of them. I don't think Sarah has ever gotten over Simcha choosing her sister Hodel over her.

I hadn't really thought about it that much until now, as my days grow fewer, but the only one to carry on my name will be Abraham. After so long, and being blessed with seven daughters, God smiled upon us and granted Golde and me a son, but now Bernice says he is in constant danger and God alone knows if he will survive, let alone marry and have children. Will he be the last generation of the Zalmans?

"Tevye! Tevye!"

Natan was shouting and running toward me. In his old age, he seemed to be in a constant state of anxiety. Rachel showed no sign of noticing him.

"What is it now, Natan? A new question about the *parsha* vexing you?"

"No, no," he puffed, trying to catch his breath. "It's, It's —"

"Well?"

"Devorah. She's back."

"My Devorah? Where? Where is she?"

"In the dining room. She just arrived. Golde's with her now."

"Thank you, Lord! Thank you for bringing my daughter home."

Natan started to tug at my sleeve. "Come already. You can talk to God later."

"Just a minute," I said, freeing myself from his grasp.

I turned to my youngest daughter, "Your sister's home Rachel." She didn't react; she didn't even change expression.

Natan was running up ahead like a horse that's broken free from a cart; energy he's never lacked.

When we got to the dining room, people were crowded around Devorah. She was eating porridge and bread hungrily. She looked pale and thin, so different from the days when she was a youngster working on the kibbutz. Her face looked as though it had aged two years for every year since I'd seen her last. Bags had formed under her eyes and crow's feet in the corners of them. Her hair was hanging loosely over her shoulders and looked dirty. Sprinkles of mud were on her cheeks.

"Papa!" Devorah stood and raced over to embrace me.

She held me a long time and then hugged her sister.

"Rachel, I missed you so much." Devorah stepped back to look at her and smiled as if nothing was wrong. "Look how big you've gotten! I hardly recognize you."

Devorah hugged Rachel again and looked over her shoulder at me with such sadness that the happiness of her return seemed to evaporate. When Devorah pulled back to look at Rachel again, the smile returned to her face.

"I have so much to tell you, but I need to rest a bit. Can I go back to your room, Papa?"

"Of course, of course."

"I have to finish making dinner, then I'll be over," Golde said.

"Go Golde," Chana said, pushing her toward Devorah. "We can manage one afternoon without you. Go and spend time with your daughter."

"It's all right, Mama," Devorah said. "Finish what you're doing. I'm just going to lie down and take a nap. By the time you're done cooking, I'll be ready to get up and we can talk. Okay?"

"Are you sure?"

"Yes, Mama." Devorah moved close to Golde and whispered in her ear, "You don't want Chana in there cooking by herself, do you? I'm hungry enough to eat just about anything but her bird-seed kugel."

"All right, sweetheart. You go and sleep. I'll see you in a little bit." Golde gave Devorah another hug and padded off to the kitchen.

Sarah came running in. "Devorah!"

"Sarah!"

The two sisters embraced.

"Look at you," Devorah said, pulling back to see how her sister had matured.

"Look at you, big sister. Have you brought news?"

"Yes, and I am dying to talk to you and catch up on all the kibbutz gossip. But I'm exhausted right now and I've got to take a nap. We'll talk later, okay?"

"Sure, sure." Sarah said, grabbing Devorah and hugging her tightly. "I missed you."

"And I missed you."

"Saraleh," I said, "take Rachel with you for dinner. I'm going to go back to the house with Devorah."

"All right, Papa. See you soon, Devorah. It's great to have you home."

Devorah and I started out of the dining room. Natan blocked the path.

"Devorah, what can you tell us about what's happening? Is it true the Germans are killing all the Jews in Europe? Are they really being imprisoned and executed?"

"Natan. I'm very tired right now. I've had a long trip. Tonight, after dinner, I'll speak to the whole kibbutz and explain what I know."

"But we've heard such terrible things. They can't be true."

"Later, Natan. Please."

"But —"

"Later Natan!" I said and shoved past him.

"Everything looks so beautiful," Devorah said when we were alone and crossing the courtyard toward the house. "I can't believe how the kibbutz has grown since I've been away. I remember when we first arrived and the only things here were some tents and a lot of rocks and swamps. You've really built something to be proud of Papa."

"Me? What did I do? Milk a few cows, pick a grape or two. Everyone has worked together to make this a land of milk and honey again, at least this little corner of our homeland."

"You have done it. I only pray that by the time the war ends there will still be some Jews alive to enjoy it."

"What do you mean?"

"When we get inside Papa. Please."

I looked at my daughter and could see that even as she was admiring the beauty of the kibbutz, and all the progress we had made since she'd been a little girl chasing tumbleweeds in the wind, that she walked as though she carried a bag of cement on her back but did not want anyone to notice.

Neither of us said another word until we were inside the house. I closed the door and said, "Sit."

"I should not tell you any of what I'm about to say," she said, starting to pace like her father, "but I can't keep it inside any longer. I have to tell someone."

"You can tell your papa."

"Oh Papa, you have no idea of the horrors that are going on in Europe, and what I've had to do."

She suddenly burst into tears.

"And what I've failed to do."

At that moment, it seemed as though the weight she was carrying had crushed her. I held her as tightly as I could without hurting her.

Then she pulled away and wiped her eyes. "I'm sorry, Papa. I usually don't cry. I can't let myself. If I did, I would cry all the time."

"What is it? What has happened?"

Devorah took a deep breath and sat. She rubbed her eyes again with her sleeve. "Papa, you mustn't repeat any of this to anyone, not even to Mama. All right?"

"You know I don't keep secrets from your mother."

She raised her eyebrow knowingly.

"All right. All right. I promise. It will be our little secret."

"You know that I have been involved in smuggling immigrants into Palestine for the Haganah. Actually, there's a more secret organization that does the work, it's called the *Mossad le'Aliya Beit.*"

"I've never heard that name. But we did know you were involved in bringing Jews to Palestine. When we heard about the *Struma* and the other ships, we were very worried about you. Bernice let us know you were safe, but we were still very scared."

"Bernice is the most wonderful person in the world. I hope one day all the Jewish people will appreciate what she has done."

"Yes, Bernice is an angel of the Lord, but couldn't someone else take your place? I know the work you're doing is important, but you've done more than your share. Why not stay here and help with the defense of the kibbutz?"

"Papa, don't you know how I long to be here with you?" She stood and resumed pacing. "You don't know what is happening to our people in Europe. Every immigrant who reaches Palestine is saved from sure death."

Devorah was starting to speak so rapidly I could barely understand her.

"Every moment we waste is a sin. The situation is much worse than anything that ever happened in Russia."

"Worse than Kishinev and the other pogroms? I can't believe —"

She grabbed me by the arms, "You must believe it!"

I was startled.

"I'm sorry, Papa," she said, rubbing her brow. "Natan is right."

"Natan the Nudnik? Natan's never been right about anything in his life."

"Well, he picked the worst time to change his luck. Hitler wants to kill every Jew in Europe. And, if he succeeds, who knows, he might try to kill every Jew on earth. Wherever the Nazis go, they arrest Jews and send them to horrible prisons. Jews are murdered in the most sickening ways, methods you couldn't imagine in your worst nightmares. Sometimes the Nazis don't even bother taking them to the camps, they just murder them on the spot."

"Women and children too?"

"Everyone with a drop of Jewish blood running through their veins. In one Lithuanian town, they forced the Jews to dig a ditch, then made them take off their clothes. Men, women and children were forced to stand naked, shivering in the snow. The Germans machine-gunned them. The bodies fell into the ditch. Then another group of Jews was lined up in front of the same ditch. And another. And another. It went on all day and all night until the ditch was full and then it was covered with dirt."

"How can this be?"

"These atrocities are being carried out all over Europe. Nazi killing squads are butchering Jews the way — no, not even the way you would slaughter cattle. Animals are treated with greater dignity."

"It's too incredible."

"That's part of the problem. The truth is so horrible, people think the reports are just Allied propaganda. I've heard stories about the Nazis forcing all the Jews in a town into a synagogue, locking the doors and then setting it on fire, burning them alive."

The image of a synagogue in flames, with voices inside wailing, forced itself before my eyes. I could see the Star of David burning and falling from the facade, and then the ceiling collapsing to silence the screams. I felt as though someone was trying to rip the heart from my chest.

"In Poland, the Jews are being herded into ghettoes. God knows what the Nazis intend for them. Many will die of starvation and disease before the Germans have the chance to murder them."

"Why doesn't anyone stop them?" I asked. "Where are the English and the Americans?"

"England and the United States are waging an all-out war against the Germans, but their strategy doesn't seem to include saving Jews. The Allies know what's happening, but Roosevelt and Churchill are like the blind mice in the nursery rhyme; when it comes to Jews, they hear no evil, see no evil and speak no evil."

"And what do you have to do with all these terrible things?"

"If we don't help the Jews escape, no one will be left to come to the Jewish state. Do you understand what I'm saying, Papa? No one!"

"But what can you do?"

"I was sent to Europe, I can't say where, to help organize the rescue effort. One of our agents leased an old, broken down cargo ship for ten times the usual asking price. I was supposed to bring a group of Jews who'd escaped from Rumania to Palestine on that ship."

"But I thought you were just a nurse who took care of sick people on the immigrant ships."

"Let's just say my duties have grown."

"So you're here. You succeeded."

"Not exactly."

She sat and put her head in her hands. I waited for her to explain.

"You don't know what we went through to get those people to the ship. A Jew named Herschel was working day and night to secure visas so people could get to our ship. He had a wife and four children. He could have left anytime he wanted, but he stayed. Papa, he stayed."

Devorah started to sob, but I didn't understand what she was trying to tell me.

Wiping away tears, she continued. "He got visas for five-hundred people. That's five-hundred lives he saved. Some people already had visas, others got them in different ways. Then we bribed every public official to allow the ship to leave. Finally, we sailed with more than one-thousand men, women and children aboard."

"So many on one ship?"

"You should have seen them, Papa. All of them were carrying their little bundles of rags, the remains of their possessions. I imagine it is what we must have looked like when we left Russia. We gave them paper bags for seasickness. The only food we had was some jam and bread. On the ship, they organized themselves into committees, just like on the kibbutz. There was a religious committee to organize prayers, a work committee to assign jobs around the ship, an entertainment committee to provide music and perform plays to keep everyone's spirits up, and an education committee to teach Hebrew."

"They'll be well prepared for life in Palestine."

"Well, one committee may have saved the ship. Just before we left the port, a fire broke out in the hold and the fire brigade reacted quickly enough to extinguish it before the whole ship went up in flames. A few people were burned, but I treated them and they all survived. A couple will be permanently disfigured. They should have gone to a hospital, but if I had sent them, they'd have been left behind and I was afraid what might happen to them."

"You had to make such decisions alone? Where were the other Haganah, I mean Mossad officers?"

"This work requires us to be on our own most of the time. Other agents helped me with some of the logistics, but I had to make a lot of decisions that no one ever taught me to make."

It was hard to imagine my little girl almost singlehandedly organizing the rescue of hundreds of people.

"God was with you, Devorah."

"Maybe, especially when you consider what those poor people had to endure. The conditions on the ship were horrible. More than one-thousand souls crammed into a space that wasn't big enough for a hundred horses. They had to sleep in shifts. People got horribly sick and I did my best to take care of them, but I had no medicine except some aspirin and morphine. Thankfully, no one died."

"It was a miracle."

"No, a miracle would be the rescue of all the Jews of Europe."

"But one-thousand more Jews are here now."

"There's a little more to the story. We were off the coast of Istanbul when British warships surrounded us. The refugees were defiant. A woman who had been a seamstress in Rumania sewed a flag of Zion and it was hoisted above the ship. Then a sheet was hung over the side of the ship that said, "Palestine or Death," while everyone stood on deck singing *Hatikvah*. It was an incredible sight."

"What were the British doing near Turkey?"

"They have spies everywhere. You wouldn't believe how much effort they put into trying to keep Jews out of Palestine. If they were doing half as much to defeat Hitler, the Jews would not be in such grave peril."

"So, what happened?"

"Well, one of the women on the ship was pregnant and the other passengers wanted me to smuggle her to shore so she would not be captured by the British and returned to Europe."

"They would send them back, knowing what the Germans are doing?"

"Yes, Papa. The British would rather Jews face certain death than create problems for them with the Arabs in Palestine."

I knew she was right. The British were indeed going to great lengths to prevent Jews from immigrating. Bernice said the legal quota is reduced every time they catch a group of illegals.

"What did you do about the pregnant lady?"

"She refused to leave. She said that she wanted to stay with her fellow Jews and see her baby born in Palestine. The other passengers tried to convince her she would never be allowed into Palestine and, if she was sent back to Rumania and captured, the Nazis would show her no mercy."

"Is that true?"

"The things I've heard they do to pregnant women are too horrible for me to repeat, Papa. But it was clear she would not be persuaded to get off the ship. Finally, I stood up in front of the group and said, 'The Lord said to Jeremiah, 'Arise ye, and let us go up to Zion . . . Behold I will bring them from the north country, and gather them from the ends of the earth, and with them the blind and the lame and the woman with child.' That ended the discussion."

"How did you know what to say?"

"Do you remember the lessons Pertschik taught us when you took him into our house in Anatevka? It was a passage he had used to try to show us how all people were equal in the eyes of the Lord. At least, that's where I first remember hearing it. Whenever you talked to us about the Book of Jeremiah, I was reminded of Pertschik's interpretation."

Pertschik did more good than I knew.

"I don't think you'll be so proud of what I did next."

"Devorah, I would be proud of you no matter what."

"Listen first. One of my orders was to avoid capture at almost any cost. If any of us are captured, we are arrested and could be forced to reveal secrets that threaten many lives."

"Forced? How?"

"The British have their ways, torture if necessary."

"Torture? Even women?"

"Yes, even women. Once the Haganah learned the British knew about our ship, they dispatched a man to smuggle me into Istanbul. I left all those people, Papa. I should have gone with them so they would not be alone when the British boarded the ship."

Devorah started to cry again. I lifted her chin and looked at the most beautiful tear-streaked face I had ever seen.

"You did what you had to do. Do you know what happened after you left the ship?

Devorah wiped her eyes on her sleeve. "Yes. The British took it to Haifa. They wanted to send it back to Europe, but the ship was leaking and they were afraid it was going to sink. I guess the *machers* in London decided they didn't want another *Salvador* incident, so, instead, they decided to arrest all the passengers. I don't know what will happen to them. Hopefully, the British will release them eventually, but who knows?"

"Devorah, you accomplished your mission! You brought all those Jews to their homeland. The British will let them go, don't worry. God would not have guided your path to this place otherwise."

"I wish I had your faith, Papa. But you still don't understand."

"God has brought you home safely, hasn't he? How did that happen?"

"Maybe God had a hand in it. After one of our agents took me off the ship, we went back to his safe house. British soldiers followed us. I slipped out the bathroom window and escaped. I don't know what happened to the other agent. I eventually got on a train and managed to get back to Haifa. My superiors told me that it had become too dangerous to smuggle immigrants by sea and said I should go home until they decided what to do next. So, here I am."

I went to Devorah and hugged her tightly. "I'm so glad you're home. God has watched over you."

She pushed away from me. "Why isn't God watching over the rest of our people? And why didn't He watch over Herschel?"

The anger in Devorah's voice shocked me.

"What happened?"

She stood up and walked over to Rachel's chair and stood holding the back, staring out the window the way her sister did each day. I heard her take a deep breath.

"Herschel sent his wife and children away with the visas in his safe. They're somewhere in Palestine. I'm going to start looking for them tomorrow."

"And Herschel?"

"He insisted on staying behind to try to help as many Jews as he could. Finally, his town was overrun by the Nazis. Herschel and the other Jews were taken to the butcher's slaughterhouse. They were stripped and forced to crawl on their hands and knees up the ramp used for animals. When they reached the end, their heads were chopped off and put in baskets. Their bodies were taken and hung on meat hooks with signs that said KOSHER MEAT. Tell me, Papa. What kind of God would let this happen?"

For the first time in my life, I had no answer.

35

Devorah told the entire kibbutz about the horrors afflicting the Jews in Europe. Though she spared them many of the gory details she shared with me, the effect was similar. For weeks afterward, the entire kibbutz was despondent.

As I have done so many times when searching for explanations to my own suffering, I turned to the Bible. After doing some research, I invited everyone to study the Book of Job with me.

I was a little disappointed that only a handful of people showed up, though it shouldn't have surprised me. Over the years I had succeeded in increasing the interest in traditions and the Holy Scriptures, but most of the *chaverim* remained uninterested at best and hostile at worst. Still, Simcha, Natan, Oren, Enoch and my children came to listen and learn.

We started by reading the book together. It's a terrible story. Poor Job loses his money, his ten sons and daughters and is afflicted with boils. His wife tells him he should curse God in the hope that the Almighty will put him out of his misery by killing him. But what does Job say?

Motel read the words, "'Should we accept only good from God and not accept evil?'"

"And," I said, "what happened when Job's friends told him to repent for the sins he committed to provoke God?"

"Job refused. He said he had not done anything wrong, that he was being punished even though he was innocent."

"Very good, Sarah."

She knew all about repentance from her experience after betraying the kibbutz.

"But God never really answers Job," Devorah said.

"When God spoke to Job, that was, in a way, an answer," Motel said, "because it reassured him of God's existence."

"Yes," Oren interjected, "but the problem wasn't faith in God's existence, it was understanding how a God could inflict such misery on Job."

"Humans are supposed to have free will, right?" Simcha said.

Everyone nodded.

"Well, if God stopped us every time we were about to commit an evil deed, we would have no free will. Evil must exist in a world where people have free will."

"That begs the question, Simcha," Motel said, taking off his glasses to clean them. "Why would God create men with evil impulses?"

"Let me tell you one answer the rabbis have suggested," I said. "Some rabbis say that our true rewards and punishments are given to us after we die. Those of us who have lived righteous lives enjoy the 'World-to-Come' and the evildoers are consigned to *gehenna*." I saw that I had everyone's attention and, at that moment, felt like all my years of study were worthwhile. "That is why Moses could die before reaching the Promised Land. In the World-to-Come, he received his true reward."

"I read something similar to that, Papa."

"Another rabbi said that no one knows when they will die, so we should perform as many good deeds as possible because, in the World-to-Come, when we are rewarded by the Almighty, we will ask, 'Why do I receive such a big reward?' God will answer, 'It is because on such and such a day, you performed such and such a good deed.' And we will be shocked to receive a big reward for a small deed and lament that we wasted so much of our lives instead of doing good deeds."

Motel obviously had been doing more than just sewing in those years of exile in Poland. He had become a learned man.

"On the other hand, Reb Motel," I said, "Maimonides disagreed completely with that type of thinking. 'No one serves the Lord after this manner,' he said, 'except vulgar men, women and children who are trained to serve God out of fear of punishment or out of greediness for a reward.'"

I saw that Aryeh was shuffling uncomfortably in his chair with a pained expression on his face.

"What is it, Aryeh? You don't seem to like any of our explanations. It's a question that has puzzled the Jewish people since before the time of Job, so you shouldn't be surprised if we fail to reach the truth tonight."

"I agree, *Zeyde*. That's why this whole discussion is ridiculous. I don't know why God allows bad things to happen to good people, or why he has turned a blind eye to the suffering here in Palestine or what Devorah says the Jews are going through in Europe. All I know is that evil is the very reason we must not lose faith in God."

"I don't understand, Aryeh."

"Don't you see, Motel? If the anti-Semites like Hitler or Stalin or the Mufti convince us, or force us to give up our trust in God, then they have won. They can destroy the Jewish people without lifting a finger to harm us. If you ask me what the response is to evil, my answer is *to believe*."

This was one time I think my smile could match Simcha's.

"Interested in another opinion?"

The voice came from the doorway. We all turned around.

"Arik. How —" Devorah shouted and ran to the dirt-covered man entering the room. She threw her arms around his neck and kissed him passionately.

"Gee, if I knew I'd get such a warm reception, I would have escaped a long time ago."

"Escaped?" Devorah said without releasing him.

"Yes, but before I tell you what happened, don't you think you should introduce me?"

Devorah took Arik by the hand and brought him to our table. Everyone stood and shook hands as they were introduced to Arik.

"You look like you've traveled a long way," Tzeitl said. "I'll get you something to eat and drink."

"*Todah rabah*," he said as Devorah pulled a chair up for him.

"Didn't they send you to prison in Africa?" she asked.

"Africa?" I said. "Where the lions are?"

Arik laughed. "Most of you last saw me at the wedding."

The memory caused me to think immediately of my poor Shoshie and the no-goodnik who left her standing at the altar.

"The British gave me a quick trial and sent me away to where they said I couldn't get into mischief." He turned to Devorah. "I told you I wouldn't die fighting for the cause, at least not as long as I knew you were here to live for."

He leaned over and kissed Devorah again.

The years on the kibbutz had made me more accustomed to public displays of affection, but I was still uncomfortable seeing a man I hadn't seen in years kissing my daughter.

"I was dispatched to a prison in Ethiopia. It wasn't too bad, really. A number of Haganah boys were there, also some of the *meshuganas* from the Irgun and the Lehi. Well, to make a very long story short, a group of us dug a tunnel out of the camp. I went out with four other men from the Haganah. Before we left, forgers in the camp made documents for us, including Guatemalan passports. We put stuffed dummies in our beds one night and made our way through the tunnel to a rendezvous where a taxi was waiting to take a group of Latin American tourists to Ethiopia. A plane met us at a small airfield and flew us to Greece. When we reached Athens, the four of us went separate ways. Naturally, we all wanted to return to Palestine, but our superiors thought it wouldn't be safe for us."

The story was so incredible I thought it was a fairy tale. The only thing missing was a confrontation with a lion.

"So, what are you doing here?" Natan asked.

"Who's he again?" Arik whispered to Devorah.

"We call him Natan the Nudnik."

"I'm not surprised," he said.

"I heard that!" Natan shouted.

"As I was saying, we were told that a lot of work needed to be done to rescue immigrants, and we could be just as useful outside of Palestine."

Tzeitl brought glasses for everyone and a pitcher of tea. She poured a glass for Arik and set a plate of bread and jam in front of him.

"Thank you."

He ate ravenously, as though it were his first meal since *Tisha Be'Av*.

"Excuse me, I haven't eaten for a while."

"That's all right. Go ahead and eat," I said. "The Good Book says news can wait, but an empty stomach cannot."

"Papa?"

"Motel, it's there, trust me."

"Where was I?"

"In Athens," Natan chimed in.

"Right, Athens. Since I was the only one of us who spoke any Arabic, it was decided that I would go to Turkey and help with land crossings."

"Turkey!" Devorah gasped. "We were so near."

"Closer than you think, sweetheart. I was in Istanbul when your ship was boarded by the Haganah. I heard the British tried to arrest you, but that you escaped. They picked up our other agent."

"What happened to him?" Devorah asked.

"Well, the Turks wouldn't let the British just arrest someone on their soil and haul them away. They insisted on getting a more formal request from London. In the meantime, our agent was locked in a Turkish jail. I paid off a few people and got him out. By the time the British found out, our man was in Switzerland. Boy were the Brits steamed."

"All right!" Aryeh shouted. Others laughed.

No wonder the British shipped Arik off to Africa. He manages to cause them a lot of trouble when he's around. I wonder how many more Ariks are doing similar things for our people.

"But what are you doing here?" Natan persisted.

"Patience Natan. As the Good Book says —"

"I have more patience for his drawn out story," Natan interrupted, "than more of your quotations."

I saw my daughters struggling to keep from laughing.

"When Devorah escaped, I had a feeling she would come here."

"So you came to be with me?" Devorah said, giving Arik another hug.

"How romantic," Tzeitl sighed.

My daughters probably fantasize about a man going to heroic lengths for them, but no man makes such a sacrifice just for a woman. At least none that I have ever known.

"Well, yes and no."

Devorah backed away.

"My first concern was the refugees. You know the British navy escorted the ship to Haifa. The Jews put up a gallant struggle, staged a hunger strike, tried to fight off the boarding party. But the British used water cannons to spray the people on the deck and forced them to disembark. We were afraid they'd put them all right back on another ship and send them home. Fortunately, they were sent to Atlit Prison."

"The one near Haifa."

"That's the one, Aryeh."

"The Haganah decided that it could not allow these people, who had escaped with their lives from the Nazis, to have their lives threatened further. Yossi and Shimshon, do you remember them? The two boys who saved my life by bringing me here when I was wounded?"

"Of course I remember," I said. Their faces were a blur, but I could still hear their voices, especially the bitter one, Dr. Susser's son Yossi.

"They were the commanders of the operation. We had a group of our men pose as physical training instructors. They infiltrated the camp and sabotaged the guns of the Arabs whom the British used as guards. Yossi and Shimshon then cut through the fence and went to the immigrants' quarters. Amazingly, the English battalion slept through the entire thing. The refugees were all led out of the camp, though many had to be nearly carried out because they refused to leave behind the bundles of earthly possessions they'd brought from their homes."

"I had the same problem when we first brought them onto the ship," Devorah said.

"Shimshon and Yossi wouldn't let me participate in the actual operation because they thought I'd been out of combat too long. As it turned out, they needn't have worried, since no one had to fire a shot."

"If you weren't there, then how do you know what happened?"

"Natan!" I yelled.

"I didn't say I wasn't there. I said I didn't participate in the operation. After everyone was evacuated from the camp, they were taken to trucks. I was in charge of leading three truckloads to a kibbutz where they were to be disguised as members."

"So, which kibbutz did you take them to?" I asked.

Arik just smiled.

Simcha jumped up. "We must go and welcome our new members. Where are they?"

"They'll be here in a few minutes. I just drove ahead to let you know they were coming and make sure there were no objections to bringing them here. I took a motorcycle, that's why I'm so muddy."

"Objections?" I said. "You have brought these Jews home. You and Devorah both."

Devorah was beaming. Arik squeezed her hand.

"You've done it, my daughter. You have saved the whole world."

36

During the day, the sky here in Palestine can be so bright you feel as if you are being bathed in the rays from God's light. After sunset, when it is safe to stare into the heavens, I feel I am so close to the Creator of the Universe that He may speak to me at any time. I am patient and can wait for a sign, like the moment in Jerusalem when the stones of the *Kotel* seemed to vibrate under my fingers.

Right now, my mind is a cauldron of terrible thoughts. I remember wishing that Oren would invent something to stop Hitler. Instead, he made a machine to wash dishes, or should I say, alternate between cleaning and breaking them. Fortunately, America has its own Orens, and they developed the atomic bomb that ended the war.

It's hard to believe that years have passed since Devorah first brought back those terrible stories about the murder of European Jewry. She's gone again. She didn't say where she was going, but I'm sure it was back to Europe. Now that the war is over, the survivors of the catastrophe are waiting to see if any country will take them in. Can you believe their liberators put them right back into camps? Jews are now "displaced persons."

The Jews of Palestine would welcome them with open arms, but we still do not have the power to bring them to their homeland. Despite the best efforts of Bernice, Weizmann, Ben-Gurion and the rest, we seem no closer to independence than when I arrived in this land that God and Lord Balfour promised us.

At least some Jews reached the Promised Land and were saved. The refugees that Devorah had brought from Europe, and Arik had liberated from prison, were indeed welcomed. Almost all of them stayed with us and have become productive members of the kibbutz. The words of one man who left, though, may have had the greatest impact on me. When he saw the barbed wire encircling the kibbutz, he said, "I never want to see another fence again."

Still, he and the others were alive, thanks, in part, to my daughter. Devorah is doing God's work. But where has God been to do His own work?

I still remember what Devorah said the day she returned. As horrible as what she told me sounded, I could not believe that she would question God. Her remark had stimulated me to hold that study session with the other *chaverim* to discuss the Book of Job, but it wasn't satisfying. The answers we came up with for why God allowed suffering make even less sense now that we know the extent of the calamity that befell our people.

I know I've questioned God all my life, about everything from why my horse went lame on the Sabbath to why I was condemned to a life of poverty. I can understand why God would be too busy to worry about Tevye the milkman, but how could He turn his back on millions of his children?

When we first heard about the camps, we couldn't believe it. Even after the horror stories Devorah had told me, I wasn't prepared for the photographs from the camps after the liberation. I believe the images will haunt me until the end of my days. I thought the pogroms in Russia were the worst acts God would permit man against his fellow man. I was wrong.

"Dear Lord, how could You turn your back on Your chosen people? How? The pictures I've seen. They come to me in my sleep. Piles of burnt bodies. Deformed skeletons that were once living, breathing humans. Mountains of hair, shoes, glasses. The tiny bodies of children in ditches."

"Did You bless me with a long life so I could witness the destruction of our people? You couldn't have taken me after the family was reunited, before this, this *churban*."

"You know I had made tremendous progress in teaching Your words to the *chaverim*. Most of them never had faith and now they feel vindicated in their original agnosticism. Some tell me there is no God, or, if there was, He must be dead. Is this supposed to be the ultimate test of faith, like asking Noah to build an ark in preparation for the flood? This can't be the reason You've kept me alive."

"Oh God, how could You take our greatest sages in such a way? I know that Akiva was murdered, and many other rabbis have been martyred, but how could You allow the destruction of so many of the teachers from Europe? And the children? What was their sin? How many would have grown to be righteous men and women? How many would have become teachers? Doctors? Farmers? How many?"

"How can this all be for the best? How can the murder of millions be for the best? How? When the Israelites cried out in Egypt, You heard their cries and freed them from bondage. Oh, Merciful God, why were You deaf to the cries from the camps? Why?"

"So, you're talking to the Almighty again, my prince," Golde shouted. "Why don't you ask why He brought me a husband who is always late? It's almost the Sabbath and . . . . Tevye, what's wrong?"

I barely heard her words. I felt like the kibbutz tractor had just rolled to a stop on my chest. I saw Golde's eyes grow wide.

"Tevye!"

37

"Why is everyone looking at me? Do I have food stuck in my beard?"

"Papa, you fainted," Sarah said.

"Fainted? What are you talking about?"

"Mama saw you collapse in the courtyard," Tzeitl said with a concerned look on her face.

I suddenly realized I was in bed staring up at the members of my family. Golde was sitting in a chair beside me rubbing her hands over and over.

"What's everybody looking at? I just fainted. It was probably the heat."

"It was more than just the heat, *Zeyde*," Leah said. "You've been working too hard. Dr. Riesman told you to take it easy. And the stress of the last few months hasn't helped."

"Papa," Hodel ordered, "you're not to work anymore. You need to rest."

"Not work? A kibbutznik who doesn't work is not a kibbutznik. I'll be all right as soon as I get out of here. I don't like hospitals, they make you sick."

I started to sit up, but my head began spinning and I fell back on the pillow.

"Well, maybe I'll rest for a little while. But I'm going back to work. I don't care what you and the rest of the committee here say."

"Hodel, you should know your father well enough to realize he's too stubborn to listen to anyone, even the doctor. If we ever need a mule, we know where to look."

"Very funny, Golde. This is the way you treat a man on his sick bed."

"A second ago you were ready to get up and work."

"A second ago you hadn't made me sick."

"I think he's feeling better," Sarah said.

"That's enough, everyone. Sick or not, he needs some rest. You can visit him again in the morning." Leah started to nudge everyone toward the door.

"Good night, Papa," each of my children and grandchildren said, and kissed me on the cheek.

"Good night, my friend. Sleep well," Simcha said, sparing me the kiss.

My family stood in the doorway waiting for Golde. I really hadn't thought about dying, but seeing those faces and knowing what was in their hearts made me feel the only reason to object if the Lord comes for me now is the desire to see my other children one more time. But someone else had something to say about my fate.

"You all go on ahead. I want to sit with your father for another minute."

Golde looked over to Leah, who shrugged, "Just don't stay too long. He really does need to rest."

"It's amazing how much she acts like Devorah," Golde said as Leah went to check on the other patients.

"An angel of the Lord," I said.

"Now, you are another story."

"What have I done? I'm not even upright at the moment." I could see from the serious look on Golde's face she was not in the mood for levity. "What's the matter?"

"You, you stubborn old ox. You're not taking care of yourself. I've invested a lot of years in you and I'm not ready to see you die. You understand me. I forbid you to die!"

"You forbid it? I wish it were in my power to obey, believe me. I'm in no hurry to leave. As the Good Book says —"

"This is no time for your quotations."

"There is a quotation for every time."

Golde began to cry. "I'm sorry, Tevye. I know how you feel about crying. It's just that I hadn't really thought about what life would be like without you before. I just took it for granted that we'd always be together."

So many years ago, in a far off place, we stood together under the *chuppah*. I was scared to death. I was going to spend the rest of my life with someone I knew practically nothing about. My father arranged the match and that was that. He made an excellent choice. The wisdom of that tradition was borne out over the decades Golde and I have enjoyed together. Oh, how everything has changed.

"We *will* always be together, Golde, in spirit if not in body. The love that has grown between us since the day we met — our wedding day — is as real and enduring as Mount Sinai. I know I haven't always been the easiest man to live with —"

"You've never been the easiest man to live with."

"Thank you very much. But, as I was saying, I know our lives haven't always been as joyous as a *Simchas Torah* celebration, but we've been blessed with wonderful children and grandchildren. We've had the opportunity to see the Promised Land, and to help rebuild our homeland. Not even Moses himself did that."

"That's true."

"And Golde, my love for you has grown like the wisdom of the sages, deeper and deeper. I did think about life without you. I didn't want to think about it, but in the dark days after Shoshana's death, I was not sure if you would survive. I realized that without you I would have been lost, even here, surrounded by so many friends."

"Really?"

"Yes, really. Until that time I don't think I understood how much you meant to me, and how much I needed you. We pray that God is our strength, our rock, but I believe He works His will through you."

Golde began weeping again.

"I know I haven't said it often enough, but I love you Golde."

"And I love you Tevye."

Golde rested her head on my chest for a long time. I stroked her hair and wondered if she believed my sentiments had come from the heart. I was surprised how easy the words came and wondered why I had not said them to her years before. Maybe I could have lightened her burden.

"Come on, *Bubbe*," Leah said. "*Zeyde* really does need to get some sleep. And so do you. I'll watch after him tonight. I'm sure he'll feel much better tomorrow. Come back before breakfast."

Golde leaned over and kissed me in a way she had not in some time. I had a sudden feeling of desperation and held her to prolong the kiss. She broke away and smiled.

"See you in the morning, Tevye. *Leila tov.*"

"*Leila tov*, Golde."

I watched Golde leave and hoped it would not be the last time I would see her.

"I meant what I said, *Zeyde*," Leah said. "You need your sleep. If you want anything, I'll be here all night. Just call." She bent over and kissed me on the cheek.

"If I knew I could get this much affection, I think I would have gotten sick years ago."

"Go to sleep."

Leah began to visit other patients and I closed my eyes. It felt good to rest.

I don't know how long I was asleep before a ghastly apparition appeared. The face looked a little like Chaim, the man who had broken Shoshana's heart and drove her to suicide. Chaim would still be a relatively young person, but the figure before me looked like an old man on the verge of death. He was nearly bald, with only wisps of hair above his ears. His cheeks were almost hollow, as though all his teeth were gone. He was so emaciated, I could see through his skin. After all these years, why was I having such a dream? Were my worst nightmares coming back to me just before dying?

I tried to shoo the ghost away, but it kept coming toward me. Then it spoke.

"Tevye. You must forgive me. I had no choice. Please, Tevye, forgive me."

I screwed my eyes shut to try to make it disappear. I felt the touch of a bony hand on my wrist.

"Tevye. I must have your forgiveness before I die. You don't know the price that I've paid for my mistake. Please, forgive me."

The ghost fell on its knees beside my bed and rested its head on my arm. I felt wetness that I realized were tears. I opened my eyes again and knew that I was not dreaming. Chaim the Socialist, the man whose father thought he was too good for my daughter, who abandoned her on her wedding night, was prostrate before me.

Through the years, I had cursed Chaim, and blamed him for Shoshana's death. This skeleton groveling at my feet had killed my precious daughter as surely as if he'd taken the glass to her wrists. Still, after all this time, I could take no comfort in the torment he had obviously suffered. I don't know if it was the passage of time or his haggard appearance that made me speak the words he sought.

"I forgive you Chaim. I forgive you."

The ashen face looked up at me. Tears were flowing down his cheeks. Up close, he looked like my image of the Angel of Death.

"Thank you. Thank you."

When he opened his mouth, I could see several of his teeth were missing and others were black.

He kissed the back of my hand. "Now I can die in peace."

He struggled to stand and started to limp away.

"No, Chaim, wait. You mustn't die. You've come too far. Please, sit with me awhile." I managed to sit up without being overcome by dizziness, and pushed a chair toward him. "I did not forgive you so you could give up on life. You've returned to your home. Everything will be all right now, you'll see."

"No, Tevye. Everything can never be all right. You don't know what I've seen, what I've done."

"Sit, please. Tell me what happened to you."

I watched Chaim pad over to the chair. He sat gingerly. He looked as though he might be toppled by a swarm of gnats.

"There is so much that is too upsetting to talk about, Tevye."

"It's okay, Chaim. Tell me what you can."

"When I left the kibbutz to see my family before the wedding, I intended to tell my father that I loved Shoshana and planned to make her my bride. Nothing he could do or say would change my mind. When I arrived at his house, everything was packed. I didn't understand, and all my father would say is that he had problems with the business and that he had to return to Germany immediately because his brother was in some sort of trouble. He said he needed me, the family needed me, and that staying in Palestine would break my mother's heart and maybe put an end to his business. I thought it was a ruse to get me away from Shoshana, but it was hard to believe he would go to such lengths just to prevent me from marrying."

I thought back to my meeting with the fat man with the cigar and obnoxious squealing laugh, and how opposed he was to the wedding. Leaving Palestine was an extreme measure, but not impossible to imagine.

"I had left the family to move to the kibbutz, but I didn't feel I could turn my back on them in their hour of need. I thought I'd be able to help solve whatever problem my father had and quickly return to the kibbutz. I wanted to write to Shoshana to explain, but my father forbade it. I wrote anyway, but don't know what happened to my letters. Knowing him, he probably paid someone to intercept them, I don't know."

I remembered we had received some letters, but I'd torn them up without opening them.

"None of us ever knew what happened to you or your family. I went to the house and it was empty."

"Please forgive me. Forgive me!"

He fell on my hand again and sobbed.

"Chaim, I've already forgiven you. The past is past. Please tell me how you came to be in this condition."

"I'm sorry."

Chaim sat up and wiped the tears away with his bony arms.

"Well, my father had not completely lied. His brother was having troubles with the business and my father and I tried to help straighten them out. Eventually we settled all the debts and started to rebuild the company. Then Hitler came to power. Soon we found our property confiscated. Like other Jews, we were stripped of our rights. My uncle kept saying not to worry, that Jews were the backbone of the nation, that Hitler wouldn't dare harm us."

"As you know now, conditions grew worse and worse. I begged my father to return to Palestine, but he became more obstinate, determined to prove that he could not be intimidated by Hitler or his jack-booted bullies. After *Kristallnacht,* he began to change his mind, but by then it was almost impossible to leave for Palestine. He thought about going to America, but his mother — my grand-mother — got sick and he couldn't leave her."

Chaim put his face in his hands. I thought he would start cry-ing again, but he just caught his breath and continued.

"I might have been able to come back, Tevye, but I couldn't leave my family, especially after the situation for German Jews had deteriorated. I knew we were in for difficult times, but I never imagined — no one did."

"You did the right thing. The Good Book says 'A wise son hears his father's instruction.'"

"Who can talk about right and wrong anymore? Was it right to steal a mouthful of bread from another prisoner to satisfy my hun-ger? Was it right to help the Nazis steal from Jews to avoid being sent to the gas chamber?"

"Chaim, you're rambling. What are you talking about?"

"I told you, I've done terrible things, Tevye. But you're right, I've gotten ahead of my story. I will spare you most of the grisly details. And there was more gore than — I'm sorry, my mind doesn't work too well these days."

"Take your time. If it's too painful —"

"I no longer feel pain. The Nazis made me numb. It helped me survive, God help me."

When Chaim ran his hand over his bald scalp, I could see a number tattooed on the inside of his forearm.

"Maybe you'd like to lie down and we can talk in the morning."

"No, I couldn't bear to spend all night thinking about what I have to tell you," he said, grabbing my arm so weakly I might not have known he had touched me if I hadn't seen him do it.

"Well, I told you my grandmother got sick. By the time she recovered, the Nazis had begun to deport Polish citizens. My grandmother was born in Cracow, so she was sent back there. She couldn't take care of herself anymore, so my father went with her. My uncle and mother were not allowed to go for almost a year. Not long after the family was reunited, Germany invaded Poland. My father told me to leave the country, but I was captured by the Nazis and sent back to Cracow."

I sat listening to Chaim's account, knowing that it would only get worse, and that millions of other Jews did not live to tell their stories. If Motel had not earned enough money to allow the family to escape Poland when they did, he, Tzeitl, Hodel and my grandchildren might have suffered a similar fate. The thought made me suddenly feel more sympathetic toward Chaim.

"I was forced to register for a work detail near town. I never believed I would look back fondly at that ordeal. By this time, my grandmother had died. I didn't know what happened to the rest of my family. When I was deported to a new camp, I lost contact with them. I was sent from camp to camp before ending up in Auschwitz. By some miracle, I found my uncle there still alive. He told me that both my parents had been gassed. I gave my uncle part of my food ration, wormy soup and some sawdust the Germans called bread, but he became too weak to work. When he collapsed, he was taken to the gas chamber."

I was surprised by the matter-of-fact tone of Chaim's voice. I guessed that was part of what he meant when he said he no longer felt pain.

"You know Tevye, Jews don't believe in hell the way Christians do. Maybe that's why it's impossible to visualize Auschwitz. It was hell. Do you know what I had to do to stay alive, Tevye? I can't even tell you half the things, but my main job was to sit in a room full of shoes."

"Shoes?"

"Yes, shoes. Piled to the ceiling. The Germans learned that some Jews from Belgium and the Netherlands were hiding diamonds and gold in the soles of their shoes. Before they were gassed, their shoes were brought to us so we could rip them apart.

Whatever we found, we turned over to the guards. One day a prisoner was caught hiding a small diamond in his mouth. A guard threw him against the wall and shot him six times, right in front of us. No one ever tried to keep anything they found again."

"You did what you had to do. No one can blame you for that."

"You don't understand. No one who wasn't there can understand."

I wanted to disagree, but I knew he was right.

"Did you escape?"

"The Soviets liberated me just in time — I was on the verge of death. Ironic, eh? A Jew saved by the Russians. I was one of the lucky ones. Most people who entered Auschwitz never left."

"And how did you get back here?"

"God's will or dumb luck. I eventually made my way back to Cracow to see if any members of my family were left. They were all gone. While I was there, I learned about a Jewish agent who was helping to arrange passage to Palestine on an old freighter. It turned out to be Devorah. She had every right to leave me to my fate in Poland after the pain I'd caused her; there were many others who she could have taken instead, but she insisted on taking care of me. Devorah brought me food and medicine. You think I look bad now, you should have seen me then. Devorah was like an angel. She brought me home."

"But why weren't you here when Arik brought the other immigrants he freed from the British prison?"

"The escape was not organized. Soldiers raced in and told us where to go. I was directed to a truck that took me to another kibbutz, one down in the Negev. It took me a little while to get back here."

He broke down again. I was afraid if he cried any more he might evaporate.

"Chaim, the past is finished. You're alive! You must be thankful for that. And you've returned to your home and your family. We will all take care of you now."

"But you still don't understand," Chaim said through his tears. "I want to join Shoshana. I want to die."

38

Chaim was right when he said I couldn't understand what he had endured, or why he wanted to die. How could someone who survived the camps and made it all the way back to our little kibbutz want to give up his life?

On one hand, I think about the catastrophe in Europe and wonder how God could let it happen. Why would he forsake so many Jews? On the other hand, maybe the Jews were like the Israelites in Egypt. When we read the Passover story in the Haggada, we don't blame God for enslaving His people; we praise His glorious name for the miracles that brought the Israelites to freedom. Maybe the miracle is that God saved as many Jews as He did, and that so many have come here to the land God promised us.

Do I dare ask why more people were not saved, why it took so long for God to hear the pleas of all the Chaims in the camps? The Israelites suffered for four-hundred years under the Pharaohs, and then wandered forty years in the desert after their liberation before they were allowed to reach this place. Chaim was luckier, if I can use such word to describe a survivor of those horrors.

While we were both in the hospital recovering, I tried to talk to Chaim about what he had to live for, how if he were to give up now, after all he'd gone through, he would give Hitler a final victory. I tried to convince him he owed it to his family to be a witness so no one would forget what was done to them, and to carry on the family name.

I spent a lot of time with Chaim, quoting from the Bible, telling jokes, holding him when the nightmares came each night. But, I must confess, none of my efforts made any difference. His life was probably saved by a more compassionate soul — my daughter Sarah.

I'm not sure I understand what motivated Sarah. Maybe it was pity, or a desire to somehow justify Shoshana's feelings toward Chaim. Maybe she felt a connection to her sister through Chaim. Whatever it was, Sarah brought Chaim back to life. I think the fact that the sister of the woman he'd wronged forgave him provided some relief from the guilt he had carried for so long, and which had intensified when he returned to the kibbutz and learned of Shoshana's suicide.

Sarah spent most of her nonworking hours with Chaim. She would bring him back to the house and they would sit with Rachel. My darling mute Rachel is probably the only person on the kibbutz who could understand Chaim's pain, and he, in turn, was the only one who appreciated hers.

Sometimes I would watch them together. Sarah would just sit silently knitting and listening to Chaim. He spoke to Rachel as though she heard every word. I thought Chaim would tell Rachel what had happened to him to show her it was possible to recover, but, as far as I know, he never did. When Chaim was with Rachel, he only spoke of happy memories; times he spent with his family, the early days on the kibbutz. By forcing himself to think about the good times, Chaim began to feel better about his own life.

It took many months, but Chaim began to regain his strength. The color returned to his skin, and he asked to work again. Before much longer, he was as productive as any member of the kibbutz.

From the day he arrived, he had been welcomed as a *chaver* who had been away on an extended trip. We were now the only family he had and, when he realized the past had not caused anyone to turn their back on him, he felt at home once again.

If you'll excuse the expression, the final step in Chaim's resurrection occurred when he and Sarah moved into the same house.

Golde wasn't happy about it, of course, but this had always been the traditional way for the *chaverim* to become joined. One day a couple would ask permission to share a house and, from that point on, the kibbutz considered them married.

How did I feel? Are you kidding? Have I ever had any say in making matches for my daughters?

So now I have another son-in-law. My other one, Motel, is now the chairman of the Executive Committee. It's been gratifying to see him and his son Aryeh talking about strategies for defending the kibbutz. Imagine, that scrawny tailor has become our general!

Watching Motel and Aryeh together also makes me long to see Abraham. It has been many years since he ran off to join the underground. So many hours we could have shared.

Bernice is very upset with him, not Abraham so much as the men he associates with now. She said the Jewish Agency had become so angry with the Irgun's actions, the Haganah had been ordered to help the British track down its members.

"Jews turning Jews into the British? I don't understand," I told her.

Bernice lit a cigarette and pumped it in and out of her mouth anxiously.

"The Haganah and the Irgun worked together for a while against the British," she explained, "but then we began to worry that the British would respond with such severity that our hope of winning support for independence would be dashed altogether. We decided the Haganah should concentrate on illegal immigration. That was when Devorah went back to Europe."

"So what did Abraham do wrong?"

"Abraham has done nothing wrong. But the Irgun is uncontrollable. Their leader won't listen to anyone."

Bernice sounded exasperated. I had read in the newspaper about some of the Irgun's activities, but hadn't realized the Jewish Agency was so upset.

"While we've been trying to reduce the level of violence in Palestine, they've been escalating it," she continued. "I'm not saying Abraham was part of any of this, but first they started attacking soldiers and then, well, you know what happened at the King David."

"I couldn't believe it when I heard the news. I still remember when you took Golde and me to see that fancy hotel across from the YMCA. I'd never seen anything like it. You said something about it being the headquarters of the British."

"One wing of the building was used by British intelligence, but the bombing killed nearly one-hundred people, some of them Jews."

"My Abraham killed Jews?"

"Tevye, did you hear what I said? I don't know that Abraham was involved in any of this."

"Bernice, please don't treat me like a child. Abraham is in the Irgun, and the Irgun has done these terrible things. He is involved."

"All right, I won't lie to you. Listen, the Irgun and the Lehi believe they have to bomb the British out of Palestine. We think that's counterproductive. Ben-Gurion was so angry after the King David bombing, he was the one who ordered that members of the Irgun be turned over to the British."

"Do you think that will happen?"

"To be honest, probably not. The Irgun is very secretive. When the British searched the whole country on 'Black Sabbath' they didn't find a single one of their leaders."

"Why are you telling me this? You don't expect me to turn my own son into the British, do you?"

"Of course not," she said crushing out her cigarette and immediately lighting another. "I'm bringing this up now for the same reason I told you about Abraham being in the Irgun in the first place, to discourage him from staying with them. I know it will be difficult, maybe impossible, but try to talk him into leaving the Irgun. Everyone in the group is fiercely loyal, but tell him the Haganah would welcome him with open arms. Tevye, we're going to need everyone working together against the British and the Arabs if we are to have our state. The time is growing near. You know the United Nations sent a commission to investigate the desires of the Arabs and Jews in Palestine."

"They had to send a commission to find out what Jews and Arabs want?"

"It was more than a formality. This new international body has to see for itself what is and is not possible here. We believe they will recommend dividing Palestine into a Jewish and an Arab state."

"Like that old British plan, the Pest Plan."

"Peel, Tevye. The Peel Plan. Yes, something like that."

"Would the Agency accept dividing our homeland? Didn't God promise all of Palestine to the Jewish people?"

"Yes, Tevye, God promised the whole land to us. But, as I told you in the past, we're not likely to have much of a choice; it's either going to be a state in part of our homeland or nothing."

"Maybe we should choose nothing rather than sacrifice what the Almighty bequeathed us."

"I don't know what our final answer will be. Some people, including my close friends, oppose partition. They agree with your point, or argue that the proposed state will be so small we won't have room for all the Jewish refugees. The hard-line ideologues, the Agency's version of Eitan and Uzi, fear that partition will lead to a decline in agriculture and a shift toward towns and a more militant and bourgeois society."

"And what do you think, Bernice?"

"Tevye, I'm inclined to take what we can get now. I agree with your sentiments, but, politically, it's just not realistic to expect any nation, or this new United Nations organization, to give us the entire country, especially when the Arabs outnumber us."

"So maybe Abraham and the Irgun are right; maybe we should fight for all of our land."

"Fight the British? The United Nations? The United States? With what, our good looks? Listen, Tevye, we're not in a position of strength here. But don't worry, we will have to fight for our state, even if it's only half of our homeland. The Arabs will never accept partition. They want their own state where they can rule over us. They'll go to war before they let us govern them."

"And then what will happen?"

"Well, if God is truly on our side, and this is the Promised Land, we will prevail. I pray that we will live in peace after that, but I'm not optimistic. As your friend the sheikh told you from the beginning, the Arabs are prepared to fight until the end of time to drive us into the sea."

So that was Bernice's reading of the political situation. We had a good chance to be granted a state by the United Nations if my son and his comrades don't sabotage the Jewish Agency's diplomatic maneuvers. But even if we win a political victory, we will probably have to secure it on the battlefield against the Arabs. It was not the way I'd envisioned living my last years.

Bernice's analyses were usually correct, but I still hoped she was exaggerating, that maybe she was purposely being pessimistic so the *yishuv* would not get its hopes up too high. The only person I knew who could give me an honest opinion of what the Arabs thought, and would do, was my old friend Sheikh Jabber. Bernice was right, he had warned me from our first meeting that his people would never be satisfied living with Jews. I had not seen him for many years, since I rarely ventured outside the kibbutz anymore, but, against the wishes of Motel and Aryeh, I left the safety of my home and went looking for the sheikh.

The Bedouins moved from place to place throughout the year, but I knew Sheikh Jabber always returned to the hills beyond our kibbutz, so it did not take long to find his tent in the familiar place. As usual, before I got too close to the encampment, I was met by an escort of the sheikh's men, who brought me to the sheikh's "home" and led me inside. I was surprised to find Ali sitting where his father had always sat.

"*Salaam aleikum.* Come in my friend. We will drink and eat. It has been a very long time," Ali said, coming over to kiss me on both cheeks.

"*Aleikumu salaam.* Yes, it has. I apologize," I said, taking my usual place on the opposite side of the carpet. A veiled woman immediately brought me some tea.

"As you can see, I am not as young as I once was, so I don't like to leave the comfort of the kibbutz."

"Man should not be confined by gates or fences, Tevye."

"I wish it were so."

"For us Bedouin, it has always been so, and always will be."

I nodded and realized the Bedouins were probably the only truly free men in the world.

"You are looking at me strangely, Tevye. Oh, I know. It *has* been a long time. My father died some time ago. I am now the master of this tent."

"Your father was a good man, may he rest in peace."

"Thank you."

Ali gestured for me to drink and I sipped my tea.

"My father usually had us come to get you. You did not come here uninvited."

"I am sorry. I did not mean to intrude. You and your father always spoke truthfully to me about what would happen in Palestine. I hoped you would do so again so that I might know what to expect in the days ahead, before I go to join your father."

"Ah, my friend you have many years ahead of you still. But I fear the future does not look good for your people. The Arabs are very upset about the number of Jews coming into the country. They have always felt you were stealing their land and their homes. Now they know it is true and fear that nothing will be left if they do not stop you now."

"What about the United Nations?"

"They believe the United Nations is nothing more than a tool to enslave them. They will never accept any decision made in New York. As my father had me tell you many years ago, the Arabs will fight as long as it takes to drive the Jews from their land. You will never have your state, and you will never be allowed to live in peace, unless you submit to their will.

"You know that we will fight back."

"Yes, I know. The outcome is in the hands of Allah."

"I am sorry that it has to be this way."

"So am I."

I was scared to ask the next question.

"Will you join in the fight against us?"

Ali closed his eyes thoughtfully. He spoke without opening them. "We have lived as peaceful neighbors for many years. The kibbutz has expanded and taken much of our grazing lands, but my father said we should be patient, that Allah would provide. I wanted to attack the kibbutz and to take back what you have stolen, but he would not let me. Now I see the wisdom of his decision. The Arabs will attack you from every side, and they will either kill every Jew or drive you from our territory. Either way, you will be gone and we will once again have back our land."

I couldn't believe my ears. From our first introduction, I knew Ali had to struggle to restrain his anger, but Sheikh Jabber had shown me nothing but kindness and hospitality. He always told me what to expect from the Arabs, but the sheikh had never given any indication that he felt any animosity toward me. Now, at the end, I learn the truth.

Just as I was about to stand up, Ali pulled out a dagger. I was shocked that after all I'd gone through God would choose to end my life this way.

Ali stood and walked toward me with the knife. I froze, feeling as though a hand had reached from the center of the earth to hold me in place so that I might be sacrificed.

I could see the hatred flaring in Ali's eyes when he knelt down beside me. I closed my eyes and prayed that it would be over quickly.

I felt my hand being grabbed. I opened one eye and saw Ali holding my hand out and gently placing the handle of the dagger in my palm.

"My father made me promise to give this to you. He wanted you to have it so that you would know he gave you a chance to defend yourself. But, if I were you, I would run away. Go back to wherever you came from while you still have the chance."

I stood up slowly. The anger was rising in me as it never had in all my years.

"This is my home. I will not run and no one will drive me away."

I stood and started to storm out of the tent. I abruptly turned around and raised the knife in the air.

Ali's eyes widened as my arm came forward.

I threw the dagger as hard as I could.

Ali let out a gasp and fell backward. The knife tip stuck in the sand between his legs.

39

"Yields of radishes are smaller than anticipated," Timur said, "but the price has risen."

The report of the Economic Committee was never the highlight of the week. Golde had to elbow me from time to time to keep me awake.

"We're doing better with sugar beets. The Committee is also considering expanding the land devoted to radishes."

Timur was droning on. Suddenly, I heard the sound of tires squealing and rocks flying as a car came to a stop outside the dining hall. A moment later, Bernice burst through the door like a woman looking for her husband in a brothel. Her head was swiveling around while everyone stared at her.

"Tevye! Tevye! Come quickly," she called out.

I could see Golde had a terrified look on her face, her intuition naturally expecting a catastrophe.

"Oh, there you are," Bernice said when she saw me struggling to get to my feet. She rushed over. "We must go immediately. There's no time to waste."

"What's happened?" Golde asked on the verge of panic. "Is it one of the children?"

"I can't explain now, Golde. We'll be back as soon as we can. Tevye, let's go. We'll talk in the car."

"But where are we going? Do I need to pack?"

"Just come quickly. You don't need anything."

Bernice was tugging at my sleeve, but I couldn't move too fast, my feet have been hurting lately and Dr. Riesman insisted I walk with a cane. She finally realized I couldn't keep up with her and slowed to my pace.

"I'm sorry, Tevye. I wouldn't rush you if it wasn't so urgent."
"What is it?"

"In the car. Please."

Bernice opened the door and helped me into the backseat. She sat beside me and, an instant later, the car spun its wheels and skidded around the courtyard and back out onto the road.

When we were beyond the kibbutz grounds, Bernice leaned over and spoke in her politician's voice to me.

"Tevye, I won't mince words. I told you that Abraham was mixed up with the wrong crowd, and I know you've never had a chance to talk to him about it, but that no longer matters. Right now, he's in prison."

"Prison!"

"I'm sorry to be the one to tell you. He was arrested and sent to Acre Prison."

"For what? What has he done?" I was in such a state of shock, words tumbled out.

"Apparently he was captured several days ago throwing a hand grenade at a British officer's car. I just found out about it a few hours ago."

"Oh Lord. Oh Lord. Bernice, what is to become of him?"

"That's the reason I came so quickly." Bernice turned away from me and stared out the window.

"What is it? What are you afraid to tell me, Bernice? Please!"

"He's been sentenced to death along with two other members of the Irgun."

I couldn't breathe.

"But we think we can prevent the sentences from being carried out," Bernice added quickly.

My chest felt like it was going to explode. I thought I might be having a heart attack.

"Tevye, breathe. Breathe. Come on, you can't help Abraham if you kill yourself with worry. That's it, calm down. We have time to talk before we get to Acre."

Every part of my body began shaking. Bernice put her arm around me and tried to ease my anxiety, but that was impossible.

"Tevye, let me explain the situation and what we have to do. Events have been spiraling out of control for weeks. First, the British flogged two Jews who were caught robbing a bank. The Irgun retaliated by whipping some British soldiers. When the British threatened to hang some of the Irgunists in prison, the Irgun announced it would do the same to Englishmen. The British carried out the death sentences and the Irgun did the same."

"But my Abraham. What was he doing throwing a grenade at a soldier?"

"As I said, Tevye, the atmosphere has grown more and more stormy. The Irgun is waging a war against the British and carrying out acts of terrorism so vile that Ben-Gurion has ordered the Haganah to capture their leaders."

"How can we turn on each other?"

"You've got to understand the impact of the Irgun's actions. They've attacked the military headquarters in Tel Aviv, the district police headquarters in Jaffa, shot soldiers on the street, blew up an officer's club. The list goes on and on. London considers us savages and rages against us, saying we are too barbaric for independence. And the bastards may be right."

"Oh Bernice, you know my years of study have taught me little of politics. I care only about my Abraham, my only son."

"Tevye, I know. I know. I just want you to understand why the British are in no mood to show any leniency toward any Jew they capture right now."

The question was suspended in the air like a seagull in a stiff breeze. I couldn't avoid it any longer.

"When is he to be hanged?"

Bernice couldn't look me in the eye. Softly, she said, "Soon."

I choked back tears. "How soon?"

"We don't know for sure. Perhaps as early as this week."

"Oh God of Abraham, Isaac and Jacob, how could this be? How could you claim another of my children?"

"Come on, Tevye, you've got to pull yourself together," Bernice said, embracing me tightly. "I came to get you so you could see each other again."

"You mean for the last time."

"No, I don't believe that. And you mustn't either, Tevye. No one I know has greater faith than you. In good times, it's easy to maintain that belief. It's in difficult times like these that true men of God — men like you, Tevye — keep their faith."

"How can I? God is taking my only son."

"Tevye, remember that after all his years of childlessness, our father Abraham was granted a son, and that he, too, thought God would take the child from him. You know what happened. Maybe it's prophetic that you named your son Abraham, I don't know. What I am sure of is that you have a chance to talk to Abraham. You must tell him to get word to the Irgun not to retaliate by taking British hostages, because the situation will only be made worse."

"What do you mean about hostages?"

"That has been the Irgun's pattern recently, especially when one of their members is due to be executed. They've been abducting soldiers and threatening to kill them to avenge the deaths of their men. Their actions are like the first nine plagues against Pharaoh; they only harden our Pharaoh in London's heart."

"Why should Abraham listen to me? We haven't spoken, haven't seen each other for years, since long before he joined the Irgun."

"You've got to try. The lunatics in charge of the Irgun don't listen to reason, or anything else, but you have to try."

"All right, I'll try."

"Good. That's not our only strategy. We are also going to ask the High Commissioner to commute Abraham's sentence."

"The British High Commissioner? Why would he listen to me?"

"Again, he might not. But I used every chit I had to get you a meeting with him after we leave the prison. Beg for leniency.

Tell him that you understand your son has committed a terrible crime."

"But has he?"

"It doesn't matter, Tevye. This is what you have to say to save his life. Tell the High Commissioner you believe Abraham has to pay for what he has done, but that life in prison would be a harsh enough penalty to impose on such a young man."

"Life in prison," I repeated, unable to comprehend how my life, and my son's life, could be turned upside down so quickly.

"When we win our independence, and I believe the time is growing nearer, we can get Abraham released. But we've got to make sure he stays alive until then. Do you understand now?"

"I think so."

"Good. We've got a long ride. Try to rest a bit."

I didn't want to rest. Talking at least kept my mind busy. Now, all I can do is torture myself with thoughts of why and how and where and what.

How could a son of mine lose his moral center and commit such terrible acts? Where did I fail? Why wasn't I a better teacher?

I want to believe, oh how I want to believe that Bernice is right, that God is testing me as He did Abraham, and that the Lord would not have granted me a son after so many years just to take him away. But I never would have believed Chaveleh or Shoshana or Rachel would be taken from me.

The incident with Rachel drove Abraham so far from the path of righteousness that I can't recognize the route. I didn't like, but at least understood, his desire to take revenge against the Arabs, but what drove him to violence against the British?

"Bernice, why is the Irgun so violent? What do they think they're accomplishing?"

"I'm tempted to be flip, and say they're only getting themselves killed and Jewish statehood postponed, but I'll try to be fair in presenting their viewpoint." She rolled down the car window, lit a cigarette and leaned back in her seat.

"Their basic philosophy is that Jews must be strong, that it is might that will bring us independence. They see the Agency as a bunch of kibitzers who talk while the British apathetically watch the Arabs murder us. To them, Ben-Gurion is a kind of Jewish Nero, fiddling while Palestine burns. They are convinced the Arabs only respect strength and that their actions demonstrate Jewish power. The Irgun believes the British will never leave unless they are bombed out."

"But what about the United Nations? Why did the British turn our fate over to them?"

"On this point, I think I probably agree with the Irgun. London doesn't believe the U.N. will be any more successful in finding a solution than anyone else. I think the prime minister expects the U.N. to throw up its hands and leave England to solve it. Then the British will feel justified in whatever they decide."

"So what is your quarrel with the Irgun?"

"I still believe our best hope lies with the international community, especially the Americans. We have to get outside help to pressure the British to leave. The Irgun's hit-and-run attacks aren't going to intimidate the mighty British army. If the English want to, they can crush us like a bug, just like they ended the Arab revolt when London became fed up with the violence. The Irgun just hurts our cause with other nations, gets good Jewish boys killed and provokes the British to retaliate against the Haganah and the Agency."

I turned away from Bernice. Staring out the window, I watched the landscape fly past as we drove down the bumpy road and thought how history repeats itself. This was how the last Jewish state collapsed, from disunity. How did our people come to be so divided? We are such a tiny minority here, we cannot afford to fight among ourselves. Even if we win our independence, how will we become one people again? We've already got three armies.

Bernice and I sat silently for some time. When we got close to Acre, I told her I'd never been there, so she started to explain the city's history.

"It was a Canaanite city that fell to all the conquerors of Palestine. When Richard the Lion-Hearted captured it in the twelfth century, it became the capital of the Crusader kingdom. One hundred years later, the Mamelukes seized it and slaughtered the Christians and Jews. The Ottoman Turks later built up the city and withstood a siege by Napoleon. Up until the development of Haifa, it was a major port. The Citadel where Abraham is held is a Crusader fortress in a corner of the city near the sea. It's considered the most impregnable prison in Palestine."

British soldiers were everywhere when we reached Acre. Bernice explained that they were on high alert expecting the Irgun to take revenge for the latest convictions.

When we got close to the edge of the old city, we were close to the sea. The sun's rays were glistening on the water. Somehow a barefoot boy had reached a rock sticking up like a tiny island, and was fishing with a wooden pole. A few minutes later we were crossing over a moat that had protected the Crusaders in the Citadel. The forbidding stone walls towered over us. I could see places where cannonballs lodged in the walls from some past war.

When we arrived at the gate, Bernice showed the guards passes she'd obtained. They looked at us skeptically and made us wait while one made a phone call, presumably to verify the authenticity of our documents. When the fellow on the phone was satisfied, he gestured for another guard to let us in. First, he took away my cane, telling me that nothing that might be used as a weapon could be brought into the prison. I never wanted the thing in the first place, so I told him to keep it.

We were led down a narrow corridor through a series of iron-barred gates. Finally, we were told to stop in front of one gate. I looked at Bernice. She just shrugged her shoulders.

A few minutes later, a guard came walking toward us.

"You have ten minutes."

"Ten minutes, but I haven't seen my son —"

"Ten minutes."

He stepped aside as he spoke and I saw a man in red pajamas waddling down the hall. He couldn't move very quickly because his feet were chained. His hands were behind his back. I knew it was my son, but I hardly recognized him. It had been so long since I'd last seen him. Now he was a grown man, taller than me and built as solidly as Jerusalem stone. His hair was still dark and tousled, like when he was a teenager, but his face was different. He had a moustache and the beginnings of a beard, but that wasn't what had changed. It was something about his expression. When he was younger, he had a playful, mischievous look. After the incident, he appeared angry all the time. But now he seemed like the picture of rage and defiance. Without speaking, his clenched jaw and unmoving eyes communicated the message that he didn't care what anyone said or thought.

"Ten minutes," another guard repeated when he brought Abraham to the front of the bars.

"The handcuffs?" Bernice asked.

"They stay on," the guard said gruffly before moving to a corner of the room just beyond earshot.

I started to reach through the bars to embrace him.

"None of that, Sir."

"But I just want to give my son a hug."

"Sorry, it's not permitted."

"But —"

"Tevye, remember we're in a prison and they are suspicious of everyone and everything," Bernice whispered.

"I'm sorry you have to see me this way, Papa. I wish we could be reunited under more pleasant circumstances."

"Seeing you under any circumstances is a blessing, Abraham. How are you?"

"I'm all right. Really, now I'm fine. But you need to get the word out to the papers about the way the British treat Jewish prisoners."

"What do you mean?"

"I mean that when I was captured the guards took everything away from me, money, watch, ring, comb. Then they began to beat me."

"No!"

"Papa, I'm not telling you this to upset you or so you'll feel sorry for me. The British say the Irgun and the Lehi are terrorists, but it's important that the world knows what barbarians they are. Soldiers punched me in the stomach until I doubled over and then straightened me up by hitting me in the face. After awhile, I was taken to a field where other prisoners had been gathered. We were stripped completely naked and savagely beaten. They hit and kicked us everywhere. I'm afraid that even if I was to survive now, I'd be no use to any wife."

"Oh God of our fathers." I squeezed my eyes shut, not wanting to see the images of my son being tortured.

"We were forced to sleep naked in the field, with only one thin blanket to cover all of us. In the morning, the blanket was drenched with our blood. One of the soldiers turned on a hose and sprayed us with freezing water. It was their idea of a shower. Then they returned our clothes and made us stand in the sun with our hands over our heads for nearly an hour. Finally, we were brought here."

"Are you hurt now?"

"No. Since I've been here, things have been better. I just sit in a tiny cell with an iron cot most of the day. They allow us outside to exercise for a few hours. The rest of the time I read the *Chumash*."

We stood inches from each other, separated by rusting iron. At that instant, I wanted nothing more in this world than to hold him in my arms the way I did when he was a baby and protect him from harm.

"Bernice told me you were arrested for throwing a grenade at a soldier."

"It wasn't just any soldier. It was the intelligence chief who has been responsible for tracking down many of our men. Papa, I don't expect you to understand. I have done what I thought was necessary to protect our people, to reestablish the Jewish kingdom in the land God promised to us."

"But by violence? Bernice and I and everyone have the same goal. Why did you have to use violence?"

"Don't you see, Papa? There is no other way. I love Bernice like an aunt, but she and the others from the Agency have been talking for years, since before I was born, and where has it gotten us? The Arabs are allowed to kill Jews with impunity; the British kept Jews from escaping from Hitler and now imprison the remnant of our people who survived in camps on Cyprus. The Arabs will never leave us in peace, and the British will never grant us independence. Don't you see that our only hope is to fight for our freedom? Just like the Maccabees."

The reference reminded me of the young boy who played Judah Maccabee in Rachel's play. Abraham was now trying to live the part.

"All I really care about is getting you out of here so you can return to your mother and your sisters, everyone who loves you."

"How is the family?"

The muscles in his face seemed to slacken. For a moment, he looked like the Abraham I knew when he was a child.

"You wouldn't believe how everyone has grown. Tzeitl is busy all the time, just like her mother used to be. Motel has become a *macher* on the kibbutz. Their children are treasures. Rebecca still likes to work with the women in the kitchen, Leah is an angel of mercy in the infirmary and little Aryeh is no longer little. He's now in charge of defending the kibbutz."

"Aryeh? Really? Is he trained?"

"He's like you, tough as cowhide."

"And Hodel and Sarah?"

"Hodel is also a leader. Everyone looks up to her, almost the way they did Jonathan. She's married now to Simcha."

"Ah, that's wonderful."

"And Sarah is also married."

"You're kidding? To whom?"

"A man named Chaim." I was about to tell him that he had once been engaged to Shoshana, then decided not to. "He's a survivor. Devorah brought him out."

"And how is my big sister?"

"We don't know where she is right now."

"Hmm, Hmm," Golde cleared her throat behind me and nodded toward the guards.

"She's been involved in some special projects. She's performed miracles. You would be proud."

"I know a little about her work and I am proud. I think she's the only one who would understand what I've done. And Mama?"

"The same. A few more gray hairs. She can still talk until the *mashiach* arrives."

A slight smile crossed Abraham's lips.

"Rachel?"

"She's gotten so big and beautiful and, well, nothing's changed."

The smile disappeared and the hard look returned to Abraham's face.

"The years. So many years have passed, that we can never get back, that I wanted us to be together."

"I know, Papa. I would have liked nothing better than to live my life on the kibbutz, just like you and Mama. Nothing could have made me happier. But God chose a different path for me the day Rachel was raped by those Arab dogs. You always told me that everything is for the best, even those acts we can't understand. So I guess this too is for the best."

I could tell he didn't say it to mock me. Maybe Abraham could see God's design for him, but it eluded me.

"You wanted to ask Abe something," Bernice prodded.

"Oh yes. Bernice explained to me what the Irgun has been doing."

"I'm sure she has," he said looking disdainfully at Bernice.

"Be respectful!"

I realized after I spoke it was a ridiculous thing to say to a man behind bars awaiting execution. "She told me the Irgun is threatening retaliation for the death sentence given to you and the others. She thinks it will just anger the British. She says that you will have a better chance of being spared if the Irgun ceases its actions."

"She says, she says. Papa, I don't mean to be disrespectful, and I know it's not just what Bernice wants, but don't you see that what you're asking is exactly what the British want? By hanging our men, they hope to silence us, to crush us. That will never happen. We are strong and we believe in what we're fighting for. They can kill me but they can't kill our cause."

"But what good will your death do?"

"Do you know what people say about the Jews in Europe, the ones sent to the camps? They say those Jews walked into the gas chambers meekly, like sheep going to slaughter. We are not sheep! Jews in Palestine, in their homeland fight back!"

He sounded a lot like Bernice when she gave one of her rousing speeches about the commitment to win our independence.

"My death will show the British that we are not afraid to die. That there is nothing they can do to stop us from achieving our goal. And like those who have gone before me, I will march to the gallows singing *Hatikvah* as a proud, unbroken Jew who wanted nothing more than to live in peace in his homeland."

"But Abraham," I was too choked up to speak.

Abraham leaned closer to the bars. "Papa, I'm sorry. I'm sorry that my death will cause you and Mama grief. But I make no apology for what I have done, and what my comrades must continue to do to win our freedom."

"Time's up," the guard shouted, and started back toward where Abraham was standing.

I thrust my arms through the bars and embraced him.

"I said none of that," the guard yelled, as he and his partner rushed over and pulled Abraham from my grasp.

I watched them drag Abraham down the hall.

"I'll be all right, Papa. Send my love to everyone. And tell them I died happy because I fought back."

"No!" I screamed. "Let me in! I just want to hug my son. Please!"

He turned and looked back at me. He smiled.

"God be with you son!"

The door slammed and he was gone.

"God be with you, Abraham," I said again, but the words just echoed in the empty room.

I slumped against the bars. Bernice came over and lifted me.

"Tevye, we've got no time for pity. We've got an appointment with the High Commissioner and he's not going to wait for us. Let's go."

Bernice pulled me toward the exit. I looked back over my shoulder through the door my son had disappeared behind. "Dear Lord, don't let my son die. Please don't take my boy."

"Come on, Tevye."

When we were back in the car, I just leaned my head against the window. My only thought was that the last time I might ever see my son was behind prison bars.

"Are you all right, Tevye?" Bernice said, taking out her cigarette and then returning it to the pack.

"Would you be all right if your only son was about to be hung?"

"Tevye, I'm not going to pretend to know what you're feeling, but you mustn't lose faith. We are going to fight for Abraham's life, and we are going to save him if I have to go to London and plead with the prime minister himself."

"Thank you, Bernice. You're a good friend."

I didn't doubt for a minute she would do what she said. I could see her barging into Whitehall and charming the socks right off the prime minister. But I didn't think it would do any good. Abraham's fate is in God's hands now.

"I know it's no consolation, but the guards usually don't allow condemned men to get even that close to visitors. I was told that you usually have to talk through a window in a solid door that is so small you can't even see each other's whole face. I insisted that you be allowed to see your son's condition."

"Do you believe what he said about being beaten? He looked all right."

"A few years ago, I wouldn't have believed it," Bernice said, nervously juggling her cigarettes. "After all, the British are supposed to be so civilized, so proper. But now, given all the other stories I've heard about their brutality, I'm sure it's true. It's one more thing to protest, and to use to shift public opinion in our favor, at least it would be if the Irgun stopped blowing things up."

"Abraham won't tell them to stop."

"To be honest, I didn't really think he would, Tevye. And even if he wanted to do it for you, the Irgun's leaders wouldn't have listened. One thing I've learned over the years, my friend, is to try to fight your battles one at a time. Our next battle is with the High Commissioner, so let's focus on that for now."

"*Biseder.*"

"Just keep two things in mind, Tevye. First, the British are in a foul mood because of all the Irgun attacks. They've imposed a curfew throughout Palestine while they hunt for the soldiers the Irgun kidnaped. Second, they have a particularly low opinion of kibbutzniks. They consider us filthy and uncultured."

I just nodded.

The rest of the journey to Jerusalem I kept my eyes closed and prayed for God to spare my son. When Golde and I went to Jerusalem, I never imagined the next time I would come would be to beg for my son's life.

When we entered the city, it was like a different place than the one I'd visited earlier. I felt no magic or wonder. Now it was just a place where a powerful man resided, another tsar intent on persecuting Jews. When we entered Government House, the office of the British High Commissioner, I felt as far from God as it was possible to be.

We were forced to wait in an outer room. I was in such a daze my surroundings were like a mirage. I was aware of chairs and desks and paintings and people in the building, but didn't really *see* anything.

Finally, we were ushered into the office. The High Commissioner came from behind his desk. I forced myself to focus. The Englishman was much taller and thinner than I. He had on a brown tweed suit and walked so stiffly he might have had a wooden plank in the back of his coat. His face was thin and angular, as though it had once been fat and then was squeezed in a vice. His bushy eyebrows were the same color gray as his hair. I instantly disliked him.

"My dear Bernice. How nice to see you again. I'm sorry it is not a happier occasion."

The English accent was so thick and hard to understand, it sounded like the words came through his nostrils.

"Thank you for seeing us on such short notice, but, as you know, a death sentence has been handed down in the case of Abraham Zalman that the Agency believes is unjustified. This is the boy's father, Tevye, who comes from the same kibbutz as I."

"I didn't know you were from a kibbutz, Bernice. You don't impress me as the outdoor, orange-picking, chicken-plucking type."

"Actually, I worked in the kitchen. But I haven't lived on the kibbutz for some time now. Tevye has been a close friend, more like family, since I first came to this country."

"Yes, well, please sit down, both of you."

Bernice and I sat in chairs facing the High Commissioner's desk, which was propped up on a pedestal so he could look down on his guests. He went back to his chair and leaned back, posing thoughtfully. The haze of smoke coming from the Englishman's pipe made me feel almost like I was in a dream — or a nightmare.

"Tea?"

"No thank you, your Excellency. I have come here to beg your Highness for leniency for my son."

"Who is?"

"You mean his name?"

The Englishman smirked and nodded. Apparently, he ignored it when Bernice told him the first time.

"Abraham Zalman, Excellency. You see I have seven daughters."

"Seven?"

"Daughters. But only one son, who I love very much. I know that he has done something wrong and must be punished, but wouldn't a prison sentence serve your purpose just as well?"

"Well, what's your name again?"

"Tevye, your Honor."

"Yes, well Tevye, I'm afraid your son has done more than just something wrong. It's not like he told a white lie or stole a piece of fruit from the market. He killed an officer of His Royal Majesty's army."

"I am very sorry. It is a terrible thing and I wish I could have prevented it, but justice does not require that my son be put to death."

"Justice? What do you know of justice? Is it just that my people cannot walk in the streets without fear of being shot, or blown up or kidnaped? Is it just that terrorists are given support and safe haven by their fellow Jews?" he said, looking sternly at Bernice.

I could see that she was growing flush and might explode. I wanted to argue also, to shout back about the fears of my people, and the injustices committed against them, but I too held my tongue.

"Your son received a trial, which is more than he and the other terrorists gave the men they attacked."

"Your Honor, I'm not asking you to excuse my son's actions. I understand that he must be punished. I am only asking that you show mercy and let him live out his days, even if it must be behind bars."

"You look like a man of God, Tevye. You know the biblical injunction against murder and the penalty for committing such a sin, an eye for an eye, and a tooth for a tooth."

"The words in the Bible are not meant to be taken literally."

"Well, I would love to argue theology with you, Tevye, but this is a matter for the legal courts, and they have already pronounced sentence."

"But surely your Honor has the power to modify their decree."

"And if I did that for your son, what should I do about all the other sons who have committed such heinous acts? They all have mothers and fathers who don't want to see them put to death."

"I can only speak for myself and my son."

"And I must speak for His Majesty's Government, which must keep order in Palestine. And that order has been undermined by your son and his associates. So, as much as I sympathize with your pain, and would like to help you —"

"Sir!" a soldier shouted as he charged into the office.

"What the devil are you doing, racing in here like a wild man?"

"I'm sorry Sir, but it's an emergency. We've just received word that there's been an escape at Acre Prison."

Bernice and I looked at each other. The High Commissioner put down his pipe.

"What kind of escape?"

"A mass one, Sir. Apparently it was well planned. A section of the prison wall was blown up from the outside."

"I thought that prison was supposed to be invulnerable?"

"We thought so, Sir."

"How many gone?"

"Over two-hundred. We have patrols hunting for the prisoners. Some have already been recaptured."

The High Commissioner stood and headed for the door. As he walked past, he turned to me. "It seems your son's fate is now in someone else's hands."

40

"And the Lord spoke unto Moses in the plains of Moab by the Jordan at Jericho, saying: 'Speak unto the children of Israel, and say unto them: When ye pass over the Jordan into the land of Canaan, then ye shall drive out all the inhabitants of the land from before you, and destroy all their figured stones and destroy all their molten images, and demolish all their high places. And ye shall drive out the inhabitants of the land, and dwell therein; for unto you have I given the land to possess it' . . . . And the Lord spoke unto Moses, saying: 'Command the children of Israel, and say unto them: When ye come into the land of Canaan, this shall be the land that shall fall unto you for an inheritance.'"

Funny that the Torah forgot to mention the United Nations would have a say in our inheritance.

"What are you mumbling about, Tevye?"

"Just reading the *parsha*."

Golde was reclining on the couch. Finally, after all these years, I had succeeded in convincing all the committees that the Sabbath should be a day of rest, even for Labor Zionists. This was probably my greatest contribution to the kibbutz.

"It talks about God's promise to give the Jews the land of Canaan. It says the Israelites will drive out the inhabitants of the land."

"Does that mean we will drive the Arabs out of Palestine, Papa?" Hodel asked, looking over from her newspaper.

"Perhaps. If this is the appointed time."

"First we have to drive out the British," Motel said from the corner, where he was arguing with Simcha.

"It's counterproductive I tell you," Simcha said, the smile gone from his face.

"The British will not leave voluntarily," Motel countered.

"But now the Irgun has aroused the world against us. That picture of the two British sergeants hanging from a tree horrified the world."

"It was retaliation. The British hung their men first."

"I'm not going to defend the British, Motel. But you could hardly expect them to give the Irgun a medal after they blew up Acre prison and freed men London considered terrorists."

"Terrorists? You call them terrorists for trying to rid us of English rule, for fighting for our freedom?"

"I didn't call them terrorists, Motel. I said that's the opinion of the British. The point is the United Nations is now going to decide our fate. How does it look to them for a bunch of Jews to go around hanging soldiers and blowing up buildings? Do you think the nations of the world are going to be impressed? They're going to say, 'those Jews are barbarians, they're not civilized enough to govern themselves.'"

"Barbarians, Simcha? First they were terrorists, now barbarians? You sound like Bernice and the other old ladies from the Jewish Agency. The British would not have even brought the question of what to do with Palestine to the United Nations if it hadn't been for the Irgun. They'd have talked and talked and talked us to death. If we hadn't spent so much time talking, maybe six million Jews would still be alive — and living in a Jewish state today."

I sat listening to Motel, still amazed that the *nebbish* I knew as a boy in Anatevka had grown to be such a firebrand. Hearing someone else say the words helped me, for the first time, to understand Abraham's feelings. I'm sure he started out just wanting to avenge his sister, but I could see how Motel's argument would now appeal to him.

I wish I could tell Abraham what I'm feeling, but he's disappeared. The British recaptured or killed most of the men who escaped from Acre Prison, but my son was never found. I pray that he escaped safely and is not lying dead in a ditch somewhere, as some of the others were when they were found. If he is alive, Bernice said, he would have gone so far underground gophers couldn't find him, because he was now one of the most wanted men in all of Palestine.

"Shh! Stop talking so loud," Sarah said from the other side of the room.

Motel and Simcha stopped arguing for a moment, then started again more softly.

Sarah and Chaim were ignoring them. Chaim was reading a poem by Bialik to Rachel, while Sarah brushed her hair. I listened to Chaim read the words of the great poet:
A different wind is blowing. Skies grow tall,
Bright distances unfold in limpid space.
Spring treads the hills, and in the village square
the earth at dawn exhales a misty warmth,
and budding shoots appear upon wet trees.
A different wind is blowing through the world.
I watched Rachel for any sign of recognition, hoping against hope that poetry could penetrate the darkness, but she did not show any sign that even the final hopeful words had reached her.
Soon in white flowers my youth will overflow —
my new-found youth entangled in old dreams,
for through them too blow currents of spring air.
To my full heart I will give utterance,
with shining tears expel my black despair.
A different wind is blowing through the world.
If only a different wind would blow for my daughter. Poor Rachel, growing older but looking the same, sitting in her chair, staring expressionless out the window. I wonder if she could sense

what her twin brother was feeling, or had any idea of what he was doing in her name. She was such a gentle child. I wouldn't be surprised if, even after the incident, she'd tell Abraham to follow the advice of Simcha instead of Motel.

"Listen to this," Hodel said from behind the newspaper. "Listen!" she shouted when Motel and Simcha kept talking. "A ship carrying forty-five hundred Jewish refugees from Sete, France was intercepted by a British warship that escorted it across the Mediterranean. The passengers threw a banner over the side, renaming the ship, *Exodus 1947*. When the *Exodus* was off the coast of Gaza, it was rammed by British destroyers. The refugees fought off the boarding party for several hours before the British used machine guns and gas bombs to board the ship. Three Jews were killed and more than a hundred wounded."

"Do you think Devorah was on it?" Golde gasped.

"I don't know," Hodel replied. "I know she's been helping refugees, but the last I heard she was still in Germany."

"What's that?" Golde said. "Devorah in Germany?"

"That's where the refugees are Mama. Wait, there's more in the newspaper."

"The ship was forced to dock in Haifa, where the refugees were loaded onto three British prison ships and forced to return to France. The three ships anchored in Sete, but the refugees refused to get off the ships. They said they would rather starve than go anywhere but Palestine.'"

"Do you think the Haganah will blow the ships up the way they did the other one, the Petrushka?"

"Not Petrushka, woman, *Patria*," I said to Golde. "No, that was a mistake. They wouldn't do that again. Besides, the British will look like the villains when the world hears they sent away refugees coming to their homeland."

"You're right, Papa. Listen to this."

"'On approaching the *Ocean Vigour*—'"

"What's that?"

"The name of one of the prison ships, Mama."

"'On approaching the *Ocean Vigour* I witnessed the most terrible spectacle I have ever seen in my life. It was a spectacle I shall never forget. On the deck, in narrow, very high cages, worse than those in a zoo, surrounded by barbed wire, were crowded together my brothers and sisters of all ages.'"

Hodel started to cry softly. I could barely hear her say, "The bastards."

"'There the sun had beaten down on their heads for eighteen days at sea. They had not even been able to lie down at night. Between the cages stood red-bereted guards isolating each cage.'"

"Stop, I don't want to hear any more," I said. "First, Hitler puts Jews in camps, gases and burns them and now the survivors are prevented from coming to their homeland, put into cages and sent back to the countries they escaped from."

"See, Simcha. These are the kind of people the British are. They would send our people back to the gas chambers just to keep them from reaching Palestine."

"Motel —"

"Mama, Papa, there's a letter for us," Tzeitl said excitedly running into the room.

"Come here, my angel," I said.

Tzeitl came over to give me a hug. She was not the scrawny little girl who used to beg to help me milk the cows. Holding her close, I could feel how much weight she'd gained over the years. She was actually on the *zaftik* side. Her hair was now completely gray, like Golde's. Where had the years gone?

I wanted to hold my baby, but the grown woman pulled away and slipped over to Golde. She handed her the letter.

"What's this, don't I get to read anything anymore?"

"Go back to your studying, Tevye," Golde said, opening the letter and starting to read.

"Don't tell me what to do woman. I want to know who that letter is from."

Golde ignored me and continued to read.

"Golde. Golde!" I said, stomping my foot on the floor.

"It's from Chava, Papa," Tzeitl said, ignoring Hodel's gesture to be quiet.

"What?" I said, feeling the blood rush to my face.

"The letter is from America."

I stormed over to where Golde was sitting and pulled the letter out of her hands and tore it up.

"What are you doing, Papa?" Hodel shrieked.

"Thank you, Lord," Golde said, clasping her hands together and looking heavenward. "Thank you."

"What's the matter with you? What's there to be thankful for?" I shouted. "You just heard what Hodel read. Jews are being sent back to camps, the British are cracking down on the *yishuv* and our fate is being left to strangers in New York."

"You were right. What happens is for the best, Tevye."

"What are you talking about?"

"Fyedka converted."

"What?"

"Fyedka converted to Judaism and they were married under a canopy."

"Are you trying to tell me —"

"Our daughter is alive and married to a Jew!" Golde shouted.

Before I could say anything, Golde ran over and hugged me. I started to push her away and she gave me a big kiss.

"And not only that, she's coming here. My baby's coming home! Praise the Lord."

I was speechless.

"That's wonderful news, Mama," Hodel said, rushing over to embrace Golde.

"They're coming here to live with us on the kibbutz. Fyedka was about to be arrested and they escaped.

"Woman, what are you talking about?" I finally managed to blurt. "Fyedka Galagan is now Jewish, he was married to my daughter under a *chuppah*, was about to be arrested and now is coming to live with us?"

"Oh, Fyedka's name isn't Fyedka anymore," Golde announced.

I was beginning to feel dizzy. "What do you mean?"

"He changed his name in America to Phil."

"Phil?"

"Phil Goldstein."

"Phil Goldstein?"

"Tevye, stop repeating everything I say. This is wonderful news. The best. Praise God. Praise the Almighty for reuniting our family."

"I still don't understand," Motel said. "Why was Fyedka, I mean Phil, going to be arrested?"

"The police discovered he was smuggling guns to Jews in Palestine," Tzeitl answered. "The United States is not allowing any weapons to be sent to us, so he and a few of his friends have been smuggling guns and ammunition in crates with farm equipment."

"How do you know?" Golde asked.

"I'm sorry, Mama, but I was afraid Papa would tear up the letter so I peeked."

I had to hold my head to keep it from falling off my shoulders. "You mean to tell me Fyedka risked going to jail to help Jews?"

"Phil," Golde corrected.

"Phil. Phil. Phil! You mean to tell me Phil has been smuggling weapons to Jews in Palestine from America?"

"That's right," Golde said. "But now they're coming here. My Chava is coming home."

Chavaleh. I can still remember the tears running down her face when she begged me to speak to her. I turned my back on my own daughter as she had turned hers on our faith and the Jewish people.

"No! It's too late. The dead cannot rise from the grave!"

"What are you saying, Tevye?" Golde said. "Have you gone mad? After all these years, you would still —"

"She's dead to us."

"No, Tevye. She is not dead! She is coming home and she *is* going to live with us. We are going to be a family again."

"I will not listen to anymore of this," I said, turning my back to Golde. The rest of the children were silent, but I could feel their eyes on my back.

"Tevye, you have told me many times that it is written that a father must have pity on his children."

Golde had begged me to forgive Chava the day that we left Anatevka. The memories rushed back.

"Did she have pity on me when she ran off? I begged the Russian priest, may his name be blotted out, to tell me where she was, but he refused. All these years of sleepless nights and heartache, she had no pity for us."

"The Bible says that God forgives those who repent," Hodel said. "Hasn't she suffered enough? Are you less forgiving than the Almighty?"

"Don't you remember when I betrayed Simcha?" Sarah asked before I could say anything. "That was a terrible sin, but I repented and the *chaverim* forgave me."

"That was different."

"It wasn't, Papa," Sarah said with a defiance I'd never heard from her.

"This is the way my children have learned to respect their father?"

"Don't you remember what you told me after Shoshana died, when I wanted to die as well?

"No."

"You told me I must choose life for the sake of my children, for the sake of Chavaleh."

"It has been too many years, Golde. The family tree has grown even as one of its limbs withered."

"Papa."

"Don't interrupt, Tzeitl."

"Papa," Tzeitl said more urgently.

"What is it?"

"The mail from America is sometimes very slow."

"What do you mean, Tzeitl?"

"Chava sent the letter several weeks ago, before she left."

"What are you saying?"

Tzeitl slowly walked to the door and opened it. Chava stood in the doorway.

Golde put her hands to her mouth and instantly began crying. She started toward the door and froze. She looked over at me.

I saw my daughter for the first time in almost thirty years. She was no longer the little freckle-faced girl I remembered. A grown woman stood only a few feet away. We stared into each other's eyes. I saw the same pleading look that was etched in my memory from the last time we spoke.

"Hello Papa."

I didn't answer.

She didn't move. Her eyes were growing misty.

Can I turn my back on my flesh and blood again? After all that has happened? How can I remain so hardhearted? I lost Shoshie and no prayer can restore her life. Poor little Rachel sitting in the corner is beyond my help. But Chava has returned to the faith, and it is now within my power to bring her back to the family.

I opened my arms.

"Chavaleh!"

My daughter ran to me and we embraced.

"Chavaleh. Chavaleh." I wanted to repeat her name over and over to make up for the years of keeping it inside.

I could see the rest of the family watching us. Golde and Hodel were wiping their eyes.

Over Chava's shoulder I saw a clean-shaven man in a suit hesitantly enter the doorway. I released Chava and looked from her to Fyedka.

Golde gasped to hold her breath. I gazed around the room. Motel had moved to Tzeitl's side and had his arm around her. She held a tissue to her nose and her cheeks were wet. Simcha was in the corner smiling. Chaim and Sarah were studying me. Rachel stared out the window, seemingly unaware of what was going on.

Chava was staring up at me with such longing. Tracks of tears flowed from each eye.

"Papa, I'd like you to meet my husband, Phil Goldstein."

I looked back at the man I'd cursed for almost a lifetime. Slowly, I held out my hand. Phil came over and grabbed it. I pulled him to me and we embraced.

4 I

It's hard to believe, but after two-thousand years of exile, we may finally have our own state again. If it is God's will, I'm sure it will come to pass, but I would feel more comfortable if He had not decided to work His will through a bunch of kibitzers from foreign lands sitting in New York.

For this momentous occasion, the whole family has once again crammed itself into our luxurious room. It is true that we finally earned enough seniority points to move to one of the newer, larger apartments, but it was still made for two people, not our entire clan. Still, it is nice to all be together — children, grandchildren, even sons-in-law — for such a momentous occasion.

"They're getting ready to start."

"Motel, do you have to sit on top of the radio?" I asked. "I know you're nearsighted, but I didn't think that affected your hearing."

"Quiet, the voting on partition is going to begin soon," Tzeitl said.

"Do you hear that Golde? My daughter is shushing me."

"She's right, shush," Golde said, looking up from sewing the flag of Zion, a blue Star of David in between two solid blue lines on a white background.

"Look who's talking."

"Quiet!" Motel shouted.

I could hear Phil — I still can't believe that Russian's now a Jew — explaining the political maneuvering.

"We didn't seem to have enough votes a few days ago, but the Americans supposedly twisted a few arms during the recess."

"But did they change enough votes?" Hodel asked him.

"I think so."

I hate to admit it, but I was impressed by Phil's knowledge of America. He worked hard while he lived there, and even lost most of his Russian accent. I can't say I've forgotten who he was, but changing his name helped almost as much as the conversion. I could see Phil was an entirely different person than the boy I'd cursed for so many years.

The image of others from that time long past suddenly flashed before me. What had happened to Lazer-Wolf, Ephraim the Matchmaker, the Rabbi? How many had gone up Hitler's chimneys like Chaim's parents? I wished they could be with us to share this glorious moment.

If only Jonathan and Pertschik had lived to see the fulfillment of their dreams. And my Shoshana.

"You are all forgetting, there will also be an Arab state," Sarah said.

"Excuse me, Sarah, but I don't think so," Phil said.

"What do you mean?"

"The Arabs have already said they will not accept partition — even if it means sacrificing their state — because they demand their own independent state in all of Palestine. Tomorrow, a war will begin. We will be outnumbered and outgunned. The British will continue to disarm us until they leave, and the Americans will not intervene on our behalf. That is why I will be going abroad to help find weapons."

"You're leaving?" Golde said without disguising her panic. "You've just returned to us."

"I'm just getting used to your new name," I said.

"It will be a short trip. And if I'm not successful, there may be nothing to return to."

"Stop scaring everyone, Phil," Chava said.

"You're right, sweetheart. We are better prepared than the Arabs think. That is one point in our favor. And we will be fighting to survive. That will give us a psychological edge. And I think we will find enough arms. You'll never guess where they're coming from though."

I looked at Phil and mouthed, "Russia."

"Close. Let's just say if we do get what we ask it will be with Stalin's blessing."

"The Lord truly works in mysterious ways. As the Good Book says —"

"Quiet, the vote is starting," Motel interrupted.

"Tevye stop pacing. We've waited this long for a state, you can wait a little longer," Golde said, increasing the tempo of her sewing.

"I'm not pacing. I'm exercising. You know Dr. Riesman told me I need exercise."

A scratchy voice on the radio announced, "Afghanistan votes no. Chile abstains. China —"

Chaim stood with Sarah in a corner opposite the rest of the family, beside Rachel, who was facing the window, giving no more indication than usual that she knew what was happening around her.

"Phil's right," Chaim whispered to Sarah. "Tomorrow there will be violence."

"I was afraid we would have a war one day," Sarah said, "but I kept hoping the Arabs would accept the U.N. decision."

"They couldn't," Chaim told her. "I understand their position. If I was an Arab, I wouldn't want to live in a Jewish state, especially if my family had lived here long before most of us settled in Palestine."

"France votes . . . wait a moment . . . France votes yes!"

The family cheered.

"That was the big one," Phil reminded everyone. He had explained earlier that the French were on the fence before the vote. They were worried about upsetting the Arabs in their North African colonies and jeopardizing the safety of the French Catholic institutions throughout the Muslim world.

"I think we can make it now," Simcha said.

"Guatemala votes yes."

"Will it be a long fight?" Rebecca asked her brother Aryeh.

"I'm afraid so. You heard Phil. We have very few trained soldiers and hardly any weapons. The Arabs will bring soldiers and guns in from all around us."

"Can we win?"

"Of course we'll win, Rebecca," I said. "As the Good Book says, 'there is a time to sow and a time to reap.' This is our time to sow. Just look at your mother."

Everyone laughed. Golde's sewing grew more frantic with each announced vote.

"Will you go to fight?" Leah asked Aryeh.

"No, I will stay and help protect the kibbutz. We must hold onto every piece of land."

"India votes no. Iran votes no."

"And yes, we will win," Aryeh said.

"The Soviet Union votes yes!"

The family cheered. I was too shocked. "Can you believe that? Russians supporting Jews. Maybe today is the day the *mashiach* will arrive."

The door of the house suddenly burst open.

It was not the *mashiach*. Instead, four soldiers came in carrying Sten guns.

"What's this? What are you doing barging into my house?"

"It's all right, Mama," Aryeh said. "These are my friends. They've come to help defend the kibbutz."

"Couldn't they knock before they come in?"

From the doorway, a female voice said, "Do I have to knock before I can come in?"

"Devorah!" Golde shouted as our daughter entered with a rifle slung over her back. "You're safe. Praise God." Golde raced to the door and threw her arms around Devorah and immediately began to weep.

"Devorah, my little soldier." I smiled so hard my face hurt.

Devorah embraced me with a steel grip. Then she went around the room hugging everyone.

"Oh, I've brought someone with me, too."

We all turned to the door and stared, waiting to see who could possibly appear next. At this point, I wouldn't have been surprised if it was Elijah himself.

A moment later, Abraham stood in the doorway dressed in olive drab fatigues with a Sten gun in his hands.

We hadn't heard any news of him since the day of the prison break six months earlier and had feared he was dead.

"I don't understand," was all I could manage to say.

Golde rushed across the threshold to hug Abraham. She held him and muttered, "Thank you Lord. Thank you."

After that day I got to spend ten minutes with Abraham in prison, I didn't think I'd ever see him again. It was as if he had been brought back from the dead. The years we lost can't be replaced, but now, at last, we have the chance to study, to pray, to talk, to be together. But until I felt his touch, I couldn't be sure I wasn't seeing a mirage.

Abraham came over to me and held out his hand. I grabbed it and pulled him to me. I held him for a long time and fought back tears.

"I was afraid you were dead."

"I'm not so easy to kill, Papa. The British did recapture or kill most of us, but I escaped and holed up with some friends. I wasn't sure when or if I'd be able to come out of hiding. The Haganah finally decided to work with us instead of against us, so I thought it was safe to surface."

"We expect the British to pull out sometime after the U.N. vote," Devorah added, "and we will need all our strength to defeat the Arabs. The Haganah and the Irgun agreed to combine forces. Abraham found me after the understanding was reached."

I reluctantly let Abraham go so he could embrace the rest of the family. Then he walked over to Rachel. He knelt before her and spoke softly.

"I've come back Rachel. You don't have to be scared anymore. No one can ever hurt you. I will make sure of that."

We all watched Abraham take Rachel's hands and kiss them. He looked into her eyes, searching for some sign of understanding. I held my breath waiting for her to speak. I think everyone in the room was doing the same, hoping our collective prayers would bring words from her mouth. She said nothing. Maybe their bond allowed them to communicate in ways the rest of us couldn't fathom.

"Sweden votes yes. Turkey votes no."

"I think we're going to make it," Motel announced.

"We will and the fight will begin," Devorah said. "That's why we're here. I'm afraid we could only spare a handful of men. Shimshon and Yossi expect the Arabs to attack the isolated kibbutzim. We are supposed to hold out for as long as possible. Most of our men are being prepared to fight in the cities, especially Jerusalem."

"This should be it," Phil said as he strained to hear the radio over the commotion.

"Yugoslavia abstains. The final vote is thirty-three votes in favor, thirteen opposed and ten abstentions. The resolution passes. We have a state!"

At that instant, we could hear the blast of a shofar outside announcing the decision.

Inside, we screamed and shouted and jumped up and down like someone had set the floor on fire. From fleeing Russian Cossacks, to cleaning up after pogroms, to being evicted from our homes in Anatevka, to starting a new life in the Palestinian wilderness, to draining malarial swamps, to taking in survivors of the catastrophe in Europe, and now, finally, to building a Jewish state. I can't believe I have lived to see it all.

I went around the room hugging and kissing everyone. The only person who didn't look happy was Abraham. I wondered if he was still capable of happiness.

"What's wrong, Abraham? Isn't this what you've been fighting for too?"

"Papa, what kind of a Jewish state have we got without Jerusalem, without Hebron, Bethlehem or the land on the other side of the Jordan River?"

"It's an imperfect state, my son. But it is what God has decreed should be ours — at least for now. Come, let's join the celebration."

I put my arm around Abraham and led him outside. The rest of the family followed. The *chaverim* were yelling and Laban was excitedly ringing the kibbutz bell. Suddenly, the throng grew eerily quiet. Softly, we could hear the words: *kol od balevav penimah nefesh yehudi homiyah.*

Phil stood beside me and was singing along off-key. He whispered in my ear, "Tevye, I've been singing this song at every Zionist rally in America, but I'm afraid I never learned Hebrew. I know *Hatikvah* means 'The Hope,' but what do the rest of the words mean?"

I put my arm around my newest son-in-law and repeated the verses:

So long as still within our breasts
The Jewish heart beats true,
So long as still towards the East,
To Zion, looks the Jew,
So long as our hopes are not yet lost —
Two thousand years we cherished them —
To live in freedom in the Land
Of Zion and Jerusalem.

When the song was over, everyone began to form circles and dance the *hora.* I was quickly pulled into the swirling mass of arms and feet. We were like the Israelites escaping Pharaoh. The U.N. had freed us from bondage and we could not control our elation.

As I was pulled around, my eyes locked on my eldest, Tzeitl, a grown woman who had blessed me with three beautiful grandchildren. She was holding on to Motel, the way she did when they announced they'd given each other a pledge to marry. He was still thin as a reed, but with a backbone of steel, stiffened from that day when he summoned the courage to ask for Tzeitl's hand.

The circle of dancers reversed itself and I found myself looking at Hodel holding the hand of my old friend Simcha. He was smiling as broadly as ever, and, for the first time since she returned, I saw a smile to match on Hodel's face. I'm sure that Pertschik is looking down at us smiling as well.

I was pulled from the outer circle into the inner ring by my grandchildren. Aryeh, Leah and Rebecca still had the youthful enthusiasm that I remembered in my own children when they were growing up in Anatevka. Devorah, Arik and Abraham forced their way into our group. I could see from the way Devorah and Arik looked at each other that they would stay together and, God willing, produce more grandchildren.

I looked at my son and wondered if he too would find a wife and settle down once the fighting was over. I had missed so much of his youth while he was fighting for our people. He is the last hope for keeping our family name alive.

Our family circle grew larger as Chava and Phil joined us. I looked at the man dancing awkwardly. I'd despised him for most of my life, the heathen who had stolen my Chavaleh. And now Phil was part of our people and Chavaleh was as precious an adult as she was a child. They never had children in America because they kept their pledge not to bring kids into such a world, but, now that we have a Jewish state, perhaps they'll change their mind and Abraham will not be the last of Tevye's family.

We were dancing so rapidly, my head felt like it was going to spin off my shoulders. The images of my family became a blur. Then I saw my Golde standing outside the circle clapping her hands and singing with rapture that I had only seen after the birth of the twins.

I broke free of the circle and started over to her, feeling out of breath from all the excitement and dancing. Suddenly, a flash of pain ripped through me. I clutched my chest. I could see Golde stop clapping. I felt like I was moving in slow motion, stumbled and then fell to the ground.

"Tevye, what is it? Tevye!" Golde screamed as she rushed across the yard to kneel over me.

The music and dancing suddenly stopped.

"Help me get him to the infirmary," I heard Devorah say as I was gently lifted.

Abraham had my legs while Arik grabbed my shoulders. They put me down on a cot. I looked up and saw the faces of everyone I loved staring down at me.

"You'll be all right, Papa," Devorah said.

"It's okay. My time has come, just as it came to Moses after God let him see the Promised Land."

"Don't talk like that," Chava said, suppressing her tears. "You'll live to be as old as Methuselah."

"I thought I already was that old. You're still my jewel, Chavaleh." Chava leaned over and hugged me.

"And Tzeitl, you grew up to be just like your mother. And I thought there could never be another." Tzeitl squeezed my hand and kissed my cheek.

"Hodel, you are stronger than any man and smarter than most. I'm glad that you have again found happiness."

"Oh Papa," she put her head on my chest and sobbed.

I stroked her hair. She got up and brushed the tears away.

"Where is Sarah?"

"I'm here, Papa."

"You take care of that socialist husband of yours. Make sure the children learn something besides Marx."

"Don't worry. They'll be scholars like you."

"Devorah."

"Yes, Papa," Devorah whispered.

"You must marry; otherwise, your mother will not have a moment's peace."

"I will Papa."

She moved away so my son could come forward.

"Abraham, you're now the man of the house. I don't expect you to have any more luck than I did getting the women to listen to you. Take care of your mother and yourself. You have made me very proud. Help build our state, so that it is a light unto the nations."

"Don't worry, Papa."

Phil wheeled Rachel into the room in her wheelchair. Her face remained impassive and I could not tell if she was looking at me or had any idea what was happening.

"Rachel, my child! I shall miss you and the quiet times we have had together. You will feel better. I will speak to the Almighty very soon and He shall help you. As the Good Book says, 'The Lord hears the prayers of the silent as loudly as those who shout to the heavens."

Motel and Phil exchanged glances, doubting the Scriptures said any such thing, but wished more than anything that it was still true.

A tear slowly snaked its way down Tevye's cheek as he tried to remember what a happy child Rachel had been. He knew this was the last time they would see each other and he thought he saw her eyes cloud over but he wasn't sure if he was just seeing unclearly though his own tears.

"Golde, come here."

The children stepped back so Golde could sit on the edge of the bed.

"Closer."

She put her head beside mine.

"Maybe I have indigestion."

"It wouldn't be the first time," Golde said.

I caressed her cheek. "Golde, we spent a lifetime together. You raised eight beautiful children and you were a good wife. I loved you the way Abraham loved Sarah. You filled my heart with happiness. As the Good Book says, 'Blessing is found in a man's house solely due to his wife.'"

"I don't need the Good Book to tell me how much you have meant to me. You've been a good husband, a loving husband. I will always love you."

"And I love you."

The family circled the bed. I looked up at their faces. My wife and children have been my greatest joy, the answer to all my prayers.

I have always tried to follow our traditions, but many have changed or been discarded. There's still one, though, that must never change.

"*Sh'ma Yisrael Adonai Eloheinu Adonai Echod.* Hear O' Israel, the Lord is God, the Lord is One."

"Dear Lord, thank you for making me a wealthy man!"

THE END

Made in the USA
Middletown, DE
30 August 2020